PEARISBUF

DISCARD

Rage of the Vampire

The follow-up to 'The Vampires of Hope's Covenant'

Hubert L Mullins

AuthorHouse™
1663 Liberty Drive, Suite 200
Bloomington, IN 47403
www.authorhouse.com
Phone: 1-800-839-8640

© 2007 Hubert L Mullins. All rights reserved.

No part of this book may be reproduced, stored in a retrieval system, or transmitted by any means without the written permission of the author.

First published by AuthorHouse 7/16/2007

ISBN: 978-1-4343-1288-4 (sc)

Cover art by Hubert H. Mullins
www.hubertlmullins.com

Printed in the United States of America
Bloomington, Indiana

This book is printed on acid-free paper.

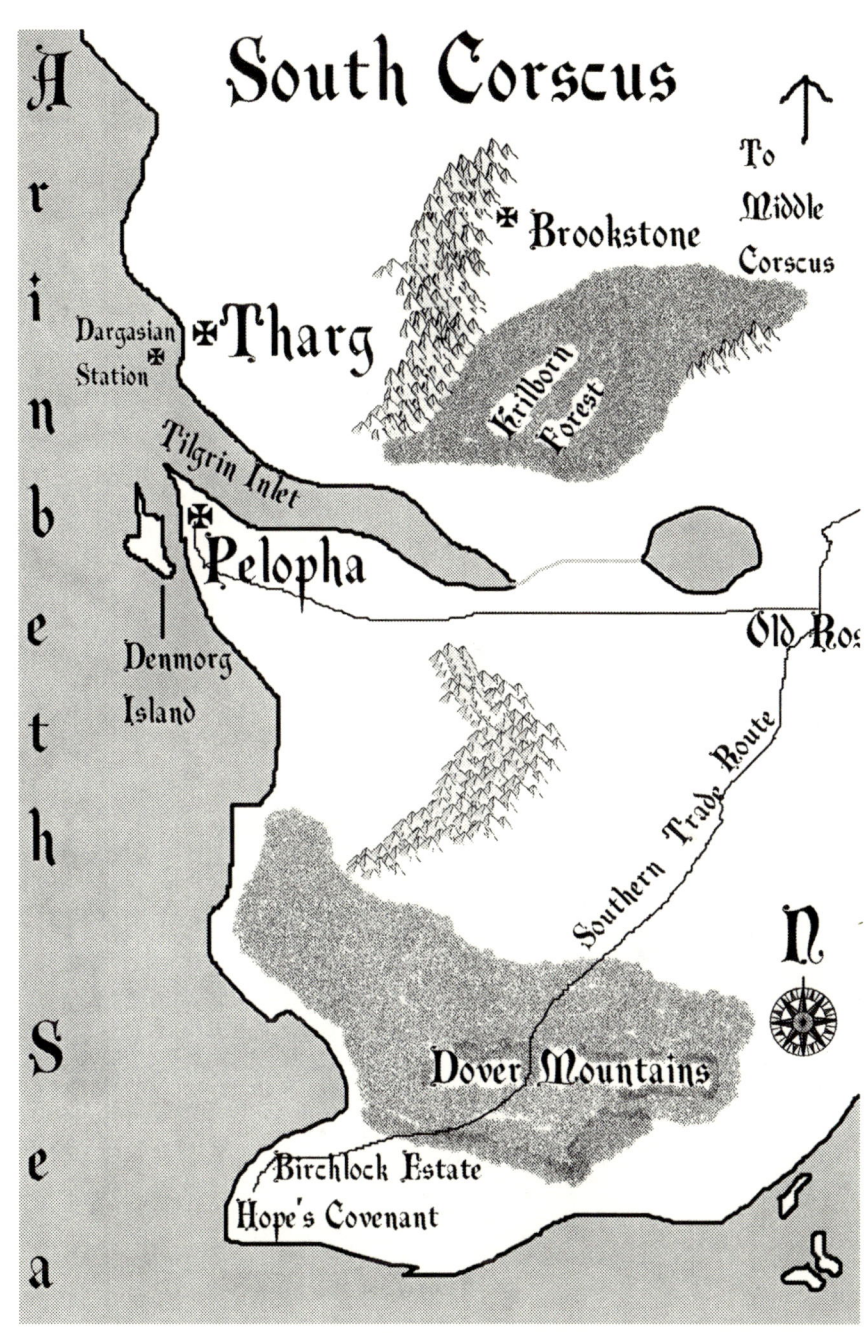

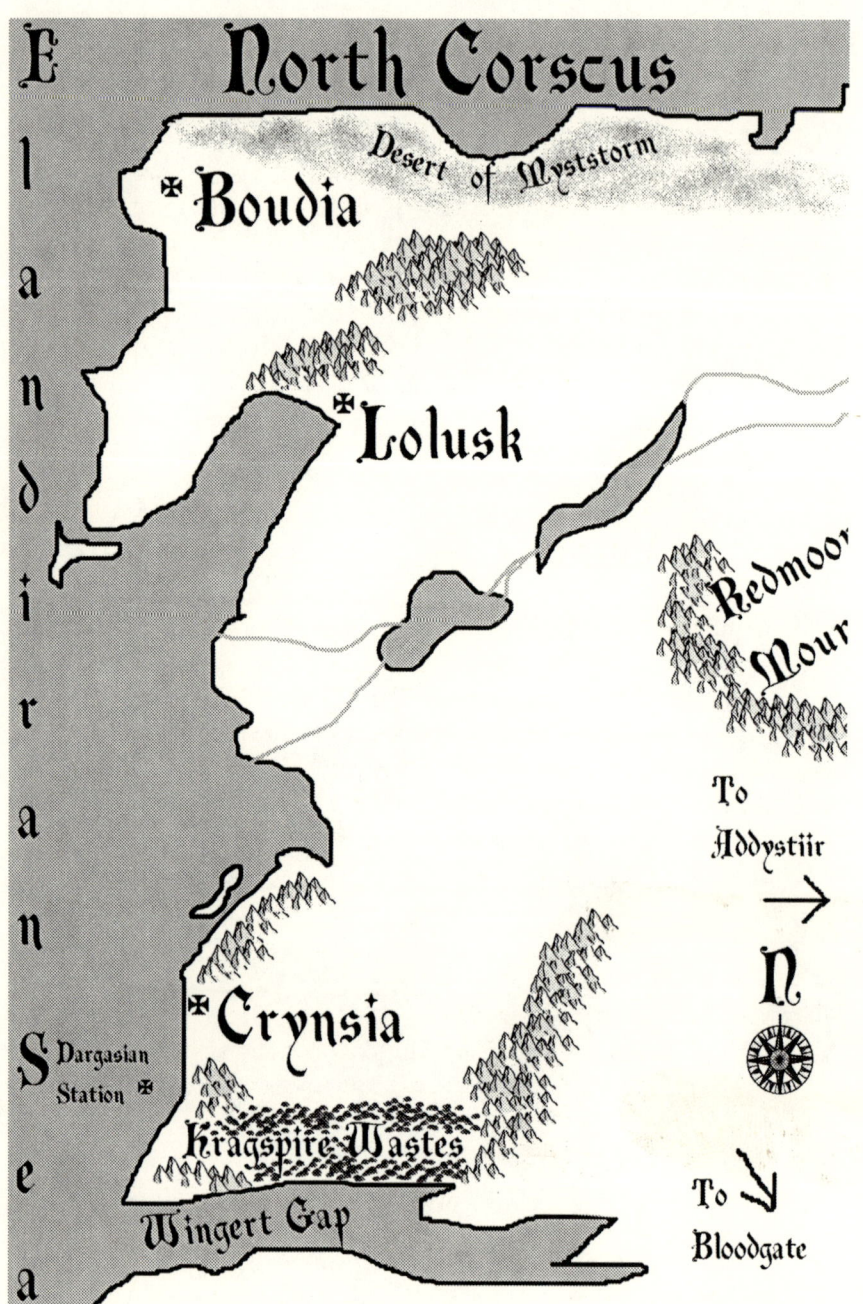

The deities who govern Mystyria...

Good

Lyluss, Her Holiness, Bearer of Light, Lady Good (Goddess of Good)
Quillian, The Heavenly Nurse, Lyluss' Shoulder (Goddess of Healing)
Symbia, Queen of Magic, The Great Sorceress (Goddess of Magic)
Dargas, Dragonmaster, The Winged Hero (God of Dragons)
Ablis, Willow's Sister, Lady of the Calm (Goddess of Seasons)
Willow, Ablis' Brother, Oakenheart (God of Nature)
Tess, The Iron Queen, The Magnificent Warrioress (Goddess of Warriors)
Heron, Immortal Thinker, The Divine Book (God of Knowledge)
Jade, Queen of the Wise, Heron's Love (Goddess of Wisdom)
Ciliath, Lady Vixen, Harlot's Queen (Goddess of Sex and Fertility)

Neutral

Telsis, The Overlord, The Structure, The First (God of Gods)
Dormi, The Gavel, Avenger of Justice (Goddess of Justice)
Ebend, Prince of Flame, Lightbringer (God of the Sun)
Lequester, The Nightfire, Queen of the Moon (Goddess of the Moon)
Amsat, The Great Thinker, Cogs (God of Technology)
Varolen, Watcher of the Sea, Lord of the Abyss (God of the Sea)
Rhagius, The Great Chalice, Drunken Lord (God of Wine)
Gailthias, Treasure Keeper, Golden Prince (God of Wealth and Treasure)
Traya, The Prodigy, Heartsong (Goddess of Music and Poetry)
Cathine, Lady Kiss, The Wondrous Lover (Goddess of Love and Beauty)

Evil

Mydian, Lord of the Underworld, The Master (God of the Underworld)
Ruin, Death Keeper, The Caretaker (God of the Dead)
Drak, Dark Child, Bane of Holiness (God of Evil)
Felorn, The Giantess, The Shattering Fist (Goddess of Destruction)
Whither, Decayer, The Rotten (God of Decay)
Jasper, The Jester, The Unseen Hand (God of Deception)
Arein, The Spiny, Mistress of Web (Goddess of Spiders)
Pralarus, Lady Poison, The Deadly Kiss (Goddess of Poison)
Knashar, Lord of Disease, The Sickly (God of Sickness and Disease)
Veil, The Hidden One, The Shadowed Hand (Goddess of Thieves)
Ny, Princess Death, Bloody Ny (Goddess of Murder)

Dedication

This book is dedicated to my mother and father, for their undying support and their unwavering encouragement.

Prologue

Mystyria was formed by *blood*. When Telsis, the god of the gods, was sculpting the rocks and carving the rivers of the world, the deities who governed it were but a thing to come. All of the gods emerged onto Mystyria through a lake of blood known as the Pool of Divinity. Despite their similarities and differences, each was woven into existence by the same method.

Some were caring and some were vengeful. Few even walked the realms as companions to the mortals while most governed from the heavens. They all shared one thing in common; their desire to leave their mark on the world. Each wanted songs sang about them in the taverns, devout followers on knees in their churches, and their names etched into the annals of history as the one, *true* power of Mystyria. In their bitter disputes and loving embraces, alliances were forged and severed.

The gods' power relied completely on their presence—their *influence* in Mystyria. Their very existence was kept stable by the amount of servants and temples they commanded. Without worshippers, they were weak, vulnerable and open to attack. In essence, the most popular gods were the most powerful.

Lyluss became known as the strongest of the good-natured gods. Her undying devotion to the weak, the needy, and the impoverished was a mighty hammer that was revered throughout Mystyria and struck terror into the hearts of her evil adversaries. She formed a union with Quillian, the goddess of healing and together they sought to vanquish the wicked, the vile, and the plague of gods that were set to rip Mystyria apart in the conquest to control it.

Mydian, the lord of the Underworld became known as the strongest of the evil-natured gods and was loved and feared at once by his followers. He formed an alliance with Drak, the true god of evil. Both wanted to lay a new foundation for the world. They believed in a Mystyria born and bred for a stronger race than man.

A fierce war was waged between the forces of good and evil resulting in millions of deaths—many on the northern barren land known as Kragspire. Mydian sent multitudes of his own servants to die, all in the sake of drawing attention away from a cave only a few miles from Lyluss' holy city of Keswing. His plan to raise a great dragon was thwarted, but it came at a price the world was not ready to pay.

Ten slayers, all good men and women devoted to Lyluss were sent to kill the beast named Gwenavaughn. Inside its lair they battled the dragon and in its dying breath, brought down the cave around them. The world knew the stories—the tales of how the slayers drank of the creature's blood to stay alive. The legend said it was the corruption flowing in their veins that made them lose all control. For most, it was true.

When the slayers broke free of their dark, dank prison, they saw Mystyria in a whole new way. In their eyes, they had been sent to die an isolated death by Lyluss and sought retaliation. They attacked her churches, killed her servants, and pillaged what they wanted from her coffers. Even other gods were assaulted—Mydian's temples and worshipers were destroyed, as well as Ebend's.

Just as those three gods grew tired of watching their interests on Mystyria crumble beneath the relentless rage of the slayers, Telsis intervened. He deemed them all to be cursed by the gods who were wronged. The mortals who drew pictures, told stories, and wrote books a thousand years later still carried the legend.

Lyluss deemed them unworthy to ever serve her again. She made them feel horrible pain whenever they saw her symbols, her churches, and her blessed trinkets and water. Ebend cursed them to fear the sun so that their savagery could not disturb the daily worship. Mydian gave them fangs and allowed them to reproduce at a prestigious rate. For drinking the precious blood of his dragon, he cursed them the same in order to live.

He also saw them as a tool—a device to wage war and convinced Ebend to remove the curse of daylight. The slayers were spared from the sun's fury but the full blunt of the curse carried on to every generation afterwards.

Their immortality, though often thought as a gift, came at a price.

Most vampires were loyal to Mydian—finding his Underworld a soothing choice for the afterlife. The dark lord promised them many things but delivered few. The slayers became known as the Greater Overlords and while most served him like the brethren to come, there were those that would not.

A thousand years after the creation of the vampire, one would dare to oppose Mydian's sovereignty on Mystyria. The prelude to the third War of Balance was marked by the actions of an unlikely heroine.

.1.

Uprising

It was an unusually cool night in Tharg. Even though it was well into spring and the sun was touching the western horizon, it was still cool. The waves of the Arinbeth Ocean crashed against the docks in the distance and the last of the lanterns had just been extinguished on Market Lane. A few children pulled a kite through the narrow, barren streets, not caring at all what had just happened a few yards up the hill. Up on Kriball Street.

A terrible fight had erupted in the Tharg Penitentiary. There was blood everywhere. All the prisoners had been herded away from the courtyard and back into their cells, eyes wide at the massacre that had taken place in front of them. Sinewy limbs and clumps of men—*strong* men were littered everywhere. A total of six unlucky, but deserving guards met their demise in the most horrific, vengeful way. And it was all at the hands of a woman.

They beat her, tried to *rape* her, but when it seemed as though her pain could be no greater, that her wounds and defilement could go no deeper, she unleashed a demon inside of her that brought death in seconds. The guards didn't have a chance to realize what was happening. The surviving three stood there, dumbfounded at how a woman—a mere *child* of a woman could do what she just did.

And then, as quickly as it started, the killing was over. The woman was finished. She sat on the ground and pulled her legs up to rest her chin. Each guard stared in shock and disbelief as this simple person rocked back and forth, as if nothing had happened—as if everything had been a dream.

One reached out and grabbed a handful of hair and pulled her back. Her face was unmoving—her eyes unaware of pain. The others thought the murderess had vacated, that the one before them was again a simple woman who needed to be beaten, who needed to be raped. They started once more, but before their crime could continue, a loud bell pulled them from their mark. It was over. The headmaster had been called and there would be many questions. Their assault—their misdeed would have to be saved for later.

The first guard grabbed her by the throat and pulled her away from the courtyard and to the south hall that would lead to the first cellblock. Her arms were at her sides and her bare feet glided across the floor. Her unblinking eyes fixed on the ceiling as her back was rubbed raw by the passing granite. The sound of keys jingling alerted her to the approach of her cell.

Tight, ruthless hands grabbed her by the hair and sat her up. A guard who was missing his front teeth smiled and wrapped his fingers around her neck.

"That little act out there is going to cost you, Kersey." He slammed her head against the bars of her cell to make sure she understood. She didn't even flinch. "Throw her in," he told the others.

Two guards grabbed her around the waist and tossed her in like a sack of potatoes. "I'm sure we'll be back. And soon," he added, and then spat in her face. Again, she didn't flinch, nor did she acknowledge what he said. The door slammed shut and locked, leaving only a pair of chuckling guards who left and paid her no further attention.

Kersey Avonwood lifted herself up and looked around. Her bed sat in the corner, though it was rarely ever used. She preferred the floor. A few slices of bread, an apple, and a jug of water were spread across a tray on the ground, attracting flies. No matter. She wouldn't eat it anyway.

She pulled her silky, black hair from her eyes and wiped the blood from them. That little act *was* going to cost her. She wasn't scared of retribution. She was scared of change. After tonight, things were *certainly* going to change. Whether it would be for the better or not, she didn't know.

Kersey's mind was getting the best of her. It was making her think things and do things that she knew she shouldn't. Tonight had not been the first time they had beaten her. It was the first time they tried to rape her, however. And it was the first time she'd murdered over it. It was the solitude, she reminded herself. She had been out of touch with the world for so long—longer than she'd been in here, in fact.

Her mind snapped away from the outside world and felt her hands were wet and sticky. There was a pool of blood forming in her lap. It was dark, crimson blood. It was *her* blood. Her fingernails were digging long tracks in her forearms. The pain was wonderful. It made her feel alive—renewed. She didn't stop. She *couldn't* stop. She wanted to touch bone, to gnaw the flesh and muscle from the ivory limbs and feel the pain wash over her. That would take away this feeling of dread—of *death*. Maybe it could take away centuries of killing and bloodshed.

"Miss Red?" came an anxious voice from beyond the window. Small pebbles started plinking to the ground below her, as the boyish individual outside tried to garner her attention. "Is anybody home?"

"Not now, Avery," she called through the bars. She couldn't stand up to look out, nor did she want to. Her burly friend who came by to see her every couple of nights picked a bad time for a visit. His gleeful, dimwitted laughter echoed as he skipped away.

There was a slight movement on her mattress. Something was on the bed, pulling at the blanket. She knew what it was—*who* it was.

She crawled across the floor, leaving bloody handprints on the cold stone and snatched the blanket away, revealing a long-dead squirrel that smelled worse than the rotting food. Its body was mangled and its fur was ripped in places, but its eyes—its eyes were pure and alive. They were unblinking and focused on her every move. It was Ruin, god of the dead, presenting himself, just as he had many times in the past.

The squirrel's body stretched, as if trying to awaken stiff bones. It sat up and hopped off the bed, limping as if it had limited use of its legs. The eyes never left her.

"Look at you," it said with an unmoving mouth. The voice of Ruin was calm and steady.

Kersey sat back against the wall, digging fresh cuts into her arm.

"Why are you here, Kersey, at the brutal hands of mortals who don't know who or what you are?" The squirrel's head tilted to the side, interested in her answer.

"Why do you keep bothering me?"

"Why do you keep ignoring reason?"

She was silent. Ruin often made a lot of sense after she had time to dwell on it, although she'd never let him know.

"I don't. You know why I stay. Please leave me." She clenched her fists and dug her nails into the palms of her hands.

"I know why you *hide*, but I don't know why you stay. I'm here to amend my offer." The squirrel crept closer on its broken legs.

"I've no need of your offers. I'm content here, as long as I'm absent of your harassment." This much was true. Even though Ruin made good points, she was here for a reason and had no intentions of leaving. She would stay here as long as time, gods, and mortals would allow her.

"You won't be content much longer, dear. Mydian now knows you are here." And in one, short sentence, he said the only thing that could motivate her to leave. Her eyes stung with the promise of tears.

"What? How do you know that?" she demanded.

"There is death wherever Mydian's servants are, and wherever there is death, there are *my* servants." The rodent managed a lopsided smile.

"I cannot die," was all she said, as calm as she could. Kersey had to stay alive. It wasn't just a rational fear of death—of *dying*. It was so much more than that.

"Oh but you will, my dear," Ruin reminded. "If you stay here, either Mydian or the mortals will see to that."

Kersey put her head on her knee and she could feel just how much she was trembling. Fear was such a useless, irritating emotion.

"You're powerful, Kersey." The squirrel was almost in her lap. "The long years passed have made you forget this. You are a force to be reckoned with. You are one of the *Ten*. Start acting like it."

She swatted the advancing squirrel away. "I've no need for savagery. I've had several lifetimes worth of it." Blood was still dripping from her fingertips.

"That may be true, but there's no changing what you are."

"I'm a person."

"Not anymore."

"Leave!" she screamed. The lanterns down the hallway flickered and went out. All the small sounds of the prison and the crickets outside the window hushed.

Kersey's attention tore from the squirrel to the hallway as the heavy footfalls of the guards approached. There was no way they could see her from the darkened passage but their faces were completely visible to her dilated eyes. They were smiling.

"Keep mindful of my offer," Ruin whispered. "I can protect you from Mydian's wrath." With that, the squirrel's head dropped and its body went limp. The eyes that once held a focused life dimmed to the dead black of a corpse.

The guard unlocked the door and stepped into the cell, grinning at just how much blood there was on the floor. Another one stood nearby, hand tensed over his sword.

"C'mon," the guard next to her said, nudging her in the ribs. "Clive wants to talk with you."

It was so calm out tonight. Looking through the window, across Hillchapel Cemetery and past deserted streets, he could see the docks at the edge of town. The gentle waves crashed against the Tharg beach, rocking the galleys and schooners from side to side. No one would have ever guessed what had just happened in the prison across the street.

Clive Porter didn't believe it himself when his aid first told him. He knew Kersey was capable of such a thing, but he didn't believe she would do it so openly—so blatantly. She had a reputation for doing strange things that should have been impossible for one in captivity. Thinking back on it, she may have been responsible for several other murders.

He didn't want to deal with this. More than that, he didn't want to be the bearer of bad news—awful, horrible news. But it was his job. Clive had worked with her for several years, had been responsible for her rehabilitation and was responsible for her actions. Her actions tonight were a sad testimony of how well her rehabilitation had gone. Why did *he* have to be in charge?

The aging man paced back and forth in Kriball Manor, waiting for the guards to bring her before him. He straightened his tunic and adjusted his tie. He ran tired fingers through his wavy, parted hair. This was probably the best he'd managed to look in quite some time. After all, he'd just arrived from a funeral.

A loud grinding sound tore him from the window. The door to the banquet hall swung open and in walked Bral Simsey, one of the Pen's guards, along with Kersey, shackled at the hands and feet. Bral offered him a smile—an eerie, *'don't worry, we nailed her, boss'* smile.

Clive motioned for Bral to seat her at the long table in the center of Kriball's massive dining hall. The guard pulled the chair out and shoved her down so hard that the water pitcher and glasses on the table rattled. She didn't seem to mind at all.

"Take those off her," Clive ordered, pointing to the shackles on her hands. Bral gave him a questioning look, but did nothing else. "You heard me, Bral, take those off her! And the ones on her feet, too." Again the burly guard was taken aback, but pulled his key ring out, nonetheless. Clive seated himself opposite of the small woman and poured himself a glass of water. Bral finished unlocking her hands and feet and started out, shackles in hand.

"Lock the door, please," Clive called. Bral threw his hand up in the air and pulled it shut. The room was strangely silent, other than the occasional flicker of the wall lanterns.

Kersey simply sat there, slumped forward with her eyes fixed on the table. Had it not been there, she would have tipped over into the floor. Her silky hair was matted and covering much of her face—a face smeared with far too much blood. Her arms didn't look any better. Each pasty limb was just as coated in thick, crimson ichor.

"Kers," Clive breathed, drumming his fingers on the table. She didn't budge. She remained emotionless, lifeless, and silent. It was her normal behaviour. Kersey was a woman of few words and those that she did speak were often troubled. He was never satisfied with her tone or answers.

Clive moved his chair back and stood, grabbing his glass of water. He walked over to where she was seated, leaned against the table and pulled out his handkerchief and dabbed it in the water. "What did you do to yourself?" he asked, and wiped the blood from her forehead. She sat back, revealing no wounds beneath the red cover.

"I'm fine," she muttered.

"As you always are." He cleaned the blood from her arm and found no wounds there, either. At one time it was strange, but Kersey had a gift for making her cuts and scrapes simply 'vanish'.

"Stop it, I said I'm fine!" She pulled her arms out of his reach and buried them beneath the bloodied, cloth tunic.

"So much blood and not a scratch on you. I would say you are more than fine." He dropped the handkerchief on the table and went back to his seat. Kersey's piercing eyes were gazing at him. Her dark stare was very unsettling, but he didn't feel threatened by it. She had never attempted to hurt him.

"So where have you been all week?" she asked, her face softening a bit. He wanted to smile but couldn't. It was sweet for her to miss him, but his reason for being away was nothing to be happy about.

This wasn't the time to dwell on things, nor was it the time to let her see him grieve.

"I've had . . . family matters to attend to. But I'm back now." Clive forced a smile.

Kersey seemed to lose interest. Her stare resumed at the blank spot on the table, her thin fingers gripping it like piano keys. She was trembling.

"So are you going to tell me what happened out there?" he asked, leaning back.

"The guards beat me and tried to rape me. I defended myself," was all she said. Her eyes flickered up for just a moment.

"Really? That won't be very convincing when I write to six families tonight to let them know their sons were savagely butchered at the hands of a woman not much bigger than a child." Clive hunkered down and tried to snatch her stare.

"Well, it's the truth."

"What are you, Kersey?" he bluntly asked. "Really, what are you?" This had plagued him for far too long and here, at her inevitable end, he wanted to know.

"I'm a person," was her only, simple answer.

"You're more than a person, girl," Clive chuckled. "You're something else. How long have you been a prisoner here, Kers?"

"Fifteen years, four months, and nine days." She didn't hesitate a second.

"And I've been here three years longer. I remember the day you came. Little ole' you tried to steal a couple of peaches from Market Lane in broad daylight. Very unusual."

"I was hungry," she offered.

"Really?" He stood and walked over to the window again. "I don't think I've ever seen you eat. But back to your time served here.

As I said, I've been here for eighteen years and after three, you came to me." He turned around and pointed at her as he spoke. "And you look today as you did back then. This prison is unkind dearest Kersey, just as you've seen tonight. A person should age twice as fast." He smirked to himself. "I certainly look older than my forty-four years."

"What is your point, Clive?" The hanging lanterns flickered slightly.

"My point . . . Kersey, is that there's too much that I don't know of you. People have sworn to have seen you outside your cell, on many occasions." This one Clive could never figure out.

Six years ago, a woman came to the prison claiming she had just watched Kersey slaughter her husband and then carry his heart away into the darkness. When Clive was awakened and told the news, he ran to the prison and up to Kersey's cell, only to find her sleeping on the floor. There had been several other incidents that were equally as puzzling and unsolved.

"We've talked about this before, Cl— "

"And those same nights you were supposedly out, there were vicious murders . . . cruel murders involving neck and chest lacerations. What do you know of this?"

"Nothing. I've told you this many, *many* times. If I could get out to kill someone, why would I come back?" Her mouth was quivering with each word. Kersey was finally keeping eye contact and Clive was starting to wish she was still staring at the table.

"I have no idea, but I'm sure you have your reasons." He flopped back down and pulled his chair closer. He sat up with his elbows on the table and stared back with a look that rivaled her own.

"Kersey, how many times have we talked in this very room?" She raised an eyebrow. "How many times have I told you stories of my childhood and of affairs outside the cell?" He tilted his head, waiting for her to come up with the genuine answer.

"Many," simply put.

"I like you, Kersey," he admitted. It was the truth. Kersey had always listened to him talk. Anytime his day had been bad, Kersey had listened. And anytime Clive needed her in the past, Kersey had listened. "For once I wished you would have opened up so I could have known who you really were."

"Why am I here?" she asked, slightly digging her nails into the table.

"Why do you think?" He couldn't meet her stare any longer.

"What's going to happen?" She leaned up, the hair finally cleared from her face.

This was the part he had dreaded from the moment those words came to him. *Kersey just killed six men.*

 She would listen to him talk no more.

"You're going to be executed, Kersey."

"What? Why?" He didn't like the strength in her voice.

"Why do you think? You butchered six guards!"

"Who tried to *rape* me!" she cried.

"It doesn't matter, Kersey! Their families aren't going to care about you. If your blood isn't splattered all over Windsycle Hill, there will be a riot in the streets." Clive couldn't take his eyes off of her. He hated himself for what he just told her but he needed to see her reaction.

But nothing happened. She pulled her hair behind her ears and stared out the window. It was unbroken. She was entranced, just as always. This was her way to escape reality. It was her way of making all the noise in the world vanish. Or so he thought.

"I cannot die," was her only reply.

"What are you looking at, Kers?" He followed her gaze outside and saw a few people standing in the narrow road between Kriball Manor and Roseberry Terrace. "There's nothing out there but Hillchapel Cemetery."

There was a low thump that resonated beneath him, as if near the cellar. Was there even a cellar under Kriball?

"There was a battle here, long ago on this very spot. Am I right?" Kersey still watched outside, never blinking, never taking her eyes from Hillchapel.

"What are you talking about, Kers?"

—THUMP.

The water in the glass and pitcher on the table rippled slightly. *What was* that?

"Here where we are sitting. A hundred men killed a dolgatha, right here." Dolgathas were large beasts that resembled ogres but had reptilian skin and a long, spiked tail. They were very rare in Southern Corscus, but up north, they were quite abundant.

Clive kept watching the window with her, as if waiting for someone to come through. There were more people outside, lingering near the manor.

"You're referring to the Tharg Uprising," he realized. "They kept the dolgatha in the holding cells of the old prison in case a riot ever broke out. It was used to restore order."

—THUMP.

"How do you know they killed it here?" he wondered. "That was almost two-hundred years—"

His words were lost when he felt the floor shift a little beneath his foot. He slid his seat back and looked under the table and noticed a thin fissure running from his chair to Kersey's. Before he had time to register it or take a closer look, something more bizarre happened.

A black vine, dotted with crimson leaves and sickly buds of browns and yellows slithered out of the crevice like a snake. Then there was another, and another until finally there was a virtual garden of nasty bulbs and black tendrils. They moved with a grace and intelligence that Clive didn't understand. Each vine pulled to the side, splitting the fissure in the marble floor even further. He looked up to Kersey, who finally decided to look his way.

"I know about it because it's still buried here." She cocked her head to the side and with that, the vines jerked toward the walls, opening up a massive hole in the floor. Pieces of marble and table flew across the room and Clive was forced backwards and out of his seat. He slammed against the ground and shielded his head as splinters of wood and marble rained down on him.

Through clenched eyes, he spotted Kersey, still sitting calmly in her chair, the table now scraps across the room. The vines in the floor parted and suddenly a massive, skeletal arm reached out and grabbed onto the nearby marble.

Another hand surfaced and together they hoisted a colossal beast from the hole. It was indeed a dolgatha. What was left of it, at least. What stood towering over him were the skeletal remains, but that was changing, if only a little.

The vines were wrapping themselves around the enormous creature and with each pass, the dolgatha's body was slightly mended. Its bones creaked and groaned as new tufts of scale and flesh sprouted. A pair of reptilian eyes bulged inside its barren sockets and glared at Clive. It was far from reconstructed, but it looked as if it had been healed enough to hold together. Enough to cause something or someone harm.

"Kersey, are you doing this?" he called. She was lifeless, as she had been most of the meeting. The dolgatha's dead eyes stayed with him, but it made no apparent move to hurt him.

"Kersey? Kersey!" he called again.

Clive slipped by the monster, clamping his eyes shut. Its hands were as big as his head. With the dolgatha's strength, it would have been quite easy to rip him limb from limb.

"Kersey!" he yelled once more to the mesmerized woman as he shook her by the shoulders. He was about to squeeze her, to break her concentration when several of the black vines wrapped around his torso and arms and jerked him back, toward the window.

He fought the enslaving tendrils, squeezing them, trying to break them, but they wouldn't give. His hand closed around one of the yellowish buds and tightened. It burst open and a brownish-black ichor that smelled of rotting flesh gushed out and ran between his fingers. He fought back the urge to dump this morning's breakfast. There was a knife in his pocket. His arm found a hole in the vines' hold and he moved quickly toward his slacks—

—when glass broke behind him and hands reached through to grab him. At first he thought it was help—thought that Bral or Harick had heard the noise but that turned out to be quite wrong. The hand was as decayed as the dolgatha. There were vines swarming all over it, too. The fingernails were dirty and jagged. Suddenly there were several men trying to squeeze through the small window, all with the help of the black vines.

They were all dead men.

Each was dressed in formal clothing that was spilling clumps of dirt. Their eyes were sunken in their heads, those *with* eyes, anyway. Some were so decayed that nothing remained but a featureless skull. These men had all been buried in Hillchapel Cemetery.

The undead dropped through the window and the vines helped them regain their footing. They climbed over Clive, using him as support and leverage to find their way into Kriball Manor. There were a total of nine, and they all turned their attention to Clive, with the dolgatha towering above them in the back.

Kersey finally stood and stared at him. He had a frantic look across his face. His heart was beating so fast. He couldn't remember the last time he was truly this fearful. Kersey approached him and the cluster of undead parted for her to pass. The vines were encircling her head like a crown, her hands like daggers, and her torso like a shield.

"Shhh," she said, bringing her finger to his lips. "I cannot die."

.2.

Orientation

If one were to describe the mood of the Infernal Underworld, it would be summed up best as 'chaotic'. Although Mydian's domain was thrown into an uproar, it wasn't normally a place of frenzy and disorder. Sure, the lava basin that filled Mount Cytop churned with the burnt, screaming bodies of the dark lord's deserters and betrayers, but overall, the Underworld was calm.

There were rumors. *Dark* rumors about war, about betrayal, and about long-standing deceit. Mydianites were gearing up for battle and it was all starting with the preparation of the Underworld. Dyne had never seen the Infernal, nor did she know the chaos was out of place. After all, one didn't die and go to Mydian's realm but once.

She had been a vampire, in the mortal realm of Mystyria and in an instant, that life was snatched away. Her skin burnt, her eyes melted, and her soul was whisked to this ominous place. When she awoke, she was on a table, her sister not far away. The passing of life to afterlife was quick, painless, and overwhelming.

"It's been this way for weeks now," Telsa said, pulling her down a shallow set of steps and into a massive, granite foyer. The black walls were gleaming against the reflection of a nearby flow of lava. It was so hot here—so hot, and eerily luminous.

"What's happening?" Dyne asked, taking notice of the soldiers darting back and forth. Some were carrying troves of blades, while others pushed huge cauldrons on wheels that were filled to the brim with smoldering steel. There were rope bridges all along the upper lofts, connecting numerous tunnels where more Mydianites moved about in similar urgency. A pair of Magma Imps was rolling barrels down a steep decline and into a dark crevice.

"I think it'd be best if Mydian told you," Telsa offered. "After all, this is all partly due to your arrival."

The Infernal Underworld stood up to all the grandeur that the songs and lore of Mystyria proclaimed. Most of it was a large, basalt city called Luthewell. This was where those faithful to the Master found themselves the moment after they took their last breath. On the border of Luthewell stood Castle Hiriam, Mydian's home and the girls' destination.

"Stop," Dyne called, tugging her sister's arm.

"What?" Telsa almost managed before being pulled into a strong embrace. Warm tears were budding on their gowns with the girls' heads buried against one another.

"I've missed you, sister," Dyne breathed through sobs. "How have you been?"

Telsa separated herself and gazed up with nostalgic eyes. A weak grin festered. It had been over three years since they'd last seen one another.

"I've been good. I'm one of Mydian's couriers now. I'm actually very well liked around here," she said, matter-of-factly. Dyne couldn't remember when her smile looked this way. There had been fangs there the last she saw.

"Of course you are," Dyne smiled, wiping a tear from her sister's eye. "And you seem happier now than I've ever known."

"Well, it's hard for you to be sick when you're already dead." For most of Telsa's life she had battled a deadly blood disease called Pinprick. It almost killed her but Dyne intervened and made her a vampire.

That was the day the animosity for lord Mydian came. Although Dyne had served him for most of her life—she felt at odds with him because of his method to 'save her life'. He *bit* her—*infested* her with the curse of the vampire. After that, he told her the only way to save Telsa was to do the same. Mydian might have delivered them both from death, but he had condemned them to a life of torment and despair.

"And look at those beautiful green eyes," Dyne said, stroking her check. "I haven't seen those in quite some time."

Telsa blushed and put a hand to her sister's solemn face. "You have the same eyes now, as well." On the eve of their vampiracy, their beautiful emerald-green eyes had been snatched away and replaced by black, lifeless dots.

In the Underworld, they were just lingering souls but their bodies appeared unchanged from a mortal's. They breathed, blinked, shed tears and ached in the bones. This was all part of the coping process. It was the part of immortality that kept the mind sane. And it was all true, Dyne realized. Telsa was dead. *She* was dead, and this was indeed the afterlife.

Her mood quickly darkened. Her thoughts drifted back to the last events of her life—the same events that passed only moments ago.

Her skin was bubbling—burning and melting from the bone. Mortals were standing all around, happily gawking at her sudden and unexpected demise. She thought of the crying; of the horrible tears that ran down her little girl's face as she watched her mommy cook on the Lylussian temple's floor.

Her *Hannah's* tears.

True, Hannah didn't belong to her, but they were related by blood. The little girl found her way into Dyne's arms a few years ago and she cared for her—fed her, bathed her, taught her how to draw pictures, but in the end, her true father ripped her away. Tranas had killed Dyne and took Hannah back.

She fought back the impulse to scream—to reach up and pull the hair from her skull, but she wouldn't allow it. It would all be for nothing. She was dead now. Even though the most traumatic event of her life happened only moments ago, it was time to put it behind her.

Dyne was visibly shaken and she could see the recognition in her sister's eyes. The young girl led her on, gentle hands pulling her arm.

"It's okay, sister," she comforted. "You needn't be concerned with Mystyria's dealings any longer." She turned around and gracefully took Dyne's other hand as well. There was a massive structure in the distance of the darkened world. "You're safe here."

She agreed. Even though the hurt would carry with her for ages to come, at least mortals weren't hunting her any more. At least now she didn't have to drink blood and avoid Lylussian temples. If there had been a sun in the Underworld, she wouldn't have had to worry about it, either. Here, she was closer to living than she had been in over three-hundred years.

Telsa guided her through a few of Luthewell's streets. There was no sky above—only a black void. The dark cobblestones were separated by tiny streams of lava that looked liked an intricate, fiery-red spider web. Small wafts of smoke lingered along the ground. Most of the homes looked like typical Mystyrian dwellings more commonly seen in cities such as Bloodgate and Crynsia. The only difference here was that the work the townsfolk did served Mydian and not themselves. Wood and steel was processed, turned into weapons, and then sent back to Mystyria for the troops to use.

Dyne and Telsa made their way up a path that looked like crushed coal. At the top sat Castle Hiriam. Its faceted stone and ominous towers rose so high that it merged with the darkness above. From here, the tortured screams of the bodies burning in Mount Cytop were but a distant noise—a simple reminder of what happened when someone was unfaithful to their god.

Magma Golems guarded the perimeter of the castle. They were colossal humanoids with a molten rock exterior and a blood-driven, beating heart interior. The halberds they carried were twice the size of the girls next to it. Luckily, the guardians let them pass—only watching with eyes that puffed black smoke.

The massive doors swung in and a low, grinding echo reverberated the grounds.

"I love the castle," Telsa said, and then pointed to the east wing that extended further than any structure on Mystyria. "My room is down that way, as well as Lorne's. Dunford lived here until he stole a statue from the foyer and now he's churning in the lava."

"Lorne," Dyne breathed, and then stopped.

"What is it?"

"I just realized something. Everyone I know is already here." Her eyes were welling with tears, but Telsa didn't seem to understand what caused it.

"What's wrong, sister?" She crept closer.

"Which way to Laraek's quarters?" Dyne asked, looking the castle over. Her fiancé, who met his death over three-hundred years ago, just before her vampiracy, was a devout follower of Mydian. Surely his room was nearby. Telsa's grim look told her otherwise.

"His soul isn't here, Dyne," she said, not meeting her sister's gaze. "He must have joined Lyluss or Quillian's cause and went to one of them when he died. No one has heard from him."

"Impossible," Dyne spat, refusing to believe such nonsense.

"It's true!" Telsa yelled, gathering attention from a patrolling Magma Golem down the hall. "There's no other explanation. If he isn't here, then he is somewhere else. Not even Mydian can see into the other gods' realms." The Magma Golem lost interest and continued down the hall, its massive feet hammering the obsidian floor.

Laraek's final resting place was in Boudia, the northernmost city on Mystyria—the one spot in the world where the sun never sat. Dyne had searched high and low to find the heart of a Greater Overlord—the first vampires—in order to gain the power to walk in the daylight. Her motivation had always been to see his grave. That was the enticement that made her get up every night.

A brief flicker of joy had come and gone. In her constant searches of Mystyria to gain allowance to see his grave, Dyne held onto one certainty: whether or not she succeeded, she would ultimately be rejoined with Laraek when she passed over. Now, even that had been ripped from her. She was at the bottom and could sink no further. All she had left, all she could do now was *exist*.

She also needed to see what Mydian needed.

"C'mon," Telsa urged, pulling her down the hall and out of the web of a thousand, saddened memories.

The throne room of Hiriam Castle was unlike any of the stories she heard as a child. Mystyrian legend proclaimed it to be a mile wide and high, with the skulls of Felornites as flooring. There was supposed to be a massive throne with two seats to the right where sat Mydian's two greatest champions—Kaider Thornsoul and Adella Bloodhoof. In reality, the audience chamber was quite different.

Most of the lavish room was dyed a bright, scarlet red. There was lush, black carpet on the floor and the walls were adorned with the mounted heads of creatures Dyne had never seen. Along the back wall was a long, yet tall window. Looking through it, the streams of lava could be seen trickling down the sides of Mount Cytop. A single figure sat at a table next to the window, drumming his fingers and watching the chaos unfold down in Luthewell.

"My lord," Telsa breathed and then knelt. Dyne was too dumbfounded that they were in the presence of a god that she didn't feel her sister tugging on her gown, coaxing her to do the same. She knelt, but watched him, still.

When Mydian turned around, her heart and mind fled three centuries in the past, to a stormy, rainy camp where her sister lay ill, death not far off. They were overlooking Keswing, just after the dissolve of the second War of Balance and Mydian, the very god who started it all, came strolling into their camp. He looked today just as he had then. The same sunken eyes, the same weathered, pale skin and the same featureless, but ominous black robe was present. Only now he didn't have seven-inch fangs.

"Rise, children," he said, smiling and holding out his hand. Dyne thought the grin to be very creepy. "I see the two of you have reunited, once again."

Dyne was too uneasy to make a move. Telsa never had the nightmares of this man—this god, and didn't know what it was like to try and push his face from mind.

Mydian approached the girls and looked them over. It was silent. Cytop was alive in the distance but the throne room was unnervingly quiet.

"And I see you finally made your way here, Emba." Dyne closed her eyes. She hadn't gone by her birth name in quite some time.

He placed his hands around her wrists, admiring her like a father on his daughter's wedding day. His touch was warm, but sent shivers down her spine, nevertheless. She had trouble meeting his stare, no matter how humble it was becoming.

Then, without warning, his kind demeanor faded. Mydian's hand lashed out and struck her across the face, stumbling her a few steps toward the door. Telsa gasped, but the small flicker of fire in the dark god's eyes stayed her hand and tongue. Dyne wasn't angry, nor was she afraid. A part of her had expected that. She already knew the reason.

"That's for murdering Arctis!" he spat, shaking the very walls. "You destroyed a plan that took centuries to conceive." His tone slowly grew gentler.

Arctis had been one of Lyluss' grand dragon slayers but after the curse he became a loathsome vampire—a servant of the dark lord.

"Say you're sorry," Telsa whispered, nudging Dyne in the ribs. She couldn't speak. She *wouldn't* speak.

"She's too headstrong for that, dear Telsa," Mydian said, backing away a bit. "Or perhaps just incredibly foolish."

"May I be a part of this, as well?" asked a taunting voice from the door. The sisters turned around and Dyne's heart raced at the sight of the large brute looking her over, his tattooed face turned into a satisfied scowl.

"You thieving maggot!" she screamed and started for him. After only a step, she hit an invisible wall that held her in place. The last time she saw this man he was on the bad end of her blade. He destroyed her little girl's sketchpad and stole her sister's sword. She wanted to wrap her fingers around his face and claw his eyes out.

It was Lorne. He was dressed in similar armor to that of Mydian's elite soldiers on Mystyria—shiny gold and flat black. He shot Dyne a wicked stare, much like the last one he ever made alive. After all, he had every reason to hate her. She killed him only a few hours ago. Apparently he had already made himself at home.

"There'll be no retribution between mortals here." was all that Mydian said just as Dyne felt the invisible hand around her waist loosen. He turned to her and added, "Especially *unjustified* retribution." What did that mean? she wondered. She had every right to slay Lorne for taking things that were so precious to her.

"I was just about to send for you, Lorne," said Mydian. "What is it that you need?"

He passed Dyne and pushed her shoulder, almost sending her to the floor. She gave his backside a foul look and gritted her teeth.

"My lord," he bowed. "Daegin wishes to contact you."

"Very well," Mydian said, walking off. "You may stay."

Lorne flashed Dyne a wicked grin and tapped his lip, motioning for her to do the same. She felt a small drop of blood where Mydian struck her. The brute stood next to her and smirked, watching the dark god pull a tiny vial from a nearby shelf.

Mydian uncorked it and tossed the contents to the floor. A red ichor oozed out and began to solidify. It was as if it were passing over an invisible human—coating every inch of him in crimson muck. When the vial was drained, there stood a slick, bloodied, and unmoving figure that looked like a slender man wearing armor.

"My darkest lord," came a voice from within the bloodied phantom. Dyne could see its mouth moving with each word. His eyes were blue and brilliant. It reminded her of a man whose flesh had been burnt to a crisp. Although it looked like a body, somewhere in the world this man was standing in front of a portal, conversing as normal from that end.

"What news have you for me, Daegin?" the dark god asked.

"A few of my men became . . . forceful with her," he answered, blood bubbles bursting in his mouth as he spoke. "It was enough for her to make a stand. She's no choice but to abandon her hiding spot."

Who could they be talking about? Dyne wondered. What person on Mystyria would be so important that Mydian, the ruler of the Underworld himself, would be summoned to hear of it?

"Do you want us to get rid of her?" Daegin asked.

Mydian chuckled. "I would *love* to be rid of her. Unfortunately, you and your men lack the capacity to deal with such a powerful enemy. Besides, your work in Tharg is too important."

"But my lord, please let us try—"

"Help is on the way," Mydian blurted out, casting an anxious eye to Dyne. He turned his attention back to the bloody phantom and asked, "What have you learned of the book's arrival?"

Daegin hesitated a moment before answering. "I was able to break into Fyrl's private chambers last week. The exchange is scheduled to happen tomorrow night. That place is locked up pretty tight, though." Dyne could see the bloody smile on his face. His teeth were gleaming white and were as brilliant as his eyes.

"You *must* use discretion, Daegin. Should Fyrl learn of your snooping, should he become fearful that it won't be safe in his company..." His voice trailed off.

"No one will ever suspect I did a thing, my lord. *This* is my specialty."

"Very good, Daegin," Mydian said. "That will be all."

The bloody man said a thank you and the solid shape was no more. It splashed across the floor and then quickly dried, shriveling up like a rotten piece of fruit. Before long, it was nothing but dark ash that disappeared into oblivion.

"Terrible things are about to happen on Mystyria," Mydian said to the room. "I fear that I've been betrayed by my fellow gods." His face was somber, like an aging old man who saw his end in sight.

"Who would do such a thing?" Lorne asked.

"Ruin," simply put. "Ruin wants to start a war."

"Why would he do that?" Dyne finally asked, gathering a look from all three. The god of the dead was supposed to be an ally, or so she thought.

"Because he sees an opportunity to undo all that I have on Mystyria," Mydian admitted. "I'm sure you've seen the uproar of my world?"

He pointed out across Luthewell and then motioned for Dyne to join him. When she was hesitant to move, Lorne and Telsa both shoved her in his direction. She sneered at Lorne and approached her dark god, keeping her eyes focused out the window.

Luthewell was bursting at the seams with life, or at least souls. There were workshops dotting the town, building siege weapons and armor, mainly cannons and ballistae.

She could remember the first time she ever saw a ballista. It wasn't until they were outside the gates of Keswing and Laraek was rolling one up the hill with two other men. She asked what it was and he told her it was a giant crossbow. Dyne had giggled by his explanation, but in truth, that's what it was. Instead of launching arrows or bolts, it launched six-foot spears. The following weeks, she became more accustomed to ballistae—the big ones that wrecked walls, all the way to the small ones that were on swivels and used to rip riders from their horses.

Her eyes fixed on the narrow road that rose from Luthewell and disappeared into the darkness of the Underworld's ceiling. There were rows of catapults and ballistae being hauled up and out of sight. Battle-ready soldiers on horseback were escorting wagons. Mydian was building weapons and training troops, then moving them up toward Mystyria. But how could he get them out? Only the Master himself was able to leave the Infernal. Mydian sealed his great domain in fearful isolation long ago, worried that the other gods would one day come to destroy him.

"What does all this have to do with me?" Dyne asked, finally looking him in the eye. She could feel Telsa's glare on her back.

"I'm moving all this equipment to Mystyria because I am being forced to protect my interests. As I said, Ruin seeks to betray me."

Why would Mydian assume Ruin was a betrayer? Dyne wondered. This had to be the first time in the history of the world. Ruin was just as evil—as foul as Mydian, and was just as alienated from the rest of the gods.

"But my lord," Lorne spoke up. "We were sent seven statues of gold and platinum from the god of the dead. What leads us to believe he will betray us?"

"Those pretentious offerings are farce!" Mydian spat, vibrating the walls. "Those were donated on false semblances of peace! Ruin has treachery on his lips!" He turned and looked to Dyne. "And I believe *she* is our proof."

She exchanged glances with Lorne and Telsa, then to Mydian. She was about to raise the question but the dark god interrupted with, "You don't know, do you?"

He focused on Telsa and added, "Didn't you tell her?"

The young girl shook her head. "No, not yet."

Mydian turned back to Dyne, a hint of curiosity in his eyes. "The thoughts of your last bit of life are still fresh in your mind, are they not?"

She nodded, forehead wrinkling in confusion. What piece of this mystery had she not been told?

"And the pain of your flesh burning, it still hurts? After all, it was only a short while ago."

Again, she nodded.

"Well to you, it was moments ago, but to the rest of the world it was an incident that happened over twelve years ago."

Her head snapped up, eyes wide with disbelief. "What?" This could *not* be. Hannah, the heart, and the murder of Arctis . . . it was all so fresh in her mind. Telsa couldn't look at her, obviously ashamed that she hadn't broken the news just yet.

"That's right, my dear," Mydian chuckled. "You died and left Mystyria over a decade ago. Your soul only recently found its way here."

"I don't understand," Dyne admitted.

"Neither do we," Telsa chimed in.

"You know what happens when you die, right?" Mydian asked. Dyne nodded that she did.

When a mortal perished on Mystyria, their soul was bound for one of the gods' worlds, depending on whom they served or betrayed in life. But every soul was sorted in a place called Upper Gothmirk. Its ruler was none other than Ruin, god of the dead.

"You see, for some reason Ruin delayed your arrival to my world."

"But why me?" she asked, eyeing her sister. "Why am I so important?"

Before he could answer, two of Mydian's servants walked in, each carrying a tall, black urn. They sat them on the table, nodded to their god, and then hastily left.

"You want to go back to Mystyria, don't you?" Mydian asked unexpectedly. She didn't say a word. "Don't you?" he repeated.

"I want *revenge*," she spoke, feeling every drop of bloody vengeance course through her veins. "I don't care what it takes as long as the man who killed us gets what he deserves."

"You know I don't just grant favors without some sort of . . . *contract*," he said tactfully.

"Trust me, I know."

"Just how bad does Dyne the great want her revenge?" he asked. "What will you do for me if I send you back to Mystyria to hunt the one who hunted you?"

"Whatever it takes," she growled. So badly she wanted to track Tranas down, no matter where twelve years of time had spat him.

"Ruin's plans are drawn against me, but he will not do it alone. He needs the help of a very special individual. I want you to *kill* her."

"Sounds simple enough. Just point me to her," she said, feeling a rush of courage that could have probably carried her up to Mystyria.

Mydian chuckled and sat on the edge of the table. "It won't be that easy, I'm afraid. She's one of the *Ten*."

"Which one?" Dyne asked, seeing the connection now with Daegin's 'all too powerful' enemy. "Alexa or Kersey?"

"I see you've learned quite a bit in your searches. Alexa is behaving like a good little girl and isn't important. I want Kersey Avonwood."

Dyne knew everything there was to know about Kersey. She had followed her for four years around Darcascis and Sorcea. Dyne had even had her childhood home in Keswing searched and ransacked. She had even been there, in Tharg, moments before Kersey had supposedly been killed.

"Why would you want her dead?" she asked. "Aren't all the Greater Overlords working for you?" She thought that was how the stories went. All of them lost their Lylussian faith and found refuge in Mydian's offerings.

"*Most* work for me, in one way or another," he said. "But Kersey is different. She is weak in mind and spirit and is of no use. But Ruin has a need for her . . . *special* talents and will most likely manipulate her into helping."

"And you want *me* to kill her?" Dyne said, almost laughing. "The only reason I bested Arctis was because I had Evan Stormwood's heart inside of me. There's no way I can do this alone."

"You won't have to. I need you to travel to Pelopha. Do you know where that is?" Mydian asked her.

She nodded. Her searches for the Greater Overlords had taken her to the cliff-side city a number of times. "Roughly eighty miles south of Tharg."

"What memory!" he exclaimed, clasping his hands together. "You will meet up with one of my most prized commanders. Along with his crew, you will have no trouble sending her soul straight to here."

"Is this even permitted?" Dyne asked, knowing it wasn't.

"Of course it's not, my dear. If Telsis learned I was sending souls back to Mystyria then I would probably be banished to Erolas." His eyes darkened and his voice grew soft, but harsh. "But these are troubling times and drastic action is a must."

Even the mortals of Mystyria knew this divine law. Once a soul passed from the world of the living to the heavenly realms beyond, they were to never return. All the gods possessed the power to send them back in one way or another, but Telsis forbade it.

"Souls?" Lorne spoke, probably just realizing why he was 'about to be sent for'.

"That's right," the dark god said, his tone now brighter. "You are going with her." He turned back to Dyne and sadistically added, "I have to make sure you don't run off and chase Tranas without first doing your job."

Lorne's face grimaced, but he nodded and bowed his head nonetheless. Dyne couldn't help but crack a smile, even though she despised this job as much as he did.

"My lord, will this Daegin be joining us?" the scowling man asked.

"I'm afraid not. Daegin is a valuable asset, which makes me very uneasy given the current mission I'm sending him on. That is why I am entrusting this job to the two of you and my men you will meet in Pelopha."

Dyne wondered just what this 'current mission' was all about. Somehow she figured it had to do with the book that was 'exchanging hands' tomorrow night.

"Could you both give us a moment?" Mydian asked Lorne and Telsa. The two bowed and left the dark god and Dyne alone in the still throne room.

He turned to the window and said, "Look."

Dyne followed his long, slender finger to a large house that sat on a rocky hill in the distance. It was nestled in the cliffs and probably had a better view of Luthewell than Castle Hiriam. There were tall, onyx chimneys sputtering orange smoke—the byproduct of brewing Craviin hops for Lorinstag Ale. It was just *so* massive.

"That is *your* mansion, Dyne," he said, smiling widely.

"Mine?" she gasped, straining for a better look.

"That's right. I had it built long ago, just for you and your family."

"My . . . *family*?" she muttered. Tears started to streak down her cheeks.

"Yes, dear. Both of your brothers, as well as your mother and father. And they will be waiting on you when you return." Mydian pulled her away from the window. "Go to Pelopha and meet my commander. He will take you to Tharg and when you make it back to my realm, *that* will be what awaits for you." He pointed again, reassuring her that it was still there.

Everything here was complete. This was the end of Dyne's—of *Emba's* saga. All the things she had done in life and in her vampiracy had led her to this place. Now that she had seen it, she would go back to Mystyria in the sake of getting to return and stay here.

Everything here was *complete*.

Everything except—

Laraek.

"It will be done, Lord Mydian," she offered and lowered her head, trying her best to not rekindle the horrible truth of things. Once again, she was giving into her dark god's will. Hopefully this time it wouldn't lead to three-hundred years worth of pain and torment. "How do I know where to find this commander once we arrive in Pelopha?"

"Make your way to the Rusted Hook Tavern and wait. Someone will show you the way." He gently tugged her in his direction. "And now I am about to bestow the greatest gift of all on you." He eyed the urns on the table. "The gift of a second life."

Daegin Crane wiped the sweat from his eyes as he closed the dimensional window to the Underworld. Mydian seemed quite pleased, as well he should. There had been much work done over the past few weeks. Kersey Avonwood had been discovered, purposely rotting inside the Pen. What were the odds?

It had been four years since Daegin had been relocated to Tharg to harvest Sania, the spawning venom, from captured vampires. He had even been given a very lofty manor, its downstairs lab, and its massive library of Mydianite lore to use at his disposal.

A week ago, he had searched the records house for the Pen to locate two thieves who stole money from one of Mydian's drop-off points. Through bribes and threats, he managed to have the men poisoned, but he also learned something else—something his dark god would be happy to know.

There wasn't a Mydianite alive who didn't know the *'Silent Order'*. If anyone located Kersey Avonwood, alert the dark god immediately. Like a good little soldier, Daegin did just that. He didn't care what Mydian's interest was in her but he knew he wanted to get involved, despite the fact that someone like her could destroy everything he worked for in Tharg.

Apparently Kersey was used to being beaten. Daegin's men, or corrupt guards as they so willingly were called, had bestowed physical pain on her routinely, never realizing who or what she was.

She endured it in the sake of keeping quiet—keeping *hidden*. And then one day, she snapped. The abuse had taken its toll and for once she fought back.

Daegin's thoughts were suddenly rippled by the annoying voice of his brother's approach. He breathed an agitated sigh. By the gods, Avery was *singing*.

"Lyluss' hand and Lyluss' might!" his childlike voice rang out. *"Fills the Infernal with wondrous plight!"* Daegin's brow furrowed. *"Bashes shields and breaks blades! Lady Good shall save the day!"* He shouted the last word with enough vigor to raise voices downstairs.

Avery was just about to start the second verse when Daegin slammed him against the wall, tight fingers around his meaty throat. A normal man of his size would have pummeled Daegin into the ground, but Avery being the slow-minded person he was, thought his brother had the upper hand and the advantage of strength. Years of constant humiliation and demoralizing took away any thoughts of self worth or retaliation.

"You are in a house full of Mydianites and you are singing a Lylussian hymn!" he screamed. Avery didn't know what he had done wrong and the crooked smile on his dirty face reassured his oblivious nature.

The mage released him and the brute fell to the floor, clutching his throat. Avery struggled to his feet, finally propping himself up in the corner and panting like a dog.

He cursed their mother for bringing that dim-witted child into the world. Avery was slow to learn and even slower to obey. They both trained at the Mydianite academy back in Bloodgate but Avery was kicked out for his lack of common sense and ability to comprehend. From then on, Daegin carried the full weight of the family legacy. The great Crane mages fell on his shoulders after their mother's death.

Taritta had been a great woman—a visionary who toiled in a small workshop in the heart of the city of the Black. She had been the first to learn the secrets of storing and maintaining vampire venom after Daegin's father had contracted the disease. She had been the key to the creation of Bloodsilver. It wasn't until several years later when Daegin took her work and brought it Tharg to advance and perfect it, and also to make sure Mydian could prosper from it.

Promise me that you'll look after Avery when I'm gone, Daegin could hear her say. She uttered those very words almost ten years ago, through bloody lips, just before he slit her throat for cavorting with agents of Felorn. Mydianites were forbidden to associate with the goddess of destruction's minions ever since the second War of Balance. Fraternizing with her servants was almost as bad as befriending Lylussians.

Murdering her was easy. Not a day went by when she praised Avery's ability to do the mundane. *Look at how well he stacks boxes!* she would say. Or, *Why can't you wash dishes or go to the store that fast, Daegin?* It seemed like no matter how hard he tried, no matter how decorated his achievements were, it was never good enough for their mother—it was never good enough against the dim-witted shadow of his loathsome brother. Her annoying voice constantly rattled in his mind, drowning him in depression and overwhelming him with frustration. It wouldn't take much to end Avery's life the same way.

Daegin used to care about things—about his mother and brother, but that faded long ago. Now the thoughts and memories were nothing more than a hindrance—an annoyance that came along with a faltering agreement that was about to crumble.

I'll look after him as long as I can use him, Daegin had said. He meant every word of it.

"Where did you learn that, anyway?" he asked his brother, returning from awful childhood memories and peeling an apple with his dagger. Avery eyed it with a vigil stare, almost spellbound.

"Hey!" Daegin shouted, pounding the hilt against the table to gather his attention. "Where did you learn that hymn?"

He pointed out the window. "Miss Red. Why, she sang it when she was a little girl, yes she did!" His squirrelly laugh was irritating.

"What did I tell you about her, Avery?" Daegin fed himself a slice of apple and raised an eyebrow. "Didn't I say to *never* go back there? To never *see* her again?" He didn't know anything about this 'Miss Red', nor did he want too. All he wanted was for Avery to stop venturing near the prison.

Now he was getting frustrated—angry at his simple-minded sibling's inability to maintain attention. He sprang from his chair and pressed the blade to his clammy neck. Avery whimpered like a scared child.

"Pay attention, Avery!" He pushed the knife harder and the silent man couldn't bring himself to swallow. "I don't want you hanging around the prison any longer! We have to take care to not be seen or followed." He squeezed the hilt tighter. "Do you understand me?"

His attention was more focused with a blade trimming the hair on his neck so he immediately nodded. Daegin drew back and resumed peeling his apple, keeping a watchful, agitated eye on his all too gleeful friend.

He didn't need this headache. If one of Fyrl Jonath's guards were to follow him here, the city watch would find a hive of Mydianites— an assortment of wizards, battlemages, warriors, and cutthroats, not to mention a lab brewing secret venom. Daegin didn't want to be the one who had to tell Mydian that the Bloodsilver had been discovered and taken because his irresponsible brother wanted to see his new friend.

Avery's hand was outstretched for a banana in the basket on the table and Daegin slid it from his reach. He frowned, his bucked teeth overlapping his bottom lip.

"But I'm hungry," he whined, fingers dancing over the table.

"Then I suppose you should've had *Miss Red* feed you." Daegin smiled and flicked a piece of apple into his mouth.

Avery's breathing was heavy and sweat was soaking the armpits of his shirt. Daegin had made him deliver a few coins to a hidden Drakish temple on the other side of the city. It had to be at least three miles away. This was the only thing Avery was good at—walking great distances and handing someone a bag of gold. The Drakin even tipped him when he stopped by.

It seemed that Drak was Mydian's only ally these days. Back when the world was new, he could have easily counted on Ruin, Knashar, and Whither to help him through any situation, but that had changed.

True, Mydian was considered evil, but who *didn't* have evil in them? Even Lyluss herself had a wicked, vengeful side and Daegin knew it. Her followers killed in her name just as Mydianites did in the Master's name. Even Ruin was blurring the lines between good and evil. If he wasn't an ally of Mydian, did that make him good? Daegin didn't think so. *There's only one type of good in this world but there are countless types of evil*, his mother had told him when he was younger. It was one of the few things she had been right about. Ruin was just another bad god on his own side.

Avery slumped back down in the corner and watched the twilight sky through the window. His simple mind was lost to the setting sun but that was only for a moment. His attention was forced away when a voice from downstairs began yelling.

It was Kerro, a battlemage just like Daegin himself. "Come see this!" he was saying over and over again.

Daegin bolted toward the steps, pushing Avery aside as he tried to cut him off and get to Kerro first. "Run along and play," he said, grabbing a handful of his brother's shirt. He did as he was told.

Kerro was standing on the second floor balcony, watching the north through a Nighteye; a magical spyglass used for seeing in the dark. He handed it to Daegin and pointed toward Kriball Street.

The Nighteye zoomed and focused on Kriball Manor, or more appropriately, behind it. There were corpses staggering around, walking in rows toward the manor house. With the power of the magical lens, every maggot-infested inch of flesh could be seen in great detail.

"A zombie infestation!" Daegin cursed. "Seal the house. Let the guards deal with it."

Kerro shook his head. "No, Daegin. This is not an outbreak. These are *not* zombies." He positioned the spyglass to what he meant. "Look."

The undead were actually helping to clear dirt from the graves and pull their comrades from the ground. Even their wounds were mending, making them more durable with each step.

But if he needed any further confirmation of what was happening, it came in the form of black vines that tilled the soil and helped excavate more bodies. Nasty tendrils and bulbs ensnared the undead and walked alongside, protecting and restoring them.

"It's her," Daegin said, passing the magical lens back to Kerro.

Her undead were different than typical zombies. When the rare undead infestation took place, all living creatures were at risk. One bite—one scratch from these demented, flesh-craving monstrosities was enough to spread the curse. Kersey's undead didn't spawn by themselves. The only way she could make new ones was to raise previously dead bodies on her own.

"Kersey?" Kerro asked. "She would be *this* bold?"

"She was probably marked for execution after slaying the guards," Daegin reminded. "She didn't have a choice if she wanted to live."

"Ready the men for an attack?" Kerro suggested, already walking off.

"No," Daegin said. "Let this be Fyrl's boys' problem for now. Lord Mydian doesn't think we are capable of killing her."

"He's right," Kerro agreed with his dark god. "She's one of *them*, after all. Mydian said that help is on the way. Let them deal with her."

"And steal our glory?" He was surprised that Kerro would suggest such a thing. Daegin huffed and walked off with his companion trailing behind. "Kersey Avonwood may be powerful but she is no god." He turned to face the battlemage. "She is *not* invincible." He plucked his quill from the inkwell and jotted down a short list of ingredients on a scrap of parchment. "I want you to gather a few items for me, Kerro." The doubtful friend snatched the list.

He looked the paper over with skeptical eyes. "Some of this will be hard to get."

"I know."

"And some will have to be stolen."

"I know."

"So you plan on capturing Kersey Avonwood?"

The last of the sun was creeping behind the Hennelshith Mountains when Daegin looked out and smiled.

"No, I plan on *killing* her."

.3.
Far From Normal

In the last fifteen years Clive had seen the dead rise twice. He fought in two separate skirmishes in the Battle of T'Gira up north. He'd witnessed firsthand what undead were capable of and what they weren't. But for some reason he'd never been afraid. He looked death in the eyes countless times. Today was a different story. He was more afraid now than he could ever remember. His arms were aching against the strain of the vines holding him in place. He licked his lips and cleared his hoarse throat. He'd been screaming for help for over ten minutes now.

The room was silent and unmoving, despite being thick with corpses. All of the vines snaking their way from the floor wrapped themselves around the dolgatha and the dead men. Kersey stood about five feet from Clive, her stare never leaving him. One of the men crept close to her ear and began whispering. He had never seen such a thing. Undead were supposed to be mindless creatures driven only by their need to kill. These were different—sophisticated in a way that should have been impossible.

Clive recognized these men. One was Tarun Shever, a guard who was killed in a prison riot about ten years ago. He remembered when he took his last breath in the Lylussian temple down on Stonechapel Street. The slash wound across his rotten neck was still visible. Kersey nodded something to him and he stepped away. His arms went to the side and he was still once more, the twisting vines the only movement.

"So you have the keys to all the cemeteries?" Kersey finally asked Clive, craning her head and putting a hand to her hip.

How did she know that? he wondered. Did Tarun just *tell* her? Did that mean these undead spoke, understood, and remembered things passed? It was true that he had the keys. Tharg guards were buried all over the place and someone had to be able to allow families in to see their fallen kin. Clive was one of the few people who had access to all of the fifty or so graveyards in the city and Tarun had known this.

"What good are the keys to you, Kers?" Clive asked, looking around to her minions. "It's obvious you don't need help getting in!"

"That's true," she admitted, her creepy gaze never dropping. "But you know this city and where each of these cemeteries can be found."

She was right. Clive knew Tharg better than most. He'd lived here his whole life. In fact, the only time he ever left was to escort prisoners to other cities. Tharg was his home. He was happy here and there was no reason, other than work, to leave. He knew where to find the keyhole for each cemetery. Kersey was starting to sound like she needed a guide.

"Why do you want to go to the cemeteries?" Clive asked, but already knew the answer. She didn't say anything, nor did she have a chance. What happened next was so fast that even the undead didn't register it until it was too late.

The door to the dining hall flew open and Bral entered, sword arched high above his head. He lunged toward Kersey and slashed downward with enough force to drive her right on top of Clive, who gasped when his head banged against the wall. He didn't think about the pain, nor did he pay any attention to the spray of blood that splattered across the floor. His mind was saddened that Kersey had just been killed—ravaged across the back by an unseen attacker.

That wasn't the case, however.

Her eyes were locked with Clive's. They were strong eyes, *angry* eyes. They were the eyes of a woman very much alive and very much ready to seek retribution for what just happened.

Sickly, black vines slithered from below the room and wrapped around Bral's arms, pulling him tight and loosening his grip on the sword. It clanked to the floor as the assaulting guard was lifted up.

Kersey turned around to face her attacker but Clive didn't care to see his face. He was too fixated on the young prisoner's back. Her simple tunic was shredded—tatters of it hanging down near her thighs. A large trail of blood was seeping from the monstrous gash, oozing to the floor from beneath the scraps of her shirt. A normal person would have already bled to death. But as Clive had known for quite some time, Kersey was far from a 'normal' person.

After a few seconds, the last drops of blood left the wound. The sounds of bone groaning and popping could be heard inside, as if her spine was mending and sliding itself back into place. The large, jagged gash running from her shoulder blade to her lower back shrank at the edges, shortening the distance. As quickly as it had appeared, the wound was gone.

Heavy footsteps sounded outside the door as more guards drew closer. The room sprang to life in response. The dolgatha turned and the vines surrounding it let go and slithered away back into the floor.

The undead men armed themselves with parts of the table, pieces of marble, and the broken water pitcher. Tarun found Bral's fallen sword and grabbed it. The vines holding the intruded guard pulled him to the side to give the dolgatha a clear shot of the doorway.

One sentry stepped through, sword drawn, and clashed with the nearest undead. Three more entered and attempted to take on the dolgatha, but that turned out to be a horrible idea. Its massive, clawed foot slammed one guard to the ground, shattering his body like a porcelain doll. The other pair were lifted and thrown into the wall where they hit in a screaming, bloody splat before sliding down.

"Kersey, stop this!" Clive yelled to deaf ears. He struggled against the vines with no luck. "What did you do to her?" this time to Bral. Two more guards entered and joined the fray.

"I did nothing," he called, trying his best to weaken the vines. Slime bursting from the bulbs was the only result.

"You tried to rape her!" Kersey looked uninterested in their conversation and lost to another trance. Bral said nothing in his defense. "She was content until this happened," Clive pointed out, watching as a guard finally managed to subdue one of the undead. "Gods only know how many of us she'll kill now that she's provoked."

Clive was wrong in thinking that things couldn't possibly get more chaotic—more bizarre. Kersey's hand hovered over the dead guard on the ground, the one who the dolgatha decided to grind into pulp. His body started to twitch until the spasms grew so intense that he was flopping around like a fish out of water. Both Clive and Bral were speechless while they watched its frenzied jerking come to a stop and then stand, its broken legs keeping it from being completely upright. It picked up its sword and surveyed the room with dead, glazed eyes and then attacked the nearest guard.

The other two who slammed into the wall exhibited similar motions as Kersey waved toward them. They eventually rose, just as the first did. Where once was nine dead men now stood eleven.

Suddenly the prison bell in the north tower started to ring. The undead didn't seem to notice but Kersey did. She snapped out of her trance and looked around. Both remaining guards fled through the door and she shook her head when one of her minions started to follow. More guards were being rallied in the prison and she knew it. She approached Tarun and whispered something in his dead ear. Together they looked at Bral, who was now shifting nervously within the confines of the vinery.

Tarun nodded and approached him, stopping only to allow the vines to loosen their grip. A tight bundle still held Bral's right arm, suspending him slightly off the ground. His feet kicked from the floor, scuffing and trying to pull away from their imprisonment.

Clive could tell what was about to happen. Tarun tightened his grip on the sword as more vines latched onto Bral's ankle, pulling him closer to the ground so that his body was taut and his arm was straight up in the air. The dead man rested the blade against the flesh of his forearm and drew back. Bral began to scream in horrid anticipation.

The warm spray of blood that met Clive in the face made him jerk his head away, teeth clenched. Bral's screaming turned to a wild howling as the stump above his elbow poured blood. The vines holding him toward the ground released and shrank away so Tarun could grab him by the collar and toss him near the doorway.

"Tell the other guards what happened here today," Kersey told him. He panted as he clutched his stump, blood pouring through his fingers. "Tell them this is what will happen if they come near me again." Bral scrambled to his feet and hastily left, leaving large globs of blood in his wake.

Tarun approached Kersey once more. Again, they whispered back and forth, only this time when the conversation was at an end, they turned to Clive. It was so unnerving that he had trouble breathing. He swallowed the lump building in his throat. What did she want? Where were the limits of her revenge? He didn't know and although he wasn't responsible for anything that happened to her tonight, he felt that his fate was going to be the same as Bral's.

Once again, Tarun nodded to Kersey and approached Clive. He clenched his jaw and looked away. Sweat was forming on his forehead and Bral's blood was stinging his eyes. His hands balled into fists at the thought that he was about to lose a limb. Thankfully, Kersey had other intentions.

The vines loosened completely, dropping him to the floor. Standing over him was Tarun, hand outstretched to help him to his feet. Clive looked past him to a nodding Kersey. The undead and dolgatha behind her were blocking the door.

Without further delay, he took the creature's dry, stiff hand in his own and allowed it to help him up.

"Why are you doing this, Kersey?" he asked, approaching her as he wiped Bral's blood away. The undead moved in front of her and the dolgatha emitted a low growl. He stopped where he was. "Did those men *really* have to die? Did Bral really have to suffer pain like that?"

For once, his questioning separated her from a trance. She pushed her way past the undead but her vines were near, ready to rip him apart should he touch her.

"You know nothing about me, Clive. And you know nothing of *pain*." Her face and voice were in a shape of anger he'd never seen or heard.

"And why did you spare me?"

"Because I need you," she grumbled.

"To help you find the other cemeteries? To help you raise more dead?" Clive swallowed another hard lump in his throat at the thought of something terrible but he didn't let her see him troubled.

"You catch on quickly," she offered, eyeing the hole that the dolgatha had created when it tunneled its way out. Kersey nodded to her minions and jumped down. It would eventually lead outside.

"I'll have my Gothmirks take you to see Nalia first," she told him from the hole, her tone suddenly gentle and angelic. "Is she home tonight?" It was odd that Kersey mentioned his sister's name. Did she really care enough about him to let him see her? Did this mean he was a captive? It was a noble gesture, although it didn't matter.

He noticed the undead were called Gothmirks. How fitting. The vines that covered them were the same weeds that were said to grow in Ruin's domain. They were called Gothmirk Tulips, namely for their tulip-like bulbs that grew sporadically along the vines.

"No, she's not home tonight," he said, looking to the ground. "She'll never be home again."

"Oh," was all Kersey said. If she wanted to question what he meant, she never let it show on her face.

It was nearly dark now and still the prison bells were ringing. Despite Bral's condition and warning, Clive was certain that the guards weren't going to simply walk away from what just happened.

This was a mistake. What was she thinking? Ruin could never protect her from Mydian. No one could. And redeem her? That hardly made sense. Her only rational choice now was to hide—to remove herself from the eyes and ears of Mystyria like she had in the past. The prison would never be safe again, nor would Tharg. She had to leave and start over. Maybe this time she could fool the dark lord for more than fifteen years.

Kersey's head hurt, as it often did when she was scared. It was the only pain she didn't like. With the pounding at her temples came a slight blurriness of vision. These problems she could take care of but it would have to wait until Clive wasn't near—wasn't *watching*.

She was happy he was here but she'd never let him know it. Clive was useful. He had the keys to the cemeteries and he was a guide for the city, but he was also much more than that. He was a friendly face—a calm voice, and a nurturing heart. Kersey needed those things. After the life she'd lived and led, she *desperately* needed those things. Clive kept her *sane*.

The corridor beneath Kriball Manor was actually the barebones structure of the old prison. After a riot, some two-hundred and twenty years ago, it was left in such disarray that it was condemned and rebuilt across the street. Thanks to the ravenous dolgatha and guards, there had been few prisoners left to move.

At the bottom of the hole were the shambled remains of a cellblock. Most of the rusted iron bars were lying in broken pieces on the muddy ground. The cells were dank and empty and it smelled like the sewers were somewhere ahead. A few bodies remained—shells of bodies that had over two centuries worth of rot and decay in them.

These bodies called out to Kersey.

Take us with you.

She obliged, allowing their mortal remains to be reawakened. The undead rose, the trail of seeping vines mending their broken bones.

Whenever Kersey heard a voice in her mind, it was a voice of reason—a voice wishing to help her. There were no rejections. She held dominion over the deceased and not one could defy her. A small part of the soul always lingered between the realms of living and dead. Kersey could summon that soul fragment and use it to gain personal knowledge. The corpse could recall events of their life and of things that happened in the presence of their body.

Clive joined Kersey by her side, clearly uneasy around the following twenty or so dead behind. She almost smiled. It was cute in the way that he flocked to her for protection.

"They won't hurt you, but stay close to me," she told him. "The guards might mistake you for one of them."

"This place hasn't been seen in hundreds of years," Clive said, looking around. The corridor was leading up, hopefully toward an exit.

"Good thing I came through. Do you think they liked being trapped here?" Kersey pointed to a newly awakened dead man who hung from a noose inside a cell. The vines wrapped around his wrenching body and pulled him free.

Clive didn't say anything. He just kept watchful and let her lead on.

She didn't get much further before her eyes locked onto a rusted fireplace poker lying on the ground in a pile of muck. It was all her mind needed to trigger another trance. They came quick and most often at very inopportune times, but when they left, Kersey was awakened with the remnants of a bad dream. They were dreadful flashbacks that centered on events that happened over a thousand years ago—before the trouble.

Before the *curse*.

The dark, muddy hallway before her melted away and her mind filled it with lush carpet, beautiful stucco woodwork and bright light filtered by stunning stain-glass windows. They glistened in the morning sun. Clive and the crowding, putrid undead disappeared and were swapped by Lylussian priests and Keswing guards. Kersey's own prison garb washed away and in its place sprouted a voluminous, blue robe.

A man stood in the corner eyeing her, the fireplace poker twirling in his fingers. He offered her a friendly smile that she returned. After all, he was still a good person at this point of his life. Her mind that stood in the dark Tharg prison wanted to scream—wanted to take the fireplace poker from his fingers and stab him through the heart, but she couldn't. The trance-induced flashback wouldn't allow her.

He approached Kersey, still playing with the poker. His long flowing robes were decorated with numerous medals and ribbons. There had been many honors bestowed on him in the last year. She briefly smiled and bowed her head. He was a priest of Lyluss too and deserved her utmost respect.

"Looks like I get the privilege of working with you," he said. His warm, genuine smile made her feel at ease—calm in the face of the danger they would soon face. Her current mind back in the muddy prison knew his kind words would betray them both, but back then, she would have believed anything he said.

"That's kind of you to say," she said, fanning herself with a handful of her robe. She was so shy and awkward around men, especially one as attractive and approachable as this one.

"My name is Brin Todrich." He offered his hand.

"I know who you are, sir. Kersey Avonwood," she returned, taking it in her own. She grinned and looked to the ground, slightly embarrassed.

"So you're the Soul-Summoner that this city has been in an uproar about?"

Kersey nodded. "I suppose my reputation precedes me?" she asked in mock arrogance.

"Of course it does," he agreed. "I will feel so much better when we're down in that dark and dismal cavern knowing you are with me. This war has torn us all apart and the world deserves someone like you." It was true that she was revered in Keswing as the "one who can bring the dead to life". Her power to do so was much different then. It wasn't as twisted, perverted, and tainted as it was today.

"What now, Kers?" Her mind was being pulled away just as several others, just as decorated, came into the room. "Kersey, what now?" the voice repeated.

The light around her was extinguished and the beautiful temple and all its inhabitants disappeared. What remained was a narrow alley in a darkened city with a score of rotting undead huddled around. The stench of death was strong in the air. Clive was shaking her shoulder as the vines circled nervously around him.

"We're outside," he said, pointing down the alley. Apparently the dolgatha found them an exit. Off in the distance were the prison's empty towers. The bells had stopped ringing and the guard posts were abandoned. They were looking for *her* now. Kersey had been entranced and there was no telling how long it had lasted this time.

There was something cold on her fingers—cold and wet. She didn't need to look down to realize she was digging more track marks into her flesh. Instead, she pulled her arms behind her and wiped them on the tattered remains of her prison shirt. The wounds would heal soon, anyway.

One of the Gothmirks crept close, its dead eyes fixed on the ground as it whispered in her ear and mind, *Ruin wants you to meet him at the Tessian statue on Bayside Street.* It pulled away and joined the ranks of its unmoving brethren.

"Where is Bayside Street?" she asked Clive. He refused to answer. His stance on justice was shielding his eyes from the true injustice that was surrounding Tharg like the plague. He knew what her Gothmirks could do and knew that more guards were going to be killed.

Vines sprang from the ground and wrapped themselves around his arms, pulling him in opposite directions just hard enough to keep him still. The undead groaned and grunted in anticipation of what might come next. The alleyway was still, other than the occasional breeze that swept through carrying straw and leaves. Hopefully most of the people of this city were off the streets and instead filling the taverns, temples, and beds.

"Help me, Clive," she pleaded with solemn eyes. "I don't want to make you a captive."

"It's a little too late for that, Kers." He looked down to his feet, as if they were about to dangle from the ground. He wasn't phased by the surrounding undead. "I won't help you kill more people." This wasn't what Kersey was asking. For once, her quest wasn't about vengeance and murder.

"I want you to help me survive," was all she said.

"I can't, Kers. You killed—"

"—guards who beat and tried to rape me. Once again, we're back at this. But tell me, Clive, does that make what I did wrong? I am to be punished for being the only person today who did what needed to be done to the ones who deserved it." He was silent, but interested. "I didn't deserve to be beaten. I didn't deserve to be nearly raped. But those guards—those vile, corrupted guards... *they deserved* to be killed." He probably didn't agree with her, but at least he saw things from her point of view.

The vines released and he dropped to the ground in a tired, defeated slump. Kersey grabbed his arm, not caring about the blood being smeared across his nice shirt, and helped him up.

"Go," she said, pointing down the alley in a direction where she had no clue as to where it would take him. "Go home."

Clive followed her finger with tiresome eyes. It must have been very inviting. He would be away from the undead, away from the prison's mess, and most importantly, away from the killer who had just abducted him.

"Well go!" she yelled, pushing him a little. She wasn't angry with him—just angry that she was letting the one who kept her centered go.

"Kers..." he breathed. "I never wanted any of this to happen to you. You have to get out of the city. Leave now and maybe they'll think you were killed."

"It's not that simple," she said, looking to the ground. "It has to be this way. My very soul depends on it."

Clive looked displeased with her answer but didn't say anything. More importantly, he didn't leave.

"Please," she implored. "Where is Bayside Street?"

He shook his head and said, "Not far. This way." He led her out of the alley, probably praying that the entourage of undead went unseen.

Kersey flicked the remaining blood from her fingertips and pulled the hair from her eyes. She needed a change of clothes and a hot bath. She wanted at least that much.

The twenty or so undead shifted in two perfect rows and followed behind her. For the sake of concealment, Kersey kept the dolgatha in the alley. The Gothmirk Tulips didn't follow either, at least not along the street. They lingered beneath the cobblestones. If needed, they would come up to do their business.

Just as she had hoped, the streets were deserted. There were people walking in the distance and a carriage could be heard around the corner, but no one was in the vicinity to see them. This time tomorrow night, everyone in the city would be aware of her presence. She was sure that Ruin would see to that.

A rustling up ahead drew her attention. The Gothmirks sprang to life and started toward the noise but she held her hand up, instructing them to stay. They were in front of a tavern called the *Drunkard*. The noise was coming from the other side and sounded like dogs snooping around in the refuse bins. Laughter and pipe music could be heard inside the inn as she hurried past it and to the alley.

It wasn't dogs, but it was garbage. A large man was knee-deep in the rotting, fly-ridden mess, vigorously rummaging through it. He held his shirttail out with one hand, using it as a basket to collect the things he found worthy of taking.

"Avery?"

He was the nice, simple-minded man who came to her window at the prison. He'd seen more of Kersey than she'd ever wanted anyone to see, but because of what he was—*who* he was, she allowed it.

Avery started at the sound of her voice and kicked a heap of garbage halfway down the alley. A pair of large, brown rats scurried away, squeaking in protest to their bothered nest. Clive looked confused by her interest in the slow man but appeared mesmerized by his size. The silhouette of him was very scary standing in the alleyway, despite how warm and gentle he was.

"Come here, Avery," Kersey ordered, motioning for him to give up the trash.

He picked up his favorite selections from the collection on his shirt and let the others fall. After stuffing his mouth with a piece of greenish meat, he humbly came to her, a wide grin on his face. There were marks all over him—cuts, bruises, and even a couple of burns that looked like mage practice. She wondered who would do such a thing.

"Miss Red?" he asked with a puffy face. "Why, you're outside… with me!" He clapped his hands together and spit food as he talked, but didn't care. Clive looked like he didn't know how to properly react to Avery's overeager personality. "Why, I haven't seen you outside since—"

"Spit that out, Avery!" Kersey demanded, holding her hand to his mouth. "That's bad for you." She raised an eyebrow and gave a nod to her waiting palm.

Avery frowned and swallowed a small bit before spitting the contents of his mouth into her hand. She threw it to the ground and then snatched the rotten apple core and half uncooked fish from his meaty fingers. He was dumbfounded by how quickly he was made empty-handed.

"What are you doing out here, Avery?" she asked, keeping a watchful eye on her ever-patient army waiting twenty feet away. The simple man looked at them too, but either didn't care or didn't realize what they were.

He glanced back to the *Drunkard*'s trash. "Daegin said to go play, so Avery goes to play!" His smile was as crooked as his posture. Normally the beefy man dwarfed Kersey but with him bending over to meet her eyes, they were nearly level.

Who was Daegin? she wondered. Maybe he was the one who was supposed to be looking after him. At the moment, he wasn't doing such a fine job.

"And why are you eating trash?" she asked.

He looked at the sloppy mess on the ground that Kersey made him give up. His hands found his stomach and he bent over slightly. "Why, I haven't eaten in two days. I'm hungry, Miss Red."

Kersey could feel herself getting angry. Luckily, it was shallow. It was very important that she didn't get too worked up. This Daegin fellow, this caretaker, wasn't looking out for Avery when he should have been. Right about now she wanted to meet him.

"You're hungry?" Her voice was strong and agitated but she didn't wait around for his answer. She walked past a clueless Clive and stood in front of the double doors of the *Drunkard*. The time for concealment was over.

The cobblestone sidewalk next to the tavern crumbled as a pair of Gothmirk Tulips broke free. The mass of dripping vines grabbed the woodwork around the doors and in a quick, violent tug, ripped them from the tavern. Clive gasped as the doors slid across the street, still wrapped in vines that were bursting with brown stench.

The undead moved quickly, hobbling into the tavern, just as soon as the way was clear. A chorus of cries and screams sounded as the music abruptly ended. And then, as quickly as the Gothmirks had entered, people began pouring out. Shrieking waitresses and barmaids, staggering, drunken customers and fluttered musicians filled the streets as the *Drunkard*'s contents dispersed into the Tharg night. Avery and Clive merely exchanged glances and both seemed to wonder if what they just saw actually happened.

After the chaos was out of earshot, one decrepit Gothmirk approached Kersey with a steaming plate of vegetables, ham, and half a loaf of bread. Another brought a pitcher of water. The undead joined the others and the vines slithered back into the ground.

Kersey handed the pitcher and plate to Avery who only stared at it with wide eyes. Without hesitation, he snatched the ham and devoured it as if someone would come along and take it if he didn't.

"I want you to listen to me, Avery," Kersey started. She put her hand over his plate to stop him from choking himself and to gain his attention. "I want you to go home or to the temple and lock the door. The city isn't going to be safe."

"What?" Clive interrupted and stepped between the two. "Why is that?"

"Calm down," she told him. "My Gothmirks aren't the reason, but they will make some bad people emerge from the shadows. You'll see."

Ruin would upset the balance in this city. Mydianites throughout Tharg would be ordered to hunt her down and attack her undead and in return, Fyrl would order his guards to hunt down the Mydianites. She was sure of this.

"Look at this, Miss Red!" Avery said and pulled a chain from beneath his shirt. The plate of food was just about to topple. Kersey reached out and tried to steady it, but quickly withdrew her hands when she saw the searing light coming from the medallion around his neck.

She tried to compose herself—to act like nothing had happened but Clive seemed to take notice of her sudden need to look away from her burly friend. A forced smile suddenly appeared on her face as she turned back to Avery, eyes on his.

"That's beautiful, Avery. Where did you get it?" she asked, ignoring the pain in her eyes and face.

"The priestess at the temple!" he exclaimed. "She gave it to me for coming to the service last night!"

Kersey was glad that Avery was happy with his Lylussian trinket. After all, she'd taught him songs, told him stories, and tried to instill faith of Her Holiness into his simple mind. She was glad he was on the true path. Even if she wasn't welcome to do so, it was a tiny delight that she could steer someone else in the right direction.

"You'd better put it beneath your shirt before you spill food on it. Now go, Avery," she told her friend once more. He nodded and ran off, splashing most of the water from the pitcher as he did.

"Thank you, Miss Red!" His voice echoed from down the alley. "See you later!" She hoped so. If she lived that long, she surely hoped so.

Back to business, she thought and turned to Clive. "Bayside Street?" He hesitated for a moment to sort through the things that just happened and then pointed past the *Drunkard*.

They kept to the back alleys, walking the narrow strips between merchant shops. On the other side was Market Lane, the busiest spot in Tharg. Even though it was after dark, the comfortable weather kept a lot of people out. After the scene in front of the tavern, Kersey felt horribly exposed. Soon, she would make a wall of a thousand undead to stand between her and any opposition. She had to survive.

A flattened cat was lying on the side of the road and Kersey waved her hand over its mangled body. It stretched its broken legs and emitted a gnarled *meow* before shaking the water from its fur and joining the ranks of her army. It purred a silent *thank you* in her mind.

When the alley opened up, a strong gust of wind hit her from her left. The waves of the Arinbeth roared as they washed against the docks. There were several small boats and two large galleys being thrown about in the moderate tumult of the ocean. All of the ships were dark and empty, their crew most likely filling the taverns.

In the middle of the preceding street stood the twenty-foot tall statue of Tess, the Iron Queen, the goddess of warriors. The mortal-turned-god held her broadsword to the sky. Her eyes were fixed on the ground, a solemn smile on her face. Beneath the statue, sitting on a bench, was a man.

He was draped in a long, green cloak and a black suit. A high fedora sat on his head. Between his legs he held a shiny, golden cane that was tipped with a snake's head. Kersey didn't need to be next to him to see the flies dancing about his head, the pale, blue skin on his hands, or the blood drenching his chest and cloak.

His head rose and looked at her with dead, focused eyes. The same eyes of the squirrel—the *same* eyes that the god of the dead carried into any cadaver he chose to inhabit. The flesh of his hands and face told Kersey that this man—this vessel that Ruin occupied didn't die long ago.

He patted the spot on the bench next to him and crossed his legs. A loud grinding sound bellowed from beneath the cloak as his stiff joints protested. Kersey hesitated but sat, nonetheless. She still couldn't believe she was actually *helping* him.

"Nice fellow. Rich man, don't you think?" Ruin was examining his sleeves, talking about the corpse he was living inside for the moment. "Got his throat slit in the alley back that way." He pointed down a passageway that led to Fyrl's massive castle while he showed her the rent flesh beneath his chin. "I guess they only wanted his money, cause he's got none."

"Why did you call me here?" Kersey asked, not caring any longer about the victim Ruin was so fond of.

"It's good to see you outside those dreadful bars," his all too-familiar calm and steady voice said. Clive was constantly stepping back, not wanting to believe with his own eyes and ears what was happening. Kersey tried not to look at him. He would want an explanation later.

"Well I'd rather be back inside," she admitted, and meant it. "There's nothing out here for me. I was *safe* there until now."

Ruin didn't say anything at first. The corpse's eyes looked like they would bulge from its skull as they focused on her arms. In a calm, inflectionless voice, he asked, "Are you still having flashbacks of Brin?" His dead fingers wrapped around her wrist and raised it to wipe the blood away.

Kersey recoiled and buried them in her lap. "That's none of your concern!" Clive gave her a questioning look that she tried her best to avoid. She cursed silently to herself and hoped she wouldn't shed tears in front of him.

"That was long ago, my dear. I'm sure he got what he deserved in the en—"

"He didn't get what he deserved because *I* didn't kill him!" The cobblestones beneath Clive's feet rippled as the vines almost broke through. He took another step back and kept his hands to his sides.

"Perhaps one day you will have your chance," Ruin uncrossed his legs and put his cane in his lap. "But for now, I have a job for you."

Kersey brushed the hair from her eyes and looked to the ground. She offered up a silent, weak nod and gave her attention. She hated the feeling of giving in.

"I want you to build an army. You can't be walking around Tharg unless you're protected. That will be a start to our goal."

"And what is your goal?" This question came from Clive. Both Kersey and Ruin looked up at him in equal surprise. He obviously didn't know whom he was addressing.

"Why, my dear boy, are *you* here?" Ruin asked him. "And why do you keep him?" this time to Kersey. She shrugged, but the reason was buried deep within.

"I need him here. With me," was all she could muster.

"You *need* him here? Kill him and raise him then." Ruin pointed to a worried Clive with the end of his cane. "You've no need of a mortal. He'll only get in your way."

"What in the hell would you know of my needs?" she cursed him. "Clive is an important part of my life and he stays, just the way he is. And if he isn't here, then I'm not going to be of any help to you." Clive looked like he didn't know whether to smile or be afraid.

Ruin folded his arms around the cane and leaned back. More blood trickled from the agitated wound on his neck. He considered what she said for a moment and finally decided it wasn't important enough to even continue speaking of.

"You have no idea, do you?" His dead eyes fixed on Clive as he spoke. "You've no clue who or what she is, do you?"

"No, I don't," he simply put it. "I've been trying to figure that out for the better part of fifteen years."

"Suffice it to say, you'll do well to *not* get on her bad side. I've seen the things she can do when she's angry, when she's upset. Her heart and mind go back a long way. Such a brilliant and eventful past, this one has."

"Is there anything else?" Kersey interrupted. Ruin knew every little dark secret of her existence and she loathed him for it, although she knew quite a few of his own. She didn't want Clive learning more than he had to. To know what Kersey was, her past, and her life would be to become madness itself.

"What is this?" Ruin pointed to her small ragtag group of undead. "What do you plan to accomplish with *these*?"

"It's a start," she argued, glad to be off the subject of herself.

"It's a *horrible* start. Most aren't even armed." Ruin pointed his cane to several Gothmirks who only carried wooden clubs or blunt pieces of rubble. They were in no condition to go against armed guards.

"It will be done then," Kersey sighed. "What then?"

"I want you to stick around the city for a night or two. You're going to be . . . breaking into Fyrl's place. For now, empty the graveyards, arm your dead." He pulled away from her and turned his nose up in a sneer, which was quite lopsided with limited facial control. "And get yourself a bath. You smell worse than I do." With that, the corpse's head fell backwards, the body went limp, and the cane slipped from its fingers. Ruin had just left the vessel. A few seconds later, it sprang to life again, picked up the cane, and joined the other Gothmirks. She was in control of it now.

A hot bath did sound nice. At the prison, she was offered a shower once a week and it was cold, unfiltered, and in the company of male inmates. There was no way she would put herself through such an experience. Kersey *could* get out of the prison when she wanted, just as Clive thought, and when she did, she took advantage of the clean water in Lake Barria.

He was eyeing the statuesque corpse that Ruin had occupied when she said, "Where is your home?"

He closed his eyes and breathed a heavy sigh before looking at her. "What?" It was obvious where this was going.

"How far are we from your home?"

"We're not going to my house, Kers," Clive assured.

One of the Gothmirks, a guard who fell in the banquet hall earlier, walked past him and whispered the directions in her ear. She smiled in satisfaction and feebly worked to suppress a laugh when

Clive threw his hands in the air and shook his head, realizing what his once friend—his once subordinate had known to tell her.

"Kers, I'll probably be executed now just for helping you," Clive pleaded. "Once Fyrl's guards realize I didn't become one of your dead, they'll come knocking at my door. What am I to tell them when they find you in my bathing chambers cleaning up?"

She cast a wicked smile. That wasn't going to happen. "They'll not get anywhere near your house. As long as you're with me, you needn't be afraid of anyone." Kersey would protect him with her last ounce of strength. There was no way she could help Ruin—no way she could put forth a foot and go into the observing and open world without him. Clive would be as guarded as her own life.

"This way," she told him, directing him to his own house.

He scoffed as he walked by and she offered a tiny, private grin to his back.

Things were going to drastically change around him soon. He would eventually see just how much of Mystyria was hidden behind the curtain. There were forces at work—forces that would control the fate of the world and they all started with Kersey. Clive was going to bear witness to the most significant change he would ever see happen to Mystyria in his lifetime. Soon, he would understand.

.4.

The World Through New Eyes

Everyone looked at them with lust and envy. The castle was full of servants; loyal to the end, but each and every one wanted to be those two. Even those with the greatest power—the greatest wealth and privileges in the Underworld would have loved a chance to visit Mystyria again.

Dyne and Lorne followed Mydian with Telsa lagging behind. They headed down a corridor away from the throne room and into a dank hall that reminded Dyne of the crypt under the Birchlock Estate. The walls were slick, wet granite and there was a putrid odor that smelled like burnt flesh. A writhing man with no skin was strapped to a table with a crowd of Magma Imps standing over top of him, dangling various instruments and cutting utensils. This was the chamber where the souls in Cytop were brought when they were needed to answer questions of happenings on Mystyria. It was a momentary reprieve from the pain and anguish they would suffer.

The god of the Infernal carried with him the two urns his aids had brought earlier. "Once you are back in Mystyria," he started, "you will find yourselves in the same spot you last remembered."

Dyne knew exactly where that was. It was still so new in her mind, despite that it happened twelve years ago. She would be in the Lylussian temple in Hope's Covenant. Lorne would be in an upstairs bedroom of the Birchlock Estate, only a mile north—right where she killed him.

"I don't believe this," he said, as if sharing the same thought. It came out so low that she barely heard him. "I was happy here. I was away from you and had a bigger purpose and now, *because* of you, I am being torn from my home, my friends, and my life."

Both had hoped they would never have to see each other again. And now, as fate would have it, they had been selected amongst a million souls to once again be together. Surely, the gods had a sense of humor. Or perhaps it was just Mydian.

"I want you to join Lorne back at the Birchlock Estate," he told Dyne. Her skin crawled at the thought. She never wanted to see that place again. She had spent only a week there but the most horrid—the most traumatic events of her life happened on its icy grounds. "I trust you remember Arctis' 'special little room'?"

How could she forget? She saw it the night she died. Arctis had been hiding in there, right under the owners' noses. He had amassed quite a collection of valuables and even took care of several wilderbears.

"What do you need from the room, my lord?" Lorne asked, giving Dyne a scornful look when she failed to speak up.

"I need you to go *through* it," he corrected. "There is a portal there that Arctis used to travel across Mystyria. It will take you to Pelopha."

Mydian led them into a massive chamber that looked like a renovated dungeon. The walls were made of dry, black granite, and the floor was dark and spotted with blood. A large drainage grate sucked in all the water from the nearby leaking pipes that ran up through the ceiling. At the center of the room stood a platform about two feet from the ground. Atop it was a massive ball of fire, illuminating every corner with a brilliant, red glow. Dyne could feel the heat from it on her face, some twenty feet away.

"If Telsis, or any of the other gods for that matter, knew I had this, I would be in severe trouble." Mydian pointed to the blazing orb.

"So that's what you've been smuggling into the Underworld these past few weeks," Telsa noticed, dumbfounded amazement on her porcelain face. "The parts for that gate."

"Gate?" Dyne asked, eyeing the hot sphere.

"That's right. This, along with your Mystyrian remains, will make it possible to send you back to the realm of the living." Mydian offered a smug smile while admiring his black-market, magical contraption.

"And our remains?" Lorne asked. Mydian shoved the urn into his arms and handed the other to Dyne.

She lifted the lid and discovered it to be filled with red-speckled white ash. A tiny gasp left her when she considered the conundrum. "This is . . . me?"

"Indeed," Mydian said. "This was neither cheap nor easy to obtain. Luckily I managed to track you down. When you are ready, take a handful and approach the sphere," he spoke to the two soon-to-be mortals.

A part of Dyne didn't want to do this. When she entered the Underworld, she felt relieved. This was it. This was the afterlife. All the bloodshed, the deceit, the need to feed and cower to the daylight was all gone. She was safe and would eventually be happy, despite the unending separation from Laraek. And now, the dark lord was making her go back to the cold, twisted, muddy and disease-infested world of the living. He was making her pick up her sword and go back to doing what she did for centuries.

Telsa's eyes were glazing over. The little girl lashed out and wrapped her arms around her. With the urn blocking, Dyne couldn't return it. There were warm tears spotting her back.

"It's okay, sister," she whispered to Telsa. "We will see each other again. You *know* this."

"It's true, I know," she cried. "But you've been without me for three years, I've been without you for *fifteen*. It feels like an eternity. I want you here with me."

"Soon, sister, soon," Dyne pulled herself away. She wanted to be here just as bad, but just as she often did in life, she had to be the strength for her sister to look up to—and to hold on to. "I love you, Telsa. I'll return and we'll never be apart again."

Telsa put on a strong face that was faltering by the second.

"Mystyria awaits, my children," Mydian said, ushering them toward the gate of fire.

Can I even draw closer? Dyne wondered. The heat was so intense from where she stood. She reached into the urn and grabbed a handful of the ash—of *herself* and kept moving forward. Lorne was right next to her.

"Try not to kill me this time," he chided.

"Try not to get in the way of my blade," she returned, finding the strength to smile just a little.

He was about to come back with what was most certainly a heated reply, but without warning, a tendril of fire shot from the orb and latched onto him. The large man screamed when it lit his flesh afire as the urn toppled to the ground. His hair started to blaze and it resembled a crown of fire. The tendril didn't recoil, nor did it ever extinguish. Instead, it drew him in, pulling him like a fisherman with his hook embedded.

Dyne was about to say something—about to back up but another reached out and struck her. The pain was unbearable. It felt like it was searing a hole straight through her torso. Her legs and arms were weakening and she thought she was about to fall. She tried to scream and as she did, ash flew from her hand, pelting her in the face and neck like tiny pebbles. It even went into her mouth, making her cough a white cloud.

She managed to turn around and see her sister standing there, watching with wide, teary eyes as she cooked. How fitting, she mused. Hannah watched her mommy die in flames. Telsa witnessed her sister's rebirth in the same fashion.

There was no turning back now. The room, along with Mydian, Telsa, and a burning Lorne wavered from her vision and was replaced by a silent darkness—a silent, unconscious, and unknowing darkness. For just a moment, Dyne Atlin—*Emba Atlin*, ceased to even exist.

Water was trickling down her face and rolling into the corner of her mouth. It dripped rhythmically and splashed against her forehead. Her body ached and there was a soreness in the pit of her stomach. Slowly, she opened her eyes and the world came into focus, if only a little.

The ceiling was leaking. She moved to the side to avoid the dripping and pain rippled up her neck and throughout her body. She tried to cry out but only a dry, hoarse cough emerged, rattling her ribcage and sending new waves of pain through her bones.

As the cough continued to jar her insides, her eyes locked onto the dreadful symbol she'd come to loathe and fear. It was the twin doves of Lyluss. With three centuries worth of instinct getting the best of her, Dyne turned her head away and brought her arms up to shield her face. How horrible an action that turned out to be.

Her arm and neck started to hurt just as bad as her torso, tiny needles of pain stabbing her in a million places. Through squinted and hesitant eyes, she turned back over, ignoring the agony in her body. She looked directly at the symbol. There was no pain. There was no burning. The power of Lyluss didn't oppose her any longer. Her shaky hands found her mouth. There were no fangs.

She tried to talk, to laugh, but only warm air came out. It was *breath*. She wasn't a vampire anymore. She was a *mortal*—a weak and slow, but living *mortal*.

Dyne braced herself for more agony and gritted her teeth as she pulled herself into a sitting position. The pain wasn't as bad now as it had been when her eyes first opened—when she first reappeared in Mystyria, a full-grown and intelligent woman.

Once upright on the floor, Dyne realized she was naked, sitting on a cold, marble surface in the dark with the sound of rain hitting the roof above. She marveled at the movement of her chest as her body took in air on its own. Her hand felt her heartbeat and she closed her eyes and enjoyed it. It was something she only knew from memories.

This was certainly the Lylussian temple, just the way she remembered it. Only now there were no broken windows, no cowering townsfolk, and no crying Hannah. Dyne couldn't bring herself to look over at the spot where the child last saw her alive.

She stood on wobbly legs and used the row of pews to find her way to the window. It was night out, she noticed from the glow of a nearby lantern post. The rain was falling hard in the streets, and perhaps the most wonderful thing of all, there was no snow.

The town was incredibly busy. She remembered Hope's Covenant having a reputation for being a cluster of scared townsfolk who only flocked to the tavern at night to congregate and stave off the unlikely attack of vampires. Tonight was much different.

There were several people out. Even the plaza with the statue of the Lylussian priestess was bustling with an open market. Children were playing in the rain, men were working on the side of a house, and an elderly couple sat on a bench beneath the awning of the Symbian church across the street, admiring the approaching storm. They weren't fearful anymore. Tranas had given them hope and made them unafraid to go outside at night. If she had been bold—and perhaps still a vampire, she could have easily taken it away from them again. She made sure to remind herself of this.

Dyne needed to feel in control again. She'd lost so much of it—so much *power* before being killed. She was used to having her way and being able to tell others what to do and how to do it. If she didn't have that back, she wouldn't be able to function.

She squinted her eyes to try and focus, but everything remained blurry. When she couldn't hone in on living heat, she realized there wasn't anything wrong with her vision. It was normal—only normal for a *mortal*. Her enhanced eyesight was gone.

Two people appeared in front of the window, quickly passing to find cover from the rain. Dyne fell to her knees and buried herself against the wall. It probably wouldn't have been a good idea for anyone to see a nude woman standing in Lyluss' house who resembled a vampire killed in that very spot twelve years ago.

There was a light blue robe draped across the nearest pew so she snatched it and wrapped it around herself. She was starting to get cold. It wasn't the same as when she was a vampire. This cold was starting to make her fingers and toes numb.

She needed to get out of here—out of the temple and out of the town. Lorne was no doubt waiting for her in a crowd of noblemen at the mansion. If she kept him standing around for long, he'd probably start killing them for fun.

Dyne pressed herself by the window and watched as a few people hurried past the temple and up toward the plaza and tavern. She buttoned the robe and pulled the hood over her head, then deftly slipped out the door, silently closing it behind her. She stood there for a moment, looking back into the temple—sure that someone would hear the door open—sure that someone would come looking for the robe they sat down while they went to wash up. No one did. She had gotten out without arousing attention.

She turned around, intent on walking the north path back up to the mansion—

—and slammed right into someone. She was stunned for just a moment. She wanted to run—to hide, but she thought for sure that at that instant there were at least a dozen eyes on her. The hood was still drawn, so that was good.

"I'm terribly sorry, priestess," came the humble reply of the man she'd just run into. All she could see was his soaked slacks and boots and the small pouch he carried in his hands. She was making sure he couldn't see her face, so that made it impossible to see his. "Ol' Ben here can be quite clumsy at times. You have yourself a good night." And with that, he was gone.

She tried to say something, to at least look normal and not appear as shaken as she was but the words still wouldn't come out. Her teeth chattered behind quivering lips—the cold settling into every newly awakened joint. Her throat was too dry—too paralyzed to talk. Besides, he was already gone, headed up the street toward the market or perhaps the tavern.

Dyne moved around to the side of the temple and raised her head just enough to look around. There were lots of people up near the market and around the Symbian temple across the street, but none were close enough to try and talk to her. She stopped at the edge of the temple's courtyard before going out into the street and approached the water running from the gutter.

Again, she looked around to make sure she wasn't witnessed and cupped her hands to gather some of the falling rainwater. Her mouth sucked it up in large gulps but she coughed most of it to the ground, not having the capacity to swallow just yet. She tried again and took small sips, quenching her immense thirst and mending the pain in her throat. Now if only she could find some food.

She decided to worry about that later. She needed to put some distance between the town and herself. Lifting her 'borrowed' robe, she stepped off the temple's sidewalk and started up the road that would lead to the Birchlock. Her bare feet sank up to the ankles in the mud but she didn't care. It would have been too much effort to find shoes.

Narrowly missing an oncoming wagon, Dyne moved to the right side of the street and gave Hope's Covenant in its entire bustling glory one final look before setting up the north path. As her muscles grew warmer and her body became more responsive, she found running to be a little easier. It didn't take long, however, for a small, insignificant fact about living to return to mind.

She had to stop several times to rest. The feelings that her lungs were going to burst were painful memories that she recalled from her mortal life. Sure, she was in great shape but the mortal body couldn't take nearly as much exertion as her vampiric machine could. This weak, limited shell was going to take some getting use to.

In the fifteen minutes it took her to get up the hill to the Birchlock, Lorne had already managed to find nearly a complete set of sullied armor, a dagger, and a wood axe. He stood out front of the main foyer, waiting for her, his new weapons sticking in the soggy ground in front of him.

The first thing she noticed was his missing tattoo. His dark skin and brown eyes were far less menacing without the large splotch of red ink adorning his face. She would have giggled with that thought in mind had it not felt like there was a little man stabbing her in the ribcage over and over. She panted heavily and felt her earlobes. There weren't any holes. Their bodies were in fact, quite new—not a blemish, mar, or bite-mark to be found.

"So I see nothing has changed," she said, looking the mansion over.

"Oh, much has changed," Lorne corrected, directing her attention to the second floor.

There were soot spots all over the house, mainly around the broken windows and doorframe. The strong, musty smell of burnt wood was apparent. All that remained of the fire damaged mansion was the outer shell. Dyne was glad it didn't look much as it did back then. She couldn't take the memories. Not now.

"Let's go," she called and started inside. She was careful to step around the broken glass. Cuts and scrapes *would* hurt now and blood loss could be a very bad thing.

Before going very far into the scorched foyer, she noticed that Lorne's footsteps didn't sound behind her. Turned back around, she saw him still standing outside, arms folded over and watching her. She rolled her eyes and headed back out.

"It sounded like you just gave me an order," he calmly said as she approached. "I don't think that is how things work now."

She gritted her teeth, feeling every ounce of the anger for him rekindle. "I said—"

And that was all she got out. Lorne's fingers snatched her throat—her painful, aching throat and lifted her against the wall, back rubbing the granite stones. For the first time in centuries, she felt what it was like to not be able to draw air—to have one's throat closed and need it opened. This feeling of submission—of being at the mercy of someone was demoralizing and infuriating.

"I do not take orders from you anymore, Dyne. Do you understand that?" She clawed at his fingers but he didn't budge. His face was turned in rage, water drenching him as it ran around his tight expression. Her feet kicked to no avail beneath her. This was a situation that she never thought she would be in. "Do you understand me, Dyne?" he repeated.

He had the advantage over her. This was obvious. Dyne was no more than a hundred and thirty pounds and her once enhanced strength was gone. But she had other talents and skills. In life, she trained longer—*harder* and when it came down to fighting, she proved time and again that she was capable of handling several such men on her own. She was better than he was and he knew it. He just needed to be reminded of it—here, today, in the pouring rain, twelve years later.

Her mind became focused even though she was on the brink of collapsing. She stopped flailing her legs and scraping at his fingers and placed her arms flush against the wall. With as much power as she could muster, she kicked him between the legs. That was all it took for his grip to loosen and drop her to the ground.

Lorne cried out in agony and fell to his knees, giving Dyne the opportunity she needed. Her fingers wrapped around his matted, drenched hair and pulled him back to deliver a violent blow straight across the jaw. His eyes clenched shut and she pounded him again, this time against the nose. Blood and water flew from her knuckles. The brute tried to get up—to gain the advantage on her again but she kicked his feet from beneath him, bringing him to his knees once again.

Dyne grabbed onto his shoulders and used him as leverage to flip over just as he tried to reach out and grab her. When she landed, she pulled his planted dagger from the muddy ground. Lorne found himself on his back, with Dyne straddling his chest, the blade held firmly across his neck. His face was bleeding profusely, running in pink streams across the granite porch. The thunder was approaching, just as she found her strength—her rage—her determination that made her who she was.

"Who gives the orders?" she screamed. Lorne failed to answer and she turned the blade so the hilt faced down and slammed it into the side of his head. He cried out in rattled pain. "Who gives the orders?" she yelled again.

"Y-you!" he submitted. He coughed a wet, sickly moan. Dyne's teeth were clenched and her hands were shaking, but that was it. Her anger was at its peak. Its threshold was much higher when she was a vampire.

"Good," she smiled, and cleared the blood from his nose. He jerked his head away from her, his pride wounded more than his body. She wiped the blood from the dagger on the leather pants beneath his armor and stood, then held her hand out to him.

Lorne scowled and spat blood on the ground. He wiped his face and surveyed his hand to see just how bad the damage was. After a few seconds of sulking, he allowed her to help him up. She pulled the massive man to his feet, which stood a foot taller than her and handed him the dagger.

"Let's go," she repeated again, shaking the pain out of her hand. She'd forgotten the hurt that came with throwing a punch. Lorne did as she asked, still spitting blood from his busted lip. His face turned into a vicious grimace whenever she faced him.

There were two dead men inside the foyer. A dwindling fire sat on the floor and a bedroll was crammed beneath the stairs. Squatters, she realized. One had a broken neck and the other a huge gash across his chest. They were nearly naked since Lorne stripped them of their armor. Dyne smirked and continued on.

There was a permanent, accurate map conveniently drawn in her head. She was just here. Even if it was twelve years ago, her mind was *just here.* She carefully watched the ground as to not step on anything sharp and headed straight into the ballroom. This was where it all started. It was where the killing began—where her minions entered for their week stay. Now, it was nothing more than a dilapidated room with no roof. The glass dome was gone; having only the charred, wooden frame to prove it was ever there. Rain poured inside and the rank smell of water and dead animals emanated from the orchestral pit. The house had been in disarray for several years.

Past the kitchen and pantry was Arctis' secret room. It was quite a wonder how it remained undiscovered for the last twelve years. The brick facade stayed in place, but one only had to pass through it to be in his private chamber. The night Dyne was here was the last time anyone ever stepped foot on the other side.

The floating orbs emanating the sound of torches burning, the lavish bed and furniture, the display cases, and the randomly strewn treasure was all still here. The empty cages that held the wilderbears sat at the far end of the massive room. Lorne and Dyne both eyed the weapon rack along the right side of the wall.

She grabbed an emerald-adorned broadsword and pulled it from its scabbard and gasped. "Gods, this is Adella Bloodhoof's sword!" Lorne was admiring it as well. Adella was Mydian's greatest champion during the first War of Balance. She was one of the first green dragon riders to enter Keswing at the start of the conflict and her, along with twenty men took the largest temple in the city. This sword was passed from Lylussian church to Lylussian church in declaration of her fall, but eventually it went missing. Just like countless other artifacts, Arctis had claimed it for himself. Dyne couldn't leave this behind.

Lorne found himself a large, double-bladed halberd that looked a lot like the one Arctis used just before Dyne killed him. After all, he had been a dragon-slayer. There was also a large crossbow with silver etchings that he slung over his other shoulder. The bolts in the attached quiver had bright red tips.

"You plan on meeting Mydian's commander wearing that?" he asked, eyeing her robe.

She looked down and tugged the fabric. "What's wrong with it?" He shook his head and sighed, then approached her. She readied herself to fight him—to make him bleed a little more, but instead, he grabbed the garment and pulled it off her. For some reason she covered herself up. Embarrassment was a new feeling, she noticed.

Lorne turned the robe around and held it out for her to see. He was right. It wouldn't be good to have this on when she met Mydian's commander. On the backside were the twin doves of Lyluss. She definitely needed to change out of that.

Luckily, there was just as much armor as weapons. Lorne found a dull black suit of chain mail and took it all, leaving the rusted and broken things on the floor. He stuffed a few daggers in the boots, the belt, and the side pouch. He was traveling heavy, but that was okay. Hopefully there wouldn't be much walking.

Dyne found a beautiful green suit of leather. As she pulled on each piece, she could feel it miraculously harden. There were beautiful designs sewn into the back of the cuirass and gauntlets and she even spotted the flowing tree of Willow, the god of nature. Across the front, just over the breastplate were the etchings of Taylom and Seva, the Oakenheart's wolves. This was no ordinary suit of armor, she noticed, feeling the hardening sensation increase. It was still easy to move in, yet it was like iron to the touch. It could probably repel arrows.

After getting suited up and scrounging enough weapons, the two threw on a couple of black robes to hide their faces. There was no telling who might recognize them. Dyne and Lorne had both made enemies and in the last twelve years, those wounds would not have had time to heal.

"So where is this portal?" Lorne asked, looking the room over.

Dyne wondered the same. There was an enormous map showing Mystyria on the wall to the left of the bed. Hope's Covenant was at the southern tip, with Pelopha a few hundred miles north on the same coast. Eighty miles past the cliff-side city and separated by the Tilgrin Inlet was Tharg. Dyne's eyes drifted to the top, to the furthest, northern point, across two continents, beyond the Ruinite city of Crynsia and found Boudia. Her heart ached at the thought of Laraek, his body now three-hundred years dead, lying in a tomb within her hometown. She wanted to go there and reminded herself that once Mydian's job was done, she would.

Lorne reached out and touched the word *'Pelopha'* on the map. As soon as his hand glided past the raised letters, the name started to shine until an intense glow filled the room. As the light grew, the map itself became transparent and what looked like cliffs and the ocean could be seen beyond. The sky was purple and day was no doubt around the corner. The map continued to fade until it was nothing more than a large doorway to the Pelopha countryside.

The two exchanged nervous glances, checked their armor and gear, and then stepped through the portal.

A full moon hung high in the black, cloudless sky above. It was absolutely quiet—unsettling even. Market Lane had shut down and the streets had been deserted. That was good. No one saw him running like a madman back toward Glendan Street—back to the safe-house.

Daegin fumbled with the keys before he got to the doors. He'd just witnessed a great thing. Mydian wouldn't be pleased to hear it, but he needed to know. All of their suspicions had just been confirmed.

The battlemage hurried up the weed-strewn steps and slipped inside the safe-house. It was as quiet as the streets. Most of Daegin's Mydianites were out—watching Kersey, the guards, the hidden temple of Felorn, and whatever else his dark god commanded.

A large smile festered on his face when he found the cask of Lylussian holy water sitting in the corner. Next to it were coils of Lydison steel chain, the strongest metal in the world. Kerro had managed to find all of the items on the list.

Daegin was just about to head to the cellar to contact his Lord when he noticed an odd smell on the air. He sniffed and realized it wasn't odd, just peculiar for lingering in this house. It was ham.

The scent was coming from the foyer. A loud grunt followed by a thick, guttural snore halted him and he rolled his eyes when he realized it was Avery. The burly man was spread out in an overstuffed chair with his feet on the table. His head was hanging back and he continued to doze with deep breaths. Across his plump belly sat a greasy plate with only an apple core rolling around each time his chest rose and fell. The very sight of him was disgusting.

"Hey!" Daegin yelled and slapped his feet off the table. Avery startled and sat upright, the plate and apple core tumbling to the ground. "Where did you get this food, Avery?"

"Why hello, Daegin," he groggily said. "What time is it?" He yawned and looked over at the wall clock above the fireplace. Could this fool even *tell* time?

"Where did the food come from?" Daegin repeated. His hand was balling into a fist behind his back. His temper wasn't as taut as it used to be. Things made him angrier much quicker today than years ago and Avery seemed to be the source of it all.

Withholding and rewarding food was how his brother was motivated. If someone else had been giving it to him, there would be no other way of getting him to do Mydian's work. His place here would be pointless.

"Miss Red gave it to me," the man hazily said between two belches. "Why, she's so sweet."

"You're lying," Daegin objected. He kicked the plate from under the table and out into view. "That's a nice plate. Not one that a prisoner would eat from."

Avery's face lit up and he clapped his hands. He bounced around in his chair like a child just presented a toy. "Why, she's out now! She's out and walking around like us!"

What was this fool talking about? Before it registered, another thought struck Daegin. Could 'Miss Red' actually be Kersey Avonwood? Impossible. Ridiculous. If this was in fact her, then why had she offered to feed Avery? Why had she talked to him through prison bars on numerous occasions?

"Avery," Daegin breathed in elevated irritation. He started swirling his finger in a circular motion about two feet in diameter. "Is *this* Miss Red?"

The empty air within the circle's ring began to shimmer and ripple like the surface of a lake until a frozen image appeared. It was an old oil painting that Daegin had seen of Kersey years ago in Bloodgate. It was when she was mortal—not bad looking and much different than the person she was today. He projected the image from his mind into the viewing portal he'd just created for Avery.

His brother's face gave him the answer. Avery started jabbering about his Miss Red and how pretty and sweet she was. Daegin didn't hear any of it. He was too busy wondering why someone as wicked—someone as corrupt as Kersey would ever care about a mortal. She had a murderous, compassionless, and vengeful heart. She'd killed thousands and done worse to thousands more.

"What did I say about her, Avery?" His voice had risen considerably. Enough so that it gathered every ounce of the large man's otherwise distracted attention.

"But Miss Red is good, she is. I like her."

Daegin wasn't sure what was making him angrier; the fact that Avery was spewing nonsense, or that he was casting Kersey Avonwood in a good light. He couldn't—*wouldn't* believe that this was her persona after the years he'd been led to think otherwise. It *had* to be a facade.

"But Miss Red—"

"What did I say?" Daegin screamed, nose to nose. His brother's breath was horrible and coming in long drafts across his face. He was looking around, searching the ground, searching his own scattered mind for something to say. Daegin smiled. This was what he wanted. If Avery wasn't going to be motivated by food, he was going to be motivated by fear.

But the next thing that happened was completely unexpected. Never would he think his brother was capable of such emotional *strength*. Avery looked up into his caretaker's eyes and said, "Why, I don't care anymore what you say, Daegin. I like Miss Red and that's that."

Daegin noticed a chain around his neck with that last, gallant remark.

With shaking fingers that were on the verge of ripping out his brother's heart, Daegin pulled the copper necklace until the trinket attached to it was on the outside of his shirt. The burly man's meaty chin was resting on his chest, gazing at the two doves flying in circles and smiling like a drunken youth eying his favorite girl across the room. He didn't even notice the higher degree of anger that Daegin had been lifted to.

The short-lived smile that had festered across Avery's goofy face didn't last long. That bit of strength—of *defiance* coupled with the bold commitment to Lyluss was all Daegin needed to let go. It was the small plug that was holding back the angry water behind the dam. His last words to his fallen mother were about to ring true.

Daegin reached out and grabbed Avery's shirt to pull him closer. His fist pummeled the beefy man's eye. It was a hard hit—one that hurt the battlemage's knuckles. Avery recoiled so hard that he tumbled backwards from the chair.

"Daegin... *no!*" he shouted, hand over his eye. There was blood running through his thick fingers as he found his footing. "You said you wouldn't again!" He was in tears, a look of betrayal and fear in his good eye.

It wasn't enough to satisfy Daegin. Avery's pain wasn't great enough and his fear wasn't deep enough. There had to be more. He drew his dagger and twirled it so the blade faced down. The cowering man's eyes locked on the gleaming knife and his mouth flew open in sudden horror.

Before Daegin could raise it above his head and hurl it, someone assaulted him and pulled it away. He jerked around to see Kerro standing there, the dagger in his hand and a scornful look on his face.

"Get out of here, Avery," Kerro called. The husky man nodded, slinging blood as he hurriedly scrambled to the door.

"How dare you stay my hand," Daegin started, but Kerro pulled him toward the cellar.

"You can kill Avery another day. Mydian needs you. *Now*."

Both men rushed down the steps and into the lab containing twenty or so servants of the dark lord. There were long tables holding beakers of Bloodsilver and a large cask of ice orbs where the Sania was stored. Three vampires sat in chairs to the east side, a matted jungle of tubing hanging from their mouths, draining their precious venom into magical flasks that kept the solution pure. Their arms and legs were chained and the Lylussian Obelisks in the corners of the room kept their powers at bay. After tonight's samples were drawn, they would each be killed. The obelisks were needed elsewhere—they were needed to help kill Kersey.

Toward the back of the expansive cellar, near two empty beer casks, sat the mirror. It was the viewing portal between Mystyria and the Infernal Underworld. There were less than a hundred in existence and Daegin was lucky enough to have one.

Mydian was already present inside, swirls of dark mist surrounding his head. He looked anxious—pressing, and Daegin felt the same. The congregation of servants looked up from their experiments and watched the conversation unfold. It wasn't every day that someone got to see and hear a god.

"My darkest lord," Daegin started. "I have much news for you."

"And I for you," Mydian said back. His voice boomed in the small room, rattling alchemy jars on a nearby shelf. "What have you learned, Daegin?"

"Ruin is most certainly in league with Kersey, my lord. My men observed a few cutthroats kill one of Fyrl's noblemen. When they left, the body got up and walked off."

"And how do you know this was Ruin?" Mydian's arms were folded over, unconvinced.

"Because he walked with a cane and sat down on a bench to wait for her. I watched her talk with him but I couldn't get close enough to hear. She had a small army standing guard. I fear that since this mortal came from Fyrl's castle, Ruin may now know of the book."

Since Ruin held dominion over the dead, he was able to search the thoughts and minds of any body he inhabited. Whatever the nobleman had known passed right into the god of the dead.

"This is very... troubling, Daegin," he said, but sounded pleased nonetheless. "But I'm glad that we now know the truth of things."

Daegin nodded. "What should I do now, my lord?"

"The spell book of Aneesa arrives tomorrow night," he said without hesitation. "I want you there when it does. Something of this power needn't be in the hands of idle gods like Felorn who will do nothing with it. It should belong to those who *want* its power. Take your men, ready your spells and charge your staves. Take it by whatever force is necessary. Do *not* let it fall into Kersey Avonwood's hands. Ruin must *not* get it." The group of mages, warriors, and alchemists behind him started murmuring amongst themselves, wondering how they were going to break into Fyrl's castle and steal something that would be so closely guarded.

The spell book was quite an artifact. Every spellcaster on Mystyria would give their soul for it, including Daegin. Its power was beyond anything in any book written since the gods formed the world.

It belonged to the great Aneesa Redblaze and was given to her by Symbia, the goddess of magic. The book and Aneesa's era passed over a thousand years ago, during the great battle at Kragspire Alps of the first War of Balance, but their legends lived on. Aneesa was killed alongside half a million others in Northern Corscus and her spell book was stolen from the battlefield. It was recovered, then lost, then recovered again, constantly shifting hands for the past thousand years.

Up until a few weeks ago, the book had passed completely out of all knowledge. Then, in the city of Lolusk, beneath a Nyian temple, it was found again. It had been buried in a shallow trove with a plethora of weapons and valuables. Now it was about to end up in Felorn, the goddess of destruction's hands. Fyrl was buying the book on her behalf. Daegin was going to have to make sure that Ruin didn't get his hands involved and at the same time, make sure Mydian came out winning.

"And from there?" Daegin asked. Once he stole the spell book, every guard in the city would be after him, not to mention Kersey herself. He hoped he could lure her to her death before it came to that.

"My men—your brethren are on their way from Pelopha. They will be arriving in Tharg in a day or so. *They* will be taking care of Kersey Avonwood. Not you." Mydian stared with an eerie, unbroken gaze.

"Very well, Lord Mydian," he assured, but the image of the dark god had already started to fade. The room was once again silent, save for the bubbling cauldrons of Dragontails and Bristleweed. Daegin wasn't about to let the Mydianites from Pelopha make off with his kill. He wanted Kersey and he would have her. *He* would be the one to bask in the glory.

"Daegin!" A man shouted from the stairs. It was Delber, one of his Mydianites. The wiry man jogged down the steps and pulled his helmet off. He was wearing the armor that Fyrl's guards wore. After all, Delber was one of his men, too. He worked the dock district down on Bayside Street but was also on the god of the Underworld's payroll. It was always good to have a lapdog that could get into the master's home.

"What is it?" he asked, watching the swirling mist inside the mirror.

"Fyrl's men are on the hunt for Mydianites. They're in the streets, knocking on doors and searching for *her*. They think Mydian is behind Kersey's escape."

Daegin smiled. This could work to their advantage. "What news have you of her?"

Delber nervously eyed the tethered vampires in the corner before answering, "She and her minions seem to be settling down for the night." He pointed to the east. "They are headed toward Abrams Hill. Kriball's own headmaster is helping her. I know him."

Fyrl didn't know how to approach a vampire like Kersey. He would send wave after wave of his own men to die and be added to her army before he realized what was happening. But if it would keep him at bay and out of Daegin's hair, then so be it. "I believe this is the perfect opportunity to keep Fyrl occupied. If he wants to try and kill

Kersey, then let's show him where to find her," he said, fishing around in his pocket for some coin.

"What will you have me do?" the corrupt guard asked.

Daegin picked up a few pieces of platinum, pulled Delber's hand up, and then pressed them into it. "Rouse as many guards as you can and *get over there*."

.5.

One of Ten

There were only a few houses at the pinnacle of Abrams Hill. One belonged to Clive, one to his sister, one to Sharisa Cafter and one sat empty. Well, two sat empty now, he sadly noted. From here, everything was out of mind and earshot. The Pen, Fyrl's castle, and Market Lane were just distant ambience of the town below.

Abrams Hill was silent now with only one person other than Clive living there. Sharisa was a young widow with too much time and money and too little respect for privacy. Clive loathed seeing her—loathed her questions and snide remarks. He avoided her at all costs and went out of his way to not be seen in the mornings and evenings when heading to and coming from work.

He was able to sneak out the back door and go down Squire Street and take an alternate route to the Pen. Sure, it added five minutes of walking to his job, but it was well worth it to avoid idle small talk with Sharisa whose house was across the street.

Unfortunately, they were coming from Bayside Street so they were near Abrams Hill to begin with. It was just a short walk up, but Sharisa would be there, on the porch, watching as Clive, a bloodied woman, and a small legion of undead ventured past her.

"I hope you realize they are not all coming to my house," Clive told Kersey and waved his hand to her following minions.

She looked insulted that he would even say such a thing. "Is it a problem?"

"Of course it's a problem!" Clive yelled in a low whisper. It was dark and silent out and they were within range for Sharisa's lingering ears to hear. "Look, at least make them stay back. I have a very *inquisitive* neighbor up above who may not take kindly to seeing them."

Kersey smiled and nodded. "As you wish."

The Gothmirks stopped long enough for them to get ahead, then followed a bit slower. When Clive looked back, he was happy that the darkness turned them into silhouettes and did a good job of hiding what they truly were.

Abrams Hill was just as he suspected. A cart filled to the brim with manure blocked half of the street. Sharisa's yard was a mess and all of her shrubbery had been tossed aside so she could expand this year's turnips and radishes. She spent more time in her yard than anyone else. Her back garden overlooked several houses on the lower streets under Abrams and it was very handy for her to pry.

Across the road sat Clive's house and beside his was Nalia's. There were no lights on like there had been last week. He was so used to coming home, listening to Nalia play the piano from the street and then going over to challenge her in a game of Hammer and Swan, her favorite card game. All of that was over now.

"Who's your little friend there, Clive?" a dreadful voice called from the right. His head whipped to Sharisa's porch and found her sitting in her swing, eyes locked on the bloodied woman.

"Which one is yours?" Kersey asked Clive, ignoring Sharisa and pointing toward the three eligible houses. He directed her to his and after she started toward it, turned his attention back to his nosey neighbor.

"Just an old friend, Sharisa."

"You know, Clive, the birds were picking at Nalia's wreath earlier today, but I took care of them." She got up and walked over to lean on the railing. The moonlight bounced off of her fair complexion. She was covered in dirt and grime. There was a lingering odor of rum on her breath.

"Thank you, Sharisa. Well, goodnight." He started to walk off but her slow-talking, soul-draining voice stopped him in his tracks.

"Such a terrible tragedy. Poor girl. Now why would she go and do a thing like that to herself?" Clive could feel her eyes on the back of his head. He stole a quick glance to the wreath on Nalia's door that was swaying gently in the light breeze. He suppressed tears—suppressed anger with Kersey only a few yards away.

"I don't know," he said and noticed the Gothmirks coming up the road. "Good night, Sharisa."

He hurried away and fumbled for his keys to let himself and Kersey inside. The small woman didn't say anything but she gave him a questioning, yet comforting look. After what seemed like an eternity on the porch, he turned the right key and let them in.

Clive touched his fire globes and instantly the house lit up. The fire globes were actually a gift from Nalia. He was horrible about keeping up with things so he often had trouble remembering where he left his tinderbox. What a good sister she'd been.

"Not that way," he said, grabbing Kersey by the arm when she started into the den. His wondering eyes looked at the blood caked across her chest. He quickly averted his gaze when she caught him staring and he said, "I've spent a fortune on new carpet in there." She shot him a questioning look but seemed to lose interest of the room nevertheless.

"Anything to eat or drink?" he asked, emptying his pockets on the fireplace mantle. "Kitchen's that way." He pointed down the hall toward the unwashed plates that covered the stove.

"No, thank you," she said and found a chair. Clive threw a blanket across it before she plopped down and then sat in the one opposite of her. He pulled his boots off and tossed them aside. The two exchanged glances at each other and out the windows for several minutes. The Gothmirks were surrounding the house like vigilant sentinels.

Clive was sure this was going to be another silent session. Just like all the other previous meetings, Kersey wouldn't have anything more to say. He was just about to give her directions to the bathing chamber when she finally spoke up.

"What happened to Nalia?" He couldn't believe she'd just asked that. He had hoped to never have to repeat his sister's fate—the fate that met her this time last week. Why did Kersey even care?

"She hung herself. Up at Fyrl's place." He couldn't look at her, despite wanting to see her reaction. Clive thought he was done grieving, but apparently that wasn't true. His heart ached at the remnants of last week's events.

He was at home, asleep upstairs, when someone started banging ferociously on his door. He rushed down and ripped it open to find one of Fyrl's guards standing there, Sharisa not far behind. The guard told him that he needed to come to the castle at once. Clive ran there as fast as he could, knowing it could only be about Nalia. After all, she was Fyrl's aid. She had always left work before Clive and was always the first one home. It had been different that night.

When he made it home, Nalia's lights were off but he thought nothing ill about it.

And then, just outside of Fyrl's personal chambers was the most horrific sight he had ever seen. That image burnt itself within the deep recesses of his mind and there it would dwell forevermore. It was his sister lying on the ground with a rope around her neck. She'd been cut down just moments before.

Clive had seen many dead bodies in his day. He'd seen several just tonight. None were as gruesome—as painful as his very own beloved sister. Her blue eyes were bloodshot and bulging from their sockets. Her skin had already paled and stiffened. There were deep gashes left by the strangling burn of the ropes. Her fingers—her *clenched* fingers, were reaching out to rip the mental anguish from her own mind. It was the same mental anguish that drove her to suicide.

"That doesn't make sense," Kersey said, a hint of concern in her voice. "Why would she do that?"

"I don't know," Clive admitted, perhaps the hundredth time. He found his flask of Timberwolf Whiskey in the chair's cushion. "The stress of working with Fyrl and keeping his secrets, I suppose." Clive took a long swig from the much-needed whiskey. "He worships Felorn, you know. This whole Tessian elegance is a facade." The evil goddess of destruction was frowned upon in the lighter cities of Mystyria. A lot of people in Tharg knew of Fyrl's treacherous way, but the money he put toward keeping the city clean, the laws that kept the streets crime-free, and the protection the guards provided all kept mouths from talking.

"And who did your sister worship?" Kersey asked, watching out the window. Sharisa was sweeping her porch but kept a watchful eye on the surrounding undead. Obviously it hadn't occurred to her what they were.

"She worshipped Quillian, just as I do." The goddess of healing's popularity nearly rivaled her ally, Lyluss'. And just like Lylussians, there were Quillianites everywhere, even in dark cities such as Bloodgate and Crynsia, although properly hidden. "And who do you worship, Kers?" It was hard to believe that question had never risen.

She just shook her head and smirked, but did eventually come to an answer. "I suppose you could call me agnostic."

"No one is that much of a fool," Clive chuckled. "Surely there is someone—or was someone that you put your faith into."

She seemed to consider what he said and laced her fingers together in her lap. "Long ago, I was a child of Lyluss. I commanded great power over the dead."

"You still do," he pointed out. "You are, after all a necromancer."

"No, no," she objected and leaned forward to make her point. "My power is twisted now. Those," she gestured out toward the Gothmirks, "are an abomination. My power was once pure and wholesome. I was a Soul-Summoner."

"A Soul-Summoner? You can't be serious." Clive had heard of them before. There were none left, supposedly.

Soul-Summoners were some of the most powerful and holy servants of Lyluss. They possessed such a cauldron of healing magic that they could literally resurrect a fallen life. The result was not undead, but a living, breathing mortal as they were before death claimed them. It was one of the most extraordinary things in the world.

"I'm very serious," she said, then grew colder, more distant. "But that was *long* ago. You can see what's left of that power now."

"Why has it been corrupted? Why can't you call on Lyluss' power?" He watched vines slither around a Gothmirk and that propelled yet another question. "Do you worship Ruin?"

"No, but it does look as though I'm *working* for him."

"What?"

"That fellow under the Iron Queen? That was Ruin."

Clive, who was in mid-drink, almost sprayed his precious carpet with the whiskey. "You're telling me that was the god of the dead?"

She nodded.

"Wha-why?'

"I'm not entirely sure myself," she offered. "All I know is that he has a plan to move against Mydian—the same damned god who wants my soul."

"What does Mydian have against you?" Clive wondered.

Kersey smiled with an unknown satisfaction. "Plenty."

After a few seconds, she stood and surveyed her surroundings, as if returning to an unusual place after being lost in a trance.

"I want a bath and you should get some sleep. We're leaving here at sunrise."

Clive nodded, a little defeated. A part of him still wanted her to just take her minions and go, but another small part was glad she wanted him to come along, although he wouldn't let her know it.

His job at the prison was finished. He had no wife. He had no children. Both of his parents were dead. His darling sister had just nearly extinguished the last of the Porter family.

His home and Kersey were all he had left in the world.

"Bathing chamber is that way," Clive said and pointed down the hall. Kersey nodded and started to walk past when he grabbed her wrist. She looked down questioningly. "Who is Brin?" he asked.

Her face darkened and for just a second, Clive thought he could see small red flames dancing in her pupils. He released her wrist when he felt her trembling. The floorboards creaked and groaned as the vines slapped at them from beneath.

"Brin was a bad, bad man," she said emotionlessly.

"Why? What did he do?" Clive wanted to see her face but she looked on. He touched her arm.

She struggled against his hand and started for the bathing chamber. "Go to bed, Clive," she called out as the bathroom door slammed shut behind her, without even touching it.

Just like any other night, Clive had trouble sleeping. Fifteen years ago, he had woken to banging on the door with the news of his grandmother's death. Seven years ago, the same with his mother. Four years ago it was his father and last week, Nalia. His mind often created false knocks on the door downstairs. The only good thing now was that there was no one left to come knocking about.

Clive groggily rolled over and reached for the flask on his nightstand and found it wasn't there. After fumbling around the bed covers, he came to the conclusion that he left it downstairs. He flipped the blankets off, turned to swing out of bed—

—and brushed against a man standing over top of him. Clive kicked off him and backtracked across the bed, ready to dart off that side—

—when he slammed into another, simply standing there.

He was about to bolt to the bottom of the bed and try and run around them but he noticed the spiraling vines from the corner of his eye. These were Gothmirks standing still and silent, their dead eyes fixed on blank spots on the walls. Kersey must have ordered them to watch over him.

After taking a few seconds to calm down, he slid himself off the edge of the bed and started toward the downstairs. Two more Gothmirks outside the door startled him fully awake and he simply passed them and jogged down the steps and into the foyer where he and Kersey had talked earlier.

It didn't take him long before he noticed the dark red stain on the floor. That certainly wasn't there when he went to bed. A small trail ran from the stain and ended near where he stood. He was about to check it out, to see if it could have been Kersey's but was stopped when a foot suddenly dangled in front of him.

It was dirty down to the mud-encrusted toenails and it jerked in a rhythmic but violent spasm. A small trickle of blood was running down the leg and dripping from the toes. It was Sharisa.

Above her, latched onto the ceiling by an unseen force was Kersey. She was holding Sharisa by the nape of the neck with one hand—its strength was incredible, and unbelievable. Her teeth were planted firmly in the side of the nosey neighbor's throat. Clive could hear slurping noises as Kersey drank from the wound. Her eyes were clamped shut but they were moving rapidly beneath their lids. Sharisa already looked dead.

"Kers?" Clive called. A surprised Kersey dropped the limp woman and she hit with a sickening *'thwack'*. The last of her blood drained across Clive's favorite rug, but he didn't see it. His friend attached to the ceiling was astonishing to him.

Kersey licked the blood from her lips and splashed it down on Clive. He cleared it from his eyes and noticed the long, protruding fangs in her mouth. A vampire—but what kind of vampire has fangs *that* long? he asked himself. Her look of anger—of disappointment of being interrupted faded and turned to cowardice and the fear of a cornered animal. She let go of the ceiling and fell toward him.

Clive readied himself to catch her, but just before she reached him, her entire body exploded into a bright green light that swarmed with a thousand mosquitoes that promptly left through the fireplace. After a moment, he could hear footsteps on the roof and the dust that fell signaled Kersey's dash across, toward the south.

He stepped over Sharisa and ran out the opened door and crossed the street to her weed-strewn yard, just in time to see Kersey on her house. He hopped the fence and trudged through the uneven garden to the back yard and watched as his friend leapt from house to house with the agility of a god.

There had been a little learned tonight of whom Kersey was and as Clive started down the street, he realized he might just get to learn *what* she was.

Kersey's fingers dug deep into the nosey neighbor's neck as she lifted her to the ceiling. She crushed her windpipe to ensure she wouldn't be screaming. Her fangs grew to her bottom lip and she pressed them into the woman's throat, feeling the flesh rending and that first, wonderful taste of new blood. It was deliciously sweet—like honey and nectar. Then again, it was always good after a three-week dry spell. Kersey could have probably gone longer, but the headaches brought on by the bloodlust would have driven her mad.

As she continued to drink, the nosey woman's hair fell to the side, revealing a golden-rimmed and diamond locket around her neck. Kersey's eyes were drawn to it and her mind was suddenly transported to a thousand years and miles away. The locket was almost like the one he'd given her. It magically flew from Sharisa's neck to her own. Hands materialized and helped to clasp it in the back.

She wasn't hanging from the ceiling and drinking blood anymore. She was in a wagon, on a bumpy road heading down a valley a few miles from Keswing.

"That's so sweet of you, Brin!" came the cheery voice of Alexa Lighthammer. Her brother Rowan looked on with equal approval. Kersey smiled to her new infatuation. It was hard to believe she'd only met Brin two weeks ago. He was perfect in every single way.

"Thank you," she told him. "Why am I so deserving?" She leaned forward and kissed him. Her mind back in Tharg almost spat blood in disgust.

"Why am *I* so deserving?" He smirked and sat back, trying to steady himself on the rough road.

Kersey peered out the window of the wagon and saw the terrain had grown very secluded. It was obvious why they hid her here. This place was a perfect shelter for something so large—so secret—so evil.

She noticed the towers of the Lylussian Academy in Keswing had disappeared from view. Ahead of them, another wagon was on the same path heading in the same direction and carrying six others who were tasked with the same job as she was.

The Kersey back in Tharg was shaking so hard that Sharisa's throat was being mutilated. Her mind wouldn't let her leave the era of the War just yet.

Brin placed his fingers on Kersey's chin and pulled her toward him. Her smile on that day before the tainting was so genuine. It was so innocent, so purpose-driven.

So foolish.

"You know I won't let anything happen to you down there, right?" His eyes were so reassuring. She nodded as the wagon came to a halt.

There were voices from the one in front as it unloaded and its passengers geared up. Someone rapped on the side of their wagon and a man appeared next to Brin's window. He was just as nice.

"Everyone ready to kill this beast and get home before dinner?" Arctis Moonbridge smiled and slapped Brin reassuringly on the arm.

She nodded and joined into their conversation but it quickly faded from her mind. The entrance to the great dragon's lair disappeared and she was back in Clive's house with him calling her name below.

Her heart sank at the knowledge of her curse being paraded in the open. Clive, in one quick glance would know her darkest secrets. She let the victim drop and then followed behind, but managed to change form and escape up the chimney and to the roof.

Kersey ran the span of the house and leaped across the street and landed on Sharisa's roof. From there she hopped down to the lower road and skipped across several more. She wanted to put as much distance between herself and Clive's house as possible and finally ended up in a dank alley that smelled of fish and hay.

How could she have been so foolish? She had marked the nosey neighbor as food from the moment she laid eyes on her. It was Kersey's intention to break into her home, feed, and then get back to Clive's house without him knowing. That all changed when the snooping lady came to talk about the fires on the east end of town with one of the Gothmirks. When she realized what they were, she turned and tried to run but Kersey wasn't about to let that happen. She pounced her like a cheetah and pulled her back inside the house, letting the Lust do the rest. That coupled with the flashback made her actions quite thoughtless—exposed.

What would Clive's reaction be to this? Sure, he had numerous inquiries as to who and what she was, but what kind of picture would his mind paint? *The things he'll think of me*, she thought. *The things he'll know I've done.* He would probably be correct on every assumption.

She wanted to go back—to explain some things, but knew that would never happen. Clive was probably so terrified or so angry that he'd never come anywhere near—

—a hand touched her shoulder.

Kersey whirled around from her squatting position and grabbed her assailant by the throat and flew with him toward the nearest wall. He crashed with a loud *'oomph'* that exploded the small glass windows in the door against his back. She was just about to decorate his neck when she saw who it was.

It was *Clive*.

He didn't run. He didn't stomp away in anger or betrayal. No, he came *looking* for her. That made all the difference in the world. She felt so bad for the fear that was mounting in his eyes right now.

Her fingers loosened and her legs faltered. She staggered away from a calming Clive and fell to her knees in defeated agony. For the first time in countless years, Kersey Avonwood let her emotions seep out. She didn't care for Clive to see her. Not anymore. This fit had been brewing for a long time and its eventual rise to the surface was inevitable.

She spotted a long sliver of broken glass and snatched it. In deep tugs, she started slicing into her forearm, feeling the fresh physical agony wash over her, dulling the mental and spiritual pain. It was exhilarating but tonight's events were not so easily extinguished. Warm blood ran down her wrist and collected into a small pool in her open palm.

"Kersey, no!" Clive yelled and stepped around her. The slicing grew more intense—so intense that clumps of her flesh were being tossed about and her own dark blood was running down the alley in a small river.

He grabbed the makeshift weapon from her and tossed it aside. She tried to claw with her own fingers but allowed him to hold her back.

"Why are you doing this to yourself, Kers?" Clive was searching her eyes and he pulled her hair away from them.

"Because I *have* to!" she cried. "I have to make the pain and memories go away!" She broke from his grasp and fell back so she didn't have to face him.

"What memories?"

She felt a comforting hand on her back and she tried to make her trembling less noticeable. She didn't answer his question but she spoke the truth of what was building.

"We were good people!" she screamed through sobs. "It changed us! The blood *changed* us! I didn't mean to kill them! I didn't mean to wreck their temples!"

That cursed dragon started it all. Her life was nothing more than a continuous downward spiral after those fateful weeks in isolation with nine others. Her very soul had been sucked from her body.

"What blood? Who did you kill? What are you talking about, Kers?" Clive was by her side, his face only inches from hers. She collapsed and closed her eyes. She couldn't talk anymore. Not tonight, anyway. Her mind, body, and heart had been drained but thank the gods, Clive was here.

He scooped her up in his arms and pressed her against the wall long enough to run his fingers through her matted hair. He cleared it from her dirty face. She could sense his warm smile as he carried her away toward his house.

.6.

The Destiny of Fear

It was the most beautiful sight she had ever seen. True, she was able to steal a glimpse when the power of the Overlord's heart beat within her chest, but this moment stood still. She wasn't being rushed to a frigid town to snatch her little girl and kill the man who murdered her sister. All of the small things in life melted away for just a moment as she watched it. There was no Lorne, no Pelopha, no thoughts of revenge, and no quest to please the god of the Underworld. There was only Dyne and the rising sun.

Morning arrived as soon as they stepped through the portal back in Hope's Covenant. The sun's radiant light was spilling across the barren countryside, its golden glow clinging to the tips of the grass and wheat like paint on a brush. This part of Southern Corscus' landscape was quite uneventful, having only a few trees in the distance as its only landmarks.

The wind was fierce. It blew across her back and pushed her toward the east, toward the wonderfully warm sun that was making Dyne reconsider the black robe. There were seagulls flying overhead, flapping their ivory wings against the strong gusts in an attempt to make it to the beach behind them.

She turned around and instantly felt a nauseating pain in the pit of her stomach. It was the ocean. Although they weren't anywhere near it, they could see it below. The portal had spit them out on a cliff that was several hundred feet high. Below the jagged cliff wall was the beach whose sand was white as bone. The Arinbeth Ocean crashed against it, pulling Dyne's mind in and out with each pass. She was *terrified* of water.

When she was only thirteen, a fisherman tried to teach her how to swim off the coast of Boudia. She was as horrified then as she was now. The fisherman grew angry at her inability to grasp the concept of keeping afloat and when he decided that the lesson was over, he tried to drown her. His fingers wrapped around her small neck and pushed her under, ignoring her nails in his forearm. It wasn't until her father's friends found them and pulled her from his murderous grasp. They killed the one who would dare drown a child and as the red water washed around her, Dyne was instilled with a fear of the ocean from that day forward.

Why is this coming back to haunt me now? she wondered, learning the reason almost instantly. She was mortal now. Her gods-given mortal fears had returned, just like hunger and thirst. It was another inconvenience she was going to have to get used to.

Dyne took a few steps back from the cliff's steep edge and knelt down in the grass. She didn't like being this high up, this close to water, with this much force blowing her small body around. Her shaky fingers wrapped around the blades of grass and it calmed her to let the moisture seep between them. Lorne chuckled above her.

"Ah, I remember this," he said and knelt down in the grass with her. He tried his best to see her eyes from beneath the overhanging hood but she wouldn't allow it. She would not let him get the best of her. "You're still afraid of the water, aren't you?"

She was still and emotionless, breathing heavily under the robes. Her fingers were now plucking the blades of grass from their roots.

"This was why we always used portals to journey between continents, wasn't it? You were deathly afraid of traveling by sea!" Lorne let out a bellowing laugh and stood, his voice echoing across the green field before them.

Dyne stood and looked past him. His laughter—his *taunting* faded from her mind as she took notice of the city on the hill a few hundred yards north. Lorne turned to see what had grabbed her attention and he stared, as well. It was Pelopha, just as it had been a century ago when she had last visited.

It sat on the highest cliff this side of the map, some eight-hundred feet up. There was no tapered path to the beach. If one were to walk to Pelopha's most westerly point, they would fall almost a thousand feet to the ocean. There were no tall buildings or towers, either. The strong winds made it impossible for high structures to last.

Across from the cliff that sported Pelopha was the Denmorg Island. It was a small landmass that stood in the water and was exactly the same elevation as Pelopha herself. Rope bridges connected the two across a hundred-foot chasm. The goddess of destruction, Felorn, broke this island off several hundred years ago.

Felorn wasn't as widely worshipped as Mydian or Ruin, but her power was still felt across the world. She was just as evil as the darkest of gods and her destructive power was legendary. Her alias was the *'Giantess'* due to her rampaging attacks on Mystyrian cities in the form of a gargantuan, ground-shattering goddess.

Years ago, there were many skirmishes inside the walls of Pelopha due to the sudden appearance of Drakish temples. The god of evil had planted his seed in the city and wanted all other religious figures out. Most of the gods and goddesses didn't care enough to send troops or use their divine powers to intervene as he tore into their temples and servants. Only Felorn opposed him.

The goddess of destruction leapt from the heavens in the form of a two-hundred foot giantess. She ripped Drak's temples apart with her bare hands and tossed them into the ocean and when she was done, she decided that Pelopha was no place for her servants. The goddess grabbed onto the land and pressed with her feet until she broke a large piece clean from the cliff. She pushed it out into the water until it was completely free to itself. She claimed this small island her own and had her servants build upon it. The giantess' footprints were still visible on the cliff wall beneath the city where she pushed off to move Denmorg further away. Locals of Pelopha called it *'Felorn's Mark'*.

Even though she didn't publicly put her hands into either of the two great Wars, many people believed she was still involved. There had always been an unspoken hostility between she and Mydian and her assassins were far too great and too well hidden to tell just how deeply they were embedded in his interests.

"Here's the road," Lorne pointed out. A stone path led all the way up to Pelopha's front gate. It ran dangerously close to the cliff's edge.

"No, I'll go this way," she said, and started up toward the city, keeping to the inland grass. It would take a little longer, but she felt much safer this way.

"Suit yourself," Lorne smirked. He headed up the stone path and was there well before she got started. The sun, the beautiful countryside, and his momentary absence made it a wonderful walk.

There were four guards in a small gatehouse just outside the city that looked at them with questioning eyes. After all, they were two securely wrapped individuals who were in the middle of nowhere without a wagon. Suspicious was definitely an understatement. Dyne was sure there was going to be trouble. Certainly Lorne was going to pull out his new halberd to see how well it sliced through bone and leather but that wasn't the case. He didn't want any more problems than the guards did.

Instead, he pulled out a small bag of coins and poured them across the gatehouse guard's folder just as he started to draw up paperwork for their arrival. The stocky, cross-eyed guard only smiled and waved his hand for the others to let them pass. Four platinum coins could buy a house in Southern Corscus or in this case, an unquestioned passage through the gates of Pelopha.

The city was remarkably quiet. It was fairly large—nearly as expansive as its northern neighbor Tharg, having a population of almost forty-thousand. The streets were packed with merchants selling all kinds of wares ranging from clothing and weapons to pets and produce. The fishing industry was very influential here. Every vender in the city seemed to sell at least some portion of trout, bait, or lines and nets.

As the two headed deeper into the eastern part of the slanting city, they saw a gradual increase in the law. There were guards everywhere. Their pauldrons and vambraces were all adorned with the open-book symbol of Heron, the god of knowledge. So their ruler was a good ruler, Dyne noted. From the looks of things, he kept the holy gods on the front row. Lyluss, Quillian, Heron, and Ebend all had temples in sight. Gods such as Mydian, Felorn, Drak, and Ruin were hidden—tucked away from the common good folk's eyes and ears.

"So how do we know where we are supposed to go?" Lorne asked, watching the sun peek through the bell tower of the Lylussian temple.

"We're to find the *Rusted Hook* Tavern," she answered, trying to remember where the inn and pub district was in this city.

"Oh?" he asked, suddenly not interested in the sun anymore. "I suppose Mydian told you that *after* I left?" He quieted down for just a moment but Dyne knew there was more on the way. "So what did the two of you talk about while your sister and I were outside?" And there it was—the pry that she'd been waiting for.

"Nothing," she told him, craning her head far back to clear the hood. She looked into his unsatisfied eyes. "If he wanted you to know, he wouldn't have asked you to leave, now would he?" Lorne shook his head, as he often did when she gave him an answer that took him nowhere.

The wide stone street quickly turned to pebble as the cropping of taverns drew near. A sudden, brief wind passed by and with it carried the most wonderful smell she could remember. It was *chicken*. The unmistakable, mouth-watering aroma of roasting chicken was thick in the air as it pulled them closer.

It seemed like there were two taverns for every person in Pelopha. The city was comprised mostly of middle-class working families who served the gods of good and such taverns were able to make a steady wage night after night. The wonderful smell was coming from the *Rusted Hook*.

A narrow bridge connected the pebble road to the small tavern on the other side of a thin crevice. She could see the ocean below. It was so far away, yet so threatening at the same time. She cupped her mouth with her hand and stepped foot on the rickety bridge, praying to any god that would listen to allow her to make it across without it snapping.

Lorne gave her a final shove to the *Rusted Hook's* doorway and she coughed from the deepest recesses of her abdomen when she was standing inside its short foyer. Her whole body was trembling. A couple of curious onlookers gave her an interested stare but quickly returned to their food, drink, and stories. It was just as quiet here as it was outside. Even the sound of beer dripping from the tap behind the bar could be heard. Lorne spotted an empty booth toward the rear and grabbed Dyne by the arm and pulled her toward it. They seated themselves next to a table where two men played cards.

"Think you gathered enough attention?" he asked as her coughing died down.

She only showed him the furrowing of her brow as she wiped the saliva from her quivering lips. This was how Lorne operated, even in life before she made him a vampire. Pick one thing that your adversary is weak at, expose it, and then use it against them. She wouldn't allow that to happen to her, too.

"Why don't you just keep quiet until we're done, eh?" Dyne asked in a stern voice.

Lorne gave a quick glance over his shoulder to make sure he was out of earshot and then leaned up. "I'm not going to sit idly and allow your constant bickering, Dyne. I never did a thing to offend you."

"You did *everything* to offend me!" she yelled, but managed to keep her voice low enough to not attract any unwanted attention. "You stole things that were precious to me!"

The night Dyne put a blade through Lorne's chest, she had learned from her courier, Dunford, that he had poured wine all over Hannah's sketchpad and then stole Telsa's sword for his own. He deserved every bit of her hatred.

"I stole nothing," he breathed. "You were so fixed on finding your precious Overlord heart that you didn't realize you were being fooled the whole time."

"Watch your mouth," she warned. "You are treading close to another incident."

"I'll not keep quiet when I'm telling the truth. Dunford made it look as though I did those things. He wanted my place. Hell, he probably wanted *your* place."

Dyne stared at her hands on the table. Was he telling the truth? Telsa had said that Dunford was punished because he stole from Mydian himself. If he was capable of that, he was surely capable of stealing from her.

"Dyne, what reason do I have to lie? Here and now, why would I continue to do such a thing?"

Lorne was right. He had nothing else to lose. If he did take those things then he had no reason to continue covering up now. The man who sat before her, the man who had once been her friend, then her deserter, then her vampiric servant, was telling the truth. She felt a small bit of guilt—of regret for what she had done but it wasn't enough to make a difference. It wasn't enough to show the true feelings on her face. Dyne was evil—evil *long* before she was a vampire and even though she was free to feel however she wanted to feel, she still didn't have to let him know that she was sorry.

By now the smell of the chicken was overpowering. It made her forget all about the queasiness the water caused, how mesmerizing the sun was, and how much Lorne's company vexed her. She wanted to eat. She needed to eat. After all, this was a new stomach that was completely empty.

"Chicken, please!" she shouted to a passing server. The simple girl jumped at the sudden outburst but nodded and headed off toward the kitchen. All of the tavern folk returned to their meals once again, hopeful that the crazy woman's antics were at an end.

Moments later, the girl reappeared, a steaming platter of roasted chicken, diced potatoes, carrots, and corn in her tiny hands. She sat those down, ran back to the kitchen, and quickly returned with two large glasses of ale. Dyne didn't even see her come back. Her face was buried beneath a few inches of chicken, ripping the meat from the bone and taking time only to savor the memories of the last time she had it.

It was in a tent, near Keswing with Laraek. A chicken had wandered into their camp so they caught it, killed it, and then roasted it in one of the barrack's makeshift ovens. Dyne's nose burned with tears at the thought of Laraek's demise only two weeks later. They had been happy there but the battle forced them to go separate ways—a decision that was fatal for Laraek and his family. She never even got to say goodbye.

Dyne's appetite had come and gone. She only managed a few bites of the roast chicken but the recall of such horrible events made it quickly vanish. After a small sip of ale, she pushed the plate aside.

There was no slowing Lorne's appetite. He dug into the chicken with his large, thick fingers and ripped the meat apart before stuffing it into his mouth. His ale was already gone and he flagged the serving girl down for another pour.

"I suppose we wait," Dyne said. Lorne nodded and continued to cram chicken into his mouth. The sun was already passing the frame at the top. It was probably close to noon. They had toured the city and found the tavern and were now waiting for Mydian's commander.

"Do you think we even have a chance of killing Kersey?"

"It depends on how many this 'commander' actually commands," Dyne offered. The Overlords had weaknesses, but she didn't know if she was capable of exploiting them. She didn't actually fancy herself as a vampire hunter, even though she'd killed quite a few. The last one—Arctis—the one with the heart, was the only one that had mattered.

"I want to do this job and be rid of her. I want to go *home*." Lorne said, grabbing his new tankard of ale.

"Home?" Dyne mused. "And what do you intend to do? Kill yourself once we're done so you can be back in the Underworld?"

"Not *that* home. I miss the Underworld already, but I long to see Bloodgate again. I want to see the Martax once more and I want to visit a few of my favorite haunts. So much has probably changed since we last visited."

"Game of King's Blade?" came a sudden, cheery voice next to Dyne. She looked over and saw a man staring back at her, his left eye obviously phony. It was bright green and shiny, as if he simply stuck an emerald in its socket to plug the hole. The other man who had been playing earlier had left—his lost coins spread across the table. Dyne shook her head but didn't let him see her face. She had played that simple card game years ago but found it to be too trivial to be taken seriously.

"Ah, that's too bad," he said, shuffling the deck and leaning his chair back on two legs. "How 'bout your friend there?" He nodded toward Lorne.

The burly man finished draining his second ale and offered the gambler an evil grin. Lorne slid over to his table while Dyne folded her arms over and watched.

"Two gold?" he asked, still shuffling the deck. Lorne nodded and flipped them on the table. The gambler smiled and then started laying down cards.

King's Blade required the cards to be laid out, faced down in a spiral pattern so each player could pick up from the outside and work their way inward. This man was doing no such thing, nor was he watching the deck. His eye was fixed on the other occupants of the tavern. He was spelling out words with each set. The gambler's cheery, happy smile faded and turned serious as he glanced to make sure Dyne and Lorne understood the message he was conveying.

The cards made an 'M', and then a 'Y'. The little charade went on until they read, 'MYDIANITE?'. Dyne and Lorne looked to each other and then uneasily nodded.

"Quite a good game, sir!" the gambler yelled in mock victory. "I'm afraid that gold is mine!" He scooped up Lorne's two coins as well as his previous winnings and headed off toward the other side of the tavern where he disappeared behind a curtain. Lorne looked frustrated of being robbed but Dyne just smiled and pushed him on.

The two passed beyond the silk partition and into another common room, although it was empty save for the bartender who was cleaning glasses. The gambler approached him and patted him on the back.

"Two for downstairs," he said. The bartender looked them over and nodded. He pulled a crowbar from beneath the counter and started prying the lid off the nearest cask. The gambler stood idly by with his hands clasped in front of him while a puzzled Dyne and Lorne tried to make sense of what was happening. A strong, salty smell filled the room as the bartender plunged his arm into the opened cask, all the way up to the shoulder. The gambler fanned the air in front of his face.

"Kurtz Malt Lager," he pointed out. "Nobody drinks that stuff 'round here!" He laughed a throaty chuckle that turned into a cough at the end.

There was an audible 'click' inside the barrel as the bartender pulled something. The wall behind him moved to the side, revealing a staircase that spiraled down. There was a faint golden light coming from below and a cold air rushed up to greet them. Obviously this was why the curtain was there.

"Follow me, children," the gambler said, motioning them toward the staircase. "By the way, name's Jonas. Jonas Sessa." He snatched a torch from a wall sconce and continued down the steps. The two 'children of Mydian' followed behind, the sounds of the bartender hammering the lid back onto the cask could be heard as the door slid shut above.

Dyne was curious as to where this passageway led. This corridor had to run straight down into the very rock of the cliff, directly below the tavern. A thick rope was attached to the ceiling of the spiraling passage and continued directly down the middle of the staircase. It would be a long drop if they fell. With that in mind, she grabbed on to it and held tight as she descended down into the darkened, narrow abyss.

Jonas led them to the bottom where it opened into a stone hallway that was just as dark as above. The air was musty and smelled of fish and saltwater. Dyne's stomach was turning at the thought of how close the water must have been.

"Guess I don't need to know your names," Jonas said, walking backwards so he could look at them. "But apparently you two must be awfully important for the dark lord to send you here after being dead and all."

"And what exactly did the dark lord say about us?" Dyne asked, grabbing her own torch from a wall sconce.

"Not a thing to us," Jonas offered. "Mydian himself probably doesn't even know about this place. Commander does all his dealings in town."

"Quite the security for your hideaway," Lorne said. Dyne followed his gaze up and noticed the floating orbs hovering above. Somewhere nearby, a litter of mages and wizards were keeping watchful eyes on their passage.

"Oh yes," Jonas agreed. "We don't let just anyone through here, not even Mydianites." He pointed to Dyne and said, "But you are allowed here because the commander has been raving about you. He truly wants to see you, my dear."

Before she could speak up to what he meant, Lorne asked, "How long have we been expected?" He swatted at the falling embers from Dyne's torch.

"Last night while the commander was training the Crossbacks at the temple in the city, a messenger arrived saying that you'd be coming."

"Crossbacks?" Lorne asked.

"Oh, yeah, quite somethin' to see. Interesting vampires. They can be lethal killers by instinct, but they are slower to learn than most. I just hope that battlemage in Tharg has enough of that elixir to make up for it. I'm sure the commander'll show you later on."

Jonas led them to the end of the corridor to a closed, wooden door. He handed his torch to Lorne and then snatched the fake eye from its socket. The dark hollow on his face was as nauseating as his yellow teeth as he smiled in adoration of his own clever trick. But before Dyne could ask what he planned to prove by taking it out, he twisted the green gem until it split into two halves. There were threads on each piece. Inside sat a small, silver key.

He quickly unlocked the wooden door and then placed it back into its ocular hiding spot. The door swung inward and the sickening sound of the nearby ocean echoed down the narrow corridor. They were literally on the beach now. Dyne didn't know if she could make it or not.

"After you," Jonas said, waving his hand and stuffing his fake eye in at the same time. Lorne passed his torch back and headed through. Dyne nervously stepped off the stone floor and onto the sand. Jonas came through and slammed the door shut so hard that it startled her and caused her to whirl around to face him, hand on her sword's hilt.

"Whoa!" Jonas said, taking a step back. "I didn't mean to alarm ye, miss." He patted her on the shoulder as he walked by and she relaxed, but only a little.

She turned around and started off, following Jonas' footprints in the sand. They were indeed on the beach, but this was a very different beach than the one she'd spied earlier from above. Behind, she could see Pelopha sitting on the cliff far off to the south, the Denmorg Island just in front. Just how far had she walked today?

The water crashed against the beach and Dyne couldn't help but feel a small bit of it on the air. Her stomach turned itself inside out as the cool moisture met her face. She circled around Lorne and walked on the other side of him, as far as she could against the base of the cliff. He dug his torch into the ground and hurried up behind her.

"And here we are," Jonas said, standing atop a small mound. Dyne and Lorne looked off to the bay that had his attention. Neither could believe their eyes.

Beneath the alcove of the cliff wall were several small buildings and huts. Some were even carved into the rock itself, reminding Dyne of the bat-like vampiric city of Gloomrift. There were rope bridges connecting some of the higher structures and a series of water-powered lifts made every point accessible. She spotted the skull-torch emblem of Mydian on several of the houses' doors and siding and in the center of the makeshift camp was a stone temple dedicated to the god of the Underworld himself.

At the end of the bay was a long pier where seven massive galleys were anchored. They were black—*completely* black from the hulls up to the crow's nests. Even the sails and rigging were ominously dark. There were very little intricacies on their sides, other than the raised letters that displayed their names. She couldn't make out the four on the far side of the pier, but the ships closest were named, *'The Black Murder', 'Adella's Pride',* and *'Mydian's Hammer'.*

"By the gods!" Lorne said, pointing to the row of ships. "Is that—"

"—the *Phantom Seven*? Why, yes it is," Jonas proudly finished for him.

The *Phantom Seven* was supposed to be a hoax, Dyne remembered. They were a fleet of seven ships that sailed under the lord of the Underworld's flag. They were myth and legend—told in stories to be the very fleet that ended the second War of Balance. They stormed the beaches of Davinshire and Sorcea and killed thousands in the name of Mydian and then, as quickly as they appeared, were gone. Powerful vampires who wanted only to carve Lyluss from the face of Mystyria made up their crew. Was this the great force that was going to kill Kersey Avonwood? She surely hoped so. Their quest suddenly didn't feel as hopeless, but in her eagerness to the addition of such help, Dyne failed to notice the method by which they would be traveling to Pelopha.

"This way, children," Jonas motioned for them to follow him toward the Mydianite hideout.

Lorne growled. "I'm getting very tired of him calling us *children*."

Dyne only grinned.

Jonas led them into a room that had been completely hollowed out of the cliff. There were support beams in every corner, hopefully strong enough to keep the weight of a couple hundred feet worth of cliff from coming down. The passage continued further into the rock and headed uphill until it once again returned to the outside. They were on the second story and could see the pier much better. It amazed Dyne that a network as large as this, and a fleet of ships as highly sought after and as secretive as the *Phantom Seven* could remain anonymous from the public eye.

There were Mydianites everywhere. Some were working on the ships while others were hoisting supplies up to the higher levels by ropes. A few were out in the knee-deep water dragging fishing nets in the tide. There was whispering all around. Everyone in the camp had taken notice of the two robed figures but didn't let it interfere with their daily activities and chores.

Jonas grabbed a bottle of wine from a crate as it was ascending past and uncorked it. He pulled up a chair and sat down, then crossed his legs and took a swig. After watching Lorne and Dyne stare for a few moments, he nodded toward two other chairs.

"Might as well get comfortable, children." He looked out toward the sea and took notice of the high-hanging sun in the sky. "It's still a few hours until sunset. Commander'll be along as soon as it's past the Arinbeth." Jonas pointed with his bottle toward the glowing orb.

"Why doesn't this commander stay here with his men?" Lorne asked.

Jonas giggled and almost spewed the wine as he did. "No, no, these are not his men. These are his *servants*. He and his lady-friend, as well as his crew all stay up in town. Their houses are up there."

A warm breeze settled over Dyne as she watched the pull of the sea. She found the chair Jonas had pointed out and sat down, motioning for Lorne to do the same.

There was a battle raging in her mind. Her subconscious had finally put things together and she didn't like the final picture. The commander wasn't a military commander. He was a *naval* commander. His men were his crew—the crew of the *Phantom Seven*. The Tilgrin Inlet to the north prevented anyone from quickly getting to Tharg by land. They planned on heading to Tharg by sea—by the *ships* that were rocking back and forth against the pier in front of her. Dyne buried her face in her hands.

"So what is all this stuff?" Lorne asked, eying the barrels that lifted up by the pulleys. There were large 'X's on them that had small red drops painted along the bottom.

"That's Bloodsilver," Jonas said. "We use it here, just like they do in the Underworld. Most of this is headed up north, to Crynsia and Bloodgate. This here is what makes the Crossbacks."

"Makes?" Dyne asked, knowing that such a thing should have been impossible. Any attempt to save Sania, to extract vampire venom, store it, and weaponize it proved futile. Man had tried countless times. Biting a mortal and injecting the poison was the only way to make a vampire. Or so she thought.

"That's right, but I'm just an ignorant boatswain. I'm not too savvy with all that magic and alchemy gibberish. The commander'll be able to explain it better than I."

Someone called Jonas' name from behind. A young girl dressed in a solid black robe rushed in from the carved doorway.

"We may have a problem," she offered and stepped out onto the balcony, her long robe dragging the floor.

"What is it?"

"There are a few Lylussian soldiers at the *Rusted Hook* asking about the commander. They asked for him by *name*."

What *was* his name? Dyne wondered. She had never asked Mydian or Jonas. It wasn't important. She did however wonder what the significance was of the Lylussian soldiers. How could they know anything about the *Phantom Seven*?

Jonas stood and put his hand on the girl's shoulders. "I need you to listen to me, Rysia." The young girl, who was probably no more than fifteen, hung on his every word and nodded, never taking her big, unblinking eyes from him. "Rouse all the Mydianites in the city's temple that you can. Tell them that they may be needed for a counterattack." The girl nodded and headed back down the corridor. After a few seconds, Dyne could see her running along the beach, back toward the city.

"What is happening?" Lorne asked Jonas.

"Lyluss has been getting bold lately," he said, settling back down in his chair. "She's eager to put an end to the dark lord's reign. She *fears* us."

"This doesn't make sense," Dyne interjected. "Why would Lyluss instigate anything? Has she ever, in the history of Mystyria, ever started any type of feud with Mydian?"

"No," Jonas offered, giving the notion only a second's worth of thought. "But then again, Lyluss isn't the only one the dark god is at odds with. There are others who would probably benefit from sealing a pact with Lady Good."

"Ruin?" Lorne asked.

Jonas nodded. "Either alone or together, they're both certainly angry about *some*thing."

.7.

The Truth of Death

"Clive, wake up! Get up, *get up!*"

There were hands on his shirt—pulling him through the bed covers and to his feet. He groggily shook himself awake and was confounded by the person who so violently separated him from his slumber. It was Kersey but he didn't recognize her at all.

Her hair had been washed and was parted nicely down the middle and tied over her shoulder. She wore a bright, yet elegant red dress that had black frills along the sleeves and neck. It was one of Nalia's. There was no blood. Her face and arms had been cleaned and naturally the scars were gone. This was the first time he'd seen her look so normal—so *beautiful*. He would have much liked to have stayed and enjoyed it but the frantic look on her face—in her eyes, made him realize something was wrong.

"We have to leave, Cl—" she started to say.

The ceiling of his bedroom suddenly splintered in a thousand pieces as a massive, burning stone came crashing down. It hit several feet from them and continued through the floor, finally landing in the den below. So much for his new carpet, he thought with a grimace.

The house smelled of smoke and the morning sun was filling into the room by means of the gaping hole in the roof.

"What's happening, Kers?" he asked her as she took his hand and led him out into the hall. There was a commotion outside. He could hear screams, swords clashing, and the roar of fire through the walls. The stench of smoke was strong here and he could see puffs of it wafting from beneath the hall doors as they passed. His house was blazing.

Another flying boulder crashed behind them, obliterating the bedroom that Clive had been soundly sleeping in just moments before. Kersey pulled him faster, dodging debris on the floor and circling past the stone that had hit earlier. The front door was missing and the windows were broken. Clive's pretty curtains—the curtains that Nalia had made herself were blazing like orange flags. A torch was lying on the scorched carpet—burning a trail all the way to the bathing chamber.

Clive couldn't believe how many there were outside. It wasn't the Gothmirks, but Fyrl's guards. They were coming up Hampton Street, a row of catapults and fire-wielding archers in their wake. There had to be nearly a hundred of them. It had taken them this long to find out where Kersey had hidden. This did not bode well for him. He would be hanged now for sure.

The Gothmirks had already engaged the guards. There were corpses all over the street and the undead were slowly thinning. After all, it was only a handful of unarmed creatures against a hundred trained and battle-ready men. Kersey had obviously been inside bathing. The look on her face told Clive that she was seeing this skirmish for the first time. It had almost been lost, but with her now taking control, the hundred guards didn't stand a chance against an army that could renew itself. She lifted her dress and approached the battle. As she did, a catapult fired and a massive, flaming rock hurtled toward her.

Before it could come down, thick tendrils sprouted from the ground and wrapped around it. They deftly pulled it harmlessly away from her. Kersey didn't even seem to notice. She flicked her hand toward the fallen men and they rose, gathered their weapons and joined her undead in the slaughtering of guards.

Suddenly a guard ran past, a dagger in his hand. He had come from Squire Street and was headed right for Kersey. Without thinking, Clive hopped his banister and gave chase. The blade was pointed out, its tip ready to skewer Kersey's neck when the guard was forced to the ground. Both men landed solidly and Clive tried his best to wrestle the dagger away.

"Clive!" the guard said. "What are you doing? Let me kill her!" It was Delber, one of the men that Fyrl had watch the ships down near Bayside.

"No!" he yelled, slamming his wrist against the hard ground. "Leave her alone and she'll not bother you!"

The guard was uninterested in hearing words of reconciliation. He looked like he didn't know how a man of Clive's rank and history could turn on his own men so quickly—and for a woman who was nothing more than a petty thief.

With a small, renewed bit of motivation, Clive managed to break the bones of Delber's hand, forcing him to release the dagger. His screams were short-lived as several vines sprouted from the ground and enveloped around every limb. Clive barely rolled off of him before they ripped him apart, spraying blood all over the sidewalk. Had Sharisa still been alive and not down the street fighting the guards, she'd have been very upset by the mess.

Clive was panting. He sat down on the ground and watched as the guards decided the battle wasn't worth their lives. Four abandoned catapults were all that remained. They retreated down Hampton and Kersey raised a hand for her minions to not follow.

She was standing over top of him, watching him, but he didn't see it. His eyes were on the ground. So much had happened. There was so much confusion and so much noise in his mind. He was helping a woman who he knew nothing about. Clive would never have done such a thing in his younger years but for some reason this woman made him at ease. Even with her undead swarming around him like a pack of hungry wolves, he still felt at ease. For some reason, she evoked happier times—happier memories from when he was a child.

"Thank you," she said and held her hand out to help him up. He took it and when she pulled, he pulled back and made her sit in the dirt with him. She plopped down and offered a weak smile, but tried to avoid his gaze as much as he tried to avoid hers.

Last night, after the episode in town, Clive brought her back to the house and put her in the first floor bedroom. He didn't ask any questions, nor did he try to clean her up. He simply pulled the covers over her tiny, sobbing body, turned off the fire globes, and went to sleep himself. Now, after his head had managed to clear just a bit, he wanted a few answers.

"So you're a vampire, then?" he bluntly assumed, watching the thick plumes of smoke bellow from the broken windows of his house. "That's why you sneak out at night. To feed?" Every accusation had been right. The townsfolk of Tharg who had witnessed her doing nasty, brutal things had been telling the truth all along.

"I guess that much is obvious," she admitted, smiling. For the first time, Clive could see her fangs. They were gleaming in the sun—the sun that should have never been able to touch them.

"Then how is it possible you are outside right now? Shouldn't you be burnt to a crisp by now?"

"I'm not like most vampires," her eyes reassured him, "I'm different."

He reached up and placed his hand above her breast. She gave him a standoffish look and slid away, but it was all he needed. There was most definitely a strong pounding in her chest.

"Why does your heart beat? Aren't all vampires *dead*?"

"*Most* vampires are dead," she corrected. "I told you, I'm different and I am very much alive."

"You have no bite marks," Clive pointed out, flipping her hair to the other shoulder.

"And you have paid far too much attention to me!" she growled, moving the hair back, an irritated look on her face. It was increasingly menacing now that she was allowing him to see her fangs. Her expression softened when she realized whom she was yelling at and answered, "I don't have them because I was never bitten." Her fangs shrank just a little.

"Exactly how is *that* possible?"

"You aren't very knowledgeable of folklore, are you Clive?" Kersey craned her head to the side in anticipation of his answer.

"Obviously not," he confessed, running his fingers through the dirt.

"I'm one of the Overlords—what the gods call the *Ten*."

"You mean the first vampires?"

She nodded.

Clive had heard of them. But then again, who hadn't? The Greater Overlords were supposedly noble and holy Lylussian Slayers who killed the dark god's dragon and became cursed by drinking its tainted blood. Ebend, the god of the sun, along with Lyluss and the god of the Underworld himself, made them what they were. *Vampires*—the first, most powerful of the breed.

"Wait. That would make you—" Clive counted on his fingers, thinking how far in the past the two great wars were. The second War ended three centuries ago, the first War seven before that. "You're over a thousand years old!"

She peered off to the sky, as a notion finally seemed to don on her. "Has it *really* been that long?"

Clive dismissed the whole idea. This was impossible. There was no one that old. Sure, there were some powerful wizards and mages out there who possessed the secrets of immortality but they were usually killed long before they could last a millennium.

There was also something else that didn't make sense. Kersey, from what Clive could tell was a good person. She helped him—she helped her friend Avery. The Greater Overlords were supposed to be the most sinister beings on the planet. It was fabled that the ten of them together had ended as many lives as the first War of Balance.

"Why are you nice?" he asked her.

"What do you mean?"

"Well, the Greater Overlords have the reputation of being evil. I remember a story being passed around that two of them went into Riverglade and killed over a thousand people in one night just because they wanted the supply of Corscun Rum."

Kersey chuckled. "I *am* evil, Clive." Her eyes told otherwise. "I may look calm and collected now, but you should have known me about six centuries ago. I killed my share of innocents, don't you worry."

She was about to get up, but then plopped back down, remembering something. "And by the way, that was two other Overlords who killed all those people in Riverglade. Alexis Lighthammer and Valen Ironwall. I was on the other side of the world at the time. And they didn't do it for the rum—they did it for *Mydian*."

"And just what did *you* do for him?" Clive thought that was whom all vampires served, whether they wanted to or not.

She lowered her head and got up. All of the Gothmirks, now totaling over a hundred swarmed around her as she walked off, completely ignoring his question. So apparently Mydian was a touchy subject. "We need to get to work," she breathed, starting down Squire Street. Clive wasn't ready to stop talking just yet.

"You're ashamed that you worked for the dark god, aren't you?" he guessed, hoping his words wouldn't prompt another episode like last night. He didn't want that demon crawling back to the surface.

She stopped as the hill started to slope downward. Her minions stopped with her and they all turned around to face him in unison. Clive didn't realize he was stepping back. Her eyes were cold, despite how beautiful she'd managed to look this morning. The protruding fangs were back and were growing ever so threatening by the second.

"I've nothing to be ashamed of," she said. "I'm *afraid*." She crept closer to him and added, "Just what do you know about the Overlords' pact with the dark god?"

Clive certainly didn't know much but he did remember stories from his childhood. His grandmother would walk with him and Nalia around the Iron Queen and the three would sit on the pier where they were treated to ghost stories night after night.

"He gave you immortality so the world would know your sins," Clive said from memory of his grandmother's tale. "And then he removed Ebend's curse of sunlight so you could do his bidding whenever he wished."

"Ah, and so the false story of the mortals carries on," she chided. "*Wrong*. Mortals seem to think that we were just *blessed* with this righteous gift of eternal life but that was not at all how it happened."

"And how did it happen?" he pressed.

"We *asked* for it." Her eyes were glazing over—the tears of last night begging to show themselves today. "We were so evil then—so *corrupt* that all we wanted to do was cause devastation and destruction. I wanted to murder everyone in my path. And for nearly eight centuries, I did. We didn't want the malice to end, so we made a deal with the dark god that he was so happy to oblige."

"What kind of deal?"

"Eternal life for the price of our souls." She looked to the ground and kicked the dirt with the shoes that Nalia once owned. "When we die, we go to the Infernal Underworld whether we want to or not. The other Overlords have done jobs for Mydian in hopes that the afterlife isn't an eternity of torment. Alexis and Valen killed over a thousand priests of Lyluss in Riverglade, Arctis and Evan hauled a dead dragon to the south, and I . . ." Her voice trailed off. "Let's just say that I ran and hid like a child. I never lifted a finger to help him. Ruin may be able to grant me amnesty."

It was all starting to make sense to Clive. Kersey was *terrified* of Mydian. She was afraid of what was going to happen when she died. This was what had set her off in the banquet hall. She was like a beast that had been backed into a corner for far too long. When the beast recognized its end was near, it turned on everything that got in its way.

But Clive could still see the good in her. He could still feel the warmth of her personality and the kindness of her heart. Was this what happened to vampires this old? Did their feelings of murder, deceit, and carnage simply fade with the passing years?

"So the others like you, the Greater Overlords, I mean, are they ... good also?"

Kersey laughed and it was a very unnerving sound. It was obvious she hadn't had much practice at it.

"I would be the exception," she assured. "My anger and hatred are buried deep down and have blossomed into depression and fear." Her face darkened when she added, "But should you ever find yourself standing this close to one of those other nine, should they still be around ... *run.*"

Clive didn't ask anything else as Kersey turned around and led her army on. The undead parted around him and followed their leader down Squire Street. He gave one last look to his engulfed home and then jogged to catch up.

Squire Street was the largest urban neighborhood in Tharg. The normally quiet hamlet was usually bustling with people walking their pets, working in their gardens and watching the sea from their second floor balconies. Today was very different. Everyone was inside; the news of the undead army sweeping through had already been heard. There were several faces pressed against windows as the Gothmirks filed down the road in three rows.

Squire Street continued on for another two hundred yards or so but Kersey stopped when she got to the signpost reading, '*Stonechapel Street*' which veered off to the east. Clive's eyes nervously shifted from her to the signpost as she contemplated where to go. He needed her to go down Stonechapel. If she went down to Brevvy Cemetery on Squire Street—

"—This way," she said, refusing his unspoken need and continued on Squire.

Clive circled around her and pointed down Stonechapel. "The cemetery is just around that bend." She followed his finger to the road that turned right up ahead, and disappeared around a cottage. Her eyes were squinting and she put a hand to her forehead as if trying to calculate just how far it was. She turned her attention back to Squire Street straight ahead.

"I feel a graveyard this way, as well." She started once more, but Clive put his hands on her shoulders. He couldn't let her go to *that* one.

"The one on Stonechapel is much closer. Let's go there first."

Her eyes were growing darker, angry at his constant determent. "I can't go to that one, Clive. We'll have to skip it."

He cursed beneath his breath as she continued down Squire without him. He knew why she wouldn't go down Stonechapel. The graveyard, which probably contained well over two-hundred rotting corpses was nestled right next to the Lylussian Temple. Kersey, being the hindered vampire that she was, couldn't stand to look in its direction, much less venture next to it. Squire Street it was, but his persuasion wasn't finished.

"Kersey, please. Let's skip Brevvy Cemetery, as well." His eyes were pleading, his tone evasive, but he could tell that she knew exactly why he was trying to coax her away from it.

"Nalia is buried here, isn't she?" Kersey realized.

He nodded. "All of my family is buried here. Nalia, my parents and my grandparents." He couldn't stand to think of his own family as one of Kersey's Gothmirks. The thoughts of their bloated corpses being draped in vinery turned his stomach. His grandparents were probably nothing more than skeletons by now. That sickened him even worse.

"I won't raise them if you don't want me to," she reassured.

"Of course I don't want you to!" Clive yelled louder than he meant to. "Please don't disturb them."

Separating Squire Street from Brevvy Cemetery was Lake Barria. The trail of undead followed them around its embankment toward the high-walled graveyard lingering to the east. There were tall, barren trees and a few windswept shrubs that were overgrown with weeds. A small dirt path led away from the cemetery gate and into a grove that was nestled next to the waterfall running into the lake.

Kersey's attention dropped from the graveyard and turned toward the grove. Clive followed her eyes to the busted lock on the gate that surrounded the rows of apple trees inside. He didn't understand why she would be interested in apple thieves.

She held her arm up and the undead stayed put. Clive followed her into the grove and was about to ask why they had stopped here—

—when someone dropped right in front. Clive took a step back when a towering man loomed over them. It was instinct that made him afraid. The large man took a step toward Kersey and Clive was ready to attack him when she yelled out.

"Avery!" She stepped up to him and put her hands on his face. Clive watched a barrage of apples fall from his shirt. He circled around and saw the horror-stricken visage of Kersey as she studied her slow friend's appearance. It was just *horrible*.

There was a huge cut that started at his eyebrow and ended near his nose. A large, puffy, black and purple ring surrounded his left eye. He was smiling, nevertheless.

"Miss Red!" he yelled and wrapped his arms around her and lifted her off the ground. She forced a smile and returned his grasp. "They locked me out, Miss Red! Why, they made it harder for me to pick apples, they did!"

Just how long did Kersey know Avery? What was it that she saw in him that made her want to befriend him? Clive believed it was his innocent nature. Maybe Kersey envied him. Avery didn't know the horrors of the world and hadn't seen the things she had probably seen. That ignorance of life—that deprivation of atrocious things was envious to Clive, as well.

"What happened to your face, Avery?" Kersey asked, ignoring his usual dim-witted comment.

"Why, can you believe that Daegin didn't like my necklace, Miss Red? He didn't want me to talk to you anymore either, but I said *no!*" He realized his collection of apples had fallen to the ground so he leaned down, picked one up, and started into it.

"So Daegin . . . *hit* you?" Her eyes were black. There were small, red flames dancing in them and her fangs seemed to grow another inch. Vines were creaking all around them as they latched onto trees and tightened, venting her anger. As usual, Avery didn't seem to notice or care. He kept stuffing his face while he nodded.

"This man will die, Clive." There was an eerie wind blowing Kersey's hair to the side that he didn't feel. Her face was so dark now—shadowed by the cloud that seemed to form over top of them.

"Let's think this through, Kers," Clive attempted to reason, but knew he was wasting his words. "I think it's atrocious that this Daegin hurt your friend in such a horrific way, but . . ." His voice trailed off when he became afraid to tell Kersey exactly what she didn't want to hear.

"...but you don't think it's horrific enough for him to die for it?" She raised an eyebrow. "Does that seem about right, Clive?"

He tried to look away but she wouldn't have it. She grabbed him by the nape of the neck and pulled him close. "Once again, you are defending someone who caused unjust brutality. When are you going to realize that this is an eye-for-an-eye world?"

Clive was speechless. In his years of serving in the prison he'd encountered many forms of justice. He'd seen the law stretched thin in places where it shouldn't have been. He did believe in eye-for-an-eye, but only if the exchange was death. Avery and Kersey were both very much alive, so he felt in his heart that their attackers should not have been condemned to die a murderer's death.

"And why would he be so brazenly hostile toward your necklace, Avery?" Kersey asked. He shrugged and started to pull it out from beneath his shirt but she rested her hand on his. She looked down, in thought and turned back to Clive. "How strong is the Mydianite presence in Tharg these days?"

He chuckled. "Mydian? There are no Mydianites in Tharg. Fyrl would have them killed on spot, either publicly in Tess' name or secretly in Felorn's."

Kersey didn't seem satisfied with the answer. She looked at Avery again and said, "There aren't many people out there who would fight a man such as this over a Lylussian trinket."

"Miss Red, can I come with you?" Avery asked, apple spewing from his mouth as he spoke. "I don't want to go back home anymore."

She shrugged toward Clive as if wanting permission to let him tag along. He rolled his eyes and threw his hands up. It wasn't up to him.

"Of course you can, Avery. I don't want you going back there, either. Just stay close to Clive and I. He's a friend. Just like you."

Avery smiled and ran up close to Kersey's 'friend'. It was much closer than he would have wished. The tall, burly man smiled his favorite, bucked tooth grin and made sure to stay evenly between Clive and his Miss Red.

"So why does he call you that, anyway?" Clive asked, heading toward the cemetery gate. "Miss Red?"

"It was on this very spot where we first met." She grinned and pointed back to the apple orchard. "I used to come here to feed, just like he did. Back then there were no fences and no lights, but Avery kept stealing so many apples that the owners put up this gate and built lantern posts."

"Lotta good that did!" he snorted, looking back.

"I was finished with my kill for the night when I turned and saw this fellow here hanging from a tree branch, watching me."

"Miss Red was messy!" he exclaimed, recalling the story as well.

"That's right," she grinned. "I was covered in blood, as you could imagine. So he named me, 'Miss Red'."

"And we talk all the time, isn't that right Miss Red?"

"That's right, Avery. You walked with me back to the prison that night and then came to visit me regularly."

He chuckled and tossed aside an apple core. "But now you're out! You're out with me!"

She winked and led them into the cemetery. Her army slowly followed behind.

The tops of the tents lining Market Lane could be seen far beyond the field of gravestones and sarcophagi. Past those was Fyrl's castle. Clive patted his pockets and realized that his keys were still at home, probably melted into a clump of iron by now. Kersey didn't seem to mind. Her Gothmirks approached the gate and three of them ripped it from its hinges.

Clive hurried through and led her to Nalia's grave, which was situated just between their parents' and grandparents'. There was even a headstone for Clive, which had been one of the last presents his mother gave him. The Porter family would hold together, even in death, she would say.

"That is . . . disturbing," Kersey pointed out.

"What?"

"You already have a tombstone with your name on it. That sends shivers up my spine."

Clive managed a smile. "Well, my mother thought it was a good idea to be prepared. You never know when the Death Keeper will come for you."

"I would still prefer to *not* see my final resting place realized before me." She turned around and flicked her wrist toward the graveyard.

For a moment, nothing happened, but shortly thereafter, there was movement all around them. Even Avery stopped eating his second apple and took notice. Vines broke through the dirt next to the graves and started to push it away. A bony hand reached up through the ground next to Clive and Kersey grabbed it and helped the decaying man up. He wore tattered Symbian robes.

All over Brevvy Cemetery the ground began to churn, the dirt loosened and the dead found their way to the surface. Their moans bellowed out in unison and Clive couldn't help to be a little afraid of what was happening. Some of the undead started breaking the doors from the sarcophagi, helping to free their entombed brethren. Avery just stood there and watched—mesmerized by the way the dead men sprang from the ground and burst from their marble and wooden prisons.

Kersey's head quickly snapped toward Clive's direction and he backed up, finding himself seated on top of Nalia's headstone. He deftly moved off and to the side as she approached.

"What?" he asked, eying her up and down. The expression on her face was frantic and questioning, as if looking for an answer to a riddle—and that answer was *beneath* her.

She dropped to her knees and pressed her ear to the ground, right where Nalia's casket lay only six feet below. Her fingers rubbed the dirt and she took handfuls of it as she listened, as if hearing a secret that was meant for her ears only.

After a moment of the bizarre behavior, she stood back up, dusted herself off, and asked, "Are you sure you don't want me to raise her?"

"Wha—of *course* I don't want you to raise her!" He couldn't believe that she thought he'd say yes to such a thing.

"Okay then," she matter-of-factly said, wiping the dirt from her fingers. "But I assure you that she has *much* to say."

What did that mean? he wondered. There was nothing that Nalia could possibly have left to say. She and Clive ended on excellent terms. The last thing he ever told her was how much he loved her, standing in the doorway of her kitchen after a night of cards. There were no regrets. No ill words that needed to be taken back. Their relationship had been strong since childhood and there could possibly be no unfinished business.

"What did she tell you?" he asked Kersey as she surveyed her new minions.

"I can barely hear her through the dirt. And the casket. Oh, and the Quillian prayer cloth around her face." Kersey stepped closer and added, "But I can tell it has to do with her death."

Clive felt fresh tears streaking his face. He never wanted to visit this sadness again. Did she want to say she was sorry for ending her own life? That had to be it. Nalia had taken a drastic step to ease her own troubles but in the same effort, managed to undo his life. She was everything to him and because she saw the only release was to kill herself, she took that along to the grave. If saying she was sorry—if regretting it was what kept her from finding eternal rest, then Clive couldn't stand in her way of obtaining it. He couldn't deny her soul its departure to Quillian's realm. He couldn't believe what he was about to say.

"Okay. I want to see her."

It only took a quick wave of her hand over the grave. Her minions circled around the two, dropped to their knees and started shoveling the loose dirt to the side with their fingers. A couple of vines sprouted from the ground and the Gothmirks gripped them with tight, stiff hands.

The vines kept growing out and as they did, additional undead grabbed them until there were two rows of Gothmirks tugging them like ropes pulling a ship to dock. Avery even stepped up and latched onto the back. With each pull, the wooden lid of the casket became more visible. Finally, the dirt had been cleared and Nalia's box was sitting on the mound where their mother was buried.

Clive took a nervous step forward as the Gothmirks ripped the lid off. He wasn't prepared for it and he quickly shielded his eyes, but the damage had been done. He *saw* her.

She had been buried in a long, green evening gown that buttoned all the way up to her chin, intentionally covering the rope-burns on her neck. The prayer cloth was lying over her face. Clive reached out with one hand and as his fingers danced over top of it—

—she sat upright and it fell to her lap. She was *looking* at him.

Her face was puffy and pale and her lips had been sewn together. Her fingers were interlaced across her lap and she slowly undid them, the sound of her hardened joints crackling.

Nalia lifted herself up and swung her legs to hop out of the coffin. Her head was tipped to the side, the bones in her neck pushing a bump through the garment. Kersey stepped up to her and took hold of the deceased woman's attention. She started whispering something in the vampire's ear.

With Nalia's lips sewn together, it was hard for her mouth to move, but Clive didn't think she spoke words anyway. Anytime a Gothmirk communicated with Kersey, it was silent. Their voices traveled right into her mind.

Kersey nodded as Nalia spoke, her eyes never leaving Clive. He watched, impatiently, his heart racing at the sight of his sister moving at her own accord. This was starting to seem like a bad idea.

He'd known that his years to come would always be haunted by that sight of her lying on Fyrl's floor with her eyes staring up at him. This image would replace that one as the most horrific he could remember.

Kersey's mouth flew open as Nalia told her something accompanied by a slash across the throat gesture.

"What? What is it?" Clive demanded.

"Do you know his name?" Kersey asked her, ignoring Clive altogether.

Nalia mouthed something that made Kersey's face darken so much that even the Gothmirks took notice of her dismay. They backed away and the vines creaked and groaned in fear and started whipping the ground like angry dragon tails.

"I see," she said and then feebly stared at Clive. "Your sister," she started, "did *not* commit suicide."

"What?"

"No, she was *murdered*, Clive."

"How, I mean, *who*? Who did this to her?"

"A man named Daegin Crane."

Clive forced his eyes to the ground. He knew what she was going to say next but he didn't know what he'd say in return.

"Do you still think he deserves to live?" Her smile was cruel and discomforting.

Clive was angry—angrier than he'd known in several years but another feeling overshadowed it. He'd been led to believe all week that Nalia had actually ended her own life. Now he knew that wasn't true. He knew that his sister did care enough to not put a lifelong burden on her dear brother. Standing in the cemetery with festering Gothmirks, a vampire, a slow, giant of a man, and his dead sister, Clive was actually *relieved*.

"There's more," Kersey said, not noticing Clive's involuntary smile. "Daegin is indeed a Mydianite. He killed your sister because he was scouting for something and she was in the wrong place at the wrong time."

"What was it?"

Kersey whispered something to Nalia and the two exchanged silent words once again. Finally the vampiress nodded. "There is a spell book arriving at Fyrl's castle tonight. Mydian wants it and Daegin is probably going to try and steal it."

"But he's not going to get it, now is he?" a steady voice from Clive's right called.

Avery was the first to see it. He drew a deep breath and laughed and pointed up to the high fence surrounding the graveyard. Clive spotted the decaying crow watching their every move. Its eyes were missing but somehow, it was still *watching*. It was Ruin, once again.

"You want us to stop him?" Kersey questioned.

The crow's skeletal wings flapped as it managed to chuckle. "No, my dear. You are going to steal it *yourself*."

"Why? What is so special about it?"

"It's Aneesa's spell book, sweet girl. You know what's special about that."

She nodded and looked to Clive. "If you'd have read a history book or two, you would know what we're talking about," she smirked. Clive grimaced in mock offense.

"Continue to raise the cemeteries and you will have no trouble walking into the castle and taking the book from under Daegin." Ruin hopped down from the fence and walked over to join the army. "Be there at sundown." With that, the body of the crow fell over and got back up as the curse of the Gothmirk took hold of its now empty vessel. Avery got down on his knees and patted it.

"I will put her back if you want, Clive." Kersey laid a gentle hand on Nalia's shoulder.

He nodded. He didn't think he could go on looking at her this way. The corpse before him did not personify his sister one bit. This was nothing but a hollow body that held onto a small fraction of her wonderful soul. This vessel needed to be in the ground, at peace, next to their parents.

Kersey motioned to the coffin and Nalia lifted herself back inside. Clive knelt down next to it as the Gothmirks were readying the lid to be nailed back on. Nalia started to lay back but saw her brother before her, eyes welling with tears at the final goodbye.

She reached up and stroked his cheek with a stiff, pale hand. Clive wrapped his own around it and forced his eyes tight, shunning the tears away. Nalia's touch was somehow warm. Through a stitched mouth, decaying vocal cords, and a guttural, toneless voice she managed, "I love you."

.8.

A Past Not Worth Remembering

There was only one thing equally as beautiful as the rising sun. It was when it set. She remembered it—remembered seeing it disappear three-hundred years ago behind the western horizon just like it was disappearing tonight. Its dying light rippled across the distant water in a beautiful, somber mosaic.

Dyne sat on the beach, just beyond the dock where the *Phantom Seven* was anchored. There was an empty bowl that once had vegetable soup in her lap and her boots were standing to the side. Her bare feet were buried beneath the sand and the sensation felt wonderful on her toes. The waves of the ocean had a calming effect that she enjoyed. Going on board the ship, however, would be an entirely different story. She still didn't think she had the courage.

Lorne's tipsy laughter could be heard over her shoulder, in one of the alcoves beneath the cliff wall. A pair of Mydianite fishermen sat with him, drinking and listening to his story of the grand siege on Sorcea. Jonas was perched on the dock, fishing and talking to two others who were stacking crates onto the *Black Murder*.

To the south, high up on the majestic cliffs sat Pelopha, a golden-dotted city that was flourishing with life as the night grew closer. A chorus of church bells could be heard, signaling the evening worship of at least a dozen temples.

Dyne sat her bowl to the side and leaned back in the sand. She was fighting the urge to cry. She wanted to go back to the Underworld, to see her sister and her family. The desire to seek revenge wasn't as great as the desire to be happy. There was no reason for her to be here other than Mydian's need to watch her suffer. Why else would the dark lord choose her to come here when he had so many other servants who were so willing and more capable? There was no other explanation.

When she was alive, he took Laraek away. As a vampire, he made it impossible for her to see where he was buried, and now, once again, he was separating her from everything else she held dear. Were the other gods this vengeful?

She was about to get up and join Lorne for a drink—a drink that she felt would steady her mind when hands wrapped around her waist and neck and pushed her back into the sand, preventing her from rising.

"I saw this beautiful girl from the corner of my eye and I just *had* to meet her." His lips hovered just over her ear. His voice was low, no more than a whisper but his breath—it was *cold*.

"Who are you? Let go of me!" She struggled to get up—to turn around and see his face but she couldn't overpower him. Weak, useless body, she cursed.

"Shhh. So much aggression, but not enough passion. She once had more than enough."

"Let me see your face."

Her mysterious attacker pulled the hair from her eyes and secured it behind her ear. "My face isn't important, only my words. I thought you were lost forever, Emba."

The newly awakened, beating heart in her chest lurched to her throat and she swallowed hard at the prospect of who was behind her. Even in a world of eerie coincidences and unusual circumstances, this was *impossible*.

"Laraek?"

He let go. She turned around and saw a hooded man before her—staring with eyes that couldn't be seen. Quickly, she reached out to snatch it away but his hand caught hers and pulled it aside. He drew the hood back on his own and let her see the smiling, pale face of her once lover. It *was* him.

It was *Laraek*.

"Gods, is it really you? What—where did you, I mean, how did you—"

"—survive?" he finished. "Isn't it obvious?" His humble smile grew until she could clearly see the corners of his mouth. There were two, bloodied fangs.

"My gods, you're a *vampire*!" Her first reaction was pity. She didn't wish that curse on anyone—certainly not her lover.

"And I have been for quite some time."

"When? How long after you last saw me did this happen?" she asked, putting a solemn hand to his face.

His eyes darkened and he pulled his robe a little tighter around his neck. "I became a vampire that same night. I was chosen by Lord Mydian, himself."

"What?" She reached out and pulled the robe away from his neck. Laraek didn't even try to fight her. Instead, he turned his head to the side and let her see the horrible, gruesome flesh that never healed. It was the same bite mark she had been given—the same mark that only a god could make. Mydian had spawned Laraek, just as he would spawn her two weeks later.

Laraek had agreed to meet Dyne and Telsa a few miles south of Boudia, in an abandoned temple of the sun god. After Telsa's sickness nearly claimed her, Dyne decided it was best to move on. She had assumed that Laraek had died with his family.

"Lord Mydian needed me, dear Emba."

He gave her hands a reassuring squeeze that did nothing to calm the anger—the sadness from rising to the surface. Why did he never make contact with her?

"So then . . .Telsa and I *waited* for you and you never showed." Her eyes were searching him for an answer that wasn't going to hurt her. She didn't think she would find it tonight.

"Yes."

"We thought you were killed . . . we thought that you were killed with your family."

"And I thought the same of you," he countered. "I only learned last night of your vampiracy, of your death, and of your recent rebirth. I certainly didn't plan for your arrival. I was told that you had been spawned just like me. That you had a job similar to mine."

What job was he talking about? Dyne and Telsa had been ordered by the dark god to kill a high priestess in Keswing who was sending Lylussian Riders to level Bloodgate's war machine. After her death, Mydian admitted defeat, but also managed to save his precious engineers and mages who were working on the mysterious, towering structure known as the Martax.

"And what did the dark god have you do?" she asked, watching Lorne and the others on the beach. Their little argument in the sand had gained onlookers.

"I founded the *Phantom Seven*." He waved his hand toward the swaying ships by the dock. "We are tasked with searching and recovering things that are of interest to Lord Mydian."

Dyne didn't care anymore about their pasts. At least not right now. She had been through so much heartache and turmoil to see this man's grave. What had already happened was unimportant. They were reunited, over three-hundred years later.

She leaned up to kiss him and buried her lips against his. It was so different now. They were so cold and so . . . distant. She didn't like it one bit. Was it because of his vampiracy, or something else? Dyne didn't know.

Laraek took her by the wrists and gently pulled her away. His eyes were somber as he watched the tow of the water behind her. The living heart inside her was sinking piece by piece by the creeping realization that he was changed—that the love he once had in his soul for her had turned to ice with the vampiric curse.

"Everything okay, miss?" Jonas asked from behind when he took notice of her dismay.

She didn't even detect his approach. Instead, she shot a quick look to Laraek and then back to him and spat, "I'm fine." The smile she managed was so weak and fabricated that it made her sick. Laraek had a vague look about him and she feared he would ask what was wrong.

Dyne managed a stronger smile and tried to kiss him, but again he pulled away, a dismal expression on his pale face. She was finally ready to question his evasiveness, but before either could say a word, the beach suddenly sprang to life with Mydianites.

They came from within the stone corridors of the camp and down the beach from Pelopha. There were hundreds of them, all wearing armor or mages' robes. Some even repelled down the cliff wall by ropes, but each of them stopped when they came to the docks. This was the *Phantom Seven's* crew. Dyne could see the respect and admiration for Laraek in the way they nodded and bowed as they approached. She looked at the ones with raised visors and spotted fangs protruding from their lips. Most of these men and women were vampires. This was the first time, other than the twisted breed inside Gloomrift, that she'd seen so many at once.

Lorne stumbled over to the two and nodded his hello to Laraek. It had been over three-centuries since he'd seen him, as well. Lorne had admired the destructive power of the *Phantom Seven* for years and that was probably what he was about to say before the violent screams on the northern beach tore everyone's attention.

"It's okay," Laraek comforted, putting a strong hand on Dyne's shoulder. Her eyes left the beach and looked at him, but he quickly averted his gaze and withdrew his hand.

There were men pushing large cages down the beach, each filled to the brim with wailing arms and terrible shrieks. They were mortals being herded like livestock. This was the vampires' food, she noticed, as they pushed them onto the dock and up the ramps of the ships. Each large vessel took one cage, enough to sustain a crew for the duration of the trip.

"Are we ready to sail?" a voice purred behind them. There were long, dainty arms wrapped around Laraek's torso as he eyed Dyne with an uncomfortable silence. A woman's head poked around his and kissed him on the cheek. It was quite dark now, but Dyne could still see her with the moon's silvery help.

She was tall and statuesque, a few inches higher than Dyne herself. Her frame was slender and she wore the close-fitted armor of Mydianite warriors. A luscious fire danced in her eyes by the way she looked at Laraek. Her long, blond hair whipped past his shoulders and circled around until her back was to Dyne.

Gods, she looks a lot like me, she thought. Even Lorne seemed to think so. He backed up a step and was eyeing the two women together, pointing silently to the similarities as Dyne scowled. In a subconscious effort to regain her individuality, she pulled the hood over her head and tied it.

Then without warning, Laraek smiled to his new friend and planted a kiss—the same kiss that Dyne had hoped for—on her bright red lips. It felt like a dozen arrows had just hit her in the chest. *So this is why he doesn't want to touch me,* she realized. *Because he doesn't have a need.*

"So sweet a kiss." Laraek smiled and pulled away. He licked his lips and tasted the blood she passed. This woman—this *thing* that he chose was a vampire, as well.

"I'm so glad to be home," she said, a look of genuine compassion in her eyes.

"Did you see any you liked?" Laraek whispered.

The statuesque woman looked to the ground and then impishly shook her head. "There was one, but it just didn't feel right. It didn't feel like . . . mine."

"You'll have more chances, my love. I'm so glad you've decided to join us tonight," Laraek said.

"I wouldn't miss it for the world!" she happily shouted. It was like grating nails to Dyne. "I've always wanted to visit Tharg." Her attention suddenly turned to the newcomers standing around on the beach, listening to her talk like a seven year old.

"Who's your friends?" she asked in a high, irritating voice, eying Dyne. She tried her best to steal a glance beneath her hood. "Anyone under there?"

"These are the ones Mydian sent, my sweetest." Laraek circled around and stood at Dyne's side. "This is Emba, and this—"

"—Dyne," she growled. "My name is *Dyne*." She presented her hand to the slender warrioress and the two exchanged a very uncomfortable smile.

"And this is Lorne," Laraek continued, trying his best to take away the awkwardness. They also shook hands but the women never took their eyes from one another.

"Em—Dyne, Lorne, this is Evangeline, my wife." The air around them seemed to thicken and not even Lorne spoke. He knew what words like that were going to stir up.

Without even so much as a question or reply, Dyne sprang on top of her and forced her to the sand. The vampiress was momentarily stunned but her head seemed to clear when Dyne began a shower of punches across her face. The Mydianites swarmed around to watch as Laraek pulled his once lover away. She grabbed a handful of Eva's hair and yanked, taking a large clump with her. The vampiress simply moaned in agitation and stood, a small bit of blood trickling from her left eye.

"I'm going to drain your last drop for that one, little girl." Eva's eyes were flaring but Laraek was on top of Dyne, shielding her from the wrath of his bride.

"No you're not, Eva." He pointed toward the corridor ahead. "Gather our things. We're leaving soon." She gave one last, vengeful look to Dyne before she left, pushing a few helpful Mydianites aside who touched her.

"What do you think you are doing?" Laraek said, low and steady. He was still on top of her, speaking right into her ear.

"Was I *nothing* to you? How could you marry after what we had?" She spit sand from her gritty mouth as she talked.

"Emba, what we had was over three centuries ago. We both disappeared from each other's lives and we both had the right to move on. I did just that. I'm sorry you've held on to the past for so long." He let her go, got up, and stormed off toward the camp.

She rolled over and spit the sand from her mouth. Lorne was standing over her, neither smiling nor relishing in her agony like he often did when something bothered her. Quite strange, she noted. Instead, he offered a hand to help her up. She shook her head and stood on her own.

"Did you *see* her?" Dyne asked, dusting herself off. She kicked the sand from her feet and stepped inside her boots.

"Oh yes. She is gorgeous." Lorne allowed a tiny smile but seemed to realize that wasn't the best thing to say. Dyne's face was telling him to recant. "But she does look a lot like you."

That didn't make her feel any better. What made her hang on to the memory of Laraek for so long? She had never asked herself that question and now, after he pointed it out, she couldn't stop asking it. But the answer had to be simple. *Love.* Obviously her love for him had outweighed his for her.

There was a pain in her chest that nearly rivaled the anguish of watching Hannah slip from her grasp some twelve years, or more precisely to *her,* two days ago. Dyne had felt so much loss in her life and every day seemed to drive the nail deeper into the coffin. Could she ever recover from such mental torment? The years had been brutal and her love for Laraek was a testament of just what kind of pain she'd endured. All her mind and heart knew were *hurt.* It would take a long time for her to get past the things she had seen, heard, and felt tonight.

Just then a loud horn swept through the camp. There were Mydianites swarming to the ships as Dyne looked to the sky toward

Pelopha. She couldn't believe what she saw but then again, she didn't fully realize what she was looking at.

There were creatures—fast moving, flying beasts headed their way. At the same time, there was a horde of people approaching along the beach, some carrying torches that were so far away that they still looked like little golden specks.

"What's happening?" Lorne asked, putting his hand on his halberd.

"I don't know," Dyne answered, but realized it wasn't good when the light caught a glimpse of one of the oncoming men rushing toward them. The holy twin dove symbol was etched on his shield. These men and women were Lylussian soldiers.

"Swoopdrakes!" Jonas called from the docks. He was frantically pointing to the flying shapes that were drawing near.

Swoopdrakes were horse-sized beasts with large, feathery wings and eagle-like beaks that carried riders long distances through the air. They were prized and revered beasts used by lighter gods such as Lyluss, Quillian, and Dormi.

The Mydianites on the beach grew more chaotic. Some were hastily loading the ship with last-minute supplies while others were readying themselves for a fight. A row of pikemen took the south flank and extended their weapons toward the horizon, ready to skewer any low-flying riders.

"All vampires to Pelopha and defend the temple! My crew head to the *Murder*!" Laraek called from behind Dyne. "We're leaving. Let the living boys and girls take care of this!"

It was too late. The swoopdrakes were in better view now and Dyne could clearly see how deadly their attack was going to be.

Lylussian archers sat atop each one with massive crossbows mounted to the saddles. Attached to the stirrups were long chains that had dangling shrapnel and spiked, metal weights. The pikemen noticed these and tried to stand—to run, but it was of no use. The Lylussian Riders knew how to deal with vampires.

A chorus of screams, heavy metal clunking light armor and flashes of white light were the result of the swoopdrakes' first flyby. The pikemen ripped through the air, some in pieces as the sharp, hammering metal slammed into them. The ten or so riders released a volley of bolts from their crossbows, several hitting their mark. Dyne watched as they pulled up and turned west to circle back around.

By now, the men on the beach had arrived. The vampires had already begun lowering their visors and covered their eyes with cloth in anticipation of Lylussian imagery. Dyne drew her sword and stood ready to impale the first soldier who came near her. She was about to be the first to make contact.

A warrior who had holy symbols on every surface of his body approached and stabbed at her with his spear. She easily dodged and shoved it to the ground, forcing him to bury the tip in the sand. Dyne took advantage and sliced him across the chest.

Another spear-wielding soldier came at her from the side and she flipped out of range and let him slide past. She tumbled forward, grabbed his weapon under her arm, and held it tight while she stabbed him in the gut.

Lorne was striking down just as many with his large halberd, although his killing was twice as messy. There were brilliant sparks of red lightning that rocked the bodies of his slain and their charred faces and smoking eye sockets could be seen beneath their armor. If Arctis had chosen to keep that halberd for himself, then it was obviously packed with power.

"We must leave," Laraek said, pulling Dyne by the shoulder. He nodded to Lorne who wiggled his blade free from the head of a smoldering warrior and followed.

"Everyone to the *Murder!*" Laraek shouted as another barrage of the swoopdrakes came through. One rider stopped and circled around to look at the three fleeing Mydianites as they headed toward their ship. Dyne struggled to keep the folds of her hood away from her eyes. She watched the rider vigilantly look toward Laraek, his mace outstretched and pointed at his head.

He was a small man whose body was completely obscured by his Lylussian faith. His bluish-white armor covered him from head to toe. He wore a crested helmet that sported decorated wings on the sides and his visor was down, revealing the twin doves over the eyes. The magnificent sword at his side was gleaming in the moonlight.

"It's him," Laraek said through squinted eyes.

"Who?" Dyne asked, watching from beneath her hood as the swoopdrake and its rider hovered above them.

"A Lylussian priest. He's been following me for weeks now. I never thought he'd find the harbor."

"Well he did, love, now let's go," Eva's galling voice rang in as she passed the three, carrying a couple of large bags.

Dyne paid no further mind to the priest as she took the woman's advice and followed. The vampires couldn't fight this many Lylussian soldiers. That cursed symbol would be the death of them all.

Laraek stopped and turned to a man who was boarding the ship opposite of the *Black Murder*. "Miral, stay put!" The vampire, who had been winding down a sail turned and offered a questioning look. "Make sure none of the Lylussian Riders leave here alive. We must keep the harbor secure." Miral nodded and hopped off the side.

"All ships remain at anchor!" he screamed to the congregation of fighting men and women, his hand shielding his face against the constant moving Lylussian symbols around him. "Make sure the *Murder* has a safe exit!"

"Are you insane?" Eva called from the deck to Laraek. "You want them to stay put? How can we dare take on Kersey without the rest of the *Seven*?"

"The *Murder* will sail for now! The rest will catch up to us after the beach is clear," Laraek replied.

There were a dozen or so crewmen on the deck of the *Murder*. They were manning the rigging, clearing the crates to the lower deck, and using the mounted ballistae to fire on the swoopdrakes. It made sense that a vessel that was totally invisible against the night sky and sea would use such weapons; hurtling spears with the force to punch holes in a ship. Cannons could easily give away one's position.

Dyne was hesitating at the narrow ramp and Laraek was pushing her forward.

"What's wrong?" he asked, watching as she eyed the water in the space between the dock and the ship. It had to be quite obvious.

"Nothing," she groaned, taking a deep breath and crossing the rickety ramp to the top deck of the ship. Eva stood by watching, a slight grin on her chiseled face. Dyne scowled and sulked off, heading toward the steps that led to the crew cabins below. There she wouldn't have to see the water.

She pulled her hood off and sheathed her sword. Laraek, Lorne, Eva, and Jonas were all standing by the edge, watching as the dock grew smaller and smaller and the battle becoming nothing more than a fleeing skirmish on the sands of Southern Corscus. They were headed to Tharg, shorthanded, to kill a vampire that would probably wipe them off the map. No matter. She buried her face in her hands and quietly wept, not caring who saw her, and not seeing the Lylussian riders make another pass high above as they watched the northbound ship.

.9.

Thieves

This was going to be *easy*. He happily watched his Mydianites perched about the high wall. Daegin shared a giddy grin with three score of them, all out of sight around the castle's hidden entrance. Kerro looked skeptical, just as he did with the prospect of trapping and killing Kersey.

They were almost a mile from Fyrl's home. The towering steeples of his castle could be seen in the distance, but this was where they were needed. This was where the exchange was going to be made. The spell book of Aneesa was about to be sold and put to use for Felorn's treacherous desires. Luckily that would never happen, Daegin thought with a smile.

Before killing Fyrl's aid, she told him all he needed to know. The place, the price it would cost, and the way the book would be delivered. It couldn't be any simpler. Fyrl didn't count on his secret getting out. He didn't think thirty Mydianites would be at his doorstep ready to take it from him before it even came close to his vault.

It wasn't in Mydian's name, either. The book would draw Kersey Avonwood away from her minions and into Daegin's nest of deception. He loved a challenge, and what better challenge than to kill one of the ten, fabled Greater Overlords? It could be done, he knew. If Ruin wanted the book bad enough then he would certainly have Kersey come for it. She would learn where Daegin lived and that would be her end. The safe house was *ready* for her.

He was so proud of himself. His mother would have only thought of something trivial that Avery had done and it would have become just as important as slaying one of the Overlords. Nevertheless, there was no reason for him to be competitive anymore—nor any reason to hold onto sibling rivalry. Taritta was gone. Avery was gone. He was alone with his personal goal to kill something greater.

The roar of beasts shook Daegin from his thoughts. It was the wagon bringing the book and it was something to behold. Six wilderbears pulled the rolling fort. Normal horses would have never been able to haul such weight. It was a solid steel vault on wheels that had only one door that was so small that occupants would have had to crawl to get inside of. On its top were two large gears that disappeared halfway into its roof. The wagon's wheels were thick Corscun Oak and bolted by rods that were several inches thick. Nothing short of hurtling it off a cliff would have made it possible to get inside.

In addition to the wagon, there were ten, crossbow-toting guards just as armored. They circled around and created a perimeter, watching the road behind them and the small wooden entrance in front. They never looked to the high walls or the trees, although it didn't matter. Kerro's spell was keeping everyone well camouflaged.

"Are you ready?" Daegin asked the three men that were huddled closest to him. Their glowing hands and staves told him they were. A chorus of whispers steadily rose on the still night as two-dozen spells were about to be put into play.

Chanting at a whisper, Daegin summoned a fire enchantment to drive the men away from the wagon, but before he could cast it, something unexpected happened. Kerro looked to him for answers but he didn't know what to say. The aid didn't mention anything about *this*.

The gears on the roof began to slowly turn. There was a heavy clicking sound inside the wagon as they came to a stop. All of the guards took a few steps back and turned to watch, as if something significant was about to happen. There was a scraping metal sound and then it happened.

A blast erupted from beneath the wagon that was so immense that the wheels lifted a foot from the ground. Daegin grabbed the wall to steady himself, fearful that it was going to rock him off of his hiding spot. The wilderbears howled and some raised up on their haunches but a nearby guard kept them steady. Smoke billowed from beneath the wagon as the armored men continued to watch.

"What's happening?" Kerro asked, watching the voluminous, black smoke rise high into the sky.

Daegin didn't know. Perhaps they weren't the only ones there. Maybe someone else was trying to steal the book. *Then why are all the guards so calm?* he asked himself.

"There's some kind of treachery here," he whispered. "Everyone attack, *now!*"

Kerro pulled out a pair of Glowbombs—small, round orbs that held a faint, red light. It was a mixture of technology and magic, but the result was a highly explosive weapon that obliterated everything within a few feet when it made contact. The days of fire and black powder were coming to an end.

The battlemage hurled the glowing orb toward the nearest guard, which exploded on impact, sending him flying against the wagon. Two other Glowbombs from the other wall darted toward more guards, causing a small blast that sent thick smoke into the air and killed whatever it touched. Three of the wilderbears were caught up in the damage. The others tried to run, but the weight of the wagon was just too much for them alone.

Daegin chanted his spell and released an arch of fire that engulfed a guard. He dropped his crossbow and ran down the path they'd just come, screaming and wailing his arms as he did.

By now, their commotion had been picked up and the small wooden door in front of the wagon swung outward, spilling out a dozen of Fyrl's men into the fray. The Mydianites jumped to the path and the fighting began. The warriors advanced, meeting Fyrl's men head-on while the battlemages kept to the back, hurling all sorts of motley colored bolts and ribbons of light.

It only took a few minutes for the skirmish to come to an end. Fyrl's men may have been well trained but they didn't know the small, rickety door would lead to a gauntlet of anxious Mydianites. Daegin himself had only subdued two of them. It was quiet once more. There were dead, burning bodies lying everywhere, including all six wilderbears. Two of the guards still sparked with magical energy as the spells died down. It was just the Mydianites, the wagon, and a black, smoke filled night.

"Get it open," Daegin grabbed Kerro by the collar and pointed to the wagon.

The battlemage pulled out his sack of Glowbombs and approached the mobile vault. He tied the drawstring around the hinges of the small, steel door and backed away.

"Everyone get back!" he yelled, grabbing one of the dead guard's crossbows. Daegin found a safe distance, plugged his ears and watched as Kerro lined up a shot and pulled the trigger.

The wagon jolted with another dazzling explosion, this one rocking it so hard that the wheels crumbled on the far side, forcing the steel box to tumble sideways. When the smoke cleared, the door was embedded in the left wall, but that wasn't their main concern. The hole in the ground was.

It was large, probably three feet in diameter and was smoking. The bottom of the wagon was also smoking, only this came from a round, steel barrel. It was the barrel of a *cannon*. Daegin hopped up on the wagon's side and looked in through the opening the Glowbombs made and saw that the massive gun was fixed to the top of the roof where it could be lowered and fired straight down through the floor. The cannon was *all* that was inside the steel beast.

"Dammit!" he cursed and jumped off. The Mydianites crowded around the hole in the ground and watched in horror as their plan crumbled to pieces. Daegin couldn't believe his eyes. The goddess of destruction and her servants were quite crafty.

About thirty yards down were the sewers. There were two men, obviously Fyrl's cohorts, hacking away at a cannonball with pickaxes. After finding a split they pulled at it until the entire steel ball broke into two halves. They dropped their tools and snatched a small bag nestled inside. One of the men looked up to Daegin and his crew, threw his hand up, and smiled before running off.

"You two, get down there!" Daegin screamed, shoving two of his men by the neck. They nodded, chanted levitation spells and slowly descended into the hole. Daegin ran his fingers through his sweat-matted hair. Fyrl had been too well planned for them.

He wiped his brow and looked to Kerro. His eyes were glowing from the night-vision spell and it made him look terrifying. They exchanged disappointed looks and glared down the street where one of the guards continued to burn in a heap of cooked flesh. The rest of Daegin's men watched the hole and road with anxious eyes.

"So now what?" Kerro asked, trying to sound as hopeful as possible.

Daegin looked at the small wooden door that led to Fyrl's castle. "If we're going to lure her back to the house, we *need* that book."

It was amusing how things could change so drastically after countless years, she thought to herself. Kersey's dominion over the dead was once a great thing. People came from all over Mystyria just to glimpse her—just to see the woman who could turn back the curse of death. She was *revered*.

She only had to use two fingers. By placing them on the temples of a fallen soldier's head and praying to Lyluss—the goddess who then still loved her, she could bring them back. People would cheer, children would gasp, and the weeping families would rejoice as sparks began to rip through the air above their fallen kin. When they woke, she was out of breath and unable to speak but they worshipped her anyway. Kersey Avonwood was almost a *god* to the poor people who lost a loved one. It wasn't anything like today.

A thousand years ago when she resurrected someone, they thanked her with their mouth and showed it with their expression. Now, they spoke directly into her mind since they were unable to form words with a rotten voice box. Their eyes were missing, bulging, or disarrayed and their lips were bloated, ripped, and clammy. They showed no emotion.

Kersey had created Gothmirks before, although never this many. She'd needed handfuls of them in the past but their numbers never grew too large to be noticed. Looking out toward the rows of dead men, women, children, cattle, domestic pets, and birds, she was amazed. This was what it was like to be a force to be reckoned with.

Their voices were overwhelming. Kersey had to use every ounce of her mental power to force their pleading wishes and rants away. She couldn't answer them all, but she could a few. Nearly every Gothmirk she'd raised had a request.

In the last few hours, she had managed to reunite a dead husband with his deceased wife who had been murdered and buried in a shallow grave a mile from his house. She answered a twelve-year old girl's plea to find her cat, which had been killed by her drunken father before he burnt their house to the ground. All three of the charred Gothmirks were behind Kersey, the cat in the little girl's blackened arms.

There had even been a king—a great ruler of the land during the first War of Balance. He had been buried here because his childhood home was by the river, long before the name Tharg came into existence. Kersey raised him and told him to visit it once more.

Even a cat—a long dead, skeletal cat had mentioned that it wanted to be with its kittens again and after hours of touring the city's graveyards, she managed to find all six. They were buried beneath urban yards and gardens, in cemeteries, and one had even been stuffed and mounted as a child's toy. It hobbled out into the streets and allowed Kersey to pull the stuffing from it so it could walk easier. All seven of them brushed against her ankle in a motion of thankfulness as a family reunited.

Avery seemed to be quite intrigued by the undead. Even though it was disturbing to most, it was still an interesting thing to see. The large man even helped a few of the corpses out of the ground. His willingness to take the hand of a dead man and pull him free was adorable. He did it because he felt like he was *helping her.*

Then there was Clive. She felt horrible for him. After such a taxing two days—a funeral, his house being burnt to the ground, and the most radical changes of his life, he had been forced to look his dead sister in the face and learn that she had been murdered. Kersey knew what that pain was like. The very first Gothmirk she'd created was her own mother. It wasn't even her intention.

A thousand years ago, after the cave but before the curse, Kersey came home to find her mother dead on the floor. She'd slit her wrists because word had traveled back that Mydian's great beast had killed the Lylussian Slayers. She couldn't bear the thought of her daughter lying dead in a cave with a ravenous dragon. Kersey knelt beside her—the bloodlust, the anger, and the need to kill was beginning to fester, but she still had a small ounce of soul left. There was still good in her and she wanted to breathe life back into her mother, just as she had hundreds in the past weeks before Gwenavaughn.

The sparks flew from her body and just when Kersey thought Lyluss had sent back the one soul she wanted most of all, the spell went horribly wrong. Her mother's milky eyes flew open and she sat up. There were thick, nauseating vines all around her and Kersey didn't know what was happening. Her mother's arms stretched out to grab her, to compassionately hold her one final time, but that was the last thing Kersey thought she wanted. This was the undead—the soldier of Ruin and the enemy of the goddess of good. The would-be vampiress drew her knife and butchered her mother, killing her for the second time in the same night. She never got over what she did, nor did she ever try to call upon Lyluss' power again.

Her mind was saved from entering a trance when Clive stepped to her side and took her arm. There was blood dripping from her elbow, coming from the deep track marks on her wrist. It was even seeping from her fingers and beneath the nails.

He wrapped her messy arm up in a piece of cloth and tied it tight to soak up the blood. She tried her best to not look embarrassed, but couldn't help it. He gave her a warm smile and stepped back toward Avery. These were the two men that mattered most to her. Even if she was doing the god of the dead's work, she was glad to at least have them by her side.

The army had grown to a few thousand by the time the sun had set. Tharg was empty now—silent against the shifting feet from score upon score of undead. There were only a few lights on inside the houses and merchant shops. People were afraid, as well they should have been. The Gothmirks, however, didn't attack unless attacked first.

There had been occasional resistance, but most of it was from afar. Earlier, men launched a barrage of arrows and threw torches but a quick shift in the Gothmirk front sent them running off into the night. No one tried to take them on directly after the guards' horrible attempt that morning. Tharg was too big a city and Fyrl's men were too spread out. It would be impossible to overthrow Kersey's army now.

This had been the most walking she had done in nearly twenty years. Her feet ached each time she stepped on the hard granite road. She only wished her power was more widespread and could keep her from trekking miles of cemetery roads. If she wanted to raise a corpse, she basically had to be next to it. Her range of ability only carried about ten feet.

"Clive!" Avery said with so much vigor that Kersey even turned around. Her friend wrapped his arm around Clive's shoulder and hugged. "Do you live here? The Giantess owns this town!" he exclaimed. Obviously Daegin had been telling him stories of Fyrl's alliance.

"Yes. Yes I do, Avery," Clive offered, trying his best to squeeze out of the uncomfortable hug. "But I suppose I don't have a house anymore, so I'm an orphan." He mocked a frown to Kersey but she didn't think it was so amusing. One look across town to the lingering trail of smoke made her heart ache.

"So now where will you go?" he asked. Kersey turned her ear to listen. She could feel Clive's eyes on the back of her head.

"Well, since I'm now probably considered a deserter and betrayer, I suppose wherever this little lady here goes," he chuckled and she smiled in hidden satisfaction. "I don't have much choice, although I could stay in that dilapidated house over across the river."

He pointed to the cluster of three decrepit homes that were situated on the bank of the Singrey River that ran into Lake Barria. Kersey didn't have to look over because she knew exactly what they were gazing at.

"Who lives there, Clive?" Kersey asked in mock oblivion.

"No one, now," he answered, his tone dark. "My grandmother lived in the house on the east, and my family lived in the one on the west."

"What about the one in the middle?" she asked.

Clive bowed his head in thought for a moment but just shrugged. "I can recall a lady living there when I was very young. She was pretty. Nalia probably wasn't even born yet. That's all I remember."

Kersey smiled. She knew more about Clive and his family than she let him think.

"Miss Red! Miss Red!" Avery shouted and ran off toward the bank.

"Avery!" Clive and Kersey both called in unison before looking to one another.

The burly man knelt down at the water's edge and just as she was about to run to him, he stood and headed back, hands full of rocks. Clive looked puzzled but she knew what he was doing now. She smiled and remembered this little game.

"I bet I can get three!" he shouted and handed her half of the rocks.

"I don't know, Avery." She grinned a little to a still confused Clive. "Three is an awful lot."

He wasn't going to be deterred. Avery stepped up to the water, bit his lip and drew back to throw the stone. He flicked his wrist sideways and the small rock shot out, bouncing once, then twice along the surface of the river before sinking.

"Good throw, Avery," she said and let her own coast across. It skipped a total of six times before sinking.

"Wow! Why, that was somethin', Miss Red!" His eyes were wide as he studied her hands.

"Care to give it a shot?" she said, tossing a stone into Clive's hands.

He instinctively caught it and shook his head. "No, I don't think so."

"Oh why not?" she asked and put her hand to her hip. She looked to Avery and added, "I don't think he can even make it skip once, Avery."

"Shouldn't we be heading to the castle?"

"Do you always have to be so serious?" Kersey asked. "Life is too harsh to not stop and have fun, even if it's only for a moment."

Clive smirked and headed to the water's edge. "That's quite amusing coming from you."

He threw his stone, which only skipped once before plummeting to the depths of the river. Avery's voice ascended higher than she had ever heard as he found great hilarity in Clive's inability to play the game.

The three kept casting stones a few minutes longer, but before Clive could even take another turn, a sudden and violent explosion rocked Kersey's thoughts. It was distant—so distant in fact that only her enhanced ears heard it. The men were too busy talking about the houses on the far bank of the river. Suddenly there were several more blasts and she thought it best to get going. The commotion was coming from the castle.

"We should leave," she said and explained what she heard.

The trip there was short but she couldn't find any suitable way for getting her army into the large estate. A massive drawbridge was raised in the front. The rear and sides of the castle were literally built into the walls of a cliff. Tharg's castle was impervious to any kind of large-scale attack, or so Kersey thought.

It wasn't until they were at Fyrl's doorstep when one of the Gothmirks, a fallen guard, approached and told her of the secret entrance. It seemed that Fyrl had a much easier way of getting inside.

The back entrance was at least a half-mile away, hidden in a valley and obscured by massive, granite walls. There had already been a skirmish. The smell of charred flesh, black powder and blood was heavy in the air. A blistered guard lay on the ground, his body still wafting smoke.

Kersey flicked her wrist and the scorched man sat up. His face was nothing more than a sickly wet, black arrangement of muscles. The dead eyes fixed on the one who just raised him. Avery didn't hesitate to help him to his feet.

"What happened here?" she whispered into his ear.

Mydianites. They attacked us, but they did not get the book. Not yet, his voice poured into her mind.

"Where is it now?" she asked, eying the wagon up ahead. She waved the remaining guards to their feet. The wilderbears tried but the overturned wagon kept them at bay.

Beneath us. Fyrl will have it put in the vault in the sub-level of the castle. Once it is there, no one will be able to get it.

"We have to hurry," Kersey told Clive as she pulled the guard's sword belt off. She shoved it into his arms. "You know how to use a sword, right?"

He nodded and fastened it around his waist. "And what about your stone-throwing friend, here?" He motioned toward Avery while making sure the belt was tight.

"Stay close to me, Avery," Kersey said. "Understand?" The simple man nodded that he did but his eyes were too fixed on the struggling wilderbears.

They couldn't have gotten far, the dead guard said. *Follow me. I will show you where to cut them off.*

.10.

The Darkest Night

The last of the vegetable soup disappeared over the ship's rear ballista and into the black water below. Dyne coughed twice and tried to draw as much air into her lungs as possible. She was sick, upset, and angered by her surroundings and wanted nothing more than to be off this ship and away from these people. She tucked her legs up around her chest and played with the end of a rope that hung from the sternpost.

She was wearing only a drab, itchy, brown dress that was stuffed in the cargo hold. It had been so hot below deck—too hot for that sweaty leather armor. Luckily Laraek pulled a large trunk next to her hammock to store her belongings.

Everything was in doubt now, including her faith in Mydian. He certainly seemed evasive as to what Ruin was up to. Why did he want this book so badly? What role would Kersey Avonwood play? There were things going on behind a deceptive curtain, but it wouldn't have been the first time. After all, the entire occupancy of the Birchlock Estate had been one big charade designed to put Dyne next to a dragon that needed her blood to live again.

Tonight was the darkest night she'd ever known. The *Murder's* crew was primarily vampires and didn't need light to see. There were only two lanterns on the entire ship and those were kept below. One was in Jonas' cabin and the other was for the mortal carpenters. A light on the upper deck was much too risky. They were invisible and silent to anyone not able to see the water breaking around the hull.

Dyne was thankful for the moon. Although it was starting to cloud over, it had given her enough light to make it out of the bowels of the ship, away from the screaming, caged mortals and the insufferable, drunken vampires.

She rested her head against her knees, trying to avoid letting the heavy rock of the ship make her stomach ache. This was a horrible way to travel, she thought. Surely man could envision ways of getting around that didn't involve going into the sea.

Laraek's ship was quite a spectacle, although Dyne had no others to compare it to. She could remember seeing merchant vessels pass by the docks of Boudia when she was a child but was too fearful to even walk along the pier after her incident with the fisherman. This was the closest she'd seen one in all its glory.

The *Murder* was over a hundred feet in length with three lower decks. There had to be at least a hundred crewmen. Most were playing cards, drinking, or rolling dice while others were snoring as the rock of the ship swung them in their hammocks. There were mounted ballistae on all sides of the main deck—each sitting atop a swivel that allowed the wielder to aim at anything that dared to oppose the ship. In addition to the deck ballistae, there were three more in the crow's nests atop the three masts. Black flags bearing the golden torch of Mydian waved gloriously as the ocean wind passed by them.

There were two raised decks—the weather and bridge deck where she sat and the forecastle deck, which was at the far end of the ship toward the bow. Laraek's cabin was beneath her, surrounded by a pair of steps that broke away from the wheel. The crew cabin entrance started beneath the forecastle deck. She had listened to the drunken squabble of the vampires long enough to pick up a few nautical terms.

Everyone was below and the ambient sounds of laughter, dice and singing crawled up the steps toward her. Surely she was alone with the sternpost, but that was wrong. The moon's fading light lasted just long enough for her to make out a figure standing against the railing a few feet from her. He was a tall, thin man looking out to the unsettling sea. A bottle of some kind of tart-smelling alcohol was clenched tightly in his hand.

"Hey," she called, wiping her chin. "How 'bout a little of that?" She pointed to the bottle but he didn't acknowledge her. He kept watching the sea and letting the rock of the ship push him back and forth.

Dyne stood on wobbly legs and grabbed his arm. "Hey!" she shouted, louder this time. The skinny man's head rose and turned to her. Even in the fleeting light of the moon she had no trouble seeing the large, black sockets that looked like burn wounds where his eyes should have been. He was looking *through* her. She started to say something and backed up a bit, not wanting the drink anymore—not wanting to even stand close to this creature—

—when she brushed against someone else.

She let out a small cry.

"Shhh," came the discomforting voice of Laraek. She closed her eyes and fought back the tears. His presence alone was enough to weaken her. So far, she had managed to avoid him the entire trip. "It's ok. He won't bother you."

He circled around and yanked the bottle from the entranced man's hand. The eyeless one didn't put up a fight, nor did he acknowledge being robbed of his beer. Laraek handed it to Dyne as the man returned his vigilant stare—or at least attention, toward the sea.

"What's wrong with him?" she pondered, and then took a long drag of the beer. It tasted far worse than it smelled so she chucked the bottle over the railing.

"Dyne, meet Marlis. This is one of the Crossbacks. I'm sure you've already heard of them."

So this is what a 'made' vampire looks like, she thought with a bit of disgust.

"Why is he so . . . unresponsive?" she wondered.

"They are always listening," Laraek said. "When the spawning procedure takes place, it causes their eyes to burn from their sockets. They are weak minded and slow to learn and think, but they also have great power and are very loyal. Their unnatural creation makes them closer to mortals than vampires. They don't even have to feed."

"They don't drink blood?" Dyne's mouth dropped. She would have loved that power when she was a vampire, although she doubted it was worth trading her eyesight.

"That's right." He grabbed Marlis' chin and pried open his mouth. There were three fangs, not two. One was abnormally short and the other two were twisted and bent. He probably couldn't even feed if he tried.

"Why are they called Crossbacks?"

Laraek spun him around and with one tug, ripped his shirt off. Marlis didn't even flinch as he was bent over the railing so Dyne could see his back.

There was a large 'X' carved into his flesh. It was singed around the edges and there were small, silver flecks inside the gashes. Thick, dried blood had hardened all along his backside.

"This wound will never heal up," Laraek assured. "The Bloodsilver is laced onto a dagger and then it is slashed across their back like you see here. The eyes burn out, the brain turns to mush and a new, although abominable vampire is created."

"Why would anyone want such a thing?" she asked, eyeing just how little and shriveled the man was. Although vampires didn't fully rely on their sight to function, it would certainly hinder them in a battle.

"They are quite useful for what they are bred. Crossbacks aren't meant to fight man or beast. They are meant to fight undead."

"And how are they useful against undead?" She also wondered why Mydian would go through so much trouble.

"I'll show you," He backed up and pulled his dagger out and turned to the Crossback. "Marlis, you will not attack me, understood?" Laraek waited for the slow man to nod an agreement and then turned his attention back to Dyne.

"What are you doing?" she asked, keeping her distance.

"Let's say your army of men and women are faced with an equal sized, or perhaps larger army of undead." He lashed out toward Dyne and grabbed her around the waist and gazed deep into her eyes. She shifted uncomfortably but he held her against the railing. "Assume I am said undead and I just attacked and killed you." He danced his blade across her chest like a puppet. "My master will come along shortly and raise you to join our army. Where once there was one undead soldier there are now two—fighting on the same side."

He backed off and twirled his dagger. She straightened her collar and pulled her hair back with a frown. She didn't understand where he was going with this—she was too enthralled by the coldness in his touch.

"Now, let's say I am the same nimble and unmerciful undead and I attack poor Marlis here." Without even a warning, Laraek reached out and plunged the dagger into the creature's chest. His scream didn't even follow though as his heart was carved and pulled free. Marlis disappeared in a brilliant flash that left Dyne speechless. She couldn't believe what she just witnessed. Laraek had just killed one of his own men for the sake of a lesson.

He got down on one knee and sifted through the white ash with the tip of his dagger. An eerie smile found its way to his mouth as his point suddenly became obvious. "You see? You can't make a pile of ash join your army."

"Why do we have to worry about the dead so much?" she questioned, watching Marlis' ashes and tattered clothes blow out to sea.

"Why do you think Mydian fears Kersey so much?" Laraek returned, sheathing his dagger.

"Fears? I assumed it was hatred. She refused to work for him so he decided he wanted her dead."

"You are close, but there's more to it." A flash of lightning cast an eerie shadow across the deck. There was certainly a storm coming. "What do you know of Kersey's power?"

"Much," she replied, just before the boom of thunder. Dyne went on to tell Laraek of all the things she'd learned over the years while hunting her and nine others.

Kersey had the ability to raise a special type of undead known as Gothmirks. She even left a few of them behind when she was supposedly killed.

"Kersey fooled Mydian into thinking his assassins put an end to her about fifteen years ago," Laraek said. "In truth, she allowed herself to be captured so she could hide from the world. She's left the confines of prison and is now looking to start trouble with the help of Ruin."

"So do we know what they are planning to do?"

"Short of starting the third War of Balance, no." The lightning and thunder were starting to pick up and the ship was being pushed around a bit more. A torrent of water splashed upon deck and ran over the sides. "But there is a book..."

Dyne recalled the conversation between Daegin and Lord Mydian. There was an exchange scheduled to happen tonight.

"Felorn is the unworthy, although rightful new owner of it, but Lord Mydian plans to snatch it away before Ruin can intervene. And you should know why. It's Aneesa Redblaze's spell book."

Of course, she thought. It all made sense now. Ruin was certainly after the book and no doubt behind so many other things. The spell book of Aneesa was powerful—so powerful and old that only a few living today would be able to read it. Ruin's plans were starting to unfold and she now knew why her soul's arrival to the Underworld had been delayed.

Only a few decades after Dyne had been cursed to vampiracy and started looking for a Greater Overlord, she stumbled onto the spell book of Aneesa herself. She carried it all across the realms in hopes of finding someone who could translate it. The spells inside were so rumored and so superior—one of them could have pointed her to the location of a Greater Overlord while another could have granted her the power to walk in daylight.

With her inability to find anyone resourceful enough to read its garbled pages, she grew frustrated and realized it was dead weight.

One night, before leaving the city of Lolusk, she buried it beneath a Nyian church along with several weapons, pieces of armor and treasure that she knew she would never return to. Dyne had been the only one who knew the book's location and she took that knowledge to the grave.

"When was the book found?" she asked Laraek, snapping out of her erratic memories.

"What?"

"It was first uncovered in Lolusk, am I right?"

"Only a few weeks ago. How did you know that?" he wondered.

"Because I buried it there almost three centuries ago. Ruin knew that once I died and went to the Underworld, I would have told Mydian where to send his servants to dig. He was buying his own people time to find it so he kept my soul imprisoned for over a decade. Once it was uncovered by chance, he let my spirit go."

"I see," Laraek said. "I wouldn't mind having that book for myself." There was a light rain falling now. The night was hot and the sporadic sprinkle of cool moisture felt wonderful on her face.

"What? Why?" she asked.

"There's got to be someone out there who can read it. Just imagine the power in those pages."

"I suppose," Dyne reluctantly agreed. She hopelessly looked for so long to find someone. The power *was* incredible, but with her limited patience she could not juggle the heart and the book at the same time.

It grew unbearably quiet. Her long golden hair was picked up by the breeze and started whipping across Laraek's face so she slid down the railing just a bit. She could feel his warm smile and for some reason she lowered her head in a yielding defeat.

"So what kept you alive all those years?" he asked her.

"You," she whispered.

"Nevermind," Laraek said, obviously not wanting to be drawn into another discussion about their history in love. She wasn't as ready to give up the conversation.

"I wanted to see your grave in Boudia so badly. I wouldn't rest. Unfortunately, someone came along and killed me before I had the privilege." Her troubled mind raced back to Tranas.

"I'm sorry your quest was all for nothing. As you can see, there's nothing more up in Boudia than an empty box and a meaningless headstone."

"Why did you have it built?"

"So the world would think I died," he answered. "The commander of the *Phantom Seven* has always remained a secret and will even after I'm gone."

There was no closure in his answer. Still, she wished she could have seen it with an unknowing mind that would have assured her that he was rotting only six feet beneath the dirt.

"Do you remember the fair? The Boudian spring fair?" she asked.

"Of course I do. I can remember thinking how preposterous it was. The world was at war and we were enjoying fun and games."

While the second War of Balance was ripping Mystyria to shreds, Boudia continued its annual tradition of holding the world's most renowned country fair. There were exotic animals, unique food and drink, and an unnatural glory that came with song and dance. People came from miles around to escape the troubles of the war and to enjoy one another's company in one of the gods' most unholy cities.

Dyne and Laraek were both fortunate enough to be pulled away from battle and were allowed a week's reprieve that came in the form of a trip home. They hadn't met yet, but on one sunny, spring day, just a stone's throw away from the wilderbear rides, the two met eyes.

"It was also the first time we saw each other," Dyne pointed out. "Just after a few days, we were so close . . . so in love."

"That was three centuries ago," he said, obviously not wanting to be dragged back into the rut that was their past.

"But do you remember what you said to me?"

"I don't recall."

"Oh, but I think you do," she said.

"So much time has passed, Dyne. I haven't dwelled on it as much as you clearly have."

His words stung a little, but her mind was too far away in too happy a place for it to bother. She remembered with vivid clarity what he had said.

"You told me that war would divide but love would unite. I carried those words with me from that day on."

"And love *did* unite our families," Laraek pointed out. "Our mothers and fathers and siblings grew to adore each other. They knew that after the war was over, we would be married. They would have never thought such . . . circumstances would draw us in separate directions."

"They never thought their children would still be alive three centuries later," Dyne said coldly, feeling the urge to drop the subject. It was only a week later when the battle turned bitter and Mydian ordered their families to be killed for losing it.

"So what was it like?" Laraek asked, resting his chin on his hand. She almost wanted to thank him for pulling her out of saddened memories.

"What was what like?"

"The Underworld. Is it as great as the stories proclaim?"

"I hardly saw it. Telsa ushered me straight to Lord Mydian. But it looked . . . *big.*" There was no other way to explain it. Mortal tongues that spat mortal words could not begin to describe a heavenly realm. "But I'm sure you'll see it one day. You are, after all, a humble servant of the Master."

Dyne hesitantly described the last events that led up to her death, twelve years ago. She told him about the heart, about Arctis, and about the long-dead dragon being guarded by abominable vampires. What she didn't mention was Tranas and certainly not Hannah. Laraek wouldn't understand. He may have wanted a baby when they were miles away, outside of Keswing but here, three hundred years later on a ship headed into a stormy night, he wouldn't have cared.

"So . . . have you been to Bloodgate lately?" Laraek asked, obviously trying to lighten the mood.

"I've only been alive for a day," she said, failing to note his humor. "Of course I haven't."

"The Martax is . . . alive these days," he said, turning around and facing the water.

Mydian's most unique and questionable creation of all time was the Martax, a tower seated in the heart of Bloodgate that rose nearly two miles into the blackened, smoggy air. It could be spotted for miles away along the barren land and it captivated anyone who saw it. Only a select few got to see inside.

It had been erected on the site of the Blood Tree, a towering oak that grew from the Pool of Divinity where the gods were rumored to have entered existence. The Blood Tree bore bloody fruit that sustained vampires through the first War up to the second until Lady Good had it destroyed.

"What do you mean by *alive*?"

"In the last few years, more and more people are going in there, working, living, and making changes that affect the city. There are strange noises from inside and steam vents sputter black smoke all along its jagged sides. Every few nights the ground rattles beneath the streets. Something is happening in there."

"And Lyluss fears this?" Dyne asked. Surely it didn't seem like a valid enough reason to go to war.

"All the gods fear this. The scariest thing in this world is the unknown. What could it be? A new weapon? A new spellshop?"

"Or maybe just a giant distillery," Dyne mused.

"Hardly. Whatever it is, it's enough to make Lyluss and Ruin put aside their differences and concentrate on Lord Mydian."

"And the other gods?"

"The other gods want no part of this. If Lyluss and Mydian go to war and these days are known in history as the third War of Balance, then Mystyria will be changed forever. This war will be the ultimate death of one of them."

"Quillian will certainly put her hands in," Dyne reminded.

"Of course she will, and I'm certain that once Daegin takes the book from her in Tharg, Felorn will, as well. This is the way of war."

"And once again, Mydian will try to take a city he can't possibly overcome and will fall back to the recesses of Bloodgate where he will wait, for centuries, to try again."

"Blasphemy!" Laraek cursed, inches from her face. Apparently the truth was sacrilege. "How could you even say such a thing about our god?"

"*Our* god?" she asked, not moving away from his menacing stare.

"Are you still loyal to Lord Mydian, Dyne?" Laraek's tone was solid and unflinching.

She had asked herself this question every day since her vampiracy. During her life she was an unyielding and devout servant of the dark god. After he bit her—after she came to fear his dark eyes, pale skin, and memories of a pain that wracked her to the core—she didn't think so.

"My loyalty is to *myself*," she answered, suddenly not caring how he would react. "I respect Lord Mydian and I have no other god in his place, but after he . . . *hurt* me . . . my religious standpoint changed."

"You should be ashamed," he sneered. "Lord Mydian granted you eternal life . . . and then, after you managed to get yourself killed, he gave you this life of mortality."

"I didn't ask for *either*!" she screamed, feeling the anger rise in her soul—the same anger that used to flow in the unbridled vampiric version of her. "I wasn't happy being a vampire. I'm certainly not happy being a mortal. All I want is to be back with Telsa, be it the Underworld or not."

Laraek chuckled and shook his head. He kicked what was left of Marlis' ash between the railing's braces and said, "You've changed so much. I can remember a time when you weren't so . . . weak. You didn't let feelings get in the way."

"And I can remember a time when you weren't such a puppet for a god who couldn't care less about you. He killed your family for no apparent reason, remember that?" It amazed Dyne how servants could still be faithful after the god they loved—the same god who was supposed to love *them*—took away the only ones who cared for them.

"My family is waiting for me in the Underworld, as are yours. You will—"

"—tell me, Laraek," she interrupted. "Does Eva share your blind faith?"

His face darkened. This was the side of him that she never got to see during their mortality. It was the side of him that came out when his anger peaked.

"Eva's loyalty to Lord Mydian is unwavering. It was her devotion to him that drew me to her a year ago."

"Oh? I would have assumed it was because we share a striking resemblance."

His head dropped and the anger in his face flooded away. This was a side that she *had* seen before. It was Laraek when he was hurt. Even though she was angry, ready to move on from his memory and let him enjoy whatever made him happy with his darling Eva, Dyne couldn't help but feel a small bit of guilt. She struck a nerve that probably hadn't been touched in three centuries. Despite that, she was still ready to use it against him. This was what she was good at—kicking people when they were down.

"You still love me, don't you?" It even hurt her to say it to him. Laraek was silent and he glanced back to the steps as if he wanted to go below deck. Before he could walk off, she grabbed his coat and repeated, "Don't you?"

"You'd best get some rest," he hastily said, a tired and defeated tone in his voice. He avoided her incisive gaze completely. "We'll be in Tharg by midnight." He jerked his coat from her grasp and headed off.

That was enough for her. Dyne was going to be in control of her feelings once again. She just needed the closure and now that she had it, her love for him would fade, just like it faded for so many people in her heartless past.

Love for Laraek had dominated her life for centuries. She had always assumed it was the source of her strength, but perhaps it was the opposite. Loving Laraek had been a driving force that kept her weak. The vampire she was could have been capable of so much more had she not let emotion—desire and sentiment of the past interfere with her daily life. She was going to change. She was going to make herself stronger as a mortal than she had ever hoped as a vampire.

.11.

To Kill Someone Deserving

Most of Fyrl's men were either up in the city or dealing with the mess Kersey's undead had caused since their rise. The path out of the bowels of the castle was quite uneventful, save for a sentry every few corridors. There was but one place the book was headed and Daegin had to get there before it did.

This was not the first time he had been inside Fyrl's vast, luxurious home. There had been several other occasions, although he never had the resources and desire to go so deep inside. He knew several guards and had stolen blueprints of the keep's layout, so he knew quite well that the book was being ushered to the vault that sat three stories up.

Daegin fumbled with a small, purple marble as he led his men down the hallway, trying his best to recall from memory where the steps to the upper floor began. The marble held a faint glow inside and cost more than the safe-house itself. It was magical, special, and their contingency plan in case things went awry.

"Stick close to me," he told Kerro who was chanting to himself. The battlemage nodded and continued preparing the rest of his spell.

The castle was silent and that was a problem. Silence usually resulted in ambush, which usually resulted in death for a lot of men. Fyrl's guards could have been leading them into a trap that would occupy them long enough so the book could be secured. Daegin halted his men, pressed his back against the wall, and peeked around the corner. There had been a shuffle up ahead of him and he wanted to see *it* before *it* saw them.

He grinned his favorite, evil smile—the one he only used when his masterful plans worked out so well that the gods themselves couldn't have aligned it any better. The two men who had nabbed the book were running down the corridor away from them, toward the staircase at the end of the moonlit hallway.

They didn't even have time to turn around. A barrage of arrows, bolts, fire streaks, and ice streams slammed into their backs, lifting them off the floor and slamming them into the wall like flaming marionettes shot from a cannon.

All of the Mydianites darted across the marble floor and hastily riffled through their belongings, sorting through weapons, clothes, and armor until finally they found the small bag containing the book.

Daegin snatched it from Kerro's hand and unraveled it. He had to see it with his own eyes. This was a piece of history—a materialized legacy that was even older than Kersey Avonwood herself. It was beautiful, but it was nothing like the legends.

Aneesa's spell book was very plain. He had expected it to be full of illuminations and have a very adorned cover and spine but it didn't. The front of the small but thick book was simply a dark, red embroidered cover with the half-moon and star symbol of Symbia. The pages were yellowed and the threading was beginning to wear out, but for a thousand year old tome, it was holding together quite nicely. Daegin assumed its slow-aging condition was partly magic. Most of the text was written in ancient Elderi. So much for trying to read it, he silently scoffed.

The mission was a success. He dropped the book into his side-pouch and clasped the pack shut. Kersey Avonwood wasn't even aware they were here, which was good. If Ruin even glimpsed the secret that Mydian knew, he would have Kersey use the book to bring great misfortune to the god of the Underworld.

That was why Daegin wanted her to come to the safe-house. If he could kill her—remove her as the thorn in Mydian's side, then his god would look quite favorably upon him. Daegin would make his mark on Mystyria as not the man who captured the essence of the vampire, but as the man who stopped the third war from undoing Mydian. He would be a *hero* to those who loved evil.

Kerro was smiling at their success. He still didn't know how Daegin planned on using it to their advantage. He didn't know that it was going to be the bait for undoing Kersey Avonwood. If anyone knew how ingenious his plan was, they may have tried to steal the glory for themselves.

Daegin was just about to suggest they head back the way they came, but the lingering smell in the room held his tongue. Everyone else noticed it too. It was the rotting, decaying stench of death.

There was a fissure on the ground and stalks of black vines were creeping into the hallway from its dark abyss.

Before Kerro's accomplished grin could even fade, tendrils of black and green wrapped around his waist and neck and hoisted him back. He flew the span of twenty feet and landed against a coat of arms on the wall and then slid down into a dizzying stupor. His eyes rolled back in his head and he shook it, trying to clear the confusion of what just happened.

The Mydianites behind Daegin sprang to life when the filtered moonlight suddenly poured into the hallway from a new opening on the side. There was a massive roar and the wall collapsed beneath the force of an undead dolgatha. Its massive, reptilian hands tore the stones away as if they were made of straw. It was covered in oozing, dripping vines.

Several undead stepped in from the newly created doorway and after a dozen or so filed inside, *she* appeared. This was the first time Daegin had actually seen her. He couldn't look away and neither could she. Her eyes were dark, foreboding and had a vengeful flare that he didn't quite understand. Daegin couldn't believe how tiny she was. She couldn't have been much taller than five feet and couldn't have weighed more than a hundred pounds. The vines were snaking along the ground, around her ankles, and creeping toward him as he backed up. A litter of undead cats by her feet hissed at the sight of him.

Just then, Avery and a man who was not a Gothmirk, stepped through the wall behind her. Daegin couldn't believe his eyes. Not only had his brother abandoned their family and their god, but he had joined ranks with the enemy. After Kersey was dead and her army was without a leader, he was surely going to come back for his betraying sibling. But if he was to do any of this, any of it at all, he first had to survive tonight.

Clive didn't believe her when she said Daegin and his men were on the other side of the wall. Apparently her powers didn't end with controlling the dead and having incredible strength. She was like an animal when she became angry—her senses were elevated and she could see their heat right through the stone. The dolgatha found its way up from the bowels of the old prison and into the sewers. It made short work of the granite wall.

He held onto Avery's shirt so the large man didn't go running off once his Miss Red headed into the opened east wing corridor. There were only a handful of Mydianites inside but the one up front was the only one that mattered. Clive already knew it was *Daegin*.

The mage was backing into his guards' arms with the approach of Kersey and her vines. If only the Mydianites could have seen through the opened portal. They would have surely turned around and ran off with their tails between their legs at the sight of a few thousand Gothmirks.

Clive was holding his sword out and didn't realize just how much he was shaking. It was the sight of his sister's killer that was making his blood boil. Daegin's end was obviously here with Kersey and her army standing over top of him but Clive was starting to want the kill. He felt that if he didn't get to be the one that swung that sword across his throat then his years to come would be filled with countless 'what ifs' and 'why nots'.

Only a few minutes after the first battlemage had sailed across the room with the help of the vines, Kersey called for the rest to be dispersed. She was thinning the human barrier that had surrounded Daegin. Mydianites flew through the air—some crashed against the wall, some were crushed against the ground and some even landed on the massive chandelier, their blood trickling down from wounds caused by the sharp crystal.

"I'm sorry, Kerro!" Daegin called across the room. Kersey and Clive both looked down the hall and saw the first battlemage the vines attacked. He was slowly getting to his feet, a look of hopelessness on his face.

A brilliant purple light gathered their attention from Daegin's corner. The battlemage slammed something onto the ground and suddenly a large, purple ring appeared next to him. A forceful wind blew through the hallway and all the small things of the room were sucked toward the swirling, purple vortex. Swords, glass from the chandelier, bodies, and even a couple of living Mydianites disappeared into the magical portal. Daegin smiled at Kersey Avonwood and let go of a wall sconce and allowed the purple haze to wash over him. Once he was gone, it shrank to the size of a coin and disappeared, leaving the room still once more.

There was a handful of Mydianites left and with the vines creating a mesh-like wall around the staircase, they had no choice but to fight for their lives. A spear, a sword, and three pairs of glowing hands were outstretched toward Kersey and her friends.

One of them chanted so loudly that he was screaming. He held his glowing hand out and without waiting around for the resulting damage, Clive quickly advanced and severed the radiant appendage with his sword. The battlemage's cries abruptly ended when a blade plunged deep within his gut.

"Back against the wall, Avery!" Clive said, switching his sword to the other hand so he could push the large man near the hole.

Another spellcaster let loose a bolt of lightning that zipped past Clive's ear and singed the hair on his temple. He slammed into the wall and dodged the next attack but it put him too close to swing his sword. Without thinking, Clive rushed him and pulled him to the floor.

The Mydianite was chanting, his hand glowing and he grabbed onto Clive's arms with what felt like burning latches. Through smoke and pain, he reached for his sword above the Mydianite's head. He held it with both hands—one at the grip and the other at the sword's tip and used his weight to create a guillotine across the man's neck. It didn't take much force for the blade to reach the floor beneath the caster's head.

Kersey's vines had started in on the others but when a blade grazed Clive's shoulder, he realized that she hadn't taken care of them all just yet. He rolled off of the headless spellcaster and found himself on his back, dodging the advancing tip of the last Mydianite's spear. He kicked off the man and gained a few inches but he was separated from his sword.

Clive was about to shield his face from an incoming jab but when he did, the attacks stopped. There wasn't a spear jutting from his face or torso, nor were there any more stabbing sounds against the floor. The blade heavily clanked to the ground and the Mydianite fell to the side, blood pouring from the side of his head.

When he moved, Avery was standing over him, a toothy grin on his face and a piece of bloodied granite in his hand. He tossed it aside and helped Clive up.

"Why, Miss Red says you're a friend of hers, so you're a friend of mine too!" he said, reassuringly.

Clive dusted himself off and sheathed his sword. Kersey wasn't paying any attention to either of them. She was too busy staring down the hall toward the one Mydianite that everyone seemed to have forgotten about.

There was only one left. The man Daegin had called Kerro.

"Where is he going?" Kersey asked him, slowly walking over rubble and broken glass to get to him. A steady drip of blood was falling from the chandelier and she let it hit her tongue, never lowering her stare from the recovering battlemage.

Kerro was on his feet, chanting, and holding his hands out toward her. The tips of his fingers began to glow as his spell neared completion. His tired, jarred face looked like he knew his end was fast approaching. With one last bit of effort, he released a blast of red light from his hands, but Kersey easily sidestepped it and advanced. Clive could tell she was angry now.

Her fingers reached up a full foot above her own head and wrapped around his face. With the strength of a thousand-year old vampire in her muscles, she snapped his neck so hard that the robe ripped. The sound of bones breaking—grinding was so loud that Avery startled.

Kerro's lifeless body dropped but Kersey still held him by the sides of his head, not letting him hit the ground. The curse of the Gothmirk suddenly filled him and his feet planted on the floor.

"Again, where is he going?" she screamed, squeezing his temples and speaking only an inch from his nose. The more helpful undead version of Kerro whispered something that made her nod. She shoved him to the side and he scrambled to get back to his feet, a blank, dead stare in his eyes.

"What did he say?" Clive asked, lowering his sword.

"Daegin has the book." Her tone turned as black as the night. "And he was the one who ratted me out to Mydian. My exposure was completely his doing."

"Well let's go find him, Kers," Clive started to say but the anger in her eyes had already made her abandon reason.

Her face turned dark and her eyes beady. Coarse, black feathers started sprouting along her flesh. The dress and boots seemed to merge into her body as more dark feathers developed all across her arms, legs, back and front. Kersey's body seemed to twist and contort and shrink until she was no longer an angry vampire. She was an angry crow that took to flight and headed out through the broken wall.

Clive ran through the opening and pushed his way past the rows of dead, standing bodies and watched her disappear into the black night. As best he could tell, she flew south. All of the Gothmirks, as if coming to the same conclusion, turned around and slowly started walking off. They knew where she was going but at this speed, it would take them all night to get there.

"Why, Miss Red turned into a bird!" Avery said, mouth gaping toward the horizon. "Did you see that, Clive?"

And hopefully this was his way of getting there faster.

"Yes Avery, I did. Do you know how to get to Daegin's house from here?" he asked the slow man. Avery grimaced and eyed the south with a hesitant uncertainty.

"I'm not going back there again, Clive. Why, Daegin is so mean to me!"

"I know, Avery, I know. But Miss Red is heading there and Daegin might try to hurt her without her friends here to help." He pointed to the slow mass of undead that was heading away from the castle. "Can you show me where he lives?"

Avery's eyes grew fearful at the thought of something happening to Miss Red. "We have to hurry then, Clive! Why, we can't let Daegin hurt Miss Red!" He started down the hill, pushing his way through the hordes of dead men, women, and animals.

Clive chased after him but felt a small bit of relief when he thought of the odds. Kersey was powerful and Daegin was a mere mortal who had already fled once tonight. Surely he couldn't best a Greater Overlord. Then again, he had no idea of what an elaborate scheme Daegin had worked up to kill such a powerful creature.

With her last bit of defiance to Laraek, she once again found herself at ease and her mind beginning to clear. She closed her eyes and let the beads of rain flow down her face, completely ignoring the uneasy rock of the ship. The thunder and lightning faded from mind and it wasn't long before she was slipping off to sleep. After all, it was the first time this body had known what it was like to rest.

A loud thump in front jarred her completely awake. Her eyes flew open and she bolted upright, dumping an inch of collected water from her lap. A violent shiver snaked its way up her spine from the drenching cold. It was still dark out—still thundering and still dumping rain on their northbound ship. A corpse had appeared in front of her. It was a man—a large man with bulging eyes and pale skin. His neck had been torn to shreds, blood seeping down the steps in slivers of pink. His clothes were matted and before she could get up, someone began dragging him toward her.

It was Eva.

The young vampiress hauled the corpse by the ankle, a bloodied, twisted smile on her delicate face. She pulled her evening meal up by the legs, grabbed his torso, and then tossed him into the water just over Dyne's shoulders. There was a solid splash that was quickly lost to the rain and thunder.

She was dressed in a long, black coat that was feebly covering a suit of grey chain mail. Her long blond hair was tied up beneath a black bonnet, making the pea-sized bite marks on her neck quite visible.

"Did I scare you?" Eva asked, wiping her chin. She stood beneath the sternpost, using the empty lantern canopy to shield her from the rain. It offered very small protection but she clung to it nevertheless.

"Hardly." Dyne settled back down and pulled the dress tighter.

"We'll be in Tharg soon. You should probably get some rest. That mortal body of yours can't take the stress that your vampiric form could."

"I'll be fine, dear," she scoffed. "Tell me, why exactly are you here? Is it to keep the deck clean and the mortal crewmen fed?"

Eva's enduring angelic smile didn't budge. "Not likely... Dyne, is it? I'm here to make sure Laraek's men keep in order while he's doing more important things aboard the ship."

"Like keeping me company by the sternpost?"

"More like making sure this ship doesn't run aground and spill your thin, mortal blood all over the rocks. Now you tell me, why exactly are *you* here?" Her smile faltered just a bit.

"It's not by choice, I assure you. Mydian himself put me here to help your crew kill Kersey."

"And just why did the dark god think we needed *your* help?" She approached Dyne from beneath the cover of the canopy. "Surely two more meatshields won't make a difference. He raised you and Lorne, a couple of vampires, from the dead and risked the Erolasian wrath of breaking Telsis' law of souls just because he wanted you to *help* us? Doesn't this all seem a little... odd to you?"

Dyne didn't know what to say, but she certainly was right. There was no rational reason for Mydian to send two souls to Mystyria for a task that the *Phantom Seven* could easily handle on its own.

"Perhaps Mydian foresaw trouble. Maybe he lacks a certain... faith in one of his servants." She tapped her foot on the wet deck, the roof of Laraek's cabin.

"What are you saying? You think Mydian believes Laraek is a betrayer?"

"You tell me. I'm sure you know more of your quest to *help* the dark god than you let on." She crossed her arms over, just as Dyne got to her feet. With Eva standing over her, she was starting to feel cornered.

"I'll tell you nothing. You've been with Laraek for the past year, not I. So if he is a traitor, I wouldn't be surprised if you shared his allegiance, as well."

"I love my god more than you will ever know," she said, putting a righteous finger against Dyne's chest. Water was running down the sides of her cheeks as she scowled her point. "As for Laraek, I cannot speak. He isn't exactly forthcoming in his dealings. After all, I woke up tonight to find that an old flame of his was going to be sailing with us."

Laraek did have many secrets. He wasn't the type of person to simply give up personal information—not even to her. There were so many things about him she never knew. So many aspects of his life she once would have loved to know, but their time was cut short and they were separated. Now, she could ask him all the questions she wanted but for some reason, she didn't feel as compelled.

"Then you have doubts about his loyalty?" Dyne pressed.

"Of course I do. He doesn't talk to his crew anymore." Eva leaned against the rail beside Dyne and she couldn't help but slide over a bit. The statuesque woman had quite an eerie aura about her. "Just between you and I, I believe he is planning on stealing the book for himself. He has grown careless, reckless even in his pursuit of it. The *Phantom Seven* is without six of its ships and it's all because of his eagerness to get to Tharg."

"And why would you tell me this?" Dyne asked. "I think you need to check your own loyalty."

"I love my husband but I honor my god above all else," she said, casting a watchful eye over her shoulder. "If he is a betrayer then I think he deserves to be caught."

"What do you think he plans on doing once he's stolen it?"

"Why sell it, of course," Eva said, laughing at such a silly question. "Any god would love to have it. I'm surprised you didn't figure that out when you carried it with you all that time."

"You are close to him," Dyne said, ignoring her dim-witted point and added, "You both sleep in the same bed. Surely you can find evidence to support such betrayal. Have you told anyone else about your suspicions?"

"No."

"Have you looked through his belongings? Do you know if he carries a journal?"

"You and Laraek share something in common," Eva answered hastily, turning her cold, glowing eyes to her. "You both have an unending barrage of annoying questions."

"In other words, no," Dyne assumed, smiling to the glaring vampiress. "Have you ever searched his cabin?" Eva's face was growing darker and darker but she seemed uninterested in what her husband's former lover suggested.

"I'm not the prying wench that you are, so no, I haven't." She boasted her arrogant, smug grin and folded her arms over.

"But Laraek *loves* this prying wench. I had him three-hundred years ago, long before you."

"And I had him only moments ago."

"The only reason Laraek has you is because you are a constant reminder of me. Now that I'm here, who knows," Dyne smiled, shrugged and looked to the starless sky, "maybe he'll be rid of you soon."

Without so much as a warning, the vampiress reached out and grabbed her face with a gloved hand and pulled her close. The pain was incredible but there was no fear.

Not yet.

"I don't know why Mydian sent you but I don't want you here. We don't need you," she growled. She pulled Dyne so close that their lips almost touched. "When we anchor in Tharg, I want you off this ship! Do you understand me?"

"No thanks, I believe Laraek is quite happy with my company," she defiantly managed through a squeezed face.

For a moment, Eva's mouth hung opened as rain dripped from her fangs. She looked Dyne over, as if inspecting a maggot-infested piece of meat. Even her nose seemed to twitch and snarl to the same effect. Her eyes studied the deck. With a hand still holding Dyne at bay, she looked back to the steps leading to the crew quarters to make sure no one was around. She gracefully pinched a fold of the drab brown dress and said, "*this* is mine."

Then, the most dreaded, most fearful, most horrifying thing that Dyne's mind could envision ... *happened*.

The angered vampiress shoved her over the railing.

Dyne's scream lasted only a second as her voice was suddenly torn apart by the crashing waves. She plummeted several feet below the frigid water before realizing just how serious her situation was. A pained childhood and a near-death experience came flooding back like the torrent of water surrounding her.

She struggled against the weight of the sea, trying her best to find her way to the surface. The turmoil of the waves was incredibly disorienting and she didn't know if she was getting closer to air or going further toward the blackened void of her death. Her lungs were about to give and she knew it was only a few seconds until she would need to breathe in, be it air or water. Dyne kept flapping her arms and somehow, by some god's miracle, her head broke through the surface.

It was so dark. In the flashes of light, she spotted the ship, moving farther and farther away. The rain was still pouring down sideways and the ocean was fiercely backed by the wind's fury. She constantly fought to stay afloat.

She couldn't swim and even if she could, there would be no way of catching the *Murder*. The anger in her heart and mind was so intense that if she were still a vampire, that power alone would probably be stripping Eva of her flesh right now.

Dyne was ready to give up the attempt of swimming—about to put her hands at her side and let Varolen's wrath take her below, when something grabbed her by the ankle.

A small screech escaped her and she thrashed her legs until someone emerged and wrapped their arms around her. Immediately, her mind raced back to the fisherman and for just a second, she could see him—his brawny shoulders, thick moustache and small, beady eyes. He was back, over three centuries later just to drown her.

But that wasn't the case. Her savior pulled her toward the ship by a rope that ran up to the sternpost.

"Wrap your arms around my neck," his voice called out. She was so disoriented and faint that she didn't realize who had said it. Nevertheless, she found the vigor in her shaky arms to do as he asked.

With incredible strength, her rescuer scaled the rope and grabbed onto the railing with Dyne on his back. When she was hovering over the deck, she let go and crashed on to it, hitting hard and banging her forehead. For just a moment, she laid there, coughing and fighting the angry urge to cry.

"Are you alright?" came the voice of Lorne. She coughed again and raised her shaky head to look up at him. He was straddling her. "Are you alright?" he repeated, and slapped her face.

Dyne spit a little bit of water from her jaws and nodded. She pushed him off of her, wheezing and struggling to regain her breath. Lorne shook his head in doubt and allowed her to sit up. They were alone on the deck.

"How much have you had to drink tonight, Dyne?" That was the wrong thing to ask, but it wasn't he who deserved the wrath of her anger.

She shot him an enraged but sobered look. Before he could recant his question, she spotted the dagger in his boot. Without so much as a word, she snatched it, stood, and ran as fast as she could down the steps and around to Laraek's cabin, the fury of the storm following.

With a well-placed, bare foot kick, she broke the door from its hinges. Eva was straddling Laraek on the bed but she turned around to see what had caused the commotion. The sounds of their laughter quickly came to an end. The vampiress' smile didn't last long as Dyne ran the span of the cabin and jabbed the blade into the side of her neck.

Laraek struggled his way out from beneath his wife, looking to Dyne with hate-filled eyes. "What are you doing?" he screamed and then pulled the knife from Eva's throat.

The vampiress' body was jolting by the sudden loss of blood, but she wouldn't die from it. Dyne's instinct of murder had always been to kill mortals, not vampires. A dagger to the neck was usually all it took. Eva clamped her hand over the wound and looked to her attacker with vengeful eyes. They were glowing.

"Hold tighter, Eva," Laraek said, pushing his wife's hand securely over the wound. Blood trickled down her nightgown and onto the pretty green bed linen. Dyne had missed. She wanted her dead—wanted her in a hundred pieces for what she just did, but Laraek wasn't going to let that happen as long as he was present.

He rushed and grabbed her around the waist, then hoisted her into the air and started toward the door. "You've caused enough trouble tonight," he yelled as he dodged masts and puddles of water. Dyne kicked and punched him the entire trip across the deck and down the steps to the crew cabins. Several vampires and mortals looked on with curious eyes as their commander carried a screaming, violent woman and plopped her down on the nearest hammock. Jonas emerged from the other side, cradling a large book and quill, obviously dumbfounded by the turmoil.

Before she had time to bounce on her new bed—before she had time to register what was happening, Laraek cuffed her ankles in shackles. He ran a chain through them and around the support beam holding the hammock.

"Now explain yourself!" he screamed. "Why did you attack Eva?" The mortal crewmen who had been soundly napping stirred awake and turned interested ears to the dispute.

"Because she tried to kill me!" Dyne screamed, pulling at the shackles on her feet. Lorne was watching from the deck, a somber look on his face. He shook his head and disappeared from the shadowy alcove.

"Why would Eva try to kill you?" Laraek asked, not seeing the simple logic of it. Was jealousy not a valid enough reason?

"I wouldn't!" came a fabricated cry behind him. The vampire turned around to see his wife, pale-faced with a rag against a still-bleeding wound. She stared at Dyne with weakened eyes. "I don't know why she would attack me . . . *again*! I never did anything to her!"

"You pushed me over the railing, you Sorcean Harlot!"

Laraek shot Eva an inquisitive look. "Is this true?"

"Of course not!" Her angry eyes took false offense. "I've been below deck, looking for more lager in the cargo hold."

He approached Dyne and leaned near her face. It was enough to make her back as far as the shackles would allow. He sniffed twice and then asked, "Just how much have you had to drink tonight?"

Dyne glowered and rolled her eyes at being asked the same thing twice. "One sip of that nasty beer your Crossback had. She *pushed* me!"

"Why would she do that?" he asked and faced his wife. Dyne was through talking. She would deal with these people on her own terms. There was no love for Laraek. Not now. He was as despicable as his bride.

"C'mon," he said, pulling her away when Dyne failed to speak up. "You need to rest now if that wound is going to heal up before we get to Tharg." He turned his attention back to Dyne. "Behave and I'll let you join us when we arrive." With that, the two headed back upstairs and toward Laraek's cabin. Eva let a thin smile slip from her pursed lips as her husband led her away.

Dyne sat back on the hammock and put her hands over her face. All of the remaining onlookers settled back down into their hammocks while the vampires kept at their card games and dice. The thunder sounded through the deck above them. The rhythmic water splashing up top would put her to sleep in no time. She hated everyone and everything right now.

With the vengeance of slaughter beating in her heart, Dyne found herself wanting to kill Kersey Avonwood even more. She had to do it—for herself. Mydian didn't care about her, so why should she care about helping him?

She felt like such a failure. She failed as a soldier—her battalion couldn't take Keswing in the second War. Her relationship with Laraek was a failure. Her ability to keep Hannah safe and out of mortal hands had been a devastating attempt, as well. The slaying of Kersey and the small trickle of self-confidence was important to her, even if it only lasted but a moment. She had to succeed at *something*.

Once Kersey was nothing more than a pile of ash and a valuable heart, Dyne would find the highest cliff and toss herself from it. She would be back with Telsa, in the Underworld, under the watch of a god who couldn't care less.

.12.

Pain

Dark red flashes of light circled around her eyes in a rhythmic pulse that was starting to make her head hurt. She didn't need this hindrance right now so she pushed it away from her mind when the beady eyes in the crow's skull locked onto his heat through the walls. He was sitting on the steps that led up to the highest floor of the house.

A part of her wished that Clive had been here. She regretted so hastily leaving Avery in his company but the anger got the best of her as it often did. When she found out that Daegin had been the loose lips of Mydian's network, she abandoned all reason and responsibility. Her fury and need to seek retaliation was leading her into a trap that she didn't even foresee. In the thousand years of her life, Kersey's immense power and perception had dimmed like a dying lantern.

There was a window opened on the second floor of Daegin's hideaway so she flew inside and transformed back into the hate-filled, miniscule woman. A Mydianite came from the corner with a sword leveled at her head but she didn't even realize how quickly her bare arms tore him apart—just like the men who tried to rape her. A stronger force—*thought* was on her mind and with that taking precedence, Kersey forgot about her actions and the environment around her.

She spotted Daegin's feet scampering up the steps to the highest level so she lifted her dress and followed, not noticing the other Mydianites watching her through the cracks of the floorboards and the walls.

The attic of the safe-house was being used as a storeroom. Coils of rope, crates, and barrels were piled all over the place. There was a strong smell of hay here and the ceiling was leaking just in front of her, splashing rhythmically on a small red book. In the corners were more stacks of boxes and sacks that were probably full of flour or sugar. Daegin was sitting in a chair to the back of the room, next to the window—watching her—*smiling* at her.

The nerve of this cold-hearted bastard, she thought. It had been many years since she enjoyed the prospect of murder. Tonight, she would savor the breaking of his body.

"Well, there it is," he said, pointing to the dampened book on the floor. His voice was antagonizing and audacious. "It's what you've come for, right?"

Kersey took a step forward, never looking to the book. Her dark, foreboding eyes were on him, watching as he casually rocked in his chair. There was a nervous twitch about him and she could see the blood in his face quickening. His heart was beating so fast. Despite the calm demeanor, it was a farce. He was *afraid*.

"I'm not here for the book. I'm here for *you*."

That made the rocking of his chair come to a stop. He sat it on all fours, stood, and drew the small dagger from his boot. Kersey couldn't help but smile. "Well come and get me," he coaxed, obviously trying his best to keep a stern, fearless face.

Something wasn't right. Kersey kept advancing the span of the room but a voice in her heart and mind told her that this was a bad idea. It crept into her ear and told her to turn the other way and go. However, a thousand-year-trained mindset would not let her abandon hatred and walk away from blazing anger.

There were Mydianites around her. They pushed the sacks of flour and the large crates away but none of them came close. Obviously they had seen what she was capable of. She wasn't concerned with anyone but the man who made her abandon her hiding spot—the man who murdered Clive's sister. Her mind and eyes were forward, ready to wipe the smug smile from his face, but that all changed when she reached the book.

She wanted to step by it—to walk around and gather it once Daegin was on the ground in no fewer than a dozen pieces. A single drop of water splashed against her head and it felt like a blistering lump of coal had struck her. It lit her hair on fire and before she could register what had happened, another hit her, this time on the shoulder.

The water seared her flesh and as a small waft of smoke emanated, the drop rolled down her chest and over her breast, scorching her skin with a thin line. She let out a scream—a real howl of pain that she hadn't felt in quite some time. There were many types of wounds in the world—mental, physical, spiritual, and in this case—the holy power of Lyluss.

It was blessed water. The holy elixir of Lady Good spelled doom for any vampire who came into contact with it. Enough of it could literally disintegrate one. This hadn't been the first time she'd had the unfortunate pain of Lyluss' power but this would be the worst of it.

Kersey fell to her knees and out of instinct, attempted to steady herself by putting her hand on the ground. Her open palm touched the small puddle of water that had collected in the dimple of the spell book. There was more smoke—so much that the nauseating smell of her own cooked flesh was beginning to make her sick.

With so much pain and so much disorientation, Kersey didn't hear Daegin's laughter. She didn't hear him barking orders to his servants and she certainly didn't see the hidden ballistae in the corners, both lining up shots toward her. The pain she felt next was greater than any she could remember.

A loud *'whoosh'* came from two separate corners of the room. Kersey recognized it as some sort of projectile weapon and managed to get to her feet, but it was too late. It wasn't the normal pain of a bow or crossbow that she was used to.

Her chest was ripped open as a heavy dart plunged into her. Another struck her through the back. Their four-foot lengths carried through, dragging chains that were murderously thick. The darts slammed into the opposite walls and anchored her in place. It was a miracle that her heart had been missed.

As if the pain could get no worse, the wounds began smoking. The chains were slick and wet and when she naturally tried to pull them out, her fingers started to burn. Even she wouldn't easily be able to break the thick, Lydison steel links. It would be useless to even try since they were doused in holy water.

Kersey's dark, crimson blood ran down her stomach and legs and dripped from her wobbly knees. The weight of the chains was incredible and she found that standing was growing harder and harder by the second. There was still water dripping on her head and neck, but she couldn't move now to get out of the way. She could still smell the singeing of her hair and could hear the tiny hisses of the strands burning.

Just then, she realized something odd. The wound on her chest—the first one caused by the water was still there. It hadn't healed, even though there had been plenty of time for it to happen. Kersey spoke a silent curse and looked to the corners of the room, now noticing the cleverly hidden obelisks. The Lylussian interrogation stones were preventing her from escaping and healing—preventing her from fighting back.

A Mydianite stepped up to her and slammed his fist into the side of her head. The force of it pushed her to the left, against the chains and made a few ribs splinter. A large splatter of blood escaped her cracked lips. She screamed again and the anger—the hatred that had finally went to sleep in the dark recesses of her heart and mind suddenly started to stir.

"Everyone look!" Daegin said to a full room. There had been more Mydianites here than she first suspected. Her eyes were growing dim—her body weak. She tried to fall to her knees but the chains kept her up, suspended in the air by a broken rib cage. She pushed the pain from her mind and tried to concentrate on what was happening around her.

"The great Kersey Avonwood is about to fall!" another man said and then spat in her face.

"Lord Mydian said we were incapable of such a thing," Daegin said, heading toward the left-hand wall. "What would he say now?"

The congregation of Mydianites cheered.

Was this her end? Kersey was closer to death now than she could ever remember. She was in the darkest place, surrounded by the vilest, most twisted people and was about to die and go to the hell that had been reserved for her a thousand years ago. It wasn't supposed to end this way. She was supposed to be acquitted, forgiven, and hopefully, eventually, *redeemed*. Here and now, she realized she wasn't worthy of such a thing.

"I think it is time for Kersey to experience the 'bath of holy reckoning'. What do you say, men?" A chorus of cheers murmured their agreement.

Daegin grabbed a rope from the wall and Kersey followed it up to the ceiling, across a pulley and to a large cask propped between the rafters above her. The rope's end was tied to the handle of the barrel's lid. A steady drip continued to fall from its cracked edge.

She swallowed a heavy lump in her throat as she realized the prospect of what was about to happen. Kersey closed her eyes. With burning hair, flesh and blood running down her body in a strong flow, she mouthed a silent prayer to a god who probably cared little about what happened to her here tonight.

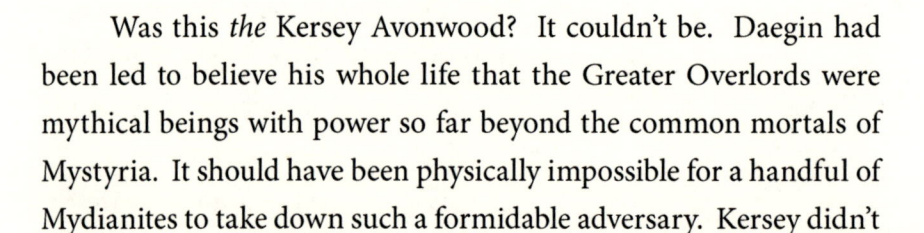

Was this *the* Kersey Avonwood? It couldn't be. Daegin had been led to believe his whole life that the Greater Overlords were mythical beings with power so far beyond the common mortals of Mystyria. It should have been physically impossible for a handful of Mydianites to take down such a formidable adversary. Kersey didn't even get to make a move.

He loved the sight of watching her so weak—so disoriented and at the mercy of mere mortals. Her arrogance and pride were probably hurting worse than her flesh right now. This woman—this vixen had survived for over a millennium and common mages with chains and water had subdued her.

There was blood everywhere. The book was covered in it and Daegin thought for sure she was going to bleed to death before he could pull the curtain and reveal his last, final act for the evening. It was going to be the literal disintegration of Kersey Avonwood.

His fingers were wrapped around the rope and he waited, intentionally until she had a chance to see what it was attached to. The recognition—the *fear* in her eyes as she watched the cask above her was priceless. There would be statues of Daegin in Bloodgate and Keswing because of this night.

The Mydianites would love him because he did a great service for their dark god. The Lylussians would love him because he managed to kill such a prominent vampire.

It was time to make history.

After Kersey had ample enough time to fill her heart and head with the dread of an inevitably painful death, Daegin pulled the rope as hard as he could. Kersey screamed out and clamped her eyes shut, ready to feel the torrent of acidic water rain down on her but it didn't happen.

The rope was still in Daegin's hand, but the handle had been ripped from the barrel. It clanked to the floor next to her and she seemed to realize that a small bit of time had been bought. The lid was separated slightly and caused a steady stream of water to run harmlessly to her side. With the apparent blood-loss taking its toll, her eyes began to flutter.

"Dammit!" he cursed and threw the rope aside. "Kill her!"

One Mydianite stepped up with his dagger drawn and before he could slice across her throat, Kersey reached out with hidden, reserved strength and snapped his neck with one hand. The rest of the men kept their distance after the sight of their twitching comrade on the ground. Daegin reminded himself that even though the obelisks were keeping her powers at bay, she still had her strength and speed.

He grabbed one of the crates and stacked it beside her, then another. Daegin continued to pile them up until he was able to climb them and reach the rafters. It was his intent to use his dagger to pry the rest of the lid from the barrel. There was probably still enough left to kill her and if not, there was certainly enough to weaken her considerably so she could be stabbed to death.

The frantic, hysterical voice calling Daegin's name from downstairs went unheard. He was atop a wobbly stack of crates and had his arm outstretched, dagger in hand, ready to pry the lid off—

—when something slammed into his rickety ladder and knocked it aside. Daegin's dagger skidded across the floor as he landed against the ground, banging his head hard enough to make the room flutter.

When he shook the grogginess away, he saw the large shape of a man come into focus. The Mydianites were headed downstairs, away from Kersey.

"Daegin, stop!" came the annoying voice of his brother. Avery picked the wrong time and the wrong place to make a stand. There was a growing stack of reasons to put an end to his dumbfounded and simple-minded life but the heaviest, lengthiest note was the interference of a job that would cost Daegin his life if he failed.

The dagger that killed Taritta—Daegin and Avery's mother, found its way back into the battlemage's hand. After tonight, the Crane family would be forever changed.

As the night grew darker, an unseasonable cold swept through the empty streets of Tharg. Clive pulled his simple shirt tighter around his body as a chill ran the length of his spine. His hand hovered over his sword's hilt, trying his best to keep it still and silent as he ran at full speed down Market Lane.

Avery was *fast*. So fast in fact, that once they were out of Fyrl's castle, Clive lost sight of him. If not for his constant wail of trepidation over his Miss Red, he might have vanished into the hushed, cold night completely.

Daegin's house was almost a mile from the castle. It was on Glendan Street, a dilapidated, sparsely populated section of the city that was perfectly suited for hiding Mydianites. There was no reason for Fyrl's guards to go here. No one cared about the safety of impoverished dwellers that put little or no taxes into Tharg's coffers.

Clive drew his sword when he saw Avery disappear into a house that sat on the corner. To an observing eye, it was obvious that it had been restored into livable quarters. The windows were only partially boarded up, giving someone enough space to see through. There were new locks on the door, as well as new gutters on the side.

What was going to happen once he was inside? When he was face to face with the one man who killed his sister, would he be able to seek vengeance? It sounded so easy in his mind but would it be just as easy to swing the borrowed sword and take a life? He didn't know. All he did know was that Kersey was in there and probably needed help.

There was little time to react to the attacker that emerged from his left. A Mydianite swung a vase, intent on breaking it against Clive's face but he had been ready. He knew it wasn't going to be as easy as walking in and rescuing his friend.

The vase exploded in a shower of glass against the wall just behind where Clive's head was a moment before. He took the opportunity and pushed the Mydianite back into swinging distance and slashed across his chest. The unarmed mage tried to mouth a spell but the spray of blood he saw was enough to disrupt his concentration. He fell hard against the ground and died.

Avery was somewhere up above, yelling Daegin's name. That was not good. If his brother had hit him just for cavorting with Kersey, then he was surely not going to be any more apologetic after she arrived to kill him. The rest of the ground floor was clear, so upstairs was the only way to go.

At the top of the staircase was yet another Mydianite who hurled a dagger that missed Clive's nose by inches. It was short work to cut him down and move on to find the steps leading to the third and final floor.

Just as he spotted the rickety, weathered stairs that would take him to the attic, a flurry of Mydianites filled it—their swords and spells ready to make sure Clive didn't make it any further.

He ran the entire length of the room, dodging the dripping blood that was seeping through the floorboards above and slashed toward the first warrior coming down the steps. The blade passed through his leg, nearly hacking to the bone. The warrior screamed out, dropped his sword, and tumbled down the rest of the steps. Clive hurriedly ran him through before the other three had a chance to attack.

A short mage with a glowing robe pulled out a wand from beneath the folds and as the tip began to shine, a noise from upstairs broke everyone's concentration. For just a moment, the fight at hand was no longer important to any of them.

It was Kersey. She was screaming *'no'* over and over again. There was so much pain and anguish in each breath. It grew so intense until there weren't even words, but only her screaming voice that steadily rose and shook the walls with her bottled fury. The windows shattered all around them. Every piece of artwork hanging on the walls fell to the floor and Clive spotted several places in the woodwork that split and cracked against the unyielding might of her rage. He couldn't help but drop his sword and cup his hands tightly around his ears.

"Daegin's going to die," one of the Mydianites said to his comrades through clenched teeth. "Mydian's glory isn't worth this." With that, they completely abandoned the fight. They dropped their weapons and ran past Clive as the horrid, dreadful screaming came to a close. He hurriedly scooped up his blade and headed up the last flight of steps.

At first, he thought that Daegin might have won—might have just put an end to the friend he was desperately trying to protect. The last, ear-piercing, glass-shattering wail could have been her dying cry of pain. Despite the horrible, disarrayed condition of her mutilated body, she was still alive. It was the sight of another's death that had set her off. Clive had hoped it wouldn't come to this.

Daegin was against the ground, a look of pure evil—of pure hatred and vengeance in his eyes as he withdrew his dagger from Avery's throat and wiped it on the dead man's slacks. The body was spread across the floor, only a few feet from Kersey. His eyes were bulging from his head, his face a thick grimace of pain. It was the first time Clive had seen him without a smile.

Kersey was sobbing gently now, letting the strength of the thick chains running through her torso hold her weight. There was a constant hiss coming from her wounds as small puffs of smoke steadily rose. Blood—*her* blood was all over the floor and water was dripping just to the right. Nearly all of her hair was gone—burnt from her scalp, revealing several blackened, bald patches. She hazily stared at Clive with weak eyes. It was the same look she gave him the day she was marked for execution. This was Kersey at rope's end with death staring her in the face and no visible option of getting away.

Clive was going to be that option.

Daegin twirled his dagger between his fingers and took notice of Kersey's helper standing next to her, panting heavily and holding out a sword that was growing heavier by the minute. The battlemage chuckled as if the very sight of him was amusing.

"You, a mortal, and helping her?" He pointed with his dagger as he spoke. "Have you no idea what she is?"

"I know exactly what she is and that's *why* I'm helping her." Clive circled around and put himself in front of her. "But I'm here to kill you by my own accord."

"Oh, and why is that?" Daegin continued to twirl his dagger, trying his best to redirect his foe's attention.

"You killed my sister last week."

The battlemage laughed and knelt by his brother. He played with the buttons on his shirt with the tip of his dagger. "Oh, that was your sister, was it? It didn't take much. I just pricked her with a drop of Venxtral. She was dead in seconds." He got back up and pointed to the ceiling and added, "But let me tell you, it was hard work lifting her up high enough to make the noose break her neck."

There was a growing fire inside of Clive. The questions he had asked himself earlier today and tonight were now distant ramblings of a weak-minded and uncertain man. It wasn't a question of whether or not he was going to seek retribution for Nalia's murder. It was now a certainty.

Daegin chuckled as his fingers lit up in a brilliant white light. He recited a three-word spell and unleashed a cold arc of magic that carried fast-moving icicles with it. The jagged, pointy projectiles hummed past Clive and splintered against the far-side wall.

He was about to unleash another wave of magic but Clive leapt through the air and pulled him to the ground by the folds of his robe. Daegin released a fireball that missed its mark and hit the ceiling, igniting the rafters above. As the fire trailed across the roof, the two men rolled on the floor, fighting for the dagger and dodging the falling embers.

Clive pounded his fist into the side of Daegin's head, making him release the blade. Before either could grab it and put it to use, the battlemage touched its hilt with one finger and in a matter of seconds, the entire blade was encased in ice. It was heavy to hold and would be impossible to use, but Clive didn't drop it just yet.

Daegin shielded his face as the block of ice came hammering toward him. It landed solidly against his forearm and yielded the sound of a break. The mage howled in pain as he tried to draw another spell from memory.

Another wave of fire spread from Daegin's fingers. This one hit the west wall and engulfed the woodwork like hay. It was growing increasingly hot. With the ceiling blazing and now the wall, the fight was going to have to come to an end. It was hard not to notice the irony of the situation. After all, this had been the second house fire that Clive had been in today.

Quickly, he crawled toward his sword and just as he reached it, Daegin jumped onto his back and tried to wrestle him away from it. Clive used his head to club the battlemage away and took the opportunity to latch onto the blade. He rolled out of the way of an oncoming firebolt and found his footing.

Daegin released one final blast of energy—a streak of lightning that enveloped Clive's sword but simply fizzled away to harmless sparks before it could do any real damage. With a weakened body came weakened magic. His ability to call upon Mydian's dark power was fleeing.

Abandoning all hope, he turned around and tried to run but Clive grabbed him by the shoulder and held him in place. With a final stab, he thrust the blade into his lower back until the cross-guard rested against his robe. Daegin spit blood as his gargled screams of pain joined the roar of the fire.

"My sister has been avenged," Clive whispered into his ear, using the sword to steer him toward Kersey. He whimpered like a puppy as his eyes locked with the one he didn't get to kill tonight. "But I'm not the only one who deserves the satisfaction of your death." With that, he shoved him off the blade and into the waiting arms of the vengeful vampiress. The sight of her hatred and anger fulfilled was a chilling spectacle.

Her blackened fingers wrapped around his neck and the last of his dying screams turned into a wet gurgle as she sank her teeth into him. Fresh blood ran down her chin as his body started to shake and convulse like a marionette being dragged by the strings. Kersey let his jolting remains drop, her eyes full of retribution and her face full of satisfied lust.

Clive sheathed his sword and stepped up to her, trying his best to figure out a way to reverse the impaling of the chains. They were embedded in the walls on one end, and raveled into the undercarriage of ballistae on the other.

"The obelisks," she breathed, her head lowered. She licked her bloody lips and weakly pointed up. "You have to move them before the fire catches."

Clive followed her shaking finger and saw a large cask of dripping water sitting between the rafters. The fire was steadily burning on both edges of the one support that was holding the barrel in place. He didn't know what the water did, but it obviously wasn't good if Daegin had taken the time to create such a trap.

"Obelisks? What obelisks?" he asked, looking the room over.

Her fingers feebly pointed to the corners of the attic. There were boxes piled up but he saw four, tall totems that were cleverly hidden behind them.

"Get rid of them. Throw them out the window." Her voice was so frail and so jumbled that he had trouble understanding her.

It was an arduous task of dragging the heavy obelisks to the only window since it was on the same side as the fire. Clive didn't understand what their importance was and why Kersey wanted them away from her, but if it helped them to escape the burning inferno, then he didn't care.

After a few minutes, he pushed the last one out. Kersey already looked better. Her face and chest had started to heal. Long strands of gorgeous, black hair sprouted on her head and grew to the length it was before. The burnt flesh on her breast and shoulder seemed to peel away, revealing unmarred skin beneath.

She grabbed the chains and ignored the smoke wafting from them. Clive could smell burnt flesh and could see the pain in her eyes as she kept pulling the links apart with her bare hands. The steel eventually gave way and split down the middle. It was equally as difficult to break the other one, but once they were both severed, she easily pulled them through her entrails and dropped them to the ground in a bloody mess.

"Avery!" she cried, falling to her knees. Clive could see the wounds closing in her torso as she pulled her departed friend close to her. She put her hands on his face and cried, completely lost in the misery that seemed to constantly trap her soul.

"Kers, c'mon," Clive urged, pulling her by the shoulder. "There's nothing we can do for him. We have to get out of here!" He surveyed the room once more, noticing just how much of the ceiling had collapsed. The house wouldn't stand much longer.

"No!" she screamed and pushed him away. Clive found himself nearly ten feet away due to her small bit of grief-induced strength. "There may still be hope!"

She put her fingers to the temples of his head and rocked back and forth—completely ignoring Clive and the raging fire. Kersey was praying.

"Please, Lyluss, Lady Good, hear me. I haven't called upon your power in nearly a thousand years but tonight, I'm in need of your healing." Her voice was thick with sadness—with hopelessness. Fresh tears were running down her face and onto Avery's. "I know that I fell from your good graces long ago but please, spare this man's life. He is a *good* soul."

There were sparks popping from her fingers. They erupted around Avery's temple and joined together in the air above his head until they grew so violent that the very force of it made the dead man's body lurch. Kersey backed up and her sadness suddenly turned around. A bright smile found her face as tears of joy ran down her cheeks. She put her hands over her mouth and Clive wondered if she really did just manage to bring Avery back to life. Did Lyluss still love her enough to grant her the powers of resurrection?

No.

The sparks died down, leaving them alone in the burning, Mydianite safe house. A thick stalk of Gothmirk tulips found its way into the room from the staircase and wrapped around Avery's arms and legs. One snaked across his chest and over his neck and with one quick and violent spasm, he sat up. His milky eyes surveyed the room and with a head that was only hanging by a thread, found Kersey and smiled. The curse of the Gothmirk had claimed him instead of holy resurrection.

"No!" Kersey screamed. "No! This isn't supposed to happen! No!" She slammed her fists into the floorboards so hard that they passed through, sending wood into the air like a mighty explosion. She screamed until it grew into a tantrum that made her stand up and pull the hair from her head. Thick clumps of it came out in her fingers and Clive didn't dare approach. He let her pace around the room, pulling hair, scratching her forearms, and voicing her horrid discontent.

There were vines everywhere—more than he had ever seen at once. They ripped through the walls, through the floor and through the ceiling and tore the house away, piece-by-piece. Her anger flowed through them—her devastation to the house mirrored her devastation to herself.

"I didn't mean to do it!" she howled into the air. "I didn't mean to hurt your servants and churches!" She was screaming regretful pleas to Lyluss concerning events that happened a millennium ago. Lady Good obviously wasn't listening. "Why can't I just be forgiven?"

"Kers, he is gone," Clive pleaded, speaking as gently as he could. By the time her fit had come to and end, she had bloodied herself, Avery, and the floor around them. She completely ignored her friend and stood, then looked the room over.

She grabbed Daegin by the neck and started whispering. His head shot up, hanging by only inches of flesh. He mouthed a few things to her and when she was done, she simply discarded him like a spent rag.

Avery's body slumped over as Kersey pulled the Gothmirk curse from him. A vine found its way into the room and wrapped around his ankles. Another took him by the wrists and together they hoisted him out the window and away from the fire's wrath.

It was just Kersey and Clive, alone in a room that was being pulled apart like a wishbone. The threat of the fire was starting to dwindle as most of the flaming lumber was being taken elsewhere.

Kersey felt horrible and probably looked worse than one of her minions. The pain she felt moments ago was fleeing but the wounds were still etched in her mind. She would be reminded of her mutilated body for a long time. But the physical pain was nothing compared to the horrible wave of mental suffering that erupted the moment Avery took his final breath.

For the first time in Kersey's life, she wanted to intervene—she wanted to make her presence known and step in to save someone she loved. She was hurt, dying and damaged and could only watch as her friend's life came to an end just inches from her. That had been the first sting in a succession of throbbing numbness and torment.

The next sting came in the form of Daegin—the one who betrayed her to Mydian and killed Clive's sister. She couldn't believe all the horrible, nasty things he was responsible for. It pained her so much to see his smiling, arrogant face. Even though he was dead by her hand, his taunting voice and corrupt allegiance to the god she hated and feared would forever be remembered.

The third and final sting wasn't supposed to be painful. It was supposed to be the glorious resurrection of Avery. It was supposed to be her unity with Lyluss. Her power went awry and the true force that she had been cursed with took over. All she was good at now was toying with death. Lyluss had truly abandoned her and that was the greatest sting of all.

All had not been lost, however. Clive, the one friend she had left—the one man she would do everything to protect, managed to save the day. He fought Daegin and his men and overcame. His caring hands ended the gruesome pain that Kersey felt. She was so thankful to have him. She was so *lucky* to have him.

Kersey bent down and scooped up the book, carefully dodging the remaining water. She used a bloodied piece of her dress to wrap it in and once it was bundled, she stood and headed downstairs. Her mind was far off, as it often was.

They didn't get far before a raspy laughter filled the house like a phantom echo. It was everywhere. Kersey froze and Clive bumped into her. That voice was unmistakable. It had been nearly a thousand years since she last heard it, but it was still fresh in her mind. It was vivid enough to scare her. Kersey shoved the book into her friend's hands and headed toward the cellar as fast as she could with Clive tagging behind.

There was a cellar below with a summoning mirror on the far wall. The withered face of Mydian shone from inside. His unmerciful eyes watched her as she descended the stairs and a wide, fangless grin sprouted on his pale, splotched face.

Her body wasn't trembling nearly as much as she would have expected. Mydian was one of the most powerful beings in all of existence and often reminded Kersey of it. His favorite method of making her listen was always to scare—with horrifying promises of what the afterlife would bring.

Ruin was building her courage, as was Clive. She had been on such a downward spiral for so long—cutting, screaming at herself, and letting her trances get the best of her. Only now was she beginning to climb back up the mountain of self-control. If she could face her fear now, there was no telling where her regained valor and motivation would take her.

She thought back to the last time she saw Mydian. It was in Kurtz, only a few years after the curse. It was during Kersey's darkest time—the era where she killed someone just for looking at her. It was a time when she was arrogant—caring far too much for beauty and appearance to cut and scrape her flesh. Her mind, although troubled and angered, was more centered and focused since it hadn't been given a millennium to go insane. She cared little for her reputation or the ones around her. It was Kersey Avonwood against the world.

Mydian found her walking down an alley after a feeding in an upstairs inn room. He presented himself, an avatar with limited strength, speed, and godhood power. It was going to be about the dragon again, she knew.

The god of the Underworld told her to meet Arctis Moonbridge outside of Keswing to help move the remains of Gwenavaughn to a very southern region of South Corscus. Naturally she refused to be an agent of anyone but herself.

Mydian grew angry and swore that she would suffer when she died—that her torment on Mystyria was nothing compared to the hardship she would endure in the Underworld. Still, Kersey was defiant. She attacked him, knowing that his mortal body could only take so much. After the avatar was dead and the god was forced back into the Underworld, she began the long and arduous task of keeping hidden. It took her from city to city, eventually ending her up in the Tharg Penitentiary.

"Kersey, Kersey," the image in the mirror began. "There aren't enough shadows in the world to hide you from me. And do you really believe that praying to Lyluss would make her listen to you? She *hates* you!"

Kersey's balance faltered, his cruel words sending an arrow straight into her heart. Fresh tears were falling down her cheeks and her arms were trembling and drawing up, ready to begin ripping the flesh from each other. Strength, she reminded herself. She knew she was stronger than this.

"And what would you suggest? That I pray to you instead? The great god of the Underworld himself?" Her voice felt so sturdy but she knew it hardly came out that way.

"Now you are seeing reason," he mocked. "Join me Kersey and I promise when you die, it will be a joyous occasion. I have a place picked out just for you." His image faded for a moment and was replaced by a beautiful mansion sitting on a rocky cliff that overlooked the fabled town of Luthewell. There was bright orange smoke wafting from the chimney.

She had seen it before. Had Mydian forgotten of the time he assured that same mansion to Alexa Lighthammer? Kersey had been there. "How many others have you promised that same house?" she asked. "Is that the reward you offer all those ignorant enough to do as you ask? I cannot be bought."

"Really? Then why does it seem that Ruin owns you?" The image of the house quickly faded and was replaced by an increasingly impatient Mydian.

"Because . . ."

"Because you think he can break the chains I have around your soul," Mydian finished for her. "Well let me tell you something, little girl. He cannot help you. I will go before Telsis and have him exiled should he try and keep a soul that is rightfully mine."

"Then Lyluss," she quickly interrupted. "Lyluss will protect me."

Mydian chuckled. "Girl, do you really think Lady Good will have you after you killed so many of her servants? After you destroyed so many of her sacred temples? No, of course not."

Kersey's strength was faltering. She was backing away but Clive stepped up and steadied her. She nervously looked to him but his smile reassured her that he was there. It was warm enough to give her the strength to not back down.

"Do you want to know why you couldn't breathe life into your little friend, Kersey? Want to know why Lyluss doesn't listen to you?"

She was silent. He had just given her plenty of reasons. She killed and destroyed so many of her valued people and structures.

"It's because you lack *compassion*. You lack the compassion for your friends and your enemies. That is what Lyluss teaches and you are not that kind of person. You never have been. You are a vampire. A weak, misguided, and self-destructive *vampire*."

"That's enough," Clive spoke up, approaching the mirror. "You know nothing about this woman."

"Join me, dear Kersey," he asked a final time, completely ignoring Clive's presence. "Together we can use Ruin's plan against him. We will wipe the god of the dead from the annals of history!" She remained quiet and after a moment he stood and pounded his hands on the table in front of him. The mirror shook and rippled in protest of his anger. "You will never make it to the north!" he screamed. "I know of the army Ruin wants you to raise but you will never come close to the Crynsian coast!"

What was he talking about? If Ruin had such a plan, he was yet to tell her.

"So tell me, Kersey," Mydian said, drawing close to the mirror. "Are you willing to endure an eternity of pain in order to help a god who doesn't care anything about you?"

She breathed a heavy sigh. She was tired of listening. Her hand was balled into a fist and she was unsure if she was about to hurt herself. A sudden rush of courage changed that. It was like there were hands on her shoulders, pushing her forward. There was a warm sensation that started at her temples and worked its way down to her toes. Strange, she thought. It was the same feeling she got whenever Lyluss was listening. Kersey found the strength to approach the mirror.

"Please send my best regards to Arctis," was uttered before the fist of an angered, rejuvenated vampire shattered the mirror in a shower of glass.

.13.

Suspicion

There were two hundred and forty-four nails that ran vertically across the ceiling of the crew deck. This had been Dyne's activity for the first hour of captivity. It was unnervingly quiet once the crew settled back down and the silence would have driven her mad. Sleep had trouble finding her with shackles on her ankles and she needed something to occupy her mind. The hammock was itchy and the soggy dress didn't help matters.

Just as she was counting the last of the nails, the ship pulled into mild weather. The rocking hammock calmed and the sound of the rain hammering the deck above her vanished as quickly as it came. Thunder was only a distant memory now of the storm she would never forget.

Now that she had been given time to think and sort her anger, not to mention dry a little, she found herself calming down. Her mind had returned to focus. Dyne's independent nature and useful cold-heartedness were seeping back to the surface and that was a good thing.

Dyne had been a grand captain for Mydian. She strategically planned over a hundred assignments, all in under a year. Her prowess on the battlefield and stealth on her own were matched by no one. If she didn't let a past relationship burden her anymore, she could finish this job and be done *tonight*.

But what about Lorne?

Something else stirred inside her. It was a feeling that she wasn't used to. It was *gratitude*. If not for him, she would have been sitting on the bottom of the Arinbeth right now. It was such a strange emotion and she couldn't remember the last time she said a heartfelt 'thank you'.

He sat only inches away from her, playing cards on a rickety table with Jonas. Both were laughing and enjoying one another's company and paying no mind to the cold, damp, and shackled woman beside them. She rested her head on the hammock and watched them, wondering what it was like to abandon all fear and hatred and just enjoy life for the moment.

Jonas caught Dyne eyeing their game and his mood darkened just a bit. He pulled the hickory pipe from his mouth and said, "I'm really sorry about what happened, miss. You have to look over Eva. She's not the friendliest soul on the ship, if you get me."

"You believe me then?" Dyne flipped over to see him better. "You believe that she tried to kill me?"

"Oh yes," he agreed, taking a drag from his pipe. He brought the bit up to his glass eye and tapped it. "How do you think *this* happened? I pried about a few things and she didn't like it."

"What did you ask? What set her off?" Dyne had to know.

"I wanted a bottle of Old Red and realized she took the last bit of it to Laraek's cabin."

"You mean *her* cabin?" Lorne chimed in, glancing a smile over his shoulder.

Jonas chuckled and shuffled the deck. "I suppose you're right. Anyway, I went after it and no sooner did I get two steps inside, she came out of nowhere and slammed me against the ground. She took her dagger and spooned my eye out and swore she'd kill me if I ever went back in there."

"Why did she get so angry that you wanted your wine back?" Lorne asked.

"It wasn't the wine," Dyne answered for him. "She was angry that he went into her cabin."

Both men looked to one another and nodded, but wasn't interested enough to press it.

"A bottle of Old Red sounds good right about now," Lorne said.

Dyne agreed and licked her lips. It sounded *awfully* good after that bitter swill she had earlier. But the ale she wanted most of all was lingering in the air, and had been the whole night.

"I'd rather have a bit of Lorinstag Ale," she said, looking for the recognition in Jonas' eye.

The hearty laugh told her that he knew exactly what it was. "Good luck with that, miss. You'll not find a bottle of that for a few hundred miles."

"I smell it," she said. That fruity scent was unmistakable.

"I doubt that. There's no Lorinstag anything on this ship. That's some pretty expensive taste there."

Dyne flipped onto her back and looked up. It was lingering *some*where. Could it be in Laraek's cabin? If the map in her head was accurate, his quarters were right above her hammock, which was nestled near the cargo hold steps, at the rear of the ship.

"Do you feel that?" Jonas asked, putting his cards down. He took one last drag of his pipe and looked around. "We've stopped."

There was a loud clanking sound just outside as the anchor was dropped into the water.

Jonas and Lorne scooped up their cards and coins when Laraek and Eva suddenly appeared, neither looking very pleased.

She was wearing chain armor and a beautiful cloak of white fur. There was a silvery bow lassoed around her body and a pair of long, slender blades was strapped to her waist. She looked much better—but not totally healed. Only the Greater Overlords could heal on demand. All the other cursed kindred had to rest no less than a few hours to be rid of such afflictions. Her wound had regenerated to a small cut but the color in her face and the unyielding look in her eyes had returned.

"We're here," Laraek said. He was suited in black armor that sported the ceremonial torch emblem of Mydian. A long black cloak rested on his shoulders. In his hand he twirled the key to Dyne's shackles. He gave her a simple smile and glanced back to his wife.

"Do you have anything you'd like to say to Eva, Dyne?" He waited patiently for her answer.

Before she could speak, Lorne noisily cleared his throat. She thought it was very annoying but also realized it was smart thinking. Dyne was quick to mouth her feelings and in this case, it wasn't a good idea. She wanted to go into town and kill Kersey. It wouldn't happen if she didn't get the shackles off her ankles.

"I'm sorry for accusing you of such nonsense, Eva," Dyne forced. The vampiress' brow furrowed in confusion and it was obvious she was wondering what the captive woman was up to.

"There," Laraek said, and turned to his wife. "Happy?"

Eva glowered as her husband took the shackles from his former lover. It was hard work for Dyne to suppress a smile.

"Get your armor on," Laraek told her. "If you're going ashore, be in the longboat in ten minutes." With that said, he started off.

But she had a plan.

"And just where am I supposed to change into it?" she demanded. Laraek and Eva turned in unison, both sharing a very irritated expression.

"Right here, just like the rest of the crew," he said. The vampires had already started donning their armor and a few even laughed by such a bold question. Eva folded her arms over, a curious look in her squinted eyes.

Dyne snickered. "Here? I think not. I am a woman and I deserve my privacy."

"Then go downstairs to the cargo hold."

"With the caged, screaming mortals? You can't be serious."

"Well it is your choice. If you want to face Kersey in that matted brown dress, be my guest." He started off once more, a trail of vampires following right behind.

"There's only one place that's private on this ship. I want to change in your cabin," she said to his back.

Eva was the first to turn around. The angered, unexpected look on her face told Dyne that she was starting to see where this was headed.

Laraek glanced to his once lover and in a defeated, accepting tone, said, "Fine. This way."

She gathered up her belongings from the chest and snatched the lantern from the card table. The scorned bride only stood there and let them pass. Dyne presented a coy smile and a quick wink before heading up the steps and across the deck behind Laraek.

It was so dark out but she could see lights about a hundred yards off from the *Murder's* starboard side. They were anchored and from this distance, probably invisible to anyone who was enjoying the clear night. She kept the lantern low, behind the railing's cover.

Laraek pushed the door to his cabin open and held his hand out. "I'm sorry but there's no lock. Someone broke it earlier tonight." He rolled his eyes and watched as Eva emerged from the second deck, staring daggers at Dyne.

"That's fine. Just make sure I'm not interrupted."

"Five minutes," he warned.

She nodded and closed the door behind her. Now that it was broken, it remained ajar. *No matter,* she thought. *This shouldn't take long.*

Dyne sat the lantern on the nearest table and quickly stripped the matted dress from her wet body. It only took a moment to don the armor. When she was in the war and sleeping in tents at Keswing's gates, she became very skilled at swiftly suiting up. Lady Good favored night attacks and she was used to getting up, getting dressed, and killing a few archers or battlemages.

Laraek's cabin was quite lush considering the small size of it. His bed, although drenched with the blood of his bride was only wide enough for one person. A thick rope was tied around the headboard, attaching it to the wall. Most of the other furniture was stationary by the same method, due to the rough ocean. There were black curtains covering all the windows—the usual safeguards of vampiric quarters.

In the corner was a cradle. She gasped for breath at the sight of it. A barrage of images flashed before her eyes at the thought of taking Hannah from her birth parents. It had been a crib much like this one—only the walls around it weren't on fire.

Dyne approached it and saw a bundle of blankets inside, as well as a carved horse and a straw doll that looked like a bear. With shaky fingers she reached down and wrapped them around the covers and yanked.

There was nothing there. No babies—only a soft, blue mattress. Dyne's breathing was a little easier, and a few things made sense now. She completely understood why Eva would react so hostilely when her personal things were in the presence of others. Dyne had been the same way. When she stole Hannah away all those years ago, she tucked her beneath her robe—hiding her from the world. There was something private about having a child that wasn't yours, as if they were for your eyes only, she thought. It wouldn't make sense to anyone else—only vampires who longed for children of their own. Eva's secret was suddenly clear, but Laraek's was still a mystery, however her sudden intrigue and dismay kept her still and unaware and she completely ignored the knock at the door.

Hands suddenly grabbed her collar and pulled her back out onto deck. Laraek shook his head with disapproval and ushered her on.

Eva made a sharp grimace and peered inside to view her crib. Her mouth opened in disgruntled anger when she saw the shuffled blankets. Dyne smiled and passed her, tossing the matted dress overboard.

Lorne and Jonas were already seated inside the longboat, an anxious look on both their faces. A group of mortal crewmen stood by, waiting for her to hop inside so they could lower them into the dark waters below. She didn't want to keep them waiting—she wanted to go kill Kersey. Giving one last check to her gear, she hurried and jumped in.

"We're meeting at a safe-house," Laraek said, handing Dyne the lantern. "Daegin Crane's place. It's a few hundred yards past the bay.

Jonas'll show you where it is." She remembered that name. He was the one Mydian talked to back in the Underworld.

There were vampires everywhere. For the first time since boarding, Dyne witnessed the amassed collection of unholy crewmen. They stood behind their commander, suited up in Mydianite steel and ready to do battle with a Greater Overlord, despite being short six ships worth of men.

"Are we to all share one longboat?" Dyne asked, but quickly realized it was a foolish question.

Laraek, as well as Eva and the brigade of vampires huddling around, leaped from the *Murder's* railing. Before they started the downward fall toward the water, each sprouted wings and transformed into a cawing, black crow that swiftly headed toward the lighted port of Tharg. How appropriate, Dyne thought when she suddenly realized the irony. The *Murder's* crew actually became a murder of crows.

A pair of mortal crewmen began lowering the longboat into the water. Dyne held her breath and watched them evenly spin the winches. Her heart was already racing and she hoped they wouldn't drop the boat too fast. It was still several feet to the surface. The davit arms wobbled gently by the weight of the three passengers but the sudden impact into the water quickly calmed her. Jonas unhooked the davit ropes before helping Lorne push off the *Murder*. Together, they began rowing toward Tharg.

It was in this very town, only a few miles north when she first and last saw Kersey Avonwood. Dyne had pulled her minions away from Brookstone and headed west. It was the same week that Tranas Anvaar killed Telsa. There was so much grief but her quest to find the heart of a Greater Overlord had grown so strong that she didn't even notice her sister's absence until two days later.

Through letters and contacts, Kersey's location had been pinpointed to an abandoned house in Tharg with a history of discarded, blood-drained corpses. For the first time, Dyne was in the right place at the right time.

Unfortunately, the Mydianites were after Kersey, as well. There was a great bounty on her head—one that would sever any alliance. Dyne found the house and watched from across the river as the assassins fought her. In the glinting moonlight, she spotted Kersey through the windows, desperately fighting for her life—or so she thought. There was a bright flash of light and she was happy in the knowledge that she would walk right in and claim the heart. Inside the room was a dead, elderly woman with her throat slashed. Standing over her were three Gothmirks and a small pile of white ash. It only took Dyne a few seconds to hack them to pieces and begin sifting through the supposed remains.

The heart was nowhere to be found.

She concluded that there had to be a remaining assassin who ran off with it. This was nothing more than another dead end because Kersey had been far too cunning and had planned her false death for weeks. A small magical orb easily created a flash and the scatter of ash. The whole world gave up looking for her that night. Even Dyne. She returned to her army and an infant Hannah and moved on to the next heart. Only a week later she found the answers that took her to the Birchlock Estate and ultimately, to her death.

The years following Kersey's supposed demise were what tore the strings holding Ruin and Mydian's relationship apart. The dark god, thinking she had died, knew her soul had to come to him. Since it didn't, the only logical explanation was that Ruin had held onto it—had *hidden* it, just as he had Dyne's. Mydian had been in the dark, just like the rest of the world and now that Kersey had emerged from the shadows of Mystyria, everyone wanted her—in one way or another

The three in the longboat didn't have to go far before the ship disappeared against the night sea. It was so quiet out. Dyne knew that something was amiss. The trouble that Mydian said Kersey would start with Ruin's help had no doubt already begun. A dead silence didn't hang on a city as large as Tharg unless something was wrong.

"Jonas, should Daegin already have the book? After all, it is supposed to arrive tonight." Her voice was no more than a whisper.

He leaned in close with each upstroke of the oars. "I'm sure he does, miss. Probably why the commander was so hasty to head on over."

Dyne rested her chin on the palms of her hands and thought about that. Lorne gave her a look that she'd seen many times. It was the same stare when he knew she had something on her mind—that something wasn't adding up from her point of view.

"What do you think?" he asked her.

"I think Laraek plans to steal the book for himself."

"Commander? You think he's trying to steal something as trivial as the spell book from Mydian?" Jonas questioned.

She explained all the things that he and Eva had told her a few hours ago and why she'd arrived at the conclusion that he was a betrayer. Mydian's reason for sending two souls back to Mystyria was a little more obvious now.

"You can't trust anyone these days," Jonas said. "Money is heavier than loyalty in days of teetering peace."

"You aren't like the rest of them, are you?" Dyne asked.

"Like the commander and his bride, you mean? No, I keep quiet, fix the holes in the ship and don't ask questions. If they want to steal gold and crave power, well . . . I can go a deck below." She liked that he didn't share Laraek's views, or Mydian's for that matter. He certainly didn't like Eva and that made him a friend to her.

Both Lorne and Dyne were able to find amusement in his simple take on life. It would probably be quite different if he had lived through the eyes of the two sitting next to him.

"What will you do if Laraek turns out to actually be a traitor?" Dyne asked Jonas.

"What will *you* do?" he returned.

She gave Lorne an uncomfortable look that was followed by a long silence.

The longboat pulled alongside the dock and Lorne quickly hopped out and tethered it to the post. Jonas joined him and together they lifted Dyne by the arms out of the boat and onto the deck. It felt *so* good to be on solid ground again. She wanted to smile so badly but knew it would make her look foolish and she didn't feel like dealing with Lorne's snide remarks.

There was only one other ship docked at the pier. It wasn't even big enough to be classified as a *ship*. Although it was much larger than their longboat and had a second deck, next to the *Murder* it would probably look like a raft. A single mast stood in the center and it probably carried a crew of only twenty men.

The three Mydianites headed up the road from the pier, letting Jonas take the lead. He directed them past a Tessian statue and through a market that looked open, only there were no people about. Fresh fruit, baskets, blankets, wooden toys, and a few weapons had been abandoned. Kersey was definitely making her presence known.

"Look at the windows," Lorne whispered.

She glanced toward a three-story house to the east and saw faces glued to every opening. They were watching them in bewilderment—in awe as they calmly walked through the streets. Had Kersey and her minions scared this town so badly?

"Daegin's safe-house is just down the road here, toward the . . . *smoke.*" Jonas' voice trailed off.

The trio held their weapons still as they picked up the pace and jogged down the dilapidated cobblestone street and onto a road that a low-hanging sign called *'Glendan'*. The look on Jonas' face told Dyne that they were at the right address.

A smoking, shattered skeleton of a house was all that remained of Daegin's hideaway. The roof and the walls seemed to have been completely ripped away, just like a little girl's doll house. The innards of the once beautiful manor were scorched, broken, and bloodied.

"Daegin!" Jonas cried, stepping into the ruined foyer. Lorne and Dyne followed, dancing past broken glass and charred furniture. "Split up," he told them. "See if you can find *anyone*. This is Kersey's doing. If there are no bodies, then she took them *with* her."

Lorne cuffed his hand to his face and drew his sword. He took a deep breath and headed up the steps to the second floor.

Most of the ground level was littered with bookshelves. Around the side of the mangled foyer was a two-story library without a roof. A thin, wooden catwalk encircled the room. A small fire burned in the middle and someone was tossing off books from the second level. Dyne stepped around and saw Laraek on a ladder, inspecting books, but only for a moment. He paused long enough to read their covers and then threw them to the ground below.

"What are you searching for?" she asked him. He started at her voice and dropped a handful of dusty, assorted manuscripts.

"Nothing," he said, regaining his composure. "What have you found?"

"We just arrived," Dyne said with a glare.

"Then search the cellar," he said flatly. "I've got this covered."

She sneered and walked off, scanning the house for the stairs. The pungent smell of Bristleweed garnered her attention and helped her find the entrance to the cellar. There were no others on the ground floor—not Jonas, Eva, or Lorne. Even the swarm of vampires that made up Laraek's crew was nowhere to be found.

The cellar had been converted into an alchemy lab. There were beakers, flasks and containers of all sorts of colored liquids and powders but the one thing that drew her attention was the shattered remains of a mirror spread across the floor to the rear.

Normally a broken mirror wouldn't gain even a second look from her—she'd shattered so many in her days as a vampire—but this one was *quite* different. This one had facial features.

She spotted an eye in one shard and then another in a shard a few feet away. There was a mouth in one and a couple of them together made up a misshaped nose. Together, the dozen or so pieces created an odd-shaped and distorted face.

"It's good to see you again, Emba," came the voice of the dark god from the mouth shard. His lips moved and seemed to zoom in and out with each word. She could see the piece vibrating on the ground as he spoke.

"My lord," was all she could say.

"I'm sure you realize now why I sent you." His voice was low and steady in the expansive room. She knew exactly the reason. It had taken her only a few hours in her former lover's company to figure it out.

"You want me to kill Laraek, don't you?"

"I want you to find out who he's *working* for," Mydian corrected. "He'll be dealt with when he dies."

"You used me," Dyne said emotionlessly.

"I had no choice. You were the only one who could slip through his defenses. Every time I tried to send someone else, they were either killed or led astray and the *Phantom Seven* remained hidden. The Lylussians were the only ones to ever get so close to him."

"So you thought I'd just climb aboard, make love to my former fiancé, learn his secrets, and then just murder him?"

"Would that be so hard?" he asked. It sounded like a joke, but both knew it wasn't.

"What has Laraek gotten himself into?"

"I'm not so sure. He certainly isn't working for Lyluss. She's chasing him with a vigilance that makes me question how badly he's scorned her. And if she is allied with Ruin, then he has to be serving someone else. This is what I need you to find out."

Mydian waited for Dyne to say something, but the words would not come. She was too busy contemplating what he said. Just when did Laraek become such a bad person?

"Kersey killed Daegin and made off with the book," the dark lord said. "You have another job now. Get that book back."

"Let me see if I understand this correctly," Dyne said, feeling the tremendous weight of work piling on her. "You want me to kill Kersey, steal the book, *and* spy on Laraek?"

Mydian smiled. "Such is the price you pay for an extravagant, luxurious afterlife."

"This is a little much for one person to do, don't you think?"

"I'm sorry but it must be done. Our very lives are on the line now."

Our lives? Did she just hear Mydian correctly? Laraek implied that Kersey was afraid of *him*. What was it that she was so capable of doing that would turn the tables on a god?

"And what if she escapes?"

The mouth zoomed in so that she only saw his top row of teeth. "She will raise an army that will wash this world in death. Blood will rain from the heavens, the Underworld, and the sea if she gets to Crynsia."

Crynsia? That was half a world away. She would have to sail past two continents to get there. Dyne still wasn't following but realized she was wasting far too much time here.

"Then I'll go after her, my lord. She'll never leave Tharg," Dyne reluctantly said and drew her sword. Once more, she was giving in to a god who didn't care about her.

"Make sure that she doesn't, dear Emba. But most of all learn what Laraek is up to." His voice and the image of the mouth faded, leaving her with the cold reflection of her solemn eyes. She tossed the shard aside, stood, and—

—ran directly into Laraek's chest.

"Who were you talking to?" he asked. Eva was standing behind him, staring at her from beneath the cover of her fur hood.

"No one," Dyne lied and walked past.

"Here," he said, and then tossed something that glinted against the glow of the fire. "Found it lying upstairs and thought you could use it." Dyne snatched it from midair and examined it between her fingers. She held the telescope up to her eye and a sudden burst of illumination enveloped her vision. A Nighteye would certainly come in handy.

"Did you find the book?" she asked him but already knew the answer.

"No, it isn't here."

"Then we better start looking for Kersey. With the condition of this place, I'm guessing she came in and took it right out of Daegin's hands." Her words were so fabricated but there was no simpler way to say it without revealing the little talk she had just had with Mydian.

"While you were playing with glass, I found her," Eva sneered.

"She's only a little way from here, but you've got to see something first," Laraek said and followed the ladies out of the cellar. Up top, they rejoined Lorne and Jonas, as well as the plethora of vampiric Mydianites. The ashen feathers from the transformation were still falling from their shoulders.

Laraek led his men out of the ruined house and down the narrow street, not paying any mind to the lack of chaos, the lack of law, and the lack of citizenship. Tharg, in just a few nights, had become a ghost town.

There was a very distinct smell of soil. The loamy odor lingered on the air and when the vampires stopped a few hundred feet up the road, Dyne saw why.

"Have you ever seen anything so strange?" Laraek asked her, pointing up ahead.

"By the gods, what's happening?" Lorne questioned, eyeing the rows of undead standing in the streets.

There were thousands of them. Each facing north, the same way that Laraek pointed Kersey to be. Every dead man, woman, child, cow, horse, or cat was as still and silent as a statue, head bowed. They were oblivious to the surrounding vampires and didn't raise one finger to fight. Dyne looked as far as the darkness and road would allow and could already tell that the line of undead went on for several hundred feet.

"Let's cut them down then!" Lorne said and pulled the halberd from his back.

"No!" Dyne quickly yelled and stepped in front. She pushed her companion aside and added, "They will defend each other should you attack. I've seen them before." That was enough to convince him to put his weapon away.

Kersey left a pack of Gothmirks behind when she was supposedly killed. They were ordered to stand their ground—only attack *when* attacked. Dyne hadn't realized that at the time and when she struck the first unmoving and unresponsive undead, the rest started in and helped their fallen kin.

"Then our first strike needs to be our last," Laraek suggested, eyeing the path up to Kersey.

.14.

Amongst A Million Souls

It never ceased to amaze Kersey by the way one's mind and heart worked. In conjunction, the two could bury you in the deepest grave of fear and depression and in the blink of an eye, could raise you up to the highest mountain of courage.

There was a fissure running straight down the middle of her soul. Part of it was keeping her scared—keeping her fearful and challenged when it came to helping Ruin in his quest to drive Mydian back into the recesses of the Underworld. The other part made her want to stand in the light and let the world—let Lyluss and all the other gods see that she was renewed. She was a different creature now, a thousand years after the killing, mutilating, and vicious carnage that shaped her.

Avery's body was lying on the ground in front of her, a few hundred yards from the house where he took his final breath. Kersey had closed his eyes and let the vines and Gothmirks carry him back to a spot that was sacred to him—that was sacred to *her*. It was the apple orchard where they first met.

She had cycled through ever feeling she had at her disposal tonight. Fear, pain, hatred, depression, and finally content. There was no happiness. There was only the brief joy of being comfortable.

This was her friend she was staring at. After so many years of killing innocents, some enemies, some not, Kersey recognized a dead body as a *friend*. In the last thousand years, only a handful of people could claim that title.

The other was standing next to her, not saying a word and letting her do what she needed to do in order to function. Clive watched the Gothmirks place Avery on the ground and then back away so the vines could slither into the orchard and do their work.

A thick stalk broke through the ground and wrapped tightly around a rather large apple tree that dominated the center of the grove. The towering giant groaned and creaked as the incredible pressure of the vines began to tug. With little effort, the roots gave way and the entire tree ripped from the ground, raining dirt on Clive, Kersey, and the horde of undead.

"I planted this tree, fifteen years ago," she said, just above a murmur. "I think it sprouted up quite nicely."

The vines discarded it just outside the grove. There was a massive hole in the ground and several tendrils were spilling into it.

A jumbled throng of them rose from its depths, wrapped tightly around a chest that was several feet long. The green, dripping tendrils deposited it on the ground next to Avery's body and unraveled, revealing the weathered, dented metal of a locked box that Kersey had planted there fifteen years ago, the same day she decided to hide in the Pen.

"I have to know something before I bury him," she stated, and then dropped to her knees before her slain friend. "I only hope I can put my troubled heart to rest."

"Are you going to try and resurrect him again, Kers? I don't think this is such a good idea. I mean, last time—"

"I don't plan on raising him," she blurted. "I just want to know where his soul went." She grabbed his bloodied shirt and pulled herself closer. "I need the satisfaction of knowing Mydian didn't get him."

Whenever Kersey created a Gothmirk, she used the small fraction of the soul that lingered between Mystyria and the heavens. That part was easy for her to control. It was the small button that she used to make them walk, kill, and protect. She needed to speak with the other part—the part that went to one of the god's realms the moment after it was sorted in Ruin's domain.

Help me, she spoke to her minions through her muddled thoughts. She was talking to their souls—the souls that were busy walking the streets of the Underworld, or enjoying the beach of Davertere Utopia, or wherever else in the heavenly cosmos they were. *I need you to help me find this man.*

She closed her eyes, ignoring the sight of her Gothmirks as they bowed their heads, each locked in a trance that looked within themselves. They were busy searching the heavens, desperately trying to find her lost friend's soul.

Even she looked—the places that she was allowed, anyway. She could see the shadows of Nubetas, Drak's world. The evil places of the heavens were easy for her to search but that power was useless for anything else. All she could see was the dark, lingering silhouette of spirits. Avery was amongst a million souls.

Miss Red? a voice suddenly purred into her head. She couldn't help but smile and drop a few tears onto his bloodied shirt.

"Avery!" she said aloud. *Avery.*

Why, hello Miss Red! I can hear you, but I can't see you. Is that okay? He sounded good—very distant, but good. She couldn't see where he was but he had managed to find *her*.

That's fine, Avery. Where are you?

For a long moment, he was silent and she grew fearful that the connection had been lost—that Avery's soul had wandered off, never to be heard again, but once he obviously surveyed his surroundings, he came back with, *It's so pretty here, Miss Red! I wish you could see it! It's warm and bright and the sky is so blue! There's a big, white castle that goes up into the clouds!*

Those words almost made her collapse on top of his corpse. She buried her face against his bloodied shirt and took a deep breath. She felt so *relieved*. Avery was in a realm known as the Whitewind Havens. The castle he saw was called Whitewind Towers. This was the realm of rule of Lyluss herself. Lady Good had accepted him into her home.

Avery, that is wonderful! You are in Lyluss' realm. After Kersey had given him the Lylussian necklace and coaxed him to go to her church a few nights, Lady Good had undoubtedly taken notice and decided to call him her own. His soul would be taken care of. He was eternally separated from Mydian and a brother who abused him. In the Whitewind Havens, Avery would find others that would love and accept him for who he was. It was just too bad that Kersey would never see him. Whitewind Havens was the one place in the universe she was forbidden.

Miss Red, I miss you!

I miss you too, Avery. Her voice faltered for just a moment and then she told him the words that she didn't believe herself, no matter how much she wanted to. *We will see each other again one day.*

I have to go Miss Red! I just met a girl and a cat who want to play with me!

Okay, Avery. Her face was streaked with tears and she felt Clive's hands on her back. It must have looked bizarre to him—a woman kneeling over a corpse, saying nothing and sobbing like a baby. *I will miss you, friend,* she managed to Avery's fading voice and presence.

I'll miss you too, Miss Red! With that, his voice descended beyond her grasp. He would never be heard on Mystyria again because she wouldn't allow it. She was going to bury him and never again call upon his spirit. Avery's afterlife was just beginning and she hoped it was everything she had always wanted for herself.

"Everything okay?" Clive asked, putting a steady hand to her shoulder.

She took it in her own and nodded. "It is now."

Vines wrapped around her departed friend's ankles and forearms and lifted him off the ground and into the hole. They began to scoop the dirt on top of him, leveling the soil until there was no evidence of a tree ever being there. Kersey muttered a short, Lylussian prayer whose words stung her throat with each syllable.

"What's in there?" Clive asked, kicking the aged chest on the ground.

"My last possessions before I went to the Pen." She tore the lock from it, then flipped open the lid. Her nimble fingers began rummaging through the various items of intrinsic and sentimental value.

There was a black pouch that she wrapped across her bloodied dress and secured around her waist. She dumped another bag of gems and coins into it, along with the spell book of Aneesa. There were two daggers, which she slipped over her ankles and attached to her shins, beneath the dress.

Most of the chest's contents were letters and papers that she used to travel across Mystyria. There were fake passes, forged trade documents, and enough fabricated identities to keep her hidden. She didn't need any of it once she came to Tharg. Up until Mydian's intervention, she had no plans of leaving. There was one item of much interest—the reason she exhumed the chest in the first place.

Clive's mouth dropped in awe as she unwrapped the beautiful lance from its silk covering. It was set in sapphires and rubies and was still as sharp as it had been a millennium ago. The dark, crimson blood of Gwenavaughn still stained its terrifying point. Kersey's fingers were shaking at the very sight of it, and just as she had feared, it prompted yet another unwanted and uncontrollable flashback.

The wobbly hands that were having trouble holding the heavy weapon quickly steadied. For the first time in her recent flashbacks, the fantasy world of her mind was just as glum—just as dark as the real world.

A muddy brown and weathered stone replaced Clive, as well as the horde of undead and the grove of apple trees. There was blood everywhere—blood and the bodies of the Mydianites who had been lingering by the beast—the same ones who had been nursing and protecting it—protecting *her.*

A blue fire sprouted in the center of the camp they had created around her belly. The flashback brought back the smell—the nauseating stench of her carcass that they'd grown accustomed to after weeks in trapped isolation.

Kersey was sitting, desperately trying to clean the blood of Gwenavaughn from her treasured lance. It wouldn't come off—it *couldn't* come off. She tried so hard and for so long until it grew into an obsession that consumed her. It kept her busy and was better than talking to the other nine who she had learned to loathe and hate with every fiber in her being.

No one said a word. Each of the doomed dragon slayers—Lyluss' prized warriors, had grown apart and turned bitter and somewhat hostile toward one another. Back then, they would have all agreed it was the lack of separation and the small confines by which they had been forced to live, but now, with hindsight staring them in the face it was clear to see that it was the *blood*.

Kersey's stomach was twisted in knots by the sight of what sat in her lap—a thousand years ago in a cave just outside of Keswing. It was a makeshift bowl of dragon meat and a helmet full of blood. This was what had kept them sustained for so many weeks but the price wasn't worth it.

"I think if we could split her claws, we could fashion some *real* mining tools," came a suggestion from Evan Stormwood.

"We tried that already, don't you remember, Evan?" came the sarcastic remark of Alexa Lighthammer. "We don't have anything strong enough to break them." She settled back against the rock, beside her brother, Rowan, who looked to Evan with an equal disappointment.

"Well, I'm going back to my tunnel. I'll not pass any more weeks in this dreaded tomb." This bold statement came from Silas Thornhook.

"No, instead you'll be spending it in the Underworld," Arctis Moonbridge said matter-of-factly. "You're digging straight down, Silas, I assure you that the surface is the other way."

"Well at least I'm digging *somewhere!*" the small man busted out. "You have done nothing but abandon hope and eat and drink more than your share of our ration!" He pointed to the dead dragon lying with its gut exposed right next to the camp.

Arctis had been a good man. Kersey had known him for several years but the blood had taken its toll on him, just as it had everyone else. What happened that day was just an example of how their minds had deteriorated over the past few weeks. He only did what the rest of them were thinking.

With a quick flick of his wrist, Arctis spun his halberd and planted it into the side of Silas' neck. The wiry man dropped to the ground, twitching and convulsing as his blood gushed across the cavern floor. Kersey watched his horrid hate-filled eyes against the dancing blue flame.

Not one of the slayers stood to help, nor did they raise a hand to Arctis. Valen Ironwall watched the ground while Ceddy Jerel and Theron Nellander continued to stuff their faces with the reddish-orange meat of Gwenavaughn. They were all evil and only cared for themselves. Kersey was no exception. Better Silas than me, she had thought.

Her mind back in the apple grove was crying and she knew why it had selected this particular flashback. It was on this day that she did something remarkable, for the last time.

For some reason, Kersey thought of the war, her family, and her friends and remembered what it was like to be revered for her faith. She hadn't called upon Lyluss' power since their entrapment and she suddenly found herself wanting to try it. Little did she know that her power to draw Lady Good's blessing was at an end and that faithful day was to be the last time Lyluss would allow her to summon souls from beyond.

Kersey put her hands on Silas' temples and after a brief spectacle of blue lightning, he was alive—his wounds mended and his eyes afire with a renewed glow. Arctis sneered and grabbed a handful of Gwenavaughn's meat from between her ribs.

Brin watched Kersey with cold eyes from across the campfire. She was smiling—happy in the knowledge that her power was still as great and worthy of such appraisal. He was the least bit impressed. It was so different than when she first met him. At one time, he envied and admired her.

"Why would you dare call upon Lyluss now? Here?" he asked, waving his hand around the cavern. Silas was still gasping for air but had managed to get to his feet and head off toward the tunnel he'd been digging in for the past two weeks with his sword and dagger.

"Because she will hear me. She will save us." Kersey believed those words so much. The others in the room looked at her like a common beggar from the streets of Keswing.

"I never realized what a stupid little girl you are." Brin stood and walked through the harmless fire and kneeled next to her.

"Why? Because I still have faith that our god has not forgotten us?" she managed, her voice faltering just a little. Her agitation had already grown as much as the rest of the doomed slayers.

"No, because you have faith in a god that has *abandoned* us. We are alone here, Kersey. I can't believe how ignorant you can be."

"But you love me," she pleaded. She wanted to believe it with all her heart but she knew better, even then.

"I *hate* you," he cursed. "Just like all the others in this room hate you." He reached out and jerked the necklace he'd given her from around her throat. She yelped a quick scream, more out of surprise than shock and sadness.

"You don't mean that!" she sobbed through angry tears, suddenly feeling the first effects of her separation from Lyluss. Maybe he was right. Maybe they were all right.

Brin knelt down and put his hands on the sides of her head and gave her a solemn, sympathetic look that eased her mind. She reached up and felt his warm fingers and started to close her eyes—feeling that his anger and misguided religious stance was passing, but it came flooding back in a way she would have never though possible for such a gentle man.

His hold on her temples tightened and in one quick, thought-shattering motion, slammed his own head into hers, throwing her back against the dark stone. She was more surprised than hurt and couldn't help but to shield her eyes and cry in her lap. The sounds of his retreating footsteps echoed in the expansive cavern.

"You'd better call upon your goddess," he chided. "Ask her to heal your wounds." Blood was seeping into her eyes from a gash across her forehead as the laughter of the others drilled into her mind.

That was the day that Kersey lost her faith in Lyluss. It wasn't the point in her life that made her evil, but it had been the first of many stepping-stones that would lead her down into the depravity of the selfish life she would come to love and adore. Brin had hurt her more than anyone possibly could but the injury to her face, pride, and faith weren't the last and certainly weren't the most brutal. Those would come just a week later.

Most of the time the flashbacks sorted themselves out. Kersey's mind would process the past events and once they made her relive the things she never wanted to see again, they faded and brought the real Mystyria back into focus. This time, she was violently shoved from those dreadful images and forced back into reality by sudden pain and shouting.

Clive was vigorously shaking her arms and pointing behind her. Kersey didn't hear a word of it, nor did she turn around. Bloody arrow tips were jutting from her chest and abdomen. There was so much movement around her—and so much light. Radiant flashes of white ignited the dark apple grove like a thunderstorm without the rain.

Frustrated by her slow response, Clive grabbed her by the shoulders and spun her around, forcing her to face the group of people standing at the summit's overlook of the orchard, just off of Glendan Street where she'd killed Daegin.

There were but a few mortals in a mix of several vampires. Most of them she'd never seen before in her life, but one stood out. She carried Adella Bloodhoof's sword—that green hilted blade was unmistakable. This one had been there when Kersey planned her own false death. From memory this woman was a vampire but the person today was breathing. Clearly a Mydianite, but why had she been returned to Mystyria? Kersey could sense her aura—could feel the things that motivated her and the things that pained her. She did not want to be here.

A sharp pain resonated throughout Kersey's torso as Clive plucked out the arrows. There was another woman at the summit, a vampire, lining up another shot, but Kersey was ready this time.

The arrow left the string and hissed with fury toward her healing chest. A vine sprouted from the ground and snatched it from the air. The vampiress looked discouraged, but drew another arrow from her quiver, nonetheless. Kersey started up the street, just after Clive pulled the last bolt through her back. The huddled group at the summit shifted nervously.

There were two women—the vampiress raining arrows and the mortal carrying Adella's sword. There were also three men—one vampire and two mortals who were armed and engaged with her minions. All of them took notice as Kersey strode toward them, her Gothmirks parting so she could slip past.

A murder of crows dropped from the sky and landed on the path in front of her, quickly changing into a torrent of vampires, their feathers falling off like dust. Kersey twirled her lance once and held it in front. She could see the fire of recognition ignite in their eyes. They knew who she was and knew what she had done with that weapon in the past. She squeezed its handle and a tingle of reassurance slithered up her spine. It was all coming back to her.

She took advantage of their momentarily enthrallment and plunged her lance into the nearest vampire's torso. It was a perfect hit and his body turned to white ash on impact. Two others darted toward her and she jabbed the lance into the ground and used its leverage to swing around and catch one of them with the tip of her boot. He toppled to the path and she drove his face into the cobblestones with her heel. A well-placed thrust was all it took to turn him to dust. Kersey sank as he magically disappeared beneath her.

The second approached, attempting to catch her off guard when the cloud of ash filled the air around them but her perception was better than his would ever be. She held her lance out at arm's length and let him do the killing for her. His twisted, pain-filled eyes screamed out at her as she hoisted him through the air and into a waiting fray of Gothmirks that tore him to shreds.

Kersey twirled her lance once more and pried a vampire who was about to feed from Clive. She separated the two by a few inches and her friend took the advantage to behead the creature and rend its heart. He smiled his thanks to her and moved on to help the undead create more flashes of light.

The vampires on the street were gone. They saw what happened when they went up against an Overlord. Only the leaders of the grunts—the throng of mortals and immortals dared to stay at the summit, waiting for her to finish the span of the road.

.15.

Alliance

It was amazing to watch so many Gothmirks in action. There were waves of them and as soon as Eva took a faulty shot at Kersey, they sprang from their prayer-like trance and started attacking. Dyne couldn't even fight at first—she was too busy marveling at their dead faces and vine-encased bodies to make a move.

They didn't fight like the living, she noticed. A human soldier was concerned with his or her own well-being and fought in, as she would call it, a 'parry-thrust, parry-slash' style. The Gothmirks didn't care about getting hurt. They didn't worry about losing a limb or getting fed upon. All they cared about was attacking until they were physically unable to do so.

Kersey had been kneeling in the middle of an apple grove, fixed upon a lance that looked like the one Dyne had seen at her side in a portrait. There was a mortal man standing nearby—watching her with a calm and silent expression that made it obvious the two were companions. It was all such an odd thing to see and comprehend—a thousand year old vampire staring vigilantly at her lance while a mortal and a legion of Gothmirk undead waited patiently.

Then the chaos exploded.

Eva had grown too impatient—too worried that the easy kill would come and pass before she could take her shot. She didn't even hit the right mark, Dyne cursed beneath her breath. A lucky arrow to the heart is all it would have taken and Kersey would have been ash before she realized something was wrong.

The vines started ripping through the ground and tearing the grove apart. All of the large apple trees had been viciously uprooted and thrown aside. She looked like a vengeful squid batting prey around a feeding tank. It was her subconscious. After all, it had happened to Dyne too when she was a vampire and thought on bad things.

Lorne stepped in front, heaving his massive halberd toward a pair of charging, undead oxen—their broken horns aimed right at his body. Laraek and Eva both drew swords and started hacking away at anything draped in the sickly smelling vinery. Even Jonas pulled out a pair of daggers and was clearing the road of the Overlord's minions.

But they all kept watchful as Kersey approached.

She looked harmless, delicate even. Dyne was at least a foot taller and had twice the physical definition. If Kersey had been a mortal, it would have been over before it had begun. Unfortunately, she was far from a mortal and was proving just how much power that little frame and quaint body could harness.

She dispatched a few of Laraek's crew with simple flourishes of her lance. Dyne had never seen such quick, effortless killing. The vampires started backing up or finding other game to hunt and left Kersey alone.

Dyne pushed her way through—parting Laraek and Jonas. With a hard swing, she brought Adella's blade across Kersey's throat but with the reflexes of a demigod, the vampiress dodged a nasty beheading. The sharp tip grazed her neck, creating a thread of blood that quickly healed.

Kersey jabbed with the blunt end of her lance—a solid hit that was supposed to topple Dyne but she easily sidestepped it and returned a vicious stab that missed its mark by inches.

"You," Kersey breathed.

Dyne was completely entranced that she spoke. Most people did very little talking when they were swinging weapons.

"You are the one who hunted me here fifteen years ago, are you not?" she asked.

"Sorry I didn't get to finish the job," Dyne said, thrusting her blade against the middle of Kersey's lance. The vampiress simply shrugged her off, still wanting to talk.

"You were alone last time. Why do you surround yourself with Mydianites tonight?" Her gentle hand patted her chest. "This is what you want, correct?"

Dyne couldn't help but cast a worried eye over her shoulder to her comrades. Lorne and Laraek were both too busy to care.

"Last time, yes. Tonight, I'm just here to kill you."

"But why? Your heart isn't in this. Your resolve feels so weak. You are being used by Mydian, aren't you?"

There was something about her words that was making Dyne lose focus. She was speaking truth, in part at least. Mydian *was* using her and she had heard enough about the tale of Gwenavaughn to know he had tried to use Kersey too. But the thing that was bothering her most was why she was being so gentle—so compassionate and not just a brute killer with a thousand years worth of saved vengeance.

"Stop talking!" Dyne screamed. Eva whipped her head around from the fight, a look of pure bewilderment in her eyes.

"Think, girl," Kersey said. "You are back from the dead, are you not? Something is amiss here. Something is out of place! There is more to this story than you've been told."

"A slice to the throat will stop that tongue from wagging," Dyne said, unreasonable to the end.

Kersey breathed a sigh and lowered her weapon for just a moment before saying, "Very well, then."

Both women took a step back to rethink their strategy. Dyne leaned back with her sword, as if to deliver a massive, over-the-shoulder slash, but this was only a ploy that she'd used many times with great success. She pulled the dagger from her boot and hurled it at the unsuspecting vampiress.

Kersey dodged the blade just in time, knocking it aside with the middle of her lance, but it was just the distraction that Dyne wanted. The toss of a simple dagger was only a diversion to the ferocious, power-swing that she harnessed right across the vampiress' throat.

There was so much blood. A dark, dismal look flashed before Kersey's eyes as she clamped the wound with a tight hand. Dyne wanted to finish her before she had a chance to heal and retaliate, so she twirled Adella's blade once and swung hard across her torso—

—when Kersey blocked the raging attack with her lance. The vampiress held it tight with both hands, shielding her face from the raining fury of Adella's blade. Her strength was faltering with the sudden loss of blood and Dyne strained to win the leverage.

It wasn't going to be that easy, she realized. Kersey healed and regained her strength too quickly. With renewed power, she pushed Dyne's blade away and in the process, slammed the handle of the lance into her face. She fell to the ground and spit blood from her throbbing lip. A slight dizziness rattled her head and it took a moment for the world to come back into focus. Kersey was going to pay for that one.

She twirled the lance and raised it above her head, ready to skewer the crouching woman with its bloody end when a mangy raven landed on her shoulder.

The mortal man who helped her ran up behind and kept the vampires away while she talked quietly to the dead bird. It nodded its head and lifted its wing to point to the west. Kersey eyed the horizon and then the bird. She whispered something and it took to flight and headed off, only to nosedive the nearest vampire.

There was a noise behind Dyne. It was something squeaking mixed with the sound of knocking, like a small stick against a rock, only it quickly repeated over and over again. She was the only one to hear it—the only one to see it.

A pair of decrepit, skeletal horses came barreling down the path above them, dragging a small, wooden carriage in their wake. Dyne rolled aside as they quickly hammered past, sparks erupting from the uprooted cobblestones.

Kersey opened the door to the carriage and let her mortal inside and then climbed atop it. She kept a constant eye on the southern horizon as she whipped the reins and sent the horses into a gallop, away from the battle and toward the west—toward the water.

The white flashes of vampires were growing thinner and not because they were wearing the Gothmirks down. Laraek's men couldn't possibly take on an army as large as Kersey's and hope to be the victor. It was foolish to even stay around and fight now that she had hastily left.

Dyne was just about to suggest they retreat—to head back to the ship empty-handed and report to Mydian that Kersey had escaped with the book when a loud '*whoosh*' passed by overhead.

It was the swoopdrakes.

They were circling the apple grove two by two, firing on the vampires with their mounted crossbows. Lanterns were tethered to their stirrups, lighting the night up in golden dots.

"Kersey is headed to the docks," Laraek assured. "We have to get back to the *Murder*. We can't allow her to leave the city."

Eva was the first to head up Glendan Street, but the dank, burning alley was filled with more than just smoke and debris. There were men running down the road, their Lylussian shields and armor reflecting the golden light of the burning house. The swoopdrakes continued to circle around, their riders blowing horns to signal the footmen to the fight.

Laraek's vampires kept fighting the undead until the soldiers made it to the grove. Lyluss' forces joined rank with Kersey—with *Ruin's* undead and fought the vampires as kinsmen. Their pact—their alliance was no longer a rumor.

Then why did Kersey run off when they showed up? Dyne wondered.

"Where is he?" Laraek asked, looking the sky over.

"Where is who?" Dyne questioned, grabbing Lorne by the arm and backing away from the mass of Lylussians who managed to break through the vampires' line.

"The priest," he growled. "The one who has been on my heels through every town I've visited for the past few weeks."

Dyne didn't see him either. She remembered his highly decorated armor and beautiful weapons and knew those wouldn't easily be missed. He clearly wasn't here so she assumed he died back at the beach in Pelopha. Laraek's constant searching of the skies told her that probably wasn't the case.

"This way," Eva said and headed out of the grove through Squire Street.

The Lylussians were everywhere, but luckily they were easily spotted. Unlike the Gothmirks, these men and women carried lanterns and torches. Squire Street was filled to the brim with them, not to mention sporadic vines and undead. Tharg was quickly closing in and Dyne hoped there would still be a path back to the *Murder*.

It was just the five of them now—Dyne, Lorne, Laraek, Eva, and Jonas. Some of the vampires were still fighting but most had decided to take to flight and head back to the ship.

Eva led them to a cluster of apartments and kicked in the door of the nearest house. Dyne sheathed her sword and followed with the men bringing up the rear. There was a staircase directly in front of them so the vampiress darted up and disappeared around the right. A fearful scream erupted and Dyne followed it around until she came to a sudden stop at the backside of Eva. She was standing there, arms at her side and quietly watching a mother clinging to her infant baby. The child was screaming—panicked by her mother's sudden outburst.

Dyne circled around and spotted the tear-blotched face of the once stern vampiress. There was hurt there—a sadness that was growing with each second that her stare remained unbroken. The terrified mother buried her face into the child's blankets and wept, fearing death at any moment.

Laraek found his way up and grabbed his wife by the shoulders and gave her a quick shake before heading past. "Eva, don't do this! Not now!" he yelled, watching the staircase below them.

Jonas was the last up and shoved a dresser across their path, cutting off the trailing Lylussians for just a moment. Lorne helped him heave an ancient armoire on top of it and after Laraek's quick comforting, headed on down the hallway.

It led to a narrow window that spanned nearly the entire height of the wall. Laraek kicked it open and led his small group of Mydianites onto the roof. He gave Dyne his hand, which she swatted to the side and then hoisted herself out.

Tharg was still. From up on the roof, the nauseating sound of the ocean could be heard. One would never suspect that an army of several thousand was walking the streets below, shifting rows of dead and decorated warriors who were working together to eradicate Mydianites. The swoopdrakes were spotted, darting behind buildings and between alleyways. The flaps of their wings were easy to hear in the unbroken silence of the night.

But an ear-piercing screech ripped through the air as one of them plummeted toward the unsuspecting group on the rooftop. Everyone jumped to the side and latched onto the shingles but Lorne had been ready.

He drove his halberd straight up in the air at just the right moment. A small spray of blood hit Dyne in the face as his magical weapon sliced cleanly through the beast's wing. It howled out in pain and fluttered its good wing but its erratic attempt to stay airborne was fruitless. It crashed against the roof and skidded to the ground before the rider could jump to safety, a trail of red lightning in its wake.

"I can see why you kept this fellow around," Laraek said, wiping blood from Dyne's eyes and pointing to Lorne. She pulled his hand away and forced a weak, agreeing smile.

"This way to the dock, ladies and gents," Jonas said, motioning toward the next house.

Dyne eased to the edge of the roof and cautiously looked down. She quickly pulled back up when an arrow hissed by her ear, tossing her golden hair like a stray breeze. In the brief look she stole of the street, she could see that the undead and Lylussians were packed shoulder to shoulder. They were going to have to roof-hop back to the ship.

"We've failed, my friends. We've failed," Jonas solemnly said, leaping across to the next house.

"Not yet," Laraek reassured, taking his wife by the hand and helping her across the two-foot gap. Dyne rolled her eyes. "But if she gets herself a boat and sets sail for the north . . . gods be with us all."

The trip to the docks was short but brutal. Clive was tossed around inside the carriage like a marble in a jar rolling down a hill. He struggled to hold onto the railing inside as the horses deftly made their way down the narrow streets. There were no windows and he couldn't tell what was happening. All he knew was what Kersey had whispered to him just before she shoved him into the wagon and left the battle.

"Lylussian soldiers want to speak with me at the docks," she had said. He was probably just as surprised as she was.

Other than the things Kersey had told him, Clive knew the hostile relationship between Lady Good and the monsters of the night. Vampires were loathed, hated, and hunted by her Holiness' servants. Why would they suddenly want to talk to one of them?

At first he thought it was a trap. The Lylussians were clearly drawing her away from her minions and into a waiting legion of soldiers who sought vampires for a living. Kersey had already fallen for one such ploy tonight. Was she about to do it again? Clive only hoped that she was smart enough to approach this meeting with a little more caution than last time.

The carriage pulled to a stop. Clive heard the boards creak on the roof as Kersey's weight shifted around and hopped off. She rapped twice on the door and her retreating footsteps sounded. The hooves of the undead horses made tiny clicks as they pattered around on the cobblestone path.

Clive stepped out of the wagon and heard the soothing draw of the ocean to his right. A small fishing vessel creaked and groaned against the pier. A horse neighed and drew attention to others on the beach.

There were three men around a golden horse-drawn wagon, all wearing the decorated armor of Lylussian priests. One of them sat atop a squatting swoopdrake, visor down but surveying Kersey with a watchful stare. His gauntleted hands firmly clamped the reins as she approached them.

"That's quite far enough," another said, stepping in front of the priest on the flying beast. Kersey stopped in her tracks and looked to the sandy beach. It must have been very painful to gaze at the cluster of Lylussian motifs on the three men, horses and wagon. "We've no desire to exchange pleasantries with a vampire such as yourself, so we will make this quick."

Clive's hand tightened around his sword. Lylussians were *good* people. Unfortunately, his view didn't sit on the same side of the table as theirs. They didn't know Kersey—they didn't know how different she was than most vampires. He surely hoped this didn't grow violent because if he were forced to kill them, he wouldn't have been able to live with himself.

"We were ordered to deliver one of our most skillful navigators to you. Tonight. *Here.*" It was clear that the speaker wasn't the leader. The priest on the swoopdrake watched their conversation without uttering one word. *He* was in charge.

"Ordered by whom?" Kersey asked. "Since when did Lyluss take orders from anyone but herself?"

"We weren't ordered by Lyluss. This request came from *your* god. From Ruin."

"I *have* no god. It certainly wouldn't be Ruin," Kersey breathed. "I just happen to be working for him in the sake of bringing an end to Mydian."

"Then it would seem that we all share something in common," the Lylussian said, waving his hand around to the other two.

"What are you saying?" Kersey asked. Clive was beginning to draw a picture of it all in his head. There was an unspoken alliance between two gods who normally traded hostilities.

"I'm saying that we share a pact with the god of the dead. He and her Holiness are *allies*." The Lylussian soldier nearly gagged on his own words.

"I assumed as much," Kersey admitted. "So where is this navigator?" she asked, looking up through squinted eyes.

The Lylussians exchanged glances and the leader on the swoopdrake nodded. The speaker backed up toward the wagon.

"We ran into trouble in Pelopha," he offered. "The navigator was . . . killed by Mydianites." He opened the door to the carriage and Clive could see the bloated body of a man whose throat had been ripped out. There was even blood dripping down the side of the wagon and across the steps. The speaker smiled and waved his hand to Kersey. "But because of your . . . special talents, we figured he was still of use."

Before he even finished the sentence, a vine slithered past his ankles and into the wagon. The speaker danced from leg to leg to dodge the snaking, stinking stalk as it withdrew the corpse from its bloody shroud. Several more vines burst through the sand and started pulling his armor away—pulling the painful motifs and symbols out of sight. With a flick of her wrist, the navigator rose and started walking toward the pier, leaving long tracks in the sand.

"He knows the waters of where you need to go. And with that, our order of business is finished. We bid you farewell." The Lylussians standing both bowed while the one mounting the swoopdrake nodded his head goodbye.

"Care to sail with me?" Kersey sadistically added, watching as the navigator climbed aboard the small fishing vessel. He began lowering the sails and looking the deck over.

"We've done our part," the speaker said, chuckling just a little. "We're only passing through. We're after a few Mydianite thieves."

"Thieves?" Kersey asked. It sounded absurd to Clive, as well. Why would these men—as decorated, skilled, and as noble as they appeared—be after simple thieves?

"I'm sure you've heard of the *Phantom Seven*? Seems they stole a few things from Lady Good. Quite valuable, if I don't say so myself."

Clive had heard of the *Phantom Seven*. It was a fleet of ships commissioned around the second War of Balance that was comprised of vampires. They had to be the ones who just attacked Kersey in the grove.

"Obviously," she sarcastically commented. "And just what did they steal that warrants the efforts of such high ranking priests such as yourselves?"

The speaker giggled and jumped upon the wagon. The other joined him and the leader on the swoopdrake tugged the reins, forcing the beast to stand up.

"We may be allies with your god, but we certainly aren't with you. Best of luck to you, Kersey Avonwood. In the coming days, you're going to need it." With that, the leader lifted his beast, stirred the sand, and then disappeared into the sky. The other two whipped the reins of the horses and their wagon headed off, toward the apple grove.

Clive and Kersey looked back and noticed that the navigator had finished preparing the fishing ship for departure. He stood by the stern, watching them, his neck still dripping blood down his shirt.

"Clive," Kersey breathed and for once he could hear just how heavy her heart was by the thickness of her voice. She looked more depressed now than she had the moment he told her she was marked for execution.

"What is it, Kers?" he asked, searching her. Their eyes locked and her red-splotched face turned humble as she approached him.

"Take this," she pleaded softly, pulling a tiny bag from her side-pouch. It landed in his hand with a heavy jingle. His brow furrowed in confusion as he untied it and peeked inside.

In a bag smaller than an apple was more money that Clive had ever seen. It was more money than had ever passed through his fingers. There were dozens of platinum coins, sapphires, a diamond the size of a chestnut and two Ruby Keses.

He couldn't help but pull the two coins out and look them over. They were made of gold and magically pressed rubies that were transparent when one looked into it. Directly in the center was the queen of Keswing from a thousand years ago, Tianava Sydith. The Ruby Keses were so expensive to make so they were only minted for a few years, primarily for royalty, and then were retired to the Lylussian vaults in the holy city. Today, they would probably rack a few thousand platinum apiece.

"What's all this?" he questioned, dropping the Keses back into their pouch. He didn't even feel safe holding them out in public with just the two of them on the beach.

"I want you to take it and get out of here." She shoved him toward the path back into town like shunning a dog after scraps. She turned her back and looked to the fishing vessel. "You don't have to go with me, Clive. I *can't* drag you along this time."

A small part of it was inviting. In his hand was enough money to start a new life. He could leave Tharg—there was no reason for him to stay any longer. The money could buy him a new house—ten houses if he so desired. It would last him a lifetime and he would never have to work again and could spend all of his time doing the things he always wanted.

That was as far as the dream went.

Clive quickly realized that those things didn't exist. He wasn't a painter or a sculptor. He didn't like to travel or mingle with friends. His life had been his family and his job. Last week, with Nalia's untimely murder, his family had been extinguished. With Kersey's escape of the prison and Clive's involvement, his job had flickered out like a dead candle. He had nothing left to take away and there was nothing he wanted that would occupy his mind and heart. There wasn't anything to fill the void. All of the money in the world wasn't going to change that one bit.

Kersey was all he had left. She was the last thing that was *his*. She was the last thing that he had to live for.

She was the last thing that he *loved*.

Her back was still to him, looking out to the blackened sea. It was so calm—so quiet. He wished that this peace would last forever but with her troubled heart and mind, he knew that turbulent, angry waters were on the horizon. He pushed the small bag back into her pouch and turned her around.

With a gentle hand around her back he pulled her close and kissed the top of her head, letting the comforting crash of the waves wash up around their ankles.

"I've come with you this far," he concluded with a warm smile. "You'll not get rid of me that easily."

.16.

What Tips the Balance

The trip back to the *Murder* took over an hour thanks to the sufficient search tactics the Lylussians exhibited. They were looking for Laraek, or so Dyne thought. Back in Pelopha he had mentioned that the priest had been after him. What was it that made him so special? Was it because he was the commander of such a prestigious fleet of enemy ships? Or was it something a little less noticeable?

When the five were back on the beach, Laraek grabbed Jonas and Lorne by the collar and took to flight, carrying them through the air and over the water like an angel. Much to Dyne's dismay, Eva grabbed her beneath the arms and hoisted her just the same.

She struggled for just a second but realized it was much faster than waiting for the mortals to row the longboat. Despite the wicked grin on her face and the eerie moonlight dancing in her eyes, Eva did just as her husband and deposited Dyne on the deck, although a bit too high.

The remaining vampires and mortal crewmen wasted no time preparing the ship to sail. The anchor was hoisted, the sails were lowered and Laraek stormed to the rear of the ship and took the wheel. Hunching, gnarled Crossbacks crowded the deck and watched

Tharg with empty eyes. There was so much chaos onboard and every one of the mortals seemed to have glimpsed Kersey and Lyluss' holy men and women.

"Are the Lylussians out to slay her as well, commander?" one of the mortals asked.

"Not quite," Laraek said.

"Kersey's heading northwest, commander," came the observant mortal once more. "We saw her leave in a fishing boat a half hour ago."

"We'll not catch her before she reaches the station," another man shouted from the bow.

"What station?" Dyne asked. If Kersey was heading northwest, then she was sailing toward the open sea.

Laraek chuckled. "You haven't traveled by sea lately, have you Dyne?"

"I've never traveled by sea until tonight," she said with a bit of venom.

Eva slipped her coat off and removed her dainty gloves. "Well you're in for a treat, dear girl." She winked and disappeared below deck. Dyne threw Lorne an uncertain look but he simply shrugged.

"Coax all the wind you can from these sails, boys!" Laraek shouted over his wife's squabble. "She'll hit the station before us, but I want our bowsprit knocking on her cabin window once we hit the Elandiran." The Elandiran Sea was near the top of the world, up around Crynsia and Boudia. Their ship would have to pass through the Arinbeth Sea and across the Faeyin Sea before they'd ever see the dark and foreboding waves of the Elandiran.

With Laraek's commanding words, the crew found their places as the *Murder* began to shove forward. Dyne stole a quick glance to his cabin before heading below deck.

Eva was nowhere to be found but there were certainly a lot of vampires. Not as many as before, but enough to crowd the crew quarters and block the passage to the far side of the deck. They were busy drawing their dark blankets and covering the cargo hatch in anticipation of the rising sun that was only a couple of hours away. Dyne didn't want to push past them, so she turned around and started to head back up when Laraek met her on the steps.

"Your hammock is that way," he said, pointing over her shoulder toward the huddle of vampires.

"I saw something quite interesting tonight," she countered, paying no mind to his ushering.

"Oh? Would it be the way Eva saved you a paddle back to the ship?"

"No, I could have rowed faster," she sarcastically corrected. "I'm talking about the baby crib in your cabin." Dyne thought for a moment about Eva's strange behavior when she saw the infant back in the apartment and made sure to bring that to Laraek's attention, as well.

He took a seat on a crate filled with bottles of water and motioned for her to do the same. After she made sure Eva wasn't about to push her way back through the entourage of vampires, she did.

"Eva . . . lost her babies when she was a mortal." For just a moment Dyne was happy—glad by the news that such a vile woman lost something dear to her, but with those feelings of anger came sadness. She knew firsthand what type of pain that caused.

"What happened?"

Laraek checked the deck himself to make sure his wife didn't make a surprise appearance. "It was years before I met her. There was a fire—in Bloodgate." He dodged her stare with the next thing he said. "Mydianites were destroying everything in the urban districts. Her family, including her twin boys was burned in their beds."

"And yet she continues to serve him." She painfully added, "Just like you and I." Dyne couldn't believe how foolhardy she could be. The lord of the Underworld at one time or another had wronged Eva, Laraek, *and* her, yet they continued to do his work. They were about to be at the forefront of the next great war, representatives to a god who did cruel things like kill his servants' families due to their inadequacies on battlefields half a world away.

But religious quandaries aside, Dyne couldn't help but feel a small pinprick of sorrow. Eva was evil and sadistic, much like herself, but the death of a child was a fate no one deserved to endure.

"So why the crib?" she asked. "This happened a long time ago, right?"

"Yes, but Eva has longed for another child. One day we will, I mean, some day we plan—"

"—on stealing one of your own?" she finished.

Laraek nodded. Vampires didn't possess the ability to father or carry children of their own.

"Eva's been away for several weeks. Tonight is the first I've seen her since she went off to Davinshire. I've been allowing her to go off and see if she can find one that she . . . connects to." He seemed almost ashamed by his words.

"Well I suppose she's well taken care of," Dyne sadistically said. "You give her shelter, blood, and even money when she makes her little excursions. You must be so proud."

"Stop with your arrogant quirks," he spat. "I want a baby just as badly as she does."

At that moment, Dyne wanted to be judgmental. She wanted to tell him that the child he wanted—that he and his *wife* wanted—was something that creatures like vampires didn't deserve. They planned on taking a baby from its bed, from its parents, and into a vampire's life, which it would never benefit from, and for some reason she scolded him for it.

But that was exactly what she had done years ago.

"I had a little girl," Dyne found herself saying. She couldn't believe she even uttered those words out loud. It was like an unspoken secret that she held on to all of Hannah's life.

"You did? And just how did you come by that?" Laraek questioned.

The look she gave him and the recognition that followed in his eyes was the only explanation needed. "I wanted a child with you so badly, but just like everything else, it was never meant to be."

"We were at war, Dyne!" yelled Laraek, but quickly hushed when a few vampires started to walk over. "You and I spent our nights in a tent, a stone's throw from Keswing's front gate. We weren't given the time and opportunity to do a lot of the things we wanted."

She looked to her lap and played with the loose hem on her boot. He was right and she shouldn't have been thinking on such things. Earlier tonight she had made a deal with herself to be a stronger person and not let the past creep up to stab her in the back. Only this time, Hannah's memory had been brought into it. That was the one exception to the rule that allowed all the barriers around her heart to be effortlessly yanked down.

"Eva and I had the one thing you and I didn't. Timing." That was the simple truth and Dyne hated him for pointing it in her face like a knife. "If you and I had met during peacetime, it would be you and I together today."

Just as he finished, the bride herself shoved her way past the vampires and up to Laraek, a red bottle of wine clenched in her delicate hand. She planted a firm kiss on his lips and stroked his cheek before heading up the steps past him, toward their cabin. Dyne stared at the weathered floor and pretended not to see them.

"Eva's a good person, Dyne. You just have to give her a chance."

She couldn't believe what she was feeling. Maybe he was right. Eva did seem like a better person now that her secret was out in the open. Looking back, Dyne realized she had instigated all of the hostility. It was she who attacked the unsuspecting bride on the beach, just for being with the man she once loved. It was an unfortunate misunderstanding about the drab brown dress that caused Eva's anger to peak and shove her over the railing. When Dyne was a vampiress she would have done the same, if not stabbing the thief in the heart first. It was so disgusting how much they were alike. That was the very pebble that shook the foundation of their unsound relationship. They were *far* too alike.

"I suppose," she admitted in a defeat that left a bad taste in the corners of her mouth.

"Good. Besides, we're all on the same side here," Laraek pointed out.

Oh really? she silently scoffed. *Well your god seems to think otherwise.*

"Laraek, is there something you need to tell me?" she asked, searching him.

He studied the ground for a moment before saying, "What do you want to hear? There's nothing left to say, Dyne."

That wasn't what she wanted. She was trying to coax him into admitting what he had done to Mydian—what he was planning on doing. This job would have been so much easier if he would have simply told her whom he was serving and why.

"Nevermind. Back at Daegin's place," she said, "you were looking for Aneesa's spell book. Weren't you?"

He glanced over at his men and then spun around to face her. "Of course. With Daegin dead, I wanted to make sure it didn't fall into *her* hands."

"Well it did."

"And what makes you so sure of that?" Laraek raised an eyebrow.

Dyne had forgotten all about her meeting with Mydian in the broken mirror along the cellar floor. Amongst other things, he had told her about Kersey's escape with the book. It was inevitable that she was headed north, to the Crynsian coast where she would finally put it to use. After all, she was one of the few old enough to read and wield its power.

"You heard your crewman," Dyne answered. "She's northbound. You know where she's going as well as I do. The trip would be pointless without the book."

Laraek nodded. "She's headed to the Kragspire Wastes to raise all the dead that's buried there. She can't do it without some sort of powerful magic."

In all the battles and conflicts that ripped across the savaged lands of Mystyria, none were as bloody or brutal as the Battle of Kragspire Alps. It was during that very clash where Aneesa Redblaze met her end and Dyne found the irony somewhat poetic that her book would once again be returned to the barren land.

Lyluss had eyed the city of Crynsia since the start of the first War, only three years earlier, and decided that whoever controlled its ports would play an essential part in maintaining Northern Corscus. The good goddess launched thousands of ships from Skyhaven and docked at the Wingert Gap, a beach just south of Kragspire where her troops could easily pass undetected through the valleys and thick forestry. Nearly a quarter of a million soldiers marched north, ready to take the unholy city of Crynsia. The allied evil gods knew such an attack would likely happen.

Fearing the loss of the seaside city, Mydian, along with the resources of Pralarus and Whither, sent nearly half a million troops south to guard the Gap and surrounding beaches. In a twist of unfortunate luck for Lyluss, the two mass forces met in the center of the Kragspire Alps.

In two days, over half a million men, women, dragons and many other forms of beasts perished. The Mydianites, along with the Venomous Daggerhands and Whitherian soldiers managed to force the Lylussians to retreat back to the Gap and into their ships. The battle was lost and for once, Mydian enjoyed a victory, despite losing most of his soldiers. It wasn't until a few years later when Lyluss sent her attack ships back to Crynsia and destroyed the ports once and for all. The Crynsian loss, coupled with the Slayers killing of Gwenavaughn forced Mydian to pull his troops out of Keswing and back to Bloodgate. The first War of Balance was over.

Before the war, the Kragspire Alps were beautiful, lush mountains with exotic wildlife and renown, unique vegetation and flora. Afterward, they were a dank, murky land where trees would not grow, where animals could not live, and where the very air carried the nauseating smell of blood. It was still that way today, a thousand years later, with nearly all of the bodies still intact—buried beneath a bloodied, muddy prison.

"Kragspire is spread out over a hundred miles or so," Dyne said, trying to remember the one time she trekked through it on her way to Crynsia. "The book must have a way of allowing her to raise undead faster or more efficiently."

"Perhaps," Laraek agreed. "Either way, we need to catch her before she gets there. My guess is that she'll take the Gap, just like Lyluss did all those years ago."

"Why would you say that?" Dyne questioned, trying her best to block out the rattle of the crewmen from up above.

"Because she can't go any farther north. Mydian and Whither have naval ships that sail those waters, not to mention the pirates and marauders. If she ventures too close to Crynsia, she's bound to run into something that could cause her trouble." He looked down and thought for a moment, then added, "No, Ruin will have her dock at a safer place where there won't be anyone looking for her. She'll head to the Wingert Gap."

"Won't Mydian be expecting this? I wouldn't be surprised if he had his soldiers holding hands all the way around Kragspire."

"That's where you're wrong," Laraek objected. "Mydian is so spooked by Lyluss and Ruin's sudden attacks that he won't move any of his troops away from his cities. Bloodgate and Xenthia are protecting their walls. There aren't enough men to venture into the middle of the continent and simply wait for an army of the dead to raise from the ground."

Laraek did make a good point. In the first war, Mydian's troops were protecting the beaches all along the western walls of North Corscus, leaving Crynsia open for an easy attack. In the second war, he moved south, taking nearly all of Bloodgate's reinforcements to the Keswing countryside of Middle Corscus. Once again, Bloodgate and Crynsia were heavily damaged and he withdrew his troops in defeat again. Dyne didn't believe that he would put his guard down a third time.

There was a heavy shudder that rocked the ship as something passed above. The lantern hanging on the post next to the water casks flickered and went out as a massive shape engulfed the doorway at the top of the stairs and then was gone. Dyne and Laraek both stood and looked up past the steps. Everyone else seemed completely oblivious as they continued in their menial tasks to keep the ship at top-notch speed.

Either they didn't just see that or they didn't care, she thought. Laraek winked and pushed his way past her.

"I guess that means we're almost there," he told one of his men. Eva emerged from the cabin at the other end of the deck, shutting the flimsy door behind her. She scanned the cloudy, dark sky above and Dyne couldn't help but to follow her stare. Whatever had just passed by the ship was gone now.

"Commander!" a mortal cried from the bridge. "They've reached the station!"

Laraek jogged up to join the navigator. Both peered out to the open sea but Dyne only saw darkness. There was nothing out there but a black, salty-smelling void. That's when she remembered her new toy, courtesy of Daegin, the man she never met.

She raced up the steps and pulled the Nighteye from her pouch. The light and clarity it produced was incredible. Its magical lens rotated and fixed on a small boat a mile or so away. Surely the *Murder* could outrun such a tiny vessel. But there was something else beyond it; something floating on the water that looked like a buoyant house.

"I hope you're ready for a long trip," Laraek said, pushing Dyne's lens down. "We're certainly bound for North Corscus now." He nodded to his navigator and hurried down the steps. "Everyone's attention!" he yelled.

The *Murder's* crew came to a stop and turned their attention to their commander who stood in the center of the ship like a professor of magic.

"We missed our chance to slay an Overlord, but we're not going to let that happen again, are we?"

There was a chorus of agreeing cheers and Eva crossed her arms over and smiled by her husband's authoritative voice. Dyne found Lorne sitting on the steps on the opposite side of the crew deck's doorway and joined him.

"She'll be in North Corscus in two days but we'll be right behind her. We'll crush her as soon as she lands." Again there was an ovation that turned into a chant but Lorne and Dyne were contemplating Laraek's last words.

They looked to one another with the most confounded, questionable stare and in the smallest, meekest voice, Dyne uttered, "*Lands?*"

.17.

The Root of Evil

It hadn't occurred to Clive that he had been without food for the past two days until he took one step into the captain's cabin aboard the *Squinted Eye*, the fishing vessel that Kersey and her undead navigator had commandeered. There was a light but pungent smell of spices coming from the round table dominating the center of the circular room. Something had rotted several hours ago, but at least a few scraps were edible.

He plucked an apple and scooped up a handful of Stalmer nuts and seated himself on the edge of the bed where he flicked silver coins into a water pitcher across the room. This kept him entertained for only a few minutes, so he pulled out the small green book that he snatched inside of Daegin's house. Kersey had made mention of Clive's lack of knowledge when it came to folklore and vampires so he figured it was the perfect item to save from the fire.

It was titled, *'The Overlords: Mystyria's Darkest Secret'*. The pages were in good condition and the binding was still tight and showed very little signs of age. Unlike the Greater Overlords it spoke of, the book itself was quite new.

Clive took a chunk from the bitter apple and thumbed through the text. His eyes scanned the bold print and black drawings as he quickly read anything bearing her name. The main reason he took the book was to gather an insight into why Kersey was the way she was. He thought her past and the circumstances of her curse were what shaped her into a killer but had there been a breaking point? Was there an event that drove her to insanity? What had been the reason for her to become a docile and depressed prisoner? He didn't know. What he did know—what he did *believe*—was that the first ounce of pain and torment she felt happened a thousand years ago, in a cave just outside of Keswing.

Whoever wrote this book believed she had died in Tharg, only fifteen years ago. In thick black ink, presumably by Daegin's hand, was written, '*Wrong! Wrong! Wrong!*'

Fifteen years ago, Clive thought. That was about the same time Kersey was caught stealing peaches and was sent to the Pen. She lived there—endured taunts and beatings—all in the sake of remaining hidden. Guards had even tried to rape her on the eve of her emotional explosion—the one that cost six men their lives for just laying an ill-intentioned finger on her.

Then he saw a name.

Amongst the ten Greater Overlords was a man named Brin Todrich. That was the name Ruin mentioned that set Kersey off. Clive had even tried to ask her about him last night but was rewarded with the same silence. Who was this man and what was his significance to her? Why did she react so hostilely toward the mere mention of his name?

There was a dark picture drawn in reddish-orange ink that was titled, '*The Eve of Gwenavaughn's slaying.*' It was a Spellink, a magical way of capturing a scene onto paper without having to even raise a brush or quill.

All ten slayers stood in front of a large, ornate door that Clive guessed to be some sort of temple inside Keswing. They looked shaken, but dignified. Each of them had been called on—called out to go and do a service for their city that would probably claim their lives. There were two women in the picture, but it was easy to distinguish Kersey's small, child-like frame from the other.

She was leaning heavily on a man who had his arm wrapped tightly around her waist. The smile on her face as she grinned to the mage conjuring the Spellink told Clive that she was very happy and very trusting of the slayer by her side. Scanning across the names along the bottom, he was in fact, Brin Todrich. Kersey was involved with him, before the slaying, a thousand years ago.

It could have been a number of things that caused her hatred toward him. After reading about the blood and the curse, every one of them changed. Even Kersey had become something of a monster. Clive had heard it from her own lips, but learning the details of her past dealings seemed to solidify it in a way that was too real for him to handle.

His hands were shaking as he read about the witnesses who saw her drag a Lylussian priestess out of her house in Sorcea and gut her in front of children. He couldn't believe that she was responsible for the great fire of Edgemount in the Year of the Traveling Monk. An entire city was nearly razed in one night just because she wanted to lose Mydianites who had been searching for her.

There was no mention in the book about Kersey's alliance with Ruin and Clive assumed it was because their pact was only recently sealed. All of the crimes and injustices that the book claimed Kersey was responsible for seemed to all be in the pursuit of escaping or fighting Mydian. Unlike all of the other Overlords, Kersey's carnage and mayhem was all done by her own accord. No one, not even an angry god could tell her what to do.

Clive was about to read more on Kersey's murderous history when he heard her humming gently outside the cabin. It was so strange and so alien that he first thought it was the wind, blowing across the single sail and through the wicker doors. He couldn't believe his ears. She was actually doing something that involved happy thoughts and happy rhythm.

The song was also a very unusual choice. It was a Quillianite hymn called *'Sisters Might'*, which was about the unwavering strength of Lyluss and Quillian's unity of goodness. Clive had heard that song many times—had heard it sang to *him* many times—and couldn't believe after all of these years it was coming back.

He pushed the door open and let himself out onto the deck. The sea was calm but the night was so dark, save for the small lantern propped by his friend's feet at the opposite end of the thirty-foot boat. Kersey was sitting against the railing of the bow, the spell book in her lap. She continued to hum the chorus of the hymn and glanced up to Clive, smiled, and focused on the book once again.

"My grandmother used to sing Nalia and I that very song when we were little." Clive sat against the door of the captain's cabin. He could see the dead navigator above her, his bloated hands gripped tightly against the massive wheel.

A warm grin found its way to Kersey's face as she slowly closed the book. Without looking up, she replied, "I know. She used to sing it to me, as well."

Clive leaned forward, wondering if he actually heard her right. Was the salty-smelling air starting to get to him?

"What?" he managed through tangled thoughts and jumbled memories.

"Your grandmother, Mima, used to sing *Sisters Might* to me as well, Clive," she answered again, as if it should have been obvious.

"You knew my grandmother?"

"Oh yes. Quite well," Kersey stood up and stretched, then added, "She was a lovely lady, but of course you already knew that."

"Why didn't you tell me?" Clive looked to his lap and said, more to himself, "Why didn't *she* tell me?"

Kersey knelt down in front of him and raised his chin so they looked into one another's eyes. "Do you remember living across the river? There were three houses. Your parents, your grandparents, and an empty one in the middle."

He nodded as she let go of his chin. His mind did the math faster than her words. "You lived in the middle house, didn't you? You were the pretty lady Nalia and I saw when we were little but you rarely came out."

Kersey smiled and nodded. "That's right. I remember when you and your sister were born." Her eyes went distant as she recollected memories from a time that didn't involve bars, guards, and frequent beatings. "I remember when your *mother* was born."

"You knew my grandmother this long?"

Again, she nodded.

"Why did you leave the house? Why did you get yourself arrested?" He knew the answer as the words were leaving his lips. Once again, he did the math in his head and remembered the odd coincidence that he thought nothing of at the time. Now, it plagued him as he struggled to realize the truth in chance.

"I was . . . forced to," she said, a hint of sadness in her voice. She sat down on the deck and Clive knew what prompted this serious mood. Robbers had killed his grandmother fifteen years ago, only two days before Kersey was arrested.

"I need to know something, Kers," he said through clenched teeth. He was getting angry, but not at her. It was the situation—the silent play that had been lived out behind the curtain. "Did you have anything to do with my grandmother's death?"

There were fresh tears running down her face but it wasn't from admittance. "They were looking for *me*," she managed through sobs. She put her hands over her face and added, "They weren't burglars. They were Mydianites who were tipped off to my location. They killed her in their searches for me."

Clive's heart slowed just a little. He didn't blame Kersey for what happened but he was still confused about the relationship between the vampiress and his grandmother.

"Why didn't they find you?" he asked.

"They did," she hastily corrected. "But your grandmother was good enough to warn me so I was able to deal with them and come up with a plan that fooled Mydian into thinking I died and went to Ruin. She's the reason I'm still alive today."

"I don't understand," Clive said, shaking a little from the cold ocean air. "Why did my grandmother care to protect you?"

She warmly grinned and looked out to the water, thinking on a pleasant, past thought. "She knew who I was—*what* I was, and she cared for me still." Her eyes were drying up with the renewed happiness of a good mortal's memory. "I'll never understand why she took such care of me. She let me watch her family—let me see what a normal life was supposed to be. I stayed around long enough to witness you and Nalia grow up and become good people, just like her. She was the one, Clive, who taught me to let go of my hate and pain. She was the one who taught me to be 'nice' as you would put it."

"Was she the reason you stayed in Tharg?" he asked.

Kersey nodded.

"Then why did you stick around once she died?"

"Because of your family. I wanted to be near you because until I met the Porters, I had forgotten what happiness was like. I was without it for a thousand years and thought it no longer existed. Your grandmother taught me otherwise. I could've picked from a thousand cells across Mystyria in which to rot but I chose Tharg. It was the one that was closest to *you*."

Clive didn't know what to say. He didn't even know what to *think*. The last fifteen years had been filled with wondering whom she really was, documenting paperwork to explain her bloodstains, and trying to figure out if she was able to get in and out of her cell. He would have never guessed that she had such close ties to his family. If Kersey had been around long enough to witness his mother's birth, then she knew his grandfather. Even Clive had never met him.

Maybe this explained the strange calm and ease that he felt whenever she was near, Clive thought. Kersey had a way of getting through—she was very much unlike the other prisoners and aside from Nalia, she was the first woman he opened up to and talked to about the menial things that went on in his daily life.

Her face flickered in the dim light produced by the lantern. Her head was cocked to the side, looking at Clive's hand. He followed her stare downward and realized she was trying to see the title of the book he was holding. It hadn't occurred to him that he brought it outside with him.

"Where did you get *that*?" she asked. Her voice didn't sound as pleasant as it had before.

"I found it at Daegin's place. I thought I would brush up on my folklore," he said with a thick grin. Kersey wasn't smiling. Instead, she sat her book aside and snatched his away.

After a few seconds of thumbing through the pages, she horridly asked, "And just how much have you read?"

"Enough," he answered, trying not to be drawn in by her questioning stare.

She looked horrified as she read bits and pieces of her own history. Most of it may have been forgotten—lost in her crowded mind and scrambled thoughts. It was the picture that seemed to affect her the most.

Kersey stopped and examined the portrait for a few seconds when Clive thought it would be best to intervene. Her breaths were labored and the lantern's glow made it easy to see the dark rings below her eyes. It was all because of him. Brin was the reason she became a killer, a murderer, a destroyer of all things. Brin was the source of her madness and despair.

It would have been impossible for Clive to see it, but the visual reference of that past relationship was the tiny flicker of the flame in her mind's memory. All of the flashbacks had been trivial and uneventful from the outside. Her body and mind started to convulse and spasm as the most nasty of all events snaked its way to the surface.

Her eyes darted back into her head and her sharp nails dug into the cover of the book with unfelt strength. She wasn't angry with Clive for showing her the picture, only upset that he would have to witness the aftermath of her most traumatic thoughts of Brin.

The fishing boat, her friend, and the endless waves of the sea transformed into the dank, dark, and foul-smelling cavern that was making her sick day after day. She was alone, rigorously grinding a stone against her lance to flake away any dry blood that she could. The blade looked the same as it had when she started and her inability to make it clean was permeating with the rest of her desperation and frustration.

Everyone else was on the other side of the cavern—past the tunnels and up near the main chamber where they felled the beast. Silas had actually managed to clear an exit with his makeshift tools. The first light in six weeks bled through the rocks and cast an eerie, ominous glow over Gwenavaughn's corpse, now merely a skeleton after the decay and the slayer's hunger. Kersey was secluded in her tiny alcove, just past the beast's tail, unaware that eight of her once friends, her once companions, finally tasted freedom.

Brin didn't care about such freedom. He wasn't worried about getting out any more. His heart had decided that the dragon's cave would be his tomb, as well as everyone else's. In his maddened, deranged mind he thought they were all betrayers for even wanting out now, after all they had been through.

Lyluss had been the reason. She had sent them to die a death that should have been reserved for false prophets and blasphemers. Gwenavaughn had been the epitome of evil—an extension of Mydian's own corruption, but Lyluss let them—*allowed* them to become that very thing.

Even Kersey had started to believe it. Her face was sore from twin black eyes, a cut along her forehead and a busted nose, and it was all thanks to the one man she had loved—the one man she thought had loved *her*. Why had Lyluss done this to two of her most devout servants? Surely Mydian wouldn't put his own children through such turmoil.

She had taken Alexa's dress. After the cave was sealed, Alexa had constantly complained about how hot it was and despite a few magical tricks to cool the place down, she still insisted that the voluminous robe was enough on its own. Kersey didn't mind. In fact, she loved the soft blue of the ruffled skirt and the silk mantle that was embellished with dove rosettes. It had been the prettiest dress in the whole world until Brin spoiled it.

He had been watching her from the shadows—from across the cavern—as she tied her hair back and scraped the stone across the lance. Sweat glistened from her skin and by the blue flame of the campfire—it cast her face in an innocent, angelic manner. She didn't see him approach and even though the past week had been littered with abuse to her face and arms, she didn't feel fear.

Not yet.

Kersey was new to the world. She had never been outside the walls of Keswing and had never seen the horror that encompassed Mystyria. The battered, bruised and tiresome vampire of the current day was a far cry from the innocence of her youth. Never in the thousand years of her life would she believe that two days after her twenty-first birthday could something that horrible happen to *her*.

It all started with a caress. Brin gently laid a hand across her face, wiping the sweat and the stress-induced tears away. She swatted as it—the cold fingers that she still thought in her heart were empty of hatred and malice. Brin's soul had left weeks ago, upon entering that dark, dismal spot in the world. She had been a fool to think he would be different—that he would change and be the loving, caring, and decorated man that he was before.

"You are so beautiful," he said, his words eating through to her spine. She felt her legs go numb—her arms heavy. Kersey threw the stone aside and sat her lance down. She closed her eyes and let his strong fingers stroke her face and hair.

At that moment she wanted to believe again that he was different—that he had abandoned all the self-loathing and all the bitterness toward her. Maybe he realized that she wasn't the enemy—that Lyluss was the true source of why they were there. Perhaps Brin was sorry for hurting her the past weeks and just wanted to make things right.

The truth came when he wrapped his fingers through her hair and pulled with all his might. Kersey's arms and legs flailed as he dragged her to the rear of her alcove, the most hidden, most distant spot away from where he thought the others would be. The entire cavern was empty now except for those two.

Kersey screamed—a resounding screech that echoed violently in the small confines of the tunnel. Brin didn't care, nor did he acknowledge. He was too intent on making sure she was pulled into his tangled web like the prey of a spider.

"I know now why Lyluss sent us here, Kersey," he said, panting. He laid his hands across her shoulders and held her down. There was so much fear in her eyes and she could feel the sting of tears burning down her cheeks. "She wanted us to be martyrs. Do you believe that?"

He was pushing himself against her, his breath warm on her face. She helplessly struggled against his weight. "No! I don't believe that! Get off of me, Brin!"

"But we won't let that become of us," he vowed. His forceful hand found its way up to her head and his fingers combed through her hair. "We will *thrive* here. We will cultivate a society and rise up against Lady Good when the time comes."

"You are mad!" she screamed. Even a thousand years later, she still found absurdity in how ludicrous and hate-driven his words had been. "I want out of this wretched hole! Get off of me!"

"No, Kersey!" he screamed back, malice thick in his voice. "Lyluss has abandoned you." He pointed up to the sky, toward Mystyria. "And out there, so has everyone else. I'm the only one left in your life. After the things we've done this past month, no one is going to want to be near you."

"Stop it!" she cried, mostly incoherent through the sobs.

"Certainly not another man. You'd best accept what you have here and now."

She tried to scream, more out of distress and anger than out of pain and fear, but that changed rather quickly.

Brin's informative, reasoning attitude suddenly darkened and Kersey didn't think he cared any more about sculpting a new life and forming a plan to get back at Lyluss. There was only hatred for *her* now. He felt wronged by her—betrayed that she wanted to leave him and pick up the pieces of her tattered life. Was it so wrong for her to want to *survive*?

Kersey was having trouble breathing and she wanted up, so she placed her foot against his chest and shoved off. For a moment, he was away from her and she was free to go but that small, fleeting chance escaped. She turned around and tried to slither away—down toward the tunnel's opening but he grabbed her hair and pulled her back.

Her fingers dug into the stone of the cavern floor, ripping at her nails and leaving thin trails of her own blood like eight strokes of a painter's brush. She howled in pain but the throbbing in her fingertips and the aching in her scalp were trivial compared to what she would feel that day—to what she would feel the rest of her life.

Brin was fumbling with something metal behind her. She felt one hand leave her sore head which made it possible to look behind and see exactly what he was doing. His other hand was around his belt, unfastening it. There was a cold stare in his eyes and an eerie, wicked grin on his face. That was when the realization came—the moment when she knew something awful was going to happen. It was in that moment that she discovered the world was a bad place full of bad people.

"Brin, no," she pleaded. He pushed her head back around, into the rock. "Please don't do this." Her voice was lost to the dusty, grimy cavern floor.

There were no more words. He wasn't interested in talking. In his mind, he was doing something right. He was mad at the world and this was the solution—procreating for the sake of bringing retribution to a goddess he thought had wronged him.

Again, she tried to escape. Her tiny, shaky fingers grabbed onto the rock and started to pull her to safety, but this time he grabbed her dress and pulled it by the mantle. The beautiful blue garment ripped beneath his fingers and she couldn't help but feel embarrassed.

She had never been naked in front of a man. The heat was rushing to her face and she could feel her skin fluster. Brin was laughing behind her. He took in a deep breath and she knew his face was buried beneath the tattered piece of dress he was holding.

Kersey tried to kick him but he caught her leg. His fingers danced all the way up her thigh and latched on. She felt a horrible sting as his nails bit into her flesh—making sure that she wasn't going to go anywhere. That quick, sharp pain lasted only a second because his ruthless, uncaring hands pulled her into a whole new world of hurt.

The greatest agony of all was the sound of her flesh being ripped. As if the pain of the experience could grow no greater, she could literally hear herself being torn apart like a child's doll. She screamed out and buried her face in her hands. She couldn't escape. Her heart was pounding too hard, her breathing was too immense and her body was paralyzed by fear. As her virginity was ripped from her, all she could do now was wait and hope he would be quick. He would probably kill her and for that, she would be grateful.

There was the sickly smell of blood. It wasn't the same as the great beast crumpled a few yards away but it was strong and very distinct. It was *her* blood. She started to reach down, to survey the damage but he grabbed her wrist and slammed it into the rocks above her head.

She couldn't feel any more pain. It wasn't possible for such a small girl to be tormented so much. There was a cold numbness that grew from her waist down and no matter what Brin did—no matter how violently he tried to defile her, he couldn't make her scream any more.

As if sensing this, he pushed her off of him and pulled his slacks up. She simply sat there, bleeding, sore, and nauseous from the heat and the smell. Brin was laughing and panting while she fought to regain her breath. For a moment, she thought he was going to say something—that he was going to make some sort of humiliating remark or ridicule her faith or faltering strength but he did no such thing. He only crawled over to her and rested his face next to hers, as if the entire thing had been just as lovely for the both of them.

That's when she found the courage and strength to take her scraping stone and strike him across the face. Brin faltered back, spitting blood from a broken jaw and while he was down, she reclaimed the feeling in her legs.

She stood and ran, crying the entire way toward the dragon's carcass. There was blood still gushing down her legs. Her balance was wobbly and it hurt to walk, but she found the opening that Silas had made. For the first time in six weeks, Kersey saw the sunlight.

She managed to run to Keswing but she didn't go home. That was when the shame started. Soon after, the self-hatred and the need for retribution against Lyluss began. Kersey believed that she deserved everything that happened in the caverns those six weeks. Her power had been twisted for a reason and Brin had been the unspoken tormentor.

After the gods knew the slayers destruction, they were summoned to the heavens to stand trial. That was the day the curse began and the last time she ever saw him. The two went separate ways, both evil and both wanting to hurt and destroy all in their path for two completely different reasons.

Kersey's entire life pivoted from that moment in the cave. The other slayers were evil because of the blood and their changed idealistic views of religion. Her evil was spawned from the most horrific event of her life. When Brin decided to rape her, he set in motion a stepping-stone that grew darker and darker as the years went on. Everything in her core—everything in her maddened and jumbled mind could be traced back to that day.

But the healing had started. It took a thousand years for someone to come along and help her see why it happened. It wasn't because Lyluss was mad or because the blood made Brin crazy. Kersey had been raped because it was the first step to her happiness. As ludicrous as it sounded, that's what she believed. If she hadn't been raped, she wouldn't have loathed the gods and attacked their churches, thus becoming cursed to vampirism. If she hadn't been granted the gift of immortality through that vampirism, she would have died ages before meeting Clive. Perhaps it was Lyluss' plan, albeit an elaborate and tiresome plan.

With that thought in mind, she returned to the present day, a little calmer, clearer minded, and with the hope of no more flashbacks.

"Kers, wake up," Clive said. He hated seeing her in these trances and this one had been by far the worse.

She had jerked violently and flailed her arms this time. There was so much blood and she tore at her face and neck. For the first time, she called out Brin's name and told him to stop.

"Clive," she breathed and coughed. She sat up, literally in a pool of her own blood and looked around. Her face was so pale and so somber.

"Are you okay, Kers?" he asked, pulling her matted hair away from her eyes.

Her distant eyes were surveying the boat, the water, and her concerned friend. The feeble dress was in tatters now, as if the gaping holes from the ballistae weren't enough.

"What did Brin do, Kers?" he asked, needing to know more than ever. If he was ever going to help her—if he ever planned on making her let go of the past, then he had to know what it was she was holding on to.

"He started it all," she answered and then spat blood into the water. Even her insides had been mangled. "Everything you see here." Her voice was becoming a growl as she spoke through clenched teeth. "It's all because of him. I loved him so much," she cried, wiping her eyes. She left a bloody mess across her cheek. "I was willing to give him all that I had and somehow he took even more."

She told him of the rape and he listened with new ears. Everything was falling into place now. Clive knew those types of men. After working in a prison so long, he saw the hate-filled and disgusting men who preyed on meek women. Kersey had been a victim of the most horrendous crime of all. Her mind's defilement was caused by her body's defilement.

"Someone like Brin needs to be punished," Clive breathed.

"Quite true," she said, a hint of righteousness in her voice. "Your grandmother may have taken away a millennium's worth of hatred and rage, but I still have a small bit tucked away. I have kept an anger that is reserved just for him and one day, he'll see it."

"I've seen this anger, even if you were too entranced to remember it. Back at Daegin's place and the grove." Clive remembered the way her vines tore the house apart and then later that night, the trees in the orchard. Her anger took on a life of its own when it was fueled by such hurt.

"*That?*" she asked, a hint of amusement in her voice. "That was nothing. Pray you never see the extent of my anger."

Her eyes watched the blood flow down the deck in steady streams and she shook her head, as if witnessing the self-mutilation for what it was worth. Clive could see the change in her face—the realization that hurting herself was what Brin would have wanted.

"Am I beyond help?" she asked with genuine fear.

"Not at all, Kers," he answered, quite seriously. "Look, anyone who has lived as long as you would certainly have to have problems. You can't expect to be level-headed after a thousand years."

She giggled, but it was weak and shallow. She'd lost so much blood and he feared that it was dangerous for her to be so close to the railing.

"We should get you out of these bloody clothes," he said. "I saw some dresses down in the cargo hold. How would you like a nice, pretty dress?"

Her stare went blank for a second but she quickly snapped out of it and smiled. "I'd love one, but I'll get it later. Let's just sit here for a moment."

"So where are we going?" he asked, feeling the sudden need to change the subject. He didn't like the way her eyes were starting to well. She smiled, nevertheless and he could tell she was just as happy to be talking about something else.

"We're headed up north, near Crynsia."

"Crynsia?" Clive didn't think he heard her correctly. He looked the small fishing vessel over—the same boat that probably never went more than a few miles off the coast. "That's a couple thousand miles away, don't you think?"

"Yes, but with the stations, we'll be there in no time."

He had forgotten about them. They made it so much easier in the last few decades to travel by sea, although he'd only used them once in his life. The god of dragons, Dargas, had blessed Mystyria by making it simple for ships to go long distances in short amounts of time.

It was unbelievable that they were going to be sailing near Crynsia. The entire idea was ludicrous. Surely Ruin had a better plan than this.

Crynsia was one of the most evil cities in the world, but then again, it was situated in the northwestern region of North Corscus, the hive of malevolence. It was roughly two hundred miles south of Boudia. Along the southeastern tip of the continent was Bloodgate. Good people like Clive were not welcome there. Worshipers to such gods as Lyluss and Quillian were hunted and killed. Ruin was widely adored and considered evil but with the recent tension between he and Mydian, claiming to be one of his servants probably didn't hold much merit either.

"What are we to do once we're in Crynsia?" Clive wondered.

"We're going *near* Crynsia, not in it," Kersey corrected. "Do you know where the Kragspire Wastes are?"

"Isn't that where the big battle took place in the first War?" He vaguely remembered a few stories.

Kersey nodded. "That's exactly right. All those bodies are still there in the blood-soaked, infertile land. I'm going to raise them."

"How are you going to do that?" he asked, knowing firsthand that her power didn't reach that far. After all, he had to escort her to the graveyards around Tharg.

Without so much as an answer, she held the spell book up. The little red text's importance was finally starting to make sense.

"It would seem that Ruin has been planning this for some time," Clive concluded.

"Oh, he has," she assured. "The other day was not the first time he tried to draw me into his scheme. He knew what this book could do."

"And what exactly is that?" Clive had never cared much about magic but he did find the process of writing it to be intriguing since there were very few spellcasters or mages in Tharg. The fact that Kersey held the oldest book of it was also something of great interest.

"There is this spell," she said, turning the book around so he could see. It didn't make any sense to him. The language was very old and beautifully written, but he couldn't be sure of its origin.

"It looks like some kind of Elderi," he offered. "But I can't read it."

"Of course not," she smirked. "*I can barely read it. It's old Elderi. This language was ancient even when I was born.*"

"What does it say?"

She turned the book back around and read it silently, then said, "It's called the *Symbian Range*. It takes normal spells and tremendously amplifies them. You could use a minor curing spell to heal thousands. Or cast a simple fireball that could devastate an entire countryside. Or—"

"—Or raise a few hundred square miles worth of corpses with a simple flick of your wrist?" Clive finished for her.

Kersey closed the book and nodded.

"And just what do you and Ruin plan to do with this army once it's risen? It will be near unstoppable."

She stood up and looked over the railing, a hesitance in her eyes and voice. "We'll be starting the third War of Balance."

Clive chuckled but he didn't find anything funny in what she said. "You say it so casually."

Kersey turned to him, far more serious this time. "For once in the history of the world, a war *needs* to be waged, Clive. Mydian has killed, starved, and tortured innocents for far too long. He is evil. He is sadistic, and he needs to be taught a lesson."

"I completely agree, Kers. But do you think that Mydian will be the only one hurt by this war?"

"Of course not," she hastily answered. "Everyone who takes up arms and goes out to fight for their god and country knows this."

"I'm not talking about them, Kers. This war will reach the homes of the innocent. Those who aren't even able to pick up a sword will be hurt or worse."

"This has to be done, Clive," she argued. "Do you see another alternative to remove Mydian from power?"

She was right. Clive didn't have a negation for such a true question. Mydian did need removed and this was the only way. He said a silent prayer to Quillian in hopes that it wouldn't be as long and demanding as the first War.

"Even if I do not raise this army, Mydian will strike at innocents anyway," she said. "He is preparing to attack with vampires."

"How do you know this?" Clive asked.

"Daegin," she told. "He's been making an elixir called Bloodsilver that creates unnatural vampires. There have been several shipments of it sent to Crynsia and Bloodgate over the past few weeks. Gods only know how many of them he has."

"Look," Clive interrupted. He was pointing out to the north, just beyond the dead navigator. Kersey ran up the steps and stood next to the wheel and gazed out to the red ball of light hovering a few miles off.

"It's the station," she offered. She gave the stern of the boat a quick glance and then another, lengthier stare. "And not a moment too soon. They are *following* us."

In just a few days time, Clive had gone from being a prison headmaster, to a hostage, to a beloved friend. Now, it seemed as though he would end up helping an instigator of war. Could he even do this? Would he go down in history as the one who helped Kersey Avonwood wage war on the god of the Underworld? He looked down and stared at the bloody deck. His thoughts turned to Nalia—to the good sister with a tight noose around the neck that was put there by a vicious Mydianite. That was the only motivation he needed. If Kersey wanted his company in destroying the dark god, he would gladly help.

.18.

Skyward

"I don't see her anymore," Dyne said, putting the Nighteye away. "Their boat was there a minute ago, and now it's gone." Lorne was watching over her shoulder but without the added visibility the magical lens created, it was hard to see any further than the waves breaking around the *Murder's* hull. There was a bright light shining from a magical lantern on a post at the floating house, but it didn't illuminate the sea at all.

Most of Laraek's crew was raising the sails and Dyne could feel the ship slowing down. Were they planning on stopping at the floating house?

She sat by the bridge and watched as the buoyant dwelling came closer and closer. The wooden structure looked rickety, making her wonder just how it stayed afloat. There was a flag and insignias on the doors bearing a dragon tooth shield. This was the symbol of Dargas, the god of dragons.

Though most dragons were evil by nature, their god was good. Telsis had created Dargas around the era of the second War of Balance to control the dragon populous. He ruled from the realm of Briarkeep Skies, a city that floated high above Mystyria. Most of his temples were in the good cities like Keswing and Skyhaven, but just like any other god, his worshipers were widespread. Dyne had no clue why this structure even existed, here, in the middle of the ocean off the coast of South Corscus.

"Jonas," Laraek called, pulling the robe over his head. "You know the routine."

The one-eyed mortal nodded and accepted a bag of jingling coins from his commander and stepped up to the bridge next to Dyne. He gave her an eerie wink and then turned his attention to the floating house.

All of the vampires left the deck and filed below. Apparently they didn't want the Dragonmaster's servants to see them. The *Murder* was easily identifiable as a Mydianite vessel and Dyne wondered just what they would think when they saw it go by.

However, it wasn't simply passing by. The navigator eased the ship *beside* the floating house. When they reached the magical lantern, Dyne could see that a ramp extended out and led up to where the *Murder* could dock with its tapered plank. Jonas jogged down the bridge and up to meet it.

There was a post with a bell on the side, so he grabbed the pull string and gave it a rough jingle that echoed across the silent sea. For a moment nothing happened, but as soon as the floorboards of the house came alive with creaks and groans, Dyne realized someone was moving inside.

Candlelight bled through the boards of a side door before it flew open. A burly man in a brown robe stepped out, carrying a simple candelabrum in one hand and a chalice in the other. The golden light danced off of his thick, coarse beard as his tiny eyes surveyed the massive, black ship docked by his house.

He sat his chalice back inside the doorway and drunkenly ambled his way up to the ramp's end. Jonas was sitting on the railing, tossing the bag of money up and down.

"Greetings, travelers," the man groggily said. Dyne could see the Dargasian symbol on his drab robe. He was a priest or a missionary of the Dragonmaster. "My, what a prosperous night! Care to donate to the Winged Hero's cause, do ye?" He held an outstretched hand.

"Prosperous?" Lorne asked him. "Have others . . . donated tonight?"

"Oh yes," he said. "Haven't seen folks in days but tonight, I gets ye two at a time!" His fat belly jiggled as a hoarse laugh exploded from his chapped lips. Afterwards, he turned serious and motioned to himself. "Well, c'mon!"

Jonas was trying his best to stifle a smile brought on by the drunken priest's slurred demeanor. He placed the coins into his palm and saluted a farewell. The Dargasian stood and started back down the ramp when he turned around and yelled, "Pull up to the marker and don't forget to raise your sails!"

Laraek and his crew had already emerged from below and started pulling the sails down. The *Murder* shoved off and Dyne grabbed her Nighteye again to look out to where they were headed.

About a hundred yards past the floating Dargasian temple, she spotted a post that was about a foot in diameter and rose nearly thirty feet into the air. At the top was a bright red flag that waved fiercely in the strong wind.

It didn't take the *Murder* long to reach the mark and she wondered what its purpose was. For what did Laraek just pay? She was about to go and ask more questions but she stopped in her tracks. A shiver brought on by the sudden, creepy ambience made her skin crawl.

That's when she heard it.

It was still far off, but it was a *large* sound. It was a steady and rhythmic thud that made everyone quiet and turn their heads to the stern of the ship. She knew this sound, although she'd never heard it on this scale or size. As it drew closer, it turned into a *'whoosh'* that she identified as wing beats.

But there are only a few things with wings this big, she thought.

Dyne looked up into the dark clouds and could see the fog was being disturbed. It twisted around like a glass of dirty water being stirred. The sound was so close to them now that whatever was causing it, created a strong gust of wind across the deck. Slack rope blew aside, a bucket rolled to one end, and Dyne struggled to keep her hair from lashing across her face.

Then, as suddenly as the sound grew, the largest pair of talons descended from the heavens and hovered just above the *Murder*. Dyne backed up and fell against the steps leading to the bridge. She instinctively held her hand over her face but there was apparently no danger here. She found her feet and noticed just how calm everyone else was. Even Lorne seemed to find peace and awe in the massive creature that was floating over their ship.

It was the largest dragon she'd ever seen. There were four paws, each hanging close to the ends of the ship. The colossal beast was covered in turquoise scales and its large underbelly heaved up and down as it took in massive breaths. Its wings were almost deafening as they slapped against the water.

Dyne followed its plated chest up but couldn't see the head through the darkness. Every few seconds it bellowed out a snort, causing a ripple across its belly. She backed away from the railing when she realized she was standing a foot from one of its gigantic claws. They were so beautiful. Any dragon she'd seen in the past always had bloody or grimy nails. This creature wasn't meant to fight.

"Here we go," Laraek called when he saw the beast clench and release its talons. Everyone latched onto something and Dyne followed suit, wrapping her arms around the railing. When she saw the dragon submerge all four paws into the ocean around the ship, she understood what was about to happen.

There was a sudden and violent shift as the beast aligned itself next to the *Murder*. With the strength of a god, it latched onto the ship's hull and started flapping its leathery wings faster. Dyne's grip on the railing tightened as it lifted the ship out of the water and continued skyward.

It grew colder as the dragon rose. Dyne could feel its constricting grip around the hull and after a moment's hesitation—it lurched forward at a speed she didn't think was possible. The wind hitting her in the face was incredible. She thought it was the most amazing experience she could remember but it didn't take long for reality to catch up and she realized it was growing far too chilly to stay outside.

"So what do you think?" Laraek asked her on their way into the crew's cabin.

"You could've warned me," she said in a light-hearted anger. "That was one scare I could have done without." The ship felt so strange. She didn't want to walk—or even move for that matter. It felt that if she jumped right now, the entire *Murder* would move with her. That thought and feeling was starting to make her nauseous. She reminded herself that flying could be no worse than sailing.

"About twenty years ago, Dargas gave a gift to Mystyria," Laraek told her, pulling the door to the crew cabins shut. "He gave us the dragon stations. He sent his beloved creatures down from Briarkeep to make sure the good people of Mystyria could travel with ease."

"Good people?" Jonas chimed in. "Think he knows we're using them too?" His chuckle followed him down the deck and to the cargo hold.

"These pack dragons pick up and drop off from three stations," Laraek continued, paying no mind to his crewman's snide antics. He took Dyne by the hand and pulled her down the hall. She turned around to look for Eva but didn't see her.

When the two made it past the vampires, past Dyne's hammock and to the end where the steps to the cargo hold started, Laraek showed her a table with a large map strewn across it. It was the western half of Mystyria.

"We just left here," he said, pointing to the 'X' that was drawn in the sea, off the coast of Tharg. "The next station is here." His finger glided up the map and stopped at the next 'X' that was in the Faeyin Sea, just a few miles from the Skyhaven coast. "But Kersey isn't going to that one. She's going to land here." Once more, his finger zipped to the top of the map and rested at the third 'X'. This station was in the Elandiran and was only a few miles from the Wingert Gap.

Everything was looking quite convenient for Kersey. Did she plan all of this on her own, or did Ruin guide her hand the entire way? Having sat in prison for more than a decade had probably dulled her mind and Dyne assumed she was nothing more than a blunt fist being driven by a higher brain. She had chased the Overlords long enough to know how most of their minds worked and how their egotistical schemes seemed to be akin to one another.

But Kersey was different.

While all of the other Greater Overlords were silently reaping havoc on Lyluss' interests, she had been hiding—doing nothing and interacting with no one. It made no sense. What was her motivation? A creature that foul was only concerned with its own well-being. Dyne knew this from experience.

Somehow, Kersey had abandoned all resemblance to an Overlord and sprouted a soul that allowed her to listen to reason—it gave her mortal-like tendencies. Ruin conveniently wedged himself between her despair and anger and somehow coaxed her into bringing an apocalypse upon the lord of the Underworld. Did she want to do it out of rage? Dyne didn't think so. She knew what awaited that woman when she passed on from Mystyria and landed in his lava-strewn world.

Kersey was helping Ruin out of fear—fear of a tortured and humiliated afterlife. Just like all of the other Overlords who were as sadistic and vile as Arctis, she deserved every moment of it. Dyne held on to his memory—his voice—and it reminded her of the time when he threatened to kill her little Hannah. Those few, but powerful words brought chilly fingers up the course of her spine.

"All of our success depends on sinking her in the water," Laraek said in a grim tone. "We are too few now and without the rest of the *Seven*, we can't attack her on her own terms. We *certainly* can't once she's risen this army."

"But look," Dyne countered, pointing to the Wingert Gap on the frayed map. She slithered her finger up through the mountains and to the Kragspire. "If they dock here, they will have at least a half-day's journey to the battle site. We can still catch her on land."

"No we can't," he corrected, shaking his head. "This trip is going to last all of today and half the overnight. If we haven't killed Kersey before sunrise tomorrow, our job is finished. We go back to Pelopha." His voice trailed off, his mind clearly on the assumption of a grand army rising from the ground and tearing their northern lands apart.

"So that's it? The grand *Phantom Seven* is useless during the day?" Dyne put her hand to her hip and waited for his heated response.

"Not at all," he huffed. "But if you want to go ashore and seize her on your own, be my guest. Feel free to take with you all seven mortals aboard."

"Perhaps I will," she stated matter-of-factly. "I scored a hit back in Tharg and I'll certainly do it again."

"Yes, and look how effective it was." Laraek rolled the map up and started down the deck with it beneath his arm. "Kersey let you go, Dyne." He stopped and turned around and she nearly slammed into him. "Don't think that small trickle of blood she put on your lips will be the last if you try to strike her again. And what did you two talk about? I noticed more words than swings back there."

"She was just taunting me," Dyne lied.

Laraek shrugged, turned and continued on, pushing his vampires out of the way. They were already in their hammocks, blankets pulled high over their heads.

The crew cabins were incredibly dark and the only light was coming from the opposite end, toward the map table and the stairs that disappeared into the cargo hold. Dyne had trouble following Laraek, but she could easily hear his voice and feel his presence. Lorne and Jonas were stashed in a corner, playing cards by the filtered glow of the lantern below them.

"Stop," Laraek told her, coming to a complete halt. She bumped into his back and could feel the cold air sifting through the door.

"What?"

"You shouldn't go outside now. We're very high up."

"So?" She was letting her voice be loud and haughty on purpose.

"So the air is quite thin and cold. It'll be frigid and hard to breathe out there. I assure you it's not a pleasant experience." He turned back to face her.

"Well it feels fine in here," she countered.

"As well it should, thanks to the air and heat stones." He pointed a long, tired finger to a couple of clear and orange rocks dangling from strings. She had seen them earlier, but just assumed them to be ugly decorations that Eva fancied.

As if there was a god of coincidence, the wife herself was on the other side of the door when Laraek pulled it open. Dyne didn't pay her any mind because she was too busy backing away from the cold wind that burst through. It reminded her of the knee-deep snow back in Hope's Covenant. She wanted away from it and away from that memory.

"Coming to bed, my darling?" Eva asked. There were icy crystals forming all along her cheeks and in her eyebrows.

"If you'll excuse me, I have a door to repair before the sun rises," Laraek said, giving Dyne a weak bow.

"What am I supposed to do all day?" she asked, tugging on his arm. He should have remembered how prone she was to boredom.

The couple smiled at one another and then Laraek turned back around. He nodded toward the back of the ship and said, "Learn how to play King's Blade."

The mortal crewmen on the *Murder* were so different than the vampires. Aside from the obvious diversities, they were laborers. Most of the vampiric kindred used their naturally strong bodies and adept senses to be soldiers of Mydian, but the human men actually kept the ship running.

Jonas was humbly whistling below them, probably cleaning the cargo deck where the caged blood slaves pleaded. There were two mortals playing cards with Lorne. One man was a short, skinny boy no more than eighteen. His blond hair was tied in the back and his matching beard was straight and cut to a point. He called himself Kraith.

The other was a tall, burly man with a shaved head and a face so matted with sweat that it looked like he'd bathed in lamp oil. His name was Timon and was the one who Dyne noticed fixed the holes and kept the rations off the floor. Both men seemed humble and happy to have new company, despite the fact that over half of their friends and fellow crewmen died back in Tharg.

There were vampires all around her—each tucked away in their deep, regenerative sleep. She remembered when she needed to do the same thing. Symbia herself could unleash an explosion from the heart of Bassex right next to a slumbering vampire and it wouldn't wake them.

The crewmen's deck was so tightly sealed that it was impossible to tell if it was day yet. Laraek left only an hour ago and all the small sounds of the ship went with him. The steady, almost hypnotic beat of the pack dragon's wings were all that could be heard outside.

Dyne rolled a barrel over to the corner and used her weight to hold it against the wall while she sat. She eyed the cards spread across the makeshift table but more importantly she watched the bottle that Timon pulled from his burlap sack.

It was Stagtart Ale. She hadn't tasted it since her mortal days. Her dry, cracking lips seemed to soothe as soon as her eyes locked onto the red liquid swaying inside.

"Well go on," Timon said, handing her the bottle when he saw her lusting gaze.

She grinned from ear to ear. That was something she hadn't genuinely done to a mortal in a long time. It was so disconcerting that she almost went into a frown the moment her cheeks started to bunch up. Nevertheless, she plucked the ale from his fingers and took a long swig. Giving the bottle's rim a light sniff, she noticed it wasn't anything like Lorinstag Ale, which she still smelled on the air. It was light and barely lingering, but it was *there*.

Her head leaned back against the wall as she let the sweet drink run down her throat. It was the best thing she'd had in years. At the moment there was nothing chasing her. There was no fighting and even though they were in the midst of a heavy haste, they were unable to do anything about it. For once in the many years of Dyne's scattered life, she was allowed to move at a pace that wasn't her own. It felt . . . *relieving*.

"You've watched us play cards for two days now," Lorne told her, dealing a hand in front of her. "Join in."

She grinned and took another sip. "I don't seem to have the coin you fellows are so fond of trading, so I'm afraid I'm out."

"Ah, it's ok, miss," Kraith offered, pulling his pile of earnings back. "Just play us one for fun."

"Fun?" she laughed. "What is the point of that?" Her tone was thick with humor.

"You know, Dyne, not everything in life has to be objective. Sometimes you can do things just to do them." Lorne pushed the hand of cards toward her edge of the table. "Try slowing down a bit and maybe the world won't bunch up on you the way it does."

She knew she should have been angry. There was a time when a comment such as that, no matter how truthful would have landed him a heavy dose of pain and suffering. Now, she was agreeing with him and actually smiling because of his honest words.

"Just when did you get so philosophical?" She scooped up the hand and arranged her suits.

"Twelve years of unlimited access to Mydian's library can teach you a lot," he smiled. "I had a nice little hovel situated just beside it."

"What was it like?" Timon asked, eyes wide and scanning both Lorne and Dyne for answers. "The Underworld is so remarkably interesting."

"Oh it is," Lorne assured, laying down a knight and two crowns. "I worked next to Hiriam and watched the Master's men train and build weapons."

"What did you do there?" Dyne asked, impatiently waiting her turn to throw her cards in.

"I made armor."

"You were a blacksmith?" Timon asked.

"One of the many," he chuckled. "I made some of the finest suits of Lydison and some of the lightest blades you've ever seen. I even shaped metal for the golems back in Bloodgate."

Dyne let a tiny grin escape at the mention of blacksmith. She would have never guessed he would do such trivial work after the kind of life he'd lived on Mystyria. But then again, there weren't many Lylussians to kill down in the Underworld.

"What's so funny?" he asked her when he saw her trying to feebly hide her toothy grin behind her cards.

"It's nothing," she managed. "It's just hard to think of you as a blacksmith."

"I'm a very good one, also," he said, quite serious. "I used to make horseshoes and greaves in my father's workshop back in Bloodgate."

"I suppose," Dyne giggled, laying her losing hand across the table. Timon shuffled and dealt again but Lorne didn't pick his up. He was watching his companion—surveying her eyes and readying the question that she knew was coming, but didn't think she had an answer for.

"And just what job would you do in the Underworld?" he asked in perfect forecast. "When you're stuck in a world without an enemy in which to stab your blade, what is Dyne the great to do?"

It was a good question. There had been a sword in her hand since the meager age of nine. Her father was a Mydianite, just as his father was before him. Fighting and combat had always been in her blood—and would be long after the days of bloodshed and carnage were over. She wasn't born with a lot of passion—despite the fact that Laraek would disagree. There weren't many things in life that she found joy and entertainment in other than those found on the battlefield. Thanks to her former lover, there was a tiny niche in her heart that she'd grown fond of. Bit by bit, Laraek had turned her into a lady but the constant moving, the looming battles, and the need to put her cares elsewhere always managed to interfere.

"I would be a seamstress." she finally came up with.

"You mean a dressmaker?" Lorne asked, trying his best to stifle his smile. He looked to the two mortals in hopes they could share his amusement but neither thought it to be funny. They could find the peace in it just as she had.

"I love them," she admitted. "I have . . . *had* a closet full of them that my mother gave to me. They were beautiful." Her eyes were distant and she looked through the table to that small closet back in

Boudia. "I had a black one with emeralds sewn up the midriff and a red one with pearls along the neckline."

"They sound beautiful, miss," Kraith said, probably uncomfortable by the eerie silence that came once Lorne's hushed grinning quickly departed.

Dyne nodded, still partly back in Boudia with the dresses. Her mind dropped those pretty garments and ran out the door—up the road and past the Drakish church and around to the Mydianite temple. That was where the Boudian fair would have been. How she wished that three centuries worth of bloodshed, deceit, and bitterness could just wash away and everything could return to those days.

She could have sat there all day reminiscing had Timon not died only a second later.

A large spear pierced the hull of the ship, just above the table. Its thick metal tip ripped through his gut and held him upright, as if he were about to deal another hand of cards. Kraith screamed and lurched to his feet, trying his best to wench the spear out of the hull—or at least his friend. It was too late. The thick shaft wouldn't budge and even if it would have, there was no time to take it out.

Another spear tore through the *Murder's* hull, this time on the other side. Its sharp end jabbed a sack of potatoes and stopped as quickly as it had entered. Dyne rushed over to it and shoved the sack aside. She stepped on one end of the spear and pulled up on the tip, snapping it in two. Her thin fingers pushed the other end out of the hull and she dropped to her stomach so she could look out.

The light was blinding after sitting for hours in the dimly lit crew cabin. There was a cold air filtering through but she didn't notice or care. She was busy looking out, through the clouds, toward the fast shapes that zipped by the small peephole.

"I think it's the—" she was about to say before two more spears impaled the hull above her. Both hit the sides of sleeping vampires, but didn't seem to cause severe damage. Dyne wiped their blood from her arm and stood. "I think it's the Lylussians," she finally finished.

"What's happening?" Jonas called from below. He rushed to the top of the steps and surveyed the damage of the hull. It looked like a sprung gauntlet in one of the dungeons beneath Pura Se. "Well this is a problem."

"We're sitting ducks in here," Lorne said, a slight hint of panic in his voice. Dyne had never heard it that way but she did agree. Inside, all they could do was watch their cabin shrink further and further as the spears continued to be launched.

"Get dressed, children," Jonas said, retreating back to the cargo hold. "If you have any heavy clothes, put them on," he continued to call from below. "Make sure you cover your face, toes, and hands."

Dyne and Lorne both found their footlockers and started pulling out the garments and armor they either stole from Arctis' room or were given by Laraek. The leather cuirass slipped over her body and hardened, just as it always did when it was donned. She pulled the long black coat over it and tied it firmly in the front. Finally, she wrapped a brown scarf snuggly around her face, leaving only a tiny slit for her eyes. The men did the same thing, grabbing jackets, gloves and scarves to keep the cold at bay when they went outside. Lorne pulled out the silver-etched crossbow he took back at the Birchlock.

Jonas reemerged from the cargo hold with four men in his wake. Each were bundled from head to toe in gear that looked like it was intended for just this purpose—cleaning the skies of Lylussian soldiers. Three of them were carrying crossbows but Jonas had a satchel that pulsed a slight reddish glow. Was he really going to use Glowbombs for this?

"We have six ballistae up on deck," he said, obviously speaking to Lorne and Dyne. "One at the bow, one at the stern, and two on the starboard and port sides. They're all loaded but reloading won't be easy with the lack of air out there, so you have one shot each. This is going to be a quick fight. Fire and don't miss." Jonas led them toward the exit and Dyne let go of her sword's hilt. She wasn't going to be running anybody through this time. Pity.

Without so much as a readying hesitation, the one-eyed, crossbow-toting Mydianite ripped the door open and stepped out onto the deck. There was a blinding light that flooded in around them, casting a golden glow halfway up the cabin floor. The swinging vampires were just beyond its cursed reach. Had they known that death was shining only inches from their hammocks, they would have probably slept one level below.

Jonas darted across, using the masts as cover—his head whipping to the sides in an attempt to spot the fast-moving swoopdrakes. Dyne struggled to free herself from the cluttered doorway that she, Lorne and five other crewmen were trying to push through. She was the first one out behind Jonas and was just as ready. Her eyes, however, were not.

The blinding sun was sitting evenly in the eastern sky over their starboard side. Its brilliant glow was cast into several golden shapes as the billowy clouds flew past. There was a constant shadow shifting across the deck that came in rhythm to the dragon's right wing.

A puff of fog came out of Dyne's mouth beneath the scarf and she shivered to force the cold out of her bones. When she tried to breathe in again, it felt like the air was being sucked from her lungs. Her chest felt heavy and it was an ordeal to keep her heart steady.

If she stayed out here long, she was sure to pass out. How bad a predicament, she thought; blinded by the light, suffocated by the wind, and forced into an unheard of aerial fight.

She raced to the nearest ballistae on the port side and lifted it. The sun was at her back and that was good. If she concentrated hard enough, she knew she could force the cold and lack of air out of her mind. She needed to focus—to bring back that mentality she had three centuries ago when she was knocking on Lyluss' front door. With that in mind, she spotted her target.

There were three of them on her side—their feathery hides an easy beacon in the throng of passing clouds. Each time the dragon's wing lifted up, they were closer. Dyne eyed the silver tips of the spears ready to be launched from their mounted crossbows and aimed at the center swoopdrake.

All three riders pulled their mounts up and evaded, but kept on course, nevertheless. Dyne followed one, careful to lead it just a bit. She had fired crossbows many times and although she was a poor student, she knew it would be hard to miss a target that large with a weapon meant to sink ships.

Suddenly the swoopdrake turned and soared right for her. The crossbow out front shifted and aimed and Dyne couldn't help but to jump to the side when she heard the audible *'whoosh'* as the spear left the string. It whipped past her and plummeted directly in the center of the deck where it wobbled back and forth like a twig caught in a storm. Dyne got to her feet, lifted the ballista back into position, found her mark, pulled the trigger, and—

—impaled the swoopdrake right between the eyes, just as it made it to the railing of the ship. She was thrown backwards when the dying beast crashed into the ballista, ripping it down to the bolts and sending it across to the other side where Lorne jumped to dodge it.

A bloodied creature was spread across the deck, jolting and screeching from the spear in its skull, but the Lylussian rider was unharmed. He stood and drew his sword. Dyne smiled and did likewise.

Even with the sun in her eyes, little air in her lungs, and a knock on the head from flying debris, she was a better swordswoman.

The Lylussian jabbed straight and Dyne caught his arm beneath hers. She spun around him with his hand locked and slammed the hilt of her blade into the back of his head. He grunted heavily as the helmet flew off, revealing a tiny string with a pebble on it around his chapped face. Quickly, he grabbed the little blue stone and pulled it back into his mouth but it was too late.

The magical air stone wasn't going to do him a bit of good once Lorne grabbed him and tossed him over the side of the ship. His garbled scream followed him a few hundred feet before the wing beats and the skirmish drowned it out.

Dyne headed to the bow of the ship and stood slack-jawed at the sight of the dragon's head. Although the passing clouds mostly obscured it, she could make out its scaled throat and the lances on its chin and cheeks. She would have loved to see its eyes. Thick green smoke expelled from its nostrils and it seemed oblivious to the fight that was erupting around it.

"There are five more," Lorne yelled through the mass of clothing over his mouth. "You and Kraith are the only two marksmen so far."

Everyone retreated to the doorway to catch their breath while the swoopdrakes circled the ship, occasionally firing bolts that ripped through wood that didn't matter. It would take much more than this to make a difference.

Jonas headed to the stern and caught one of the riders trailing alongside the ship. He picked up a Glowbomb from his pouch, tested its weight once and hurled it over the railing at an unseen target. There was a vicious explosion that washed the deck with black smoke and for just a second, Dyne could see yellow feathers being tossed against the fury of the wind. The entire smoking mass, as well as the explosion seemed to suck away into the distance, putting the dragon's speed into an astonishing perspective.

"Four to go," Jonas triumphantly said.

From the doorway, Dyne spotted the dreaded priest that had been chasing Laraek, flying level with the ship, just beyond the dragon's left wing. The twin doves across his lowered visor glinted against the sunlight. No doubt beneath that helmet was an air stone in his mouth and surveying eyes—watching the ship for vulnerability.

It didn't take him long to find one.

He turned his swoopdrake and sped toward the *Murder*. Nearly all the mortals, as well as Lorne and Jonas were on the starboard side, taking shots at the three Lylussians who were deliberately drawing their attention away from the priest.

Dyne rushed toward the middle of the ship with her sword drawn and outreached, ready to clip the paws of the passing beast, to topple the rider and keep him from making a devastating blow—

—but missed by only a few inches.

The Lylussian zipped across the deck and fired his crossbow. Its bolt landed solidly in the torso of Kraith. The mortal who Dyne had just played a hand of cards with screamed and dropped his weapon but the rider wasn't finished just yet. He had readied an attack that made sure the victim didn't walk away.

Attached to the spear was a chain that hooked to the swoopdrake's saddle. As soon as the rider passed across the deck and the slack tightened, Kraith was pulled up like a kite. In an attempt to keep himself stationary, he latched onto one of the mortal's arms and pulled them to their death. He vanished over the railing in a flurry of shrieks.

Dyne watched the priest circle around, carrying a twitching Kraith in his wake. It didn't take long for him to slide off the spear and fall to Mystyria. Luckily he would be dead before he hit the water a few thousand feet below, Dyne morbidly thought.

The battle raged on, claiming two more swoopdrakes and three mortals. Blood painted the deck, the sails, the dragon's belly, and all of the fighters who still fired bolts, arrows, and spears into the air.

It was down to the priest and one other. They regrouped and Dyne could see them talking and pointing to the ship. She squinted her eyes to try and make out their intentions. In the past, she'd needed to spy enemy commanders directing their battalions so she picked up on hand gestures in an extraordinary way.

"Uh oh," she said, more to herself than anyone on board. Lorne happened to be reloading his crossbow right behind her.

"Uh oh?" he asked, laying a bolt across it.

"Kill them!" she screamed when she saw them approaching. "Don't let them get near the ship!" She knew exactly what they were planning and was surprised that neither party had thought about it until now.

She raced to the nearest starboard ballista while Jonas took the one next to it. Lorne and the last mortal lined up between them and readied their weapons.

Everyone released their projectiles at once. Lorne and the mortal's bolts hissed harmlessly between the advancing swoopdrakes.

Dyne's spear grazed the priest's calf but Jonas' had managed to hit the other directly in the chest. The Lylussian flew from his mount, screaming all the way to Mystyria. The rogue swoopdrake, now free of its reins, took to the air and soared above the dragon.

The priest spiraled out of control but released a shot that hit its mark. He flew right over their heads, across the deck and through to the other side.

The spear plunged into the dragon's hind leg.

There was a loud, vibrating wail as the creature lit up in pain. Its nostrils flared and its head rose to the sky. In an instinctive withdraw to the attack, it released the front end of the ship on the starboard side.

Dyne thought for sure that the *Murder* was slipping from its grasp—that it wasn't going to be able to hold the weight up with three feet and that they were going to plummet to Mystyria. Everyone on deck tumbled toward the bow of the ship. The mortal with the crossbow spiraled off the edge and vanished into the thick clouds below. Lorne grabbed Dyne by the ankle as they slid across to the forecastle deck.

The *Murder* was almost vertical—its stern high in the air and its bow toward the water. Dyne rolled up the steps and felt herself free-falling, which she thought was away from the ship and to her death. It turned out to only be from the deck to the bow railing.

She landed with a solid thump against the bars and her heart felt like it was going to lurch from her chest. She couldn't breathe and she was on the verge of collapse. On top of the already steep mountain of perils, Lorne followed her path to the railing and landed on top of her, pushing what little air in her lungs out through her nose.

Her eyes were weak and her face was pressed tightly against the railing but she could see *through* it, through the clouds and down to the water—probably the Faeyin—that was ten-thousand feet below. She was literally lying parallel with Mystyria. The cliff-side city of Pelopha didn't feel so scary in her mind anymore.

With all of her might, she lifted herself up—with Lorne on her back, with gravity, the wind, and the cold fighting her—

—and she heard the railing snap.

She closed her eyes. This had to be a dream. No one would put her through this and let her be spared over and over again.

"Get off of me!" she screamed to her heavy companion. It was his extra weight that was going to kill them both. "We have to get off this railing!"

The splintering increased and Dyne spied the crack running up the length of the banister. There was another snap, and then another and she clamped her eyes even harder. This was her end. This was where her journey on Mystyria ended and she would return to the Underworld a failure.

That might have been her story but that chapter would not be written today.

The dragon's cawing ceased and it regained its composure. It reached out and steadied the ship, lifting and leveling the front end. Dyne rolled away from the railing and rested her back against the deck. It was safe once more—if only for a moment. The splintered railing quietly broke off and fell from the front of the ship.

She opened her eyes and looked behind her. The priest was still flying around—upside down to her. Quickly, she scrambled to her feet when she saw him circling toward the rear of the ship. There was no air left in her, or strength but somehow, she found some. Her mind pushed all the mortal inadequacies away and she went to do what she needed to do.

Lorne and Jonas were standing in her way but she shoved them aside in her spree to the stern of the *Murder*. The priest was almost there and just as she got to the final ballista with a readied shot, he was passing by with one of his own.

The spear ejected from his crossbow and landed just to the right of her. Dyne didn't even flinch. It wouldn't have mattered if his shot had been spot on. There was no way she was going to miss. Her chapped fingers wrapped around the trigger and pulled.

There was a loud *'whoosh'* as the spear zipped beneath the course of the dragon's tail and hurled right toward its aerial mark. In the last moment before impact, he saw it and pulled the reins of the swoopdrake, coaxing the beast to lift higher in the sky. The spear jabbed into the haunch of the creature, a splatter of blood exploding from the wound. It cried out in pain which was nothing compared to the dragon's agonizing scream moments ago. The swoopdrake spiraled out of control as large globs of blood poured from its injured leg. It steadily lost elevation and continued to descend toward Mystyria until it completely vanished from view.

Dyne jogged back toward the crew deck, desperately trying to suck air into her lungs. She wasn't going to make it and Lorne knew it, so he hurried across and dragged her the rest of the way inside. Jonas was already there, unwrapping his face and hands. She should have been happy with the successful repel of the attack but she couldn't revel in it. She was too busy wondering just what was going on around her—just as she had back in the Birchlock.

"Why did they attack us?" she managed through large gasps of air. "I understand why back in Pelopha and Tharg, but why did they pursue us with such determination?"

"They're working with Kersey and they don't want us chasing after her," Jonas offered, breathing heavily.

"This is true, but it doesn't explain why they are being so risky. We are but a minor problem to her. I don't think Lyluss let six of her men just die in order to keep us off Kersey's back. They know that we don't have the book." Dyne walked to the doorway again and looked through, despite the fact that it was shut. Her mind's eyes were crawling across the bloodied deck and into the cabin that rested on the other end—the cabin where two people just slept through a life-threatening battle.

"But what *are* we carrying?" she asked Jonas. He looked clueless, just as she figured he would. "There's something aboard this ship that Lyluss so badly wants."

.19.

Something in Common

The rest of the day turned out to be incredibly boring but that was just fine. There were no more attacks and the ship seemed to be lower now than it had been just hours ago. Breathing on deck was a little less strenuous and the biting cold no longer brought back the memories of waist-high snow in Hope's Covenant.

There were only three souls stirring around the ship since the battle. Lorne, Dyne, and Jonas had managed to repel the attack but they had been the only ones to make it through. It was unnervingly quiet. Every now and again, she could hear the whispers of the caged mortals below but other than that, it was silent.

She had even managed to get in a few hours of real sleep. It came surprisingly easy since she chose a hammock and not the cold rain and wind this time. Lorne also settled down for once, stripping all his gear and basking in the glorious defeat of the Lylussians. Only Jonas seemed to adhere to a schedule; life on the ship had become all too routine to him.

He turned out to be quite a cook. That had been his job aboard the *Murder*. Dyne had assumed that all his time spent below deck was to help plot routes and fix holes and make sure the floors were clean.

Instead, he was slaving over stoves—cooking for his fellow mortals and even the caged blood slaves who would be food themselves come nightfall.

The smell wafting up from the kitchen was so inviting. Dyne could hardly contain herself when she saw Jonas coming up the steps with a platter of freshly baked cinnamon bread and a beer braised chicken. The one-eyed man smiled and was happy to serve her. That was something she wasn't used to.

Dyne was a harsh, cold person before she was a vampire. When she received the curse, that persona intensified and made her a loathsome creature that most could not stand to be around. She didn't care. The people who got to see her—to talk to her and know her company were scarce.

The simple, mortal body of hers was making her feel the strangest things. She understood the fear and the jealousy because she remembered those in her days before vampirism. What she didn't understand was why she smiled when Jonas brought her food. Or why she cared enough to listen to Lorne talk about things that didn't concern her. Why was she becoming more approachable and not just a sinister witch who wanted to destroy all in her path?

It had to be hindsight, she concluded. Dyne had already lived one mortal life. She made it to the grand age of twenty-seven years before she was spawned into a vampire. Once the curse of blood was flowing through her veins, she lasted another three hundred and ten. Now, with the experience of several amassed lifetimes, she could analyze her character with a bit more intelligence.

She knew that her self-pitying and arrogance got in the way of most everything she strived to achieve. If only she'd listened to the smarter people around her, she would have probably gotten her Overlord heart and been happier by the outcome. Death in a small, coastal town wouldn't have been on her plate. She would not have known *failure*.

But then again, there would have been no Hannah. Dyne reminded herself that all of her actions—all of her feelings, and all of her desires shaped her path into finding that little girl. No matter how many foolish decisions she made, she knew that the events of her life made her who she was—a mother who loved her little girl.

"So what's in the bag for ye, after all this?" Jonas asked, sitting across from her and watching her eat.

"You mean what will I do once our job is done?"

He nodded.

"I have revenge to tend to," she replied. "The one who sent me to the Underworld has an appointment with the Deathkeeper."

"I see," Jonas said, a slightly troubled look in his eyes. "But after that . . . after you have your retribution, then what?"

"I suppose I'll find a nice little hovel to settle down and live."

"Oh really?" Lorne smirked from the doorway. "Dyne the great wants to start a family, does she? This is truly hard to believe."

"Is it?" she asked, a small bit of surprise in her voice. "My whole reason for living was to start a family. I wanted Hannah and I also wanted to see Laraek's grave. I wanted *closure*. All of the killing, all of the murder and bloodshed wasn't going to leave me alone until I had that unknowing voice out of my head."

"You had to see his grave for yourself?" Jonas asked.

"That's right. And now that I know he's not in it, I can move on with my life." She looked down into her lap and suppressed a tear and added, "Despite having my little girl ripped away from me."

Lorne was about to say something to those words of strength but Jonas cut him off. "C'mon, now Lorne, leave the poor girl be," he said, placing a reassuring hand on her shoulder. "She's been through a lot in the last few days." He turned to face her and said, "I think that's a wonderful idea, Dyne. Go off and start a family."

"Thank you," she said. The words felt like acid on her tongue. She certainly wasn't used to saying that.

Lorne patted her head in a feeble attempt to say sorry and then left.

He had been cleaning up the deck—pulling spears out of the wood, washing away the blood, and pushing the swoopdrake overboard. The door was open but the sun had already started to make its descent, so the golden light across the floor was limited.

"If I may ask a question," Jonas started. "If you do not have unwavering allegiance to Lord Mydian, then why are you here? Why didn't you just disappear in Tharg or Pelopha and go track down your killer?"

Surely it wasn't because of Lorne, she thought. Mydian may have put him here to watch over her but he must have forgotten how her brute commander ended up in the Underworld in the first place. Dyne could easily kill him and if she couldn't, it wouldn't have been hard to elude him in the busy morning flow of Pelopha. "I guess you could say it's for personal achievement. I want to kill Kersey Avonwood and make sure the book doesn't end up in . . . unworthy hands," she stated coldly.

"Ah, I see. So then this is a hunt for you?"

"I suppose you could call it that," she answered. There was a small part of her that wanted to hear what Kersey had to say. The things she mentioned back in Tharg were quite interesting and someone as old as she would probably know more about what was happening on Mystyria than anyone else. Gathering the book was also important to her. Even if Kersey raised her army and threw Mystyria into the third War of Balance, Dyne still wanted the satisfaction of knowing it was in her own hands.

"So you're not here for Lord Mydian at all then, are you?"

"'Fraid not," Dyne answered. Although the dark god wanted to know who Laraek served, she wasn't going to do it for *him*. She had started to loathe him for the person he had become. He was a tiresome creature that was so fixated on killing Kersey and snatching the book from her pile of ash. He didn't care about anything but himself and his damnable bride. It was eerie by how similar he was to the way Dyne used to be when she was a vampire. He was walking the same walk she had for the last three-hundred years—the seclusion, the resentment, and the obsessions—they were all a part of her at one time.

"So why are *you* here? I'm assuming it *is* for Lord Mydian, correct?" Dyne asked, feeling the desire to make small talk for the first time ever.

"That's right, but don't worry, I won't bully my religious beliefs on you." He chuckled and was about to stand but Dyne pulled him back down into his seat.

"Wait," she pleaded. "Tell me, why are you so humble? Mydian's servants are usually nothing like you."

"Well, I had a different upbringing than most of his followers," Jonas said. "My family worshipped Whither." He settled back against the wall and recollected a story from his sordid childhood. "I lived in Addystiir, along with my mother and brothers. We were coming home from temple one night when Felornite priestesses attacked the city. You know how they attack, right?"

Dyne nodded that she did. Felornites assaulted cities and people the same way their goddess did—in the form of gargantuan warriors. They would take potions or cast spells to augment their size. Nothing was more destructive than a band of giant, angry priestesses ripping apart a city with their bare hands.

"I lost my entire family that night. One of those priestesses just happened to be storming by on her way to destroy one of Mydian's temples when she sadistically kicked our house. I was only seven and could remember watching the foundation rip from the ground and then, in an instant, it was flying through the air toward the river. My family was just one of many who died that night.

"The next day, every temple in the city turned its back on me. I was a young, hungry little boy with nowhere to go. I was a Whitherian and considered an outcast in Addystiir. When I knocked on the Mydianites' door, however, they welcomed me with open arms. Outcasts befriending outcasts.

"They gave me food, a bath, and even a place to stay until I was old enough to make it on my own. I was a missionary for the Master for six years before the *Seven*."

"I suppose you owe Mydian your life then, don't you?" Dyne asked.

"Not really. The Master was good to me. He took me in, made me his own, but then again, I'm sure any of the good natured gods would have done the same, had they been around." He pulled his chair a little closer. "What I'm saying is that Mydian is the god *I* chose. You may have your reasons to doubt him, to doubt your faith and beliefs, but that is your decision to make. The gods don't tell us who we can and can't worship, although they try. It's up to you to decide what you do with your life. Don't let anyone else choose for you, no matter how powerful, frightening, or convincing they are."

Jonas was right. No matter how many bad or good things Mydian promised Dyne, he still had no control of her faith. Just as she had told Laraek, her loyalty was to herself.

Not one god was worthy of her love.

"Anyone care to explain why my wife and I woke up on the floor of our cabin?" Laraek asked the three playing King's Blade.

Dyne didn't even look up from her cards. She just sat there, waited her turn, and listened to the impatient tapping of his foot.

"The Lylussians," Jonas said.

Eva let out a small gasp that Dyne thought was very annoying. While she was sleeping and enjoying the silent embrace of her husband, the rest of the crew was dying to save the ship.

"Where are Kraith and Timon?" Laraek asked, watching his vampires stir from their slumber. It didn't take them long to throw on their chain mail and leather and head outside.

"A few miles that way," Dyne said, kicking the floorboards. "We cleaned up and discarded the bodies. You're welcome." She stood, ready to walk off and get some fresh air but he held her in place.

"Jonas, Lorne, why don't the two of you help me ready the sails." They looked up at him and then to each other and realized the room needed to be clear for just a moment. Dyne growled as they headed past her with Laraek trailing. Her once lover gave her a quick nod and a friendly wink before leaving her alone with Eva.

"What?" Dyne asked, taking her seat and scooping up the cards. Eva's face wasn't as stern. Her soft expression was very unusual and slightly troubling.

"I learned that you and I have something in common," she gingerly said.

"Oh?" Dyne spread the cards out to play Anvil.

"Yes, we both share the compassion for children. You and I were both mothers."

"That does not mean we are *alike*," she breathed.

"I just want to know something. How did you . . . choose? What made you pick her from any other?" Dyne had never really thought about it. She didn't think it had anything to do with picking the right child. In truth, Hannah had been the first baby she'd seen since her vampiracy. The aura that surrounded her, the ability to detect one's own lifeline drew her in.

"My little girl was my heir. I felt her the moment I stepped into the house," Dyne admitted.

"Then you are lucky. I believe my bloodline has ended. Most of my family lived up in Boudia. Do you know where that is?"

"You're joking, right?" Dyne asked with a hint of hesitation. "That's my hometown, as well as your husband's."

"I didn't know that. I suppose trivial things such as origin don't cross the minds of vampires," she said. That was where she was wrong. Dyne knew first-hand that origin was something she thought about quite frequently when the vampiric curse swam in her veins.

"Where in Boudia did you live? And just how old are you?" Dyne wondered.

"I'm old enough," she laughed. Judging from her natural appearance, Dyne would have guessed she was around twenty at the time of her spawning. "But my family lived on Palace Street. There isn't a person alive in North Corscus who doesn't know where that is." Boudia's Palace Street stretched for five miles. Even Dyne herself grew up on the south end, near the temple district.

"That's true," Dyne said, not liking the fact that she was actually being put to good moods in the presence of this woman. It was the same person who pushed her over the railing just nights ago. "You don't sound Boudian. Laraek and I both have thick accents."

"My family lived in Boudia. I grew up in Bloodgate, a missionary for Mydian."

"Is that so? My father was a missionary when he wasn't defending the city in the Master's glory."

"Really? I hardly knew my father," Eva said, a warm smile surfaced as she seemed to recall a distant, happy memory. "He abandoned us while I was still so young."

"I'm sorry to hear that," Dyne said. The words felt forced, but she could sense her own sincerity, if only a little.

"It's ok. He got what he deserved for it," she said, an eerie, vacant look in her eyes.

"So why are you here?" Dyne asked, not caring anymore about her past or secrets of retribution. "And why are you being so polite?"

There were butterflies in her stomach. A loud rattle vibrated the walls of the cabin as the dragon started to descend. Dyne grabbed a handful of the sack she was sitting on and pressed her back against the wall. This was a very odd feeling that she didn't like.

"I suppose I'm trying to apologize," Eva said, obviously unphased by the dropping ship. "Until now I just saw you as a threat who might come along and snatch my husband away."

"Well you needn't worry about that, trust me," Dyne said, drumming her fingers against the table.

"I know, I know. Now I see that you and I both lost something. We both had our children taken from us." Her eyes were glazed, her skin paling. "I can't hate someone who has been through that." Dyne had thought something just like that only a day ago.

The cabin door opened and down came Laraek. His wooden smile showed that he had coaxed his wife into the apology. At least Dyne felt the genuine sincerity of it. "Everybody hold on—"

Before he could finish, there was a sudden drop that made Dyne's stomach turn in knots. The playing cards literally lifted a few inches from the table and then settled back down. There was a loud splash outside and a small trickle of water seeped through the roof. They had just been deposited into the sea. Dyne listened to the dragon's wing beats fade into the distance.

"Our last chance to take Kersey is upon us, girls." He motioned for them to follow him outside.

Dyne was about to trail after Eva but the sudden smell of Lorinstag Ale tickled her nose. It was back and stronger than ever. She followed it to the end of the crew cabin, just above the steps that led down to the cargo. There was a drip of pale green liquid splashing onto the floor. It fell in steady drops from the ceiling. She cupped her hand and held it out to gather a small bit and when she passed her tongue over her palm, she found it was indeed Lorinstag Ale. It was her favorite, expensive rarity. Apparently a bottle of it had broken above, in Laraek's cabin. She wanted to stay there and lap up all that wished to fall, but knew someone would eventually come looking for her, so she jogged down the cabin and up to the main deck.

It was quite warm out. The night air stirred chaotically around the ship as Jonas hurried to untie all the sails. Without the other mortals—the men who kept the ship running like Kraith and Timon—they were off to a much slower start. Laraek and Eva stood up by the bridge and Lorne was seated between the starboard ballistae. Most of the vampires were just lingering on deck, talking about Kersey, about the War that was no doubt in motion, and what they were going to do when it was all over.

Dyne made her way up to the bridge, offering Lorne a small, gentle smile that made her feel awkward. Eva stepped aside and humbly let her pass. All eyes were trained on the sea ahead, to the small fishing vessel that was still out of sight.

"She's not far off," Laraek told her. "We *will* catch up."

"We don't have half the crew we did before," Dyne pointed out. "Can we still do this?"

He dropped his head and looked down to the bowsprit. He gave Eva a worried gaze and then turned back to Dyne. "The world'll certainly change if we don't try."

.20.

A Shadow on the Wind

The beauty of the Pack Dragons never ceased to amaze her. Although they began soaring over Mystyria's waters only years before her imprisonment, Kersey still managed to travel enough to enjoy them. They were all shades of colors—mainly turquoise and lavender, but every so often a bright green or yellow one emerged from the heavens and carried off a ship. Dargas loved his great beasts—*servants*, just as any god should.

One of the most interesting and perhaps majestic qualities of the great winged creatures was their docility. They were incapable of harm and wouldn't even raise a claw to defend their own hides. They were incredibly intelligent. The bright lavender beast that was hauling their fishing vessel knew that the ship was too small to carry high up and that Clive wouldn't have been able to breathe, therefore it kept low, just a few hundred feet from the passing waves.

Dargas taught his beasts to serve mankind—observe them, and never become like their more sadistic and loathsome brothers. Most dragons, after all, were quite hostile. They mainly served whatever would feed them or pay them the best, depending on their intelligence. Not all dragons spoke and thought—but those that could, did so very well.

Many times Kersey had fed from the Pack Dragons. Their only response was a low, guttural growl that only recognized the slight prick of pain. She loved their blood—it was so pristine and pure. It was one of the most untainted things left on Mystyria. Human blood and anything that fell beneath it was tarnished by the world and its ways.

For the first time since traveling by Dargas' creatures, Kersey chose not to dine. She was in the presence of Clive and the sight—the notion that she would sink her teeth into the hindquarters of the dragon would probably be very unsettling.

His world had been turned upside since the prison—all because of her. At least he was safe now and content with what he had. Clive had nothing left on Mystyria but her. What an honor, she sarcastically thought. Kersey the mad, Kersey the Greater Overlord, and Kersey the failed Soul-Summoner was some poor, unfortunate mortal's prize. A part of her wanted to cry when she thought on the prospect that he would have been safer—and happier had she just left him there. There was another part that said no.

Clive would have continued his solitary life. He would wake up, dodge Sharisa on his way to work, deal with unruly inmates, and then come home. That would be his routine until the end of his days. Kersey knew what repetition was like. She knew how it could drive the mind around in circles. Along with a habitual life came a *boring* life that lacked meaning and purpose. It was something she had dealt with for the better part of a millennium. No, the more she thought about it, the more she realized she had *saved* him.

During the long and boring trip, the two had managed to talk quite a bit. She wasn't used to spending that much time with someone—not since she'd become a vampire, at least. Clive talked more about his family, mainly Nalia, and Kersey could tell just how heartbroken he was upon her death. He told her about the funeral—about how there was no one left in the family to come and pay their respects other than two girl friends of his sister that he'd never met.

Kersey even opened up a little herself. She talked about *her* family, although she had repressed so much fear and hate after the curse. There were so many spots of her history that she had simply forgotten. The vivid images of her mother's death were still very fresh but certain things, like the death of her brother, the friends who had died during the war, and all those buildings that were destroyed and then one day rebuilt were all blank spots in her brain. She didn't even remember what year after the curse that she left Keswing. It always amazed her by the way the mind could remember the bad things in great detail and lose track of all the little good memories.

Their undead navigator left his post for only a moment to drop sail and then quickly returned to keep them on course. The dragon had sat them down only moments ago and Clive was watching it leave from the bow of the ship. It was nearly impossible in this kind of darkness. They were in the blackest place of the world.

Their fishing vessel had been deposited at the Dargasian station in the Elandiran Sea, only twenty or so miles from Crynsia. Ruin wasn't ignorant enough to send them in that direction so Kersey's best intuitive guess told her that they were headed east, toward the Wingert Gap. It was the one place Mydian probably wasn't. Lyluss herself had even used that beach as a camp since it was too risky of a spot for the dark god to try and defend.

"Learn anything worthwhile?" Clive finally asked, breaking the two-hour silence that followed the moment after she decided to pick up the spell book.

"Much!" she excitedly said. Oh, and she had.

Aneesa's book was a work of pure genius. After all, the goddess of magic had crafted it herself. It astonished Kersey that such a powerful item would even be entrusted to a mortal. Didn't the Queen of Magic ever think that it might some day fall into the wrong hands? Kersey giggled to herself. She would probably be thinking that just this moment if she happened to look down from the heavens and see who had it.

Kersey stood up and held the book outstretched. The language was so deep—so intricate and precise that it was almost a hymn. Each syllable of every spell was like humming the chorus to a very fast-paced and delicate song. She had never been put off by the difficulties of magic and she wasn't about to start now.

With fingers dangling above her, she began to recite the words of one such spell. She spied Clive from the corner of her eye looking ever so astonished and thought it was well justified. The words she was speaking at that moment made no sense and even to those trained in magic, it still sounded like drunken gibberish.

When the last syllable of the last word rolled off her tongue, a dim light ignited the tips of her fingers. Kersey closed the book and examined her hands. She could feel the magic working and as soon as it was finished, the light faded, placing her once again on a starless, cloudless stage.

"What did that just do?" Clive asked, examining her fingers.

"Watch," she said, looking around. "Show me the navigator!" she called out to no one in particular.

Suddenly a thin trail of light left her finger and circled around Clive, up the steps to the bridge and ended when it touched the backside of their dead navigator. The light danced and lingered in place, clearly marking a path right to the point she instructed.

"That's hardly useful," Clive said.

"Oh?" she uttered, almost choking on her own words. The power was so incredibly potent. She wiggled her finger and cleared the spell. "Show me the lost treasure of Pura Se!" she commanded again.

This time, the thin trail glided from her finger and into the darkness of the water. It kept snaking its way out until it disappeared far off to the south. If they so chose to do so, they could have followed that trail to the fabled treasure of the Pura Se white knights. The *Vivid Direction* spell of Aneesa was quite extraordinary.

Clive smiled and rested his back against the bow. "Now that's impressive. But I hope it'll be worthy enough to get Ruin off of your back." His tone was so cheerful but his face told Kersey otherwise. Even though he was at ease, he was still probably homesick.

"Are you going to go back to Tharg? When everything is said and done, I mean?" she asked.

He snickered. "I don't know. There's not much there. I mean, the city will probably cave in from all the holes in the ground now."

"You have your family's resting place," she pointed out.

"I suppose. But a granite headstone is no reason to stick around a town that has nothing left for you. What about you?"

"What?"

"What are *you* going to do when everything is 'said and done'?"

Kersey sat back down against the starboard railing. "I'll either die and go to Lyluss' home or I'll die and be tortured in Mydian's." In her heart, it was that simple.

Clive's face was thick with discouragement when he asked, "Is there an option that doesn't involve you dying?"

She smirked but her eyes were distant as she thought about what he just said.

Kersey's life was of little value—to her and to the gods who wanted her. Ruin only needed her ability to raise the dead. It didn't matter if she lived or died in the process—as long as she did her job. She had long ago accepted the fact that this was how her life was supposed to be—a rag that was used to wipe up a mess and then thrown away like the piece of garbage it was. She had said three little words the night she escaped the prison but she never really believed anyone would care to listen:

I cannot die.

What kind of world would it be where Kersey Avonwood did her job, was forgiven, and then allowed to live? That thought never crossed her mind but she was starting to want it—to forge a life that was full of optimism, of—

I cannot die

—dreams and desires that she never got when she was a mortal. Clive was unknowingly whispering hope into her ear. He had been such a help this entire trip and he didn't even know it.

"You were quite the swordsman back there," she said. "Had run-ins with vampires in the past, I assume?"

He chuckled when he saw her jokingly, relaxed expression. "Hardly. I would remember their interesting light display when they die. I only killed three of them. Your helpers took care of the rest. I'm afraid I'm a little rusty when it comes to swinging a blade."

"There'll be plenty more flashes of light to . . . interest you, I'm sure." She didn't like the somberness that followed those words. They weren't done fighting. Clive was smiling—his mouth trying its best to stifle the grim frown that should have been there. It had been his choice to stay and fight and she was overwhelmed that one person on Mystyria would care enough to put their life on the line for her.

"Thank you," she said, almost defeated. It stung her throat and she felt a sudden guilt because she hadn't bothered to express it yet.

"For what?" he asked, genuinely curious.

"For staying with me. For *saving* me. Gods, for just being you and helping me make sense of my muddled mind." There were tears mounting in her eyes but for once, it wasn't sadness, a beating, or a rape that brought them on. These were joyful. Kersey rested her head in her hand and put another one across her chest. Her heart was pounding so hard now—reminding her for the first time in ages just how alive she was. It was almost as if it had stopped a millennium ago and just this moment begun anew.

"I love you, Clive."

An uncomfortable silence settled across the deck. "What?" he asked, crawling toward her on his knees. She had whispered it so faintly, so delicately that she knew he didn't hear. It was more for her ears anyway. Kersey had always loved Clive but she never had a reason to say so. It was probably the prison bars. Or the shackles. Or the constant bloody hands and face, she reminded herself.

Out of the darkness, a spear whipped past, interrupting her chance to say it again. It lodged into the bridge railing and the navigator looked on, oblivious to the sudden assault on their borrowed vessel. It didn't take long for Clive and Kersey, the tender moment now passed, to get to their feet and face the empty black of the sea behind them.

Empty to Clive, at least.

Kersey, with her enhanced vision, saw quite clearly what was happening. Her eyes narrowed into slits and she spotted the large ship drawing closer, silent and incredibly swift. There were a few vampires standing around—eyeless, monstrous vampires—but none dared to fly off and board the tiny fishing vessel. Kersey knew they would try and sink it first. She saw the blond woman on the bridge—the one who she spoke with, looking through the lens of a Nighteye right back at her. *Pity. I would have liked to have talked to her once more,* she thought.

Another spear fired, this one passing through the railing and ending up all the way at the door of the captain's cabin. Clive narrowly missed having his knees sliced. He had a confused, but clearly distressed look about him as he drew his sword. "Pirates?"

"No, it's a shadow on the wind. It's *them*," she said, heading back to the cabin. She grabbed him by the collar and pulled him along. "The Mydianites from Tharg."

"Where are you taking me?" he said, trying his best to drag his feet. Kersey showed a tiny bit of her strength and pushed him inside.

"Wait here," she said, looking over her shoulder. The ship was getting closer, the etching on the side now easily readable as *'The Black Murder'*. "You've no use on the deck other than target practice for *them*." With that, she shut the door before he could offer up one word of objection.

This fight wouldn't last long, she mused. It wouldn't even be a fight. There would be one less ship sitting in the Elandiran after tonight. Her mind reached out and found many things lurking beneath their slow-moving vessel. The sounds of the water crashing around the hull, the shouting vampires and launching spears were tiny echoes in her mind now compared to the hammering voices of the deep.

Kersey made her way back to the stern of the ship, paying little mind to the spears that rocked past her and thudded harmlessly into the bridge steps and cabin. When she stepped upon the railing and held her arms out, she thought for a brief moment that the Mydianites would take an easy shot and knock her down from her pedestal. In truth, they were bewildered by her unusual behavior and seemed to stop firing long enough to watch. The black ship was so close now—literally dwarfing their tiny fishing boat.

With arms outstretched, Kersey recited another spell she had learned earlier. Her memory for enchantment was excellent—she'd mastered healing spells and disease wards in such little time that she was rushed to the Keswing infirmary the day the first War of Balance broke out to help aid the veteran healers and priests.

An orange halo formed over her head and the voices of the dead beneath her doubled. They were all crying out—crying for a chance to come up and do whatever it was she would have them do. Kersey wanted to use each and every one of them, but there was one voice that made her smile. She didn't even know what it belonged to, only that it sounded . . . *large*.

I can stop them in their tracks, mistress of the dead, it called. *Just say the word.* The voice was so deep and so detached from Mystyria. It had been dead for a long time—sitting, waiting in the prison of its mortal remains for a chance to climb to the surface and make a difference. She completely related.

Kersey flicked her wrist to the magic spot, some one hundred yards away from the *Murder* and instantly the water began to bubble like a pot of boiling potatoes. The torrent of ripples grew so intense that it looked like something massive would emerge from the blackened depths and for a moment, she was certain that it would. However, the bubbles revealed nothing of the terrifying creature that was now awakened. It made a thick, silent trail in the water as it slowly stalked the starboard edge of the *Murder*.

Gods be with anyone aboard that doomed vessel, she sadistically thought.

Up close, the fishing vessel looked a bit larger than Dyne had originally thought. Sure, it was miniscule situated in the shadow of the *Murder*, but it wasn't just a tiny boat that was going to be easily crippled by ballistae spears.

It was no match for the *Murder's* speed. Once the vessel was spotted on the open sea—still swaying from the dragon's drop—it was but a small effort to turn sail and bear down on its course. They would be in boarding range in just a few seconds but Dyne didn't think anyone on the *Murder* had enough guts to try and take Kersey on directly. Laraek would see her underwater first, so the ballistae up front continued to drill holes into the hull.

Kersey and her mortal friend had been sitting on the deck, talking and completely oblivious to the creeping death that was stalking behind them. Dyne watched through the Nighteye as they scrambled the moment the *Murder* opened fire. Kersey shoved the man into the cabin—a strange, protective notion that made no sense. Why on Mystyria would she care to protect a *mortal*? The history books *had* to be right, Dyne concluded. Kersey was an evil, vile creature that had no business being among the rest of the world. Despite having a seemingly empathetic relationship, the vampiress still had a heart of ice that Dyne wanted to shatter in a million pieces—for herself.

Not for Mydian.

With the mortal safely tucked away, Kersey returned to the stern of the boat and stood atop the railing. Her arms flailed as she recited the words to some unknown—but probably powerful piece of magic. When the orange halo encircled her crown, Dyne stepped down and yelled, "She's casting!"

Laraek raced to the front and leaned over the bowsprit—eying Kersey with a weathered, contemplating gaze. He shook his head and said, "Well, she's done now."

"Not much of a spell," said Eva. She stood by Dyne's side, looking up to the forecastle deck where Laraek stood. Lorne and Jonas were not far behind, both peeking over the starboard side toward the front—waiting for her tiny boat to be overshadowed by theirs.

Neither of them saw what was coming just off to their right.

Everyone was so enthralled that Kersey was so close that the tread of bubbles coming toward their ship went unnoticed. It was nearly as wide as the *Murder* herself—but it moved slowly—stealthily trying to take them from behind. Dyne licked her lips and was reminded of the sound that brewed Hippersnouts made in the Boudian distillery and that was what prompted her to raise the Nighteye and look starboard.

"Laraek!" she screamed out, the moment her eyes fixed upon it. The Nighteye turned the water a light grey that made the advancing shape beneath it turn black. It was gigantic—several times longer than the *Murder* and roughly just as thick. She could see the back end moving side-to-side—wading through the water like a lizard.

By the time she made out the contours of its frame, Laraek had already darted to the starboard side and looked over. Dyne remembered vampiric vision—much like the Nighteye only stronger and didn't make one's arm tired from holding up a metal tube. He saw the shape clear as she had and the fearful, frantic look on his face made her incredibly worried.

"Hard to port!" he yelled to the vampire manning the wheel. The pale creature spun with all his might—desperately trying to turn the ship to the left to avoid a collision from whatever beast Kersey had managed to awaken.

They weren't moving nearly fast enough. If not for the orientation of the fishing boat ahead, Dyne would have never guessed they were veering to the side. The bubbles lurched on—closing the distance between it and the *Murder*. She took a few steps back, suddenly not feeling safe at the railing any more. Lorne was by her side, halberd at the ready.

The frothy sound of the shape suddenly dissipated. Dyne held the Nighteye up again and cautiously peeked over the side. It was gone—vanished to the depths of the Elandiran. Kersey's power over it must have faded. The sheer size of it must have been tiresome to her. Dyne breathed a sigh of relief and for just a moment the deck was silent.

The vampires—the fifteen or so that had survived the night—stood around and looked to one another for an explanation to the sudden calm. Only three were Crossbacks, their swollen eye-sockets gazing out toward an unsettling sea. Laraek and Eva exchanged nervous glances and Lorne continued to study the murky depths over the railing. The soft crash of the water against the hull and weathered creaks of the ship's wood were the only sounds.

Then there was a dull thud beneath them.

It wasn't much—only a distant vibration that was muted by the water—like something scraping against the hull. There was a rough grinding and suddenly something erupted from the sea in a violent splash. A chorus of swords being drawn sounded across the deck as everyone readied themselves for the unexpected. There was something in the air—something that the water expelled—that was twisting wildly and flying high above the ship. If the moon hadn't silhouetted it, Dyne would have never saw it.

Then, as quickly as it shot up—the object began to fall. Water was tumbling off of its shiny, wooden surface. It spun and swiveled and expelled water and everyone backed up as it came crashing down and hit the deck in a solid *'thwack'* that nearly toppled Dyne to her knees.

It was their rudder.

"Uh oh," Laraek almost said before the ship was pounded from below.

The *Murder* groaned in angry protest as she began to turn on her side. Barrels, crates, and sacks that had been restacked after the Lylussian attack found themselves sliding to the port side, most of them going overboard. Dyne ran the span of the ship, Nighteye drawn, but found nothing more than the grey sea. This creature—whatever it called itself—was beneath them.

After a few seconds of being pushed aside, she thought for sure that the water was going to reach the deck and begin to flood down to the cabins and cargo hold. Or worse than that, the creature was going to keep pushing and flip them completely over. However, once the panicked cries ended and most of the deck cargo went overboard, the ship leveled back out and the sea turned calm again.

"We have to do something!" Dyne yelled, but felt powerless. This kind of battle had no way of winning.

"Feel free to jump in and save us," Laraek said, the thickest sarcasm she'd ever heard. She shot him a cold look and continued to scan the sea. Most everyone was watching the water from the wrong side. It hadn't occurred to anyone that Kersey might have summoned more than just the large, devastating beast to wreck the ship. They certainly didn't see the scaly humanoid creatures that were climbing over the railing and onto the deck.

Dyne could *smell* it. There was the stench of death nearby—the same smell that wafted from the rows of undead that constantly surrounded Kersey. That smell had been left behind in Tharg but now, in the water, thousands of miles away, it was back.

She began to head toward the bow when suddenly a sword sliced through the railing where she'd just been leaning. At first she was dumbfounded by the sight of the blade—a thick scimitar made of wood and lined with some sort of large jagged teeth. She knew what the beast was that held it, although she'd never seen one before; certainly not an undead one.

It was a Ken'shar, a seven-foot tall lizard-like creature. There were human features—legs, arms, and torso—but every inch was covered in green and brown scale. Its reptilian hands and feet were webbed and its eyes were narrow and yellow. They lived in colonies beneath the sea—scavengers who attacked ships and stole only things that could be used to protect them or help turn the tables on the next vessel that passed by.

This particular one was little more than the shell of a Ken'shar. Its scales were either missing or turning a putrid black that was thick with algae. Its bloated belly and slit throat told Dyne that it failed on the last boarding mission. A forked tongue hung lifeless from the corner of its mouth and its long-dead eyes were empty sockets that saw nothing. A corroded chest plate hung across its scaly breast—held there only by a couple of decaying leather straps.

Out of instinct, Dyne kicked the creature in the midsection and sent it flying overboard, its scimitar dropping to the deck. She turned around, ready to tell Lorne or Laraek to be on the lookout but no explanation was needed. The deck was crawling with such creatures.

Not only were there Ken'shar, but also men—soldiers, pirates, and merchants that had their guts torn open or their throats slit ear to ear. Apparently Kersey found the site of a skirmish—a sunken ship or a fishing boat. The Ken'shar probably attacked it, the men fought back, and this was their dead, all coming back to do battle—only this time they were on the same side.

There was another hard knock against the *Murder* and everyone lost their footing as it leaned toward the sea. Luckily, the vampires held on but most of the men and Ken'shar—with years worth of seaweed and muck clinging to them—slipped and went over.

Dyne drew her sword when she saw scaly hands latch onto the railing in front of her. She raised it high above and brought it down on its wrists, severing the creature from its grasp on the *Murder*. She grinned by the way the long dead hands were still clenched around the railing when another thump jarred the ship—causing her to tumble and lose hold on her sword.

The *Murder* started to go on its side once again and she watched—horrified—as Adella's priceless blade slid across the deck. She scrambled to her feet and chased after it, dodging vampires, Jonas, and oncoming Ken'shar and men as she finally made it to the edge of the railing and watched as the blade teetered on the rim of the wood. Dyne dropped to her knees, slid toward the falling grip—

—and grabbed it just before it was lost to the Elandiran forever.

She breathed a heavy sigh and tightened her hold on the blade. She was just about to pull herself back up on deck when the water beneath her exploded and a skeletal, slimy shark broke through. Its chipped teeth and hollow skull made it look like it was smiling.

Dyne's eyes widened and she deftly pulled herself out of harm's way as the shark's jaws closed around air. It returned to the dark depths and reminded her that falling overboard would be a very bad thing.

When she got to her feet, the first thing she noticed was the large, skeletal tentacle that was slowly and unnoticeably rising out of the water behind the ship. Everyone else was too busy fighting the Ken'shar and dead men who continued to swarm the deck. They were no match for Laraek's men but the creature surfacing behind was certainly another story.

The tentacle was tipped with long barbs at the end that made Dyne realize it was actually a tail. Water was pouring down its skeletal links as it continued to rise well above the *Murder's* tallest mast. It lurched to the side and she knew it was winding up—garnering strength to let loose another attack that was going to cripple the ship even further.

"Everybody down!" she screamed, a little too late. Only she and Lorne managed to kiss the deck fast enough.

The tail swept across with so much force that it broke through all three masts, splintering them like twigs. A couple of white flashes lit up the night as two of Laraek's men found themselves in halves. There was a heavy groaning and she saw the shadows of the masts starting to change. They were *falling*.

For a second, she stood dumbfounded—watching as an unseen assailant ripped their ship apart. She was so awestruck that the masts were collapsing like timbers that she didn't feel Lorne and Jonas grab her by the shoulders and pull her into the crew cabin.

There was a jarring thump that cracked the deck open as one of the masts landed squarely on top of them. It pushed its way through and finally ended up at their feet—the weight far too much for the forecastle to handle. They could see that the other two had fallen to the sides, in the water. Everyone on deck was pressed to the railing, recovering from the falling sails and ballistae. There was now such a clear, uninhibited view of the creature that was steadily rising out of the water.

Its massive skull was as wide as the *Murder* herself. There were empty eye sockets that dumped water onto the deck that had the same anger as it probably had years ago when it was killed. Its teeth were sickly yellows and greens and were the size of broadswords. There were long tusks across its cheeks, chin, and forehead. Dyne couldn't believe Kersey had managed to find one of these. It was a sapphire dragon.

Gods, this is too many dragons for one day, she thought.

The beast grabbed onto Laraek's cabin with two, massive claws and started to pull the ship aside. Everyone braced themselves once more, but now that the creature was out of the water, it wasn't going to be as easy for it to topple them.

Jonas and Laraek armed the side ballistae, turned to the monster, and fired into its feet. The beast let go of the *Murder* and held its claws up, a small, coarse growl escaping its dead maw. Both men desperately hurried to reload but the dragon felt too little pain—and too much anger.

Laraek abandoned his ballista when the dragon brought its foot down. He rolled aside as the massive appendage broke through the upper deck and ripped up the hammocks below. A large puff of flour shot up from the hole. Dyne was growing worried by its strength. If the dragon went just two more decks down, it would punch a hole in the hull of the ship.

She battled through two Ken'shar and one dead man to get to Laraek's position. She grabbed him by the sleeve and jerked him inside his cabin. "We have to get off this ship! There's not going to be anything worth salvaging." Her voice was troubled but strong.

"Go right ahead. I'm not abandoning the *Murder*!" he screamed over the sound of the splintering deck. He kept a watchful eye on his wife standing by the steps up to the devastated forecastle. She was having no trouble keeping the Ken'shar off of her.

The beast's fist hammered down again, this time on the roof above them. Open sky poured in as the quarterdeck, along with the sternpost and wheel was completely ripped off. The dragon simply discarded it in the water. By now the remaining vampires and Lorne had resorted to using flaming spears. He launched them from his ballista, scoring several clean hits, but with the water and the drenching seaweed clinging to the beast, they did little more than anger it further.

Her hiding spot was no longer safe. With the roof gone and nothing holding the sides up but air, Dyne knew the next hit would be right where she was laying. Water trickled down from the dragon's slimy throat as she rolled onto her back and looked up at it. One of the Crossbacks was sitting squarely on its nose, hacking wildly with an axe while the beast yelled out in a crude rumble. It sounded more like a low horn than that of a creature. This was the best opportunity to move.

Laraek got to his feet first and headed to the only loaded ballista left. Dyne scowled at his back for leaving her behind but got up and followed suit, nevertheless. Moving across the deck was an adventure. In most places the debris created such an obstacle that she had to climb over ballistae pieces, deck wood, and sails. In other spots, it was missing, revealing the cabins below. It would be a miracle if their ship stayed afloat.

Dyne spotted a crossbow sitting up on the demolished forecastle deck and she wanted to grab it, but getting there would be no easy feat. She sheathed her sword; it was only getting in the way. A Gothmirk man slashed across her midsection, narrowly missing her naval. She reached out and shoved his slimy body over the railing and continued up the battered steps to the crossbow.

The dragon screeched and pulled the vampire from its nose and in one quick motion, bit him in half. His short-lived cry only carried for a moment before the ash scattered through the skeletal jaw of his killer.

Jonas was sitting beneath the ruined steps, a bottle of ale between his legs. His ballista was floating in the water next to the ship and with it, his courage. Dyne had never seen such defeat in a man's face before. That was a feeling she had never known—not even now, in the shackles of a mortal body. She didn't understand what he was feeling or thinking. All that she knew was that it made her angry.

"What are you doing?" she screamed, reaching up and nabbing the crossbow from the forecastle. "We need you to help kill this thing."

"Will Mydian take care of me?" he asked, eyes distant as he took a drag from his bottle.

"What? Now isn't the time for this, Jonas." She could see the misery in his eyes.

"I know you have your doubts about the Master, but do you think he honestly cares about *me*? To see *this* happen to one of his most devout followers?"

Dyne eyed the dragon and made sure its attacks were still at the far end of the ship. "Lord Mydian took you in once, Jonas. The Master most certainly loves you." Those words stung her tongue but she thought they were probably true. Someone like Jonas, as blissfully unaware of what Mydian did to his servants, would no doubt be held in high esteem.

"Where are you going to go when you die, Dyne?" he asked.

"I'm not entirely sure," she answered. "I'll probably burn in Cytop for the very thoughts I've had this week, but then again, I think I've earned enough reprieve for having to deal with your commander and his lovely bride." She was smiling, but Jonas wasn't. He probably didn't even hear her. His eyes were fixed on the dragon, the bottle now at his side.

He was weeping and for just a moment, Dyne's inner instinct to ridicule came to the surface, but then she realized something. She actually liked Jonas. He was one of the first people she had ever sat down and talked with—not as a subordinate or a servant—but as a friend. A companion. Dyne was starting to see the core of living—of where the power of being a mortal came from.

"So you'll burn or be forgiven," he said, and then looked deep into her. "Well, either way, I suppose I'll be seeing you in the Underworld. Goodbye, Dyne."

Before she could say a word, he darted out from beneath the stairs, leaving the bottle and dragging a glowing sack along with him. She wanted to say something; to scream out and try to stop him but it was too late. Her heart and mind didn't know how to react to such a thing. Only Hannah had made her aware of what the feeling of loss meant.

Jonas stepped upon the railing and waved his hands to get the dragon's attention. It stopped its attack for just a moment to take notice—its skull darting back and forth as if trying to understand what this fool of a man was doing. Everyone backed up while it lowered down to the deck, level with the one who dared to make a stand. Dyne continued to watch from her hiding spot, shaky fingers letting the crossbow fall.

The dragon's skull quickly rose back out of reach and then slammed down on top of Jonas, its jaws open wide to rip him apart with the fury of a hundred, grinding teeth. There was a scream inside its mouth that stopped the fighting on deck. Even the Gothmirk men and Ken'shar seemed to take notice of the horrible mutilation occurring twenty feet above them.

Blood was running over the dragon's jaw and Dyne could see Jonas inside—could see the pain in his eyes as he looked right back at her. She couldn't take it any longer and she dropped to her knees and lowered her head on the first step.

Then it happened.

There was a colossal explosion that made her look up so fast that she bumped her head on the step above. The dragon's skull was flying apart—landing in the sea and on the *Murder*. Its skeletal body writhed for just a moment and then stiffened before disappearing into the black water. Pieces of the shattered skull floated as far as she could see; small beacons that were still burning. A loud ringing echoed in her ear and she shook her head to clear it. Jonas had ended his life with an entire sack of Glowbombs but it had saved their own in the process.

She returned to the deck and helped the remaining four vampires, along with Lorne, Laraek, and Eva, clear the rest of the Gothmirks. She only prayed that Kersey didn't find another one of those dragons clinging to the bottom of the sea.

For once in her life, Dyne was saddened by death. She climbed her way up to the forecastle and simply sat there. Everyone else was trying to make sense of what had happened and how they were ever going to get moving again but for some reason she didn't care. Was she becoming a good person? Preposterous, she mused.

In her mind, she was no longer aligned with Mydian. That alone should have made her good, but that notion was silly when she thought about it. There were so many forms of evil in the world. Once she figured out her place in it, and once she believed her own allegiance to herself, she would simply take up another one.

.21.

The Light of a New Day

The damage to the *Murder* had been substantial but by the grace of the gods, she had stayed afloat. The majority of the upper deck had been ripped to shreds, revealing the cabin deck below. In a few places, the destruction was so severe that the cargo-hold floor could be seen. Only two blood slaves lasted the duration of the trip, but the dragon had pummeled them beneath the weight of the upper deck. All that remained now was a large, twisted blood-covered cage. Laraek had thoroughly checked out the integrity of the hull and came to the conclusion that they were safe—at least for now.

Dyne had helped clear some of the wreckage but not because she wanted to get the ship back in order. She knew that the grief of Jonas had shown on her face and she didn't want Lorne or anybody else to question it. So, if she stayed busy, that would give her a reason to stay quiet.

"Well this is just lovely," Laraek sarcastically said, kicking the rudder that sat in the middle of their ruined deck. "Do you know how difficult this will be to fix?" he asked Dyne. Before she could answer, he added, "Have any clue how hard it will be to raise the one mast we have left?" He pointed to the middle one—the same one that had crashed down on the crew cabin steps.

"But I'm sure you'll think of something," Eva purred. She kissed him on the cheek, smiled at Dyne, and then was off toward his shell of a cabin.

"What about the rest of the *Seven*?" Lorne asked. Dyne had completely forgotten about them.

"They will come along, eventually, but there is no guarantee they will spot us."

"How far is land from here?" Dyne asked. She couldn't find her Nighteye after the attack and as far as she could tell, it was black all around.

"Too far for you to swim and for us to fly, if that's what you mean," Laraek answered. "We are stuck here, friends."

"We've failed, then," Lorne said, sitting on the rudder. "We've failed Lord Mydian."

"That we have," Laraek agreed. "Kersey will have her army in just a few hours. Mydian just may lose this war because of us."

"And what if he does? Why should his fate fall on our shoulders?" Dyne asked, feeling the anger rise in her voice.

"Watch your mouth," Laraek said.

"No! In the last week . . . to me, at least, I've been from one end of Mystyria, to the Underworld, and now up to the other end. It has taken me this long, through this much tribulation to realize that *I* am in control of my destiny. Mydian has put me through so much hell. And for what? Just to chase after a girl who didn't play by his rules a thousand years ago? Since when did our courage, our desire to make ourselves proud sell for so little?"

"Just how much have you had to drink?" Laraek asked.

"We all want to kill Kersey, right?" she asked, ignoring her former lover's grating tone. Instead, she pointed to him and said, "You want the spell book, don't you?" Before he could spit a reply, she added, "Then let's go and do it. Let's kill Kersey. Let's take the book from her. Not for Mydian. Not for the glory of the Master, but for *ourselves*. An army of dutiful undead may already be up there, in the hills, surrounding her, but I say we keep after her. We've faced this kind of danger before." Dyne chuckled weakly. "Besides, we're all going to end up together in the Underworld anyway."

"Well, it may be sooner than we think!" Eva shouted. She was pointing to the horizon but Dyne couldn't see anything. Laraek and the other vampires scrambled to their feet and she was just about to question it when their faces snarled and they let loose a low growl that made her arms break out in gooseflesh.

The sky was a pretty purple, the telltale color of the approaching sunrise.

Laraek had a frantic look on his face as he rubbed his neck and paced back and forth. "This is not good," he said. "Look at this!" He was pointing to the horrible condition of the ship. "Our cabin is ripped wide open. The entire crew deck is littered with holes and all the cargo, the sheets and blankets went overboard. There is no decent spot on this ship to hide from the sun."

"What are you going to do?" Lorne asked. Dyne remembered how fearful he had always been when the sun crept close to being a danger.

Laraek turned to the four worried vampires and said, "Tie up."

The creatures darted back and forth, searching for ropes and chains. Eva cut the rigging from the fallen mast and tossed her husband a length of it before gathering herself some. Laraek tied one end around the bow of a ballista. It probably weighed two hundred pounds. He then tied the other end to his ankle.

Every vampire on deck followed suit, each keeping a worried eye on the horizon. The sun would be peaking over the water in a matter of minutes. After all of the light-sensitive creatures managed to tether themselves to an anchor, they stepped up to the railing and swung over to sit on it. Dyne finally realized what they were going to do.

Laraek turned to her and said, "If anyone comes by, just say that the ship was attacked by marauders and that help is already on the way. Hide our flags. We'll be back at sunset." With that, he jumped over and let the heavy wood carry him below, away from the harmful reach of the sun. The rest of the vampires, as well as Eva did the same.

It was only Lorne and Dyne now. All of the other mortals aboard the *Murder* had perished in only two days' time. Jonas had been the last. With that thought in mind, she felt something *'plink'* against the metal heel of her boot. She bent down and picked up the small, emerald orb.

It was his eye.

She played with it between her fingers and ambled her way over to the forecastle steps where Lorne had already started on a bottle of ale. She sat next to him and looked out toward the ruined cabin that Laraek and his wife had shared. The sun was just starting to come over the horizon and she closed her eyes with a renewed hope, thinking on what it would be like to not feel like such a failure—to not serve anyone but herself.

"Everything alright?" Lorne asked as sleep began to wrap its arms around her.

"It will be," she answered and clenched the glass eye.

"Clive, wake up! Get up, *get up!*"

He had heard those words before, only last time they were uttered so urgently, so demanding that he found himself on his feet and out of a burning house in seconds. This time, however, they were hushed and slow, as if her telling him to wake up was a secret.

It was day out now and Clive had actually been enjoying a brief spell of shuteye. There was too much light bleeding in from the window of the cabin so it made the two shadowed figures standing between him and the doorway impossible to discern. When his sleepy mind counted one extra that should have been inside, he sat upright and cleared the grogginess from his mind.

Kersey was bent over, below the windows' view before she sat down on the bed and put a finger to her mouth. Clive leaned to look past her and saw it was the dead navigator who also stood inside. He was a mess—dried blood from head to toe, a large slit across the throat, and a beaten, weathered face from the biting wind of the dragon ride.

"What's going on, Kers?"

As soon as he spoke, there was a resounding "hello?" from outside. He quickly threw the covers off and grabbed his boots from beneath the bed. Kersey ducked and made her way over to the window and peered out. Clive hopped over to join, trying to don every piece of clothing he had at once.

There was a ship—not as large as the *Murder,* but one much bigger than their tiny vessel—sitting squarely across their bow. It was preventing them from sailing. Clive noticed the black flag bearing a red 'X' with a white sword on one side and a golden torch on the other. He didn't recognize the origin, but Kersey certainly did.

"They're Mydianites from Crynsia," she told him. "That flag is the symbol of the House of Knives, from Tsiral Crool. Crynsia's ruler."

"Well, what are they doing here?" he asked.

There was a man on board their boat. He was a thin, scrawny one with sweat-matted hair and red, sun-burnt skin. His tiny blue eyes were peering into the cabin—the one spot where people on the fishing vessel could hide.

"Probably just looking for easy loot, but go find out for sure," Kersey said, as if it would be that easy.

"What? You can't be serious. They are probably *looking* for us!"

"They're looking for *me*!" she corrected. "I don't want to kill them and risk their ship being missed."

"Kers, these Mydianites probably don't even know what you look like."

"True, but either way, we're going to have trouble if they see him." Her tiny fingers pointed to the half-butchered navigator—the *standing and aware* half-butchered navigator. She then laid a hand across her own chest and added, "And they certainly aren't going to just leave an innocent, young girl alone in the open water."

Kersey was right, although Clive didn't know if she meant it sincerely or sarcastically. Anyone who sailed the seas this far north weren't looking for honest trade. There were no fishermen or merchants—there were pirates and murderers. This was the darkest place on Mystyria, he reminded himself.

"Anybody in there?" the man called from behind the mast.

"Wait here," Clive said, laying his sword across the bed. He grabbed one of Kersey's knives and stuffed it into the back of his slacks and threw his shirt over top of it. After making sure she and the navigator were out of view, he pulled the door open and stepped foot on deck.

There were more men outside than the one on their boat. They were all crowded around the Mydianite vessel—all watching and listening with great interest as to why this tiny fishing boat was way out in their territory.

"Mornin' to ye," came the cheery voice of the sun-burnt man. He was looking the deck over—looking for others, for weapons, and probably for valuables. This wasn't going to end well, Clive thought. Someone was probably going to die today and for such a small, insignificant reason.

"Is there a problem?" Clive asked, leaning against the door of the cabin. The Mydianite was checking their sail and rigging, pulling on it, testing its strength and durability. He smiled, as if oblivious to the question.

"You're a long way from port, my friend. Where'd ye come from?"

Clive wasn't good at lying on the spot—came from working in the justice system, but this was one time when his life could have very well depended on it. His mind was flooded with answers but he needed one that made sense—a town that was near, a port that wasn't far off, a place where they very well could have come from and he managed to say—

"Crynsia."

That was a bad idea. While it would have probably been easier just to say they had ridden in on the dragon, it would have taken much longer to explain why. These Mydianites, had they heard of Kersey, would have known that she would have been traveling by exactly those means. Still, the answer Clive gave didn't help their situation at all because now, on top of a messy lie, he was probably going to have to answer questions about a city he had never been to and knew nothing about.

"Quite a long way from Crynsia, aren't we?" His face was musing and Clive knew he could tell it was a lie. But then again, he probably expected it. Everyone with a ship on these waters had *something* to hide.

Clive wasn't even sure how far away Crynsia was. He wouldn't know how to operate the ship in order to get back there even if that's where their port was. All he did know was that he was sitting on a very unsteady foundation of lies that was about to topple at any moment.

"Well you have to go where the fish are," he managed and smiled just a little. It sounded good, at least to him.

The man looked all the way back to his companions on the ship and then to the edges of the fishing vessel. "Where are your nets?" he asked.

Clive could feel the heat rushing to his face. There were none. Since the rightful proprietor of the fishing vessel was probably somewhere in Tharg when it was stolen, all of the equipment on board had been carried off. There were no nets, no fishing poles, not even a meager scrounging of bait. They were on a fishing boat with no means to fish. Still, he had to keep the ruse going.

"We haven't started today," he offered. "We were still asleep when you came aboard and—"

"*We?*" the Mydianite asked.

That was the end of the ploy. They were caught and Clive knew it. This man—this Mydianite had been a little too clever or perhaps just taking advantage of his sleepy, slow-moving mind. Either way, the next question was going to be painfully obvious.

"Care if I look inside the cabin?" he said with positive certainty.

There wasn't much they could do now, he thought. Hopefully Kersey was listening by the door and knew what was about to happen. They would let the Mydianite in, let him look around, and then kill him behind the closed door. After that, they would have to fight to get their boat free of the Crynsian ship.

Clive nodded and backed away from the door. The scrawny man threw back the flap of his coat and rested his hand on the hilt of his sword. He noticed Clive's dismay and felt that he needed to add, "Can never be too careful, ye know?"

"Trust me, I do," he returned.

He was expecting the Mydianite to draw his sword and attack the Gothmirk as soon as the door opened but that didn't happen. Clive's view was blocked by the scrawny fellow's back but he could briefly see Kersey sitting on the bed, a large robe wrapped around her. Thank the gods that the bloody dress had been thrown overboard last night along with the rags they used to clean the deck.

After the two men filed into the cabin, Clive saw the Gothmirk was nowhere to be found, the covers were pulled, and his sword had been hidden. He searched the room high and low and wondered if Kersey had managed to stuff him beneath the bed.

"Why 'ello, miss," he said, tipping his invisible hat. Kersey gave a shallow nod and threw her hand up slightly. When the Mydianite turned his back to her, she looked Clive in the eyes and motioned toward the small closet at the rear of the cabin. That was where the Gothmirk had been stowed.

The scrawny man was searching their entire cabin, as if admiring a new home before the big purchase. He checked his teeth in the oval mirror on the right wall and stopped at the table to grab one of the

Stalmer nuts. His eyes lit up when he saw the silver coins sitting in the water pitcher, so he scooped them up and deposited them in his pocket.

Clive was growing frustrated but wasn't ready to do anything until Kersey gave the word. If she wanted to kill them all, she would. So far, their newest passenger wasn't doing anything that was dangerous or threatening. Luckily, the purse holding all the money, as well as Kersey's lance, was tucked safely below in the cargo hold beneath a big blanket.

When the Mydianite got past the table, he noticed the little red book sitting on the chair. Clive and Kersey exchanged equal looks of uneasiness. She sat up straighter, eyes narrowed against his toasted fingers and dirty nails as he plopped down on the chair and started thumbing through it.

His peeling forehead wrinkled in confusion as he tried to make sense of the archaic writing. He bit his tongue and shook his head but finally just opened up with a hearty laugh. "Who in their right mind can read this 'ere mess?" He closed it and slapped it down on the table with enough force to rattle the pitcher and nuts.

For just a moment he sat there, stretched his legs, yawned and laced his fingers together on his lap. He surveyed the room but eventually his eyes came to rest on the door of the closet. This was where the objection was going to come. Clive knew that once he was denied permission to look in there, he was going to turn hostile and call his men over.

It was the longest, most uncomfortable pause in the world. Clive was certain it lasted twenty minutes or so in his mind, but in truth, it was more like twenty seconds. The Mydianite stood, looked at the door once more and then said, "I suppose everything is in order here. Now go catch some fish." With that, he left, boarded his ship—with a few silver coins belonging to them—and was off. The Crynsian vessel, propelled by rowers, circled the fishing vessel and headed north.

Clive sat in the chair where he had just been and breathed a little easier. He pulled out his knife and laid it on top of the book. Kersey threw off her robe and opened the closet for the Gothmirk to come out. He was wedged in tightly—his arms and legs in awkward positions that would have been tiresome for a living being.

"We're not far from our dock," Kersey said, making sure the Crynsian ship was far enough for the Gothmirk to go back on deck.

"How do you know?" Clive asked, realizing just as much that being out in these waters in just a tiny fishing boat was suicide.

"I don't. He does." She pointed out the opened door to the navigator as he pulled down the sail. "He says it's only a mile or so east of here. After all, we've been in the Gap all morning."

Clive had seen enough maps of Northern Corscus to know that the Wingert Gap was a stretch of jagged beach that went inland about seventy miles. When he stepped back out onto the deck, he looked off to their port side and could see land. It didn't look like much from here—no more than sand and rocks—but there were massive mountains looming in the distance beyond. The clouds hovered just below their caps and he was sure this was the Kragspire. There were no birds—at least none that he could see, and it was eerily quiet.

"Oh the majesty," Kersey sarcastically noted, viewing the landscape with equal bitterness.

Northern Corscus' countryside was just as hospitable as its people. Over half of it was nothing more than long stretches of desert and the other half was wind-eroded rocks and burnt forestry. There had been more battles on North Corscus soil than any other. Those who lived here cared little for the land—those who didn't, cared even less.

There were actually trees beyond the beach—a small patch of forest that disappeared up the embankment toward the foothills that would eventually lead to the ominous mountains beyond. Their navigator was bringing them right to the front door.

Kersey headed below deck to gather her things and then joined Clive by the railing of the starboard side. The boat hit the sand with a solid *'thump'*, driving the stern at least twenty feet onto land. Had they been leaving the same way, they would have had to wait until the tide came to carry it back out to sea. Clive wasn't entirely sure how they *would* be leaving—or if they even would at all.

He slid his blade into its scabbard and hopped over, landing in the shallow water with a tiny splash. It was cold—but it felt so good. The air here was hot and humid and the bugs made his skin feel so disgusting. A lingering odor of blood wafted down from the mountain.

"Well, which way?" he asked Kersey, carrying her off the side of the boat and up the beach where she wouldn't get her new dress wet.

"I'm not entirely sure," she said. She pointed up to where the tree line began and added, "Maybe that way? I'm almost certain that is north."

"Actually that is north*west*," a voice corrected from behind. Clive grabbed his sword and whirled around. There was the biggest spider he'd ever seen—nearly the size of a horse. He drew his blade, took a swing and quickly had it knocked aside by two of the arachnid's legs.

"Stop that, boy," it said, but this time Clive recognized the calm voice. It was Ruin.

The spider's legs moved its segmented body side to side in an almost hypnotic motion. There were deep slash wounds across its rough back and it was shy one mandible. It was a Reef Spider—a type of arachnid that blended into the corals of the shallow water and attacked fishermen, swimmers, or whoever else dared enter the clear blue that it called home. Apparently this creature had a run in with a blade long before Ruin found it.

"I see you're still toting around your mortal bodyguard," his voice purred out.

Kersey folded her arms over. "Well he's served a much greater purpose than you, which as I can tell, is only to play games and tease with riddles."

"Oh Kersey, this is what I *adore* about you." He passed Clive and pushed him aside with one leg. "Your ability to see the truth in a completely unhindered way."

"Why don't you just tell us why we're here?" Clive asked, circling back around so the spider's dead eyes could look at him.

"Well, *she* is here because she is going to be the death of Mydian. You . . . well, I'm not sure why *you* are here, my boy."

"What do you mean by the death of Mydian?" Kersey asked.

The spider rubbed its crusty chin with a leg and said, "I mean you and your army are going to destroy him. Plain and simple."

"How?" she asked.

"Your army is going to cut down Mydianites wherever they are found. The Gothmirks will take Crynsia, Xenthia, and even Bloodgate. Without temples and servants, Mydian will be powerless."

"Why is this war being fought?" Kersey asked. "Why are you and Lyluss instigating such a thing?"

The spider's mandible twitched before it answered. "Because I'm tired of watching my own people starve and be killed by Mydianites who attack trade routes and unjustly claim lands for their own. I have witnessed the Master's self-righteous methods through two wars already. I want it to end. I want him to never recover."

"And Lyluss?" she asked.

"Lyluss has her own reason. You should ask her the next time the two of you talk."

Kersey's face darkened just a bit and Clive didn't know if it was from anger or embarrassment. She probably would have loved to talk with Lady Good. Clive wondered if Lyluss' reason was because of the Mydianite thieves who had been trailing them.

"You are almost finished, dear Kersey," Ruin said, his voice a purr. "The sweet escape of fear is upon you. Finish your job and I will hold to my word. You will not suffer in the Underworld."

A single tear streaked down her face and she gazed up at the mountain behind her. She weakly nodded and said, "Tell me what to do then."

"I need you . . . and your friend to walk in that direction there and don't stop until you're ten miles from here." The spider pointed a half-severed leg in the direction of the trees. Northwest it was.

"Ten miles?" Clive thought, already tired at just thinking it.

"That's right, lad. Oh, and mostly uphill, as well." The spider patted him across the chest. "I guess that's the price you pay for being *mortal*." Clive sneered and stared up at the woods.

"And after the ten mile hike?" Kersey asked.

"You'll be at the summit. There's an old, abandoned Drakish temple there. This is where you will use the spell you learned. In this spot the dead will be thick. Your magic will trickle across the fields and mountains and find them wherever they sleep."

"And then?" she pressed.

The spider crept close and surrounded her with its thick, hairy legs. It used two of them to pull her into the most hideous, grotesque embrace Clive had ever seen. Ruin leaned in and whispered, "And then you'll be free to live your life as you choose."

.22.
Isolation and Congregation

The morning hours went by slowly, but then again so had the day before. Dyne didn't like so much idle time—so much sitting around and waiting for the next step. She felt helpless and at a loss of control.

There was very little shade on the *Murder*. After the sea dragon ripped it apart like a straw hut, the ship turned into a long, hundred-foot plank. Sure, the cargo deck was mostly intact but it was sweltering hot down there and had the distinct odor of rotten fish. Dyne had never ventured past the steps of the crew cabin. The smell was enough to keep her from checking out Laraek's assortment of wine and ale.

She and Lorne decided to spend most of the day up toward the bow, along the steps leading to the devastated forecastle deck. He stood by her side, leaning over and pelting bolts into the water with his crossbow. The Ken'shar and the dead men had been killed before sunrise but the Gothmirk sharks were still there.

Their rotted, tattered fins could be seen breaking through the water and every so often, one of them would ram the ship. It didn't make a difference but the bone-against-wood sound had grown annoying after five hours. They seemed to be testing them—hoping they would grow bold and reckless enough to jump ship and swim to land.

Things weren't that bad yet.

"Why don't they attack the vampires chained below us?" Lorne asked.

"Because they are regenerating. Don't you remember how cold and inert the body goes? I'm willing to bet the sharks can't even see them."

The sun was sitting high in the sky, scorching the flesh on their faces. Dyne patted her taut forehead and felt tiny needles of pain. She knew her skin was ruddy from the heat's unending fury and that it would hurt much worse the same time tomorrow. Luckily, there was still plenty of fresh drinking water stowed away near her hammock and Lorne had been kind enough to carry it out to their spot.

It was hard for her to accept her feelings toward him. She was *grateful*. He had saved her life, several times in the past few days, and she was thankful for his presence. Things had certainly taken a change since their arrival—since their brawl back in Hope's Covenant.

"Thank you," she found herself saying. It tasted like bitter poison in her mouth.

"For what?" he asked, wrinkling his nose in confusion. He sat by her side and loaded up another shot.

Dyne hesitated for a long moment. She wasn't good at this sort of thing. She had hoped that he would have said a simple, "you're welcome" and that would have been the end of it.

"For saving my life. Countless times now." She was playing with Jonas' glass eye and she bounced it against the step as she talked.

He leaned over close to see her face but she kept it hidden by her sweat-matted hair. "That's something I never thought I'd hear Dyne the great say."

"I agree with you there."

"It's these bodies," he said, rubbing his chest. "They're weak and powerless."

"I *don't* agree with you there," she said. "I think these bodies are more powerful than our vampiric ones could have ever been."

He raised an eyebrow in disbelief, his forehead becoming scrunched lines of red and white.

"We are more in tune with our character now Lorne, don't you see? I know my limitations and that could very well save my life. We aren't just a blunt club without emotions letting our bodies do all the work; bashing, breaking, and causing panic. No, now we have intuition and feeling to guide us. We are capable of so much more than these vampires below us."

"I suppose," Lorne said. "But I still wouldn't mind being able to take to flight and be off this deck."

Dyne giggled. "So true, my friend." She had used that very trick on countless occasions to save her life, but even if they still possessed it, they were too far out.

For the next hour, Lorne continued to pelt the sharks with his crossbow until his bolts had been spent. He reluctantly tossed his quiver at one of the passing monstrosities and then put the weapon down. Dyne continued to play with Jonas' eye but kept watchful of the exposed cabin at the other end of the ship. Laraek's cabin.

There was something down there and she knew it. Ever since the Lylussians attack in the air ended, her gut told her that Laraek was hiding something aboard the ship. He had too many vampires—too many snooping crewmen that made their living by checking the ship over for abnormalities. If something was hidden on board, it had to be in there, under his protection.

Except now.

Dyne stood and made her way across the deck to the demolished cabin. Lorne followed once the sharks seemed to lose interest and swim off. He didn't know or understand what she was searching for but at that point, she thought he might care.

"Lorne, if Laraek were to sell the book to another god, who would you guess it to be?" she asked.

"Any one of those squabbling powers up there in the heavens would pay a fortune for it. Why?"

"Because I think there are more gods involved in this war other than Mydian, Ruin, and Lyluss."

"And what would make you think this?" he asked.

"Because Mydian himself thinks the same."

"What?" His tone was almost comical.

"Back in Tharg, I talked to Mydian inside Daegin's house. Laraek is a traitor, Lorne." She pulled the covers off the bed.

"He wants you to kill him, doesn't he?" Lorne concluded.

"Not exactly. He wants me to find out who he is serving. Who he plans on giving the book to."

"And why did he pick us for this job?"

"He picked *me* for this job. You are here to make sure I don't run off without first doing it. The *Phantom Seven* wouldn't open their door to just anyone. Mydian knew that Laraek would want to see me and would let me onto his ship with no questions."

"And what have you learned so far?"

"Not much, but that's why we're here." She waved her hand across what was left of the cabin.

"For someone who doesn't seem loyal to the Master, you sure are going out of your way to help him."

"I'm done taking Mydian's word. I want proof that Laraek is a traitor for *myself*."

"I don't think that's it at all. You're angry that he doesn't still love you, aren't you?"

"Stop it."

"And you'll probably kill him because that's the only way you know how to deal with such a thing."

Dyne grabbed him by the throat and pushed him against the only wall that still remained. His eyes were somber but his normal provoking laughter was absent. "What of it?" she allowed. "He's a traitor and you know what should become of traitors, don't you, Lorne?"

"You have similar resentment for Lord Mydian, as well," he pointed out. "Just because you haven't chosen another god doesn't mean you still haven't walked away from this one. You will both be judged the same by the Master, Dyne."

The anger grew in her face but she didn't allow it take over. She reminded herself of how the mortal body was better—stronger and superior. She even allowed a tiny grin as she released his throat. "Then so be it," she said, and turned around.

This wasn't the time to be fighting over such petty things. There was something hidden here that Lyluss wanted—that Lyluss probably wanted *back*. Laraek had even said that the *Phantom Seven* was tasked with recovering things that Mydian sought. Perhaps they stole something from one of Lady Good's temples.

She checked beneath the bed and under the cradle. There was nothing but an empty bottle and a collection of shells. Most of the clutter on the desk in the corner had blown out to sea. If Lyluss wanted paperwork, she was going to have to scour the entire Elandiran.

In a nightstand next to the bed was a folded piece of cloth that turned out to be a coat of arms from Boudia. It was a cross between Dyne and Laraek's family crests. Her heart fluttered for just a moment at the sight of it but she didn't allow Lorne to see. She loved the piece—its tattered, yellow letters and silk embroidery were exquisite. Without even realizing, she balled it up and stuffed it into her pouch.

There were several armoires tethered to the wall, but they contained mostly dresses, slacks, and shirts and were of noble fashion. There was a small closet that had more shoes than Dyne had ever seen in her life, as well as more dresses and frilly hats. Eva had quite extravagant taste and Laraek seemed obliged to pay the bill for it.

"What exactly are you looking for?" Lorne asked, but continued to help sift through the junk nevertheless.

"I'm not sure. But whatever it is, the Lylussians died for it."

"It's probably scattered across the Elandiran by now. This room is in shambles."

The drawers of the armoires were checked, rechecked, and then thrown overboard. Dyne even pulled out her dagger and gutted the mattress to make sure there was nothing hidden amongst the stuffing. She was ready to give up and go back to her spot on the steps but she noticed something odd.

"Do you see any Lorinstag Ale?" she asked.

Lorne searched the room over before answering, "No."

"Neither do I, but I surely smell it." She knew it had to be here somewhere.

From the deck below, she had caught the green goodness as it fell from the ceiling—or more appropriately—this cabin.

Dyne dropped to her knees and jerked the massive silk rug from the floor. She balled it up and tossed it overboard. Her face lit up when she saw the hinged door, simply locked with a copper latch.

Quickly, she unbolted it and pulled the trapdoor up, basking in the wonderful aroma of Lorinstag Ale. It was so strong—so potent. There was a small box inside that was wedged tightly in place by a Lylussian spear. With strong hands, Lorne ripped the chest from its hiding place and sat it aside. The box was sticky with Lorinstag Ale and when he popped the lock off with his dagger, Dyne saw why.

Inside was a shattered bottle of the sweet draught, the broken end of the spear wedged within the wood-grain. The chest's pretty satin lining was ruined. Half of the box's contents were wrapped in a beautiful, black silk cloth. Dyne's face lit up with recognition and confusion when he pulled it free. Beneath were little trinkets that she'd seen before, but she didn't know why they would be here.

There were three small keys, each richly adorned—having several Lylussian motifs and an assortment of exquisite jewels. Attached to each was a small tag with a city name and number on it. Laraek's box contained keys *one*, *two*, and *four* and were marked with Hope's Covenant, Skyhaven, and Davinshire.

"By the gods," Dyne said. "Lylussian Warding Keys? Why would Laraek have these? They're just like the two that locked Gloomrift." She remembered vividly the keys that were needed to unlock the crypt beneath the Birchlock Estate. There had been two of them— one Dyne had found on her own in Lorinstag and Arctis Moonbridge had uncovered the other. The key that came from Lorinstag had been blessed with several wards and safeguards and prevented vampires from touching them. She wondered if these had those powers as well.

"I think these are the *new* ones that lock Gloomrift," Lorne said, studying the runes. Two of them were covered in dried blood.

"That's ridiculous," she said. "Why would it be locked again? Gloomrift was emptied out after I went there. Tranas and his friends took their source of blood away and after I killed Arctis, the remaining vampires would have had no choice but to leave."

"The remaining vampires died shortly thereafter and Gloomrift *was* relocked with four keys this time, not two. I believe these are three of those four."

"That doesn't make any sense. And how do you know these things? I killed you before I even stepped foot inside Gloomrift," she pointed out.

"I know these things because I hear the rumors of the Underworld. I was there twelve years, mind you. Gwenavaughn, Gloomrift, and the vampires all had a greater meaning than what you originally thought, Dyne."

"And how is that?" she wondered. Gwenavaughn was moved to Gloomrift by the vampires who had been imprisoned there. She was supposed to be raised to march out and attack Keswing.

"When Arctis and Evan moved Gwenavaughn's remains to Hope's Covenant, it was to *secure* Gloomrift."

"Are you saying there is more buried in Gloomrift than just a dragon carcass?"

"Isn't it obvious? Why didn't Lyluss just remove the skeleton and be done with that hole in the ground? She locked it back because of what Arctis and his vampires found down there."

"And that is?"

"A passage to the Underworld. It has been there since the beginning of time, hidden away far beneath the streets of Gloomrift and is protected by a mile-high gate of bone and steel. Gwenavaughn was to be raised in order to protect the gate on the Mystyrian side."

"Then I came along and unlocked Gloomrift, forcing Lyluss to conjure more keys. Now Laraek has been tracking them down, killing all in his path to claim them," Dyne realized, rubbing the dried splotch of blood.

"All he needs is one more and the gate to the Underworld will be exposed," Lorne said.

"So this is why he wants the book," she said. "He can't find the fourth one so he needs Aneesa's powerful magic to point him in the right direction."

"That is how it seems, yes,"

"Look at this," she said, grabbing the black silk cloth. With gentle fingers, she spread it out across the debris-strewn floor of the cabin and stared with a blank expression at the insignia. There was a large hammer shattering the ground.

It was the mark and symbol of Felorn, the goddess of destruction.

"The Giantess?" Lorne asked. "Laraek is serving the *Giantess*?"

"Obviously so. Felorn has the wool pulled over Ruin and Lyluss' eyes. They think Mydian took these keys. She is instigating the war!"

"And she'll just sit back and let them tear each other, the heavens, and Mystyria apart. Felorn wants to take over Mydian's realm. Do you remember all of those troops heading up that winding road in the Infernal? That road must have led to the other side of the gate beneath Gloomrift. It all makes sense now! They were preparing to defend the Underworld!"

Dyne scooped up all three keys and placed them inside her pouch. She threw the silk inside the case, picked it up, and tossed it overboard.

"Just what do you think you are doing?" Lorne asked.

"I don't know," she said. "But I don't want to just leave them here."

"I'm sure Laraek is going to notice they're gone."

Just then, Dyne heard something different among the crash of the waves and the groaning of the ship. It was something *rolling*. She looked to Lorne and both shared a puzzled stare as they tried to place what the weird noise was.

She dropped to her knees and narrowed her eyes toward the far end of the ship. A small green gem quickly moved from the forecastle steps down to the cabin where they sat. It was picking up speed as it went and by the time it made it to her fingers, it was bouncing up and down with great force. The shadows on the deck had changed—moved, and the horizon had started to shift.

They both exchanged a worried stare and Lorne uttered, "Oh no."

Dyne scrambled to her feet and ran the span of the deck—jumping over debris and holes where needed until she disappeared down to the crew cabins. She continued down the steps that would take her to the cargo hold when—

—she stepped in ankle-high water.

Lorne's heavy footfalls sounded behind her and she could feel him gasp over her shoulder. At the far end of the cargo hold, past the empty mortal cages was water—deep water that wasn't there before. Dyne could hear a faint knocking sound below and couldn't help but to investigate.

The water rippled each time the knock came and as she neared it, one of the sharks ripped through the murky surface and snapped at her. Luckily Lorne was close enough to pull her back, out of the maw of an angry, undead monster. It simply sat there, jaw snapping, unable to do further damage without the water to carry it along.

"Dammit!" Lorne cursed. "These things have punched a hole in the hull!"

"You mean . . ."

"We're sinking? Yes." He shoved her back toward the steps and out onto the deck. Lorne looked the ship over and called her attention to the stern. It was further out of the water than it should have been. There was a clear line around the hull where the water-worn wood was much darker. The stern had risen at least a foot higher since the attack.

"What are we going to do now?" she asked, realizing that they left their only longboat back in Tharg.

Lorne looked around. There was nothing but open water as far as the eye could see in all directions. Angry, undead sharks continued to circle their ship as one end rose into the air and the other was pulled beneath the depths of the Elandiran. He put his hand to his sunburned face and said, "The *Murder will* sink. I suggest we pray that help shows up before we end up in the water."

A horrible fear washed over Dyne. She knew she couldn't swim and certainly not with ravenous sharks just waiting for them to drop a limb in the water. She wished she could hurry the setting of the sun. The vampires would at least be able to pull them off the deck and into the air. She went and retrieved the eye she'd grown fond of playing with and settled back down on the steps and smirked. Just whom was she supposed to pray to for help?

Kersey remembered what the Kragspire was like before—during the days when its landscape was hospitable. There used to be dense forests of black Corscun oaks, rivers that teemed with fish, and a majestic array of mountains that rivaled anything on the two southern continents. Time, an angry war, and the infectious seep of blood changed all of that.

The beautiful, dark oaks kept their color but the foliage burned to a crisp. One catapult after another hurled flaming stones into the forest, leaving it a withered, shriveled blemish on the map. After the battle, the blood of the dead—the quarter *million* dead—leaked into the ground and turned the soil to a crimson mud that never washed away. The overwhelming coppery smell wafted from every surface.

After the blood tainted the land, it washed into the rivers. For weeks the water flowed red, killing everything in its polluted path. The animals that depended on the river's catch soon left the Kragspire and headed south. Those that stayed around learned to adapt to the blood—and became something more degraded than the land itself.

Clive kept a few steps behind Kersey, carefully watching the trees and the sporadic rock formation for any signs of life. She knew there wouldn't be any. If living creatures found their way to this part of the world, they were looking for them.

"I believe that's it," Kersey said, pointing off in the distance.

They were on the mountain, several miles away from where the boat left them and it had just started to become an ordeal. The trip had taken several hours, party due to the strong winds coming down from the summit. Also, Kersey had picked the one pair of shoes from Clive's closet that the wilderness should have never seen. Her poor, aching feet made her want to sit every half-mile.

The terrain was growing sharper by the step. Most of the withering trees were giving way to grey rock that crumbled like chalk. Both of them left bloody footprints the moment they stepped off the forest floor and onto the rock-strewn mountain.

Kersey pointed to the steeple of a church—still a long way off, but close enough to discern the closed fist atop it. That was the symbol of Drak, the god of evil.

Though Mystyria and the gods would both concur that Mydian was the *true* god of evil, only one such creature possessed the title and birthright.

That was Drak.

He was the eldest and most powerful of the gods—created by Telsis around the same time Lyluss was woven into existence. For the first part of his godhood, Drak fought against the good-natured deities, driving them south, away from his temples in Northern Corscus. With the help of Mydian and Whither, he forged an empire that stood against all that was good and holy. And then, as quickly as it came to fruition, it was gone—the god of evil seemed to suddenly disappear.

For years he fed the world lies—stories telling of how he was only a mythological creation thought up by the good gods to steal power away from the bad ones. In truth, he decided that Mystyria wasn't worth fighting for as his other kindred had for so many years. Despite having numerous temples and servants, Drak let the world believe that he was nothing more than a child's story. Kersey always believed that one day—when the world was at its dying end—and with the right reason—he would return to his throne in Bloodgate—and rule alongside Mydian. Or at least rule in his stead, she thought with a bit of optimism.

Clive nodded that he saw the crumbling steeple and put his hands to his knees, breathing in heavy strides. She had almost forgotten how limited the human body could be—as Ruin so truthfully put it, *'that was the price you pay for being mortal'*.

"Do you want me to carry you?" she asked, wiping the sweat from her brow. The sweltering heat was starting to annoy her.

Clive stood up and laughed. "You're joking, right?"

She returned his humble manner and said, "Of course," but she wasn't joking at all. Instead, she offered her hand and pulled him a few feet toward the ledge of the summit.

From here to the top it was going to take both hands to make it up. Sure, Kersey knew she could simply change form to a bird and be there in seconds, but she wasn't about to leave Clive behind, not even for a moment. He had stayed with her this long. The least she could do was return the favor.

Kersey took a few steps and balanced herself against a rotten tree stump and then pulled Clive to her spot. She used that method all the way up the mountain. Slow, but it kept them together and put less work on his already tiring body. They were rising above the tree line—the open sea could be seen in the distance, but that wasn't what was important now. All the things behind them faded from existence. All that mattered was the abandoned Drakish Temple ahead.

It was sitting haphazardly on the side of the cliff, a row of faltering support beams keeping it from tumbling to the charred forest below. The windows were mostly broken but the colored fragments revealed that at one time they were probably beautiful. Most of the foundation was stone—a dark brown granite that Kersey had never seen used before. She also noticed that the roof shared some of the fire damage as the woods below. For an abandoned church a thousand years old, it surely held together quite nicely.

Only it *wasn't* abandoned, at all.

Kersey and Clive walked through the back door of the temple and didn't notice its rows of weed-covered pews, or the cracked marble floors, or even the degrading statue of Drak himself. What they did notice were the three men, two women, and little girl that were sitting on the floor in the corner.

She could hear Clive pull his sword out behind her—certain that these were Mydianites waiting to ambush them—but that wasn't the truth at all. These people looked genuinely happy to see them—to see *her*. Even the child shot up with an ecstatic glee that Kersey found to be eerily ominous. When was the last time she'd even been *near* a child?

When one of the men stood, she could see the silhouette of a skull drawn onto his shirt. It had only one dark circle for an eye. This was the symbol of Ruin. This was the mark that his servants adorned and lived by.

Kersey held her hand out at arm's length to Clive and nodded for him to sheath his weapon. Even though he did as she asked, his fingers continued to caress the hilt.

"Kersey Avonwood, I presume?" came the reply of one of the men. He was nervously bowing—drawing closer but keeping his distance like a cat that's untrusting of a new friend. She could only nod.

He looked back to his congregation and shared in the gleeful approval that erupted. She didn't understand it at all. Why on Mystyria would anyone be this happy to see *her*?

"My name is Pendar," the man announced. "And this is my family." He gave a quick wave to the nodding and saluting patrons sitting behind him. The child smiled with a blank look on her face. "We've been waiting here for quite some time."

"Waiting?" she asked. "For me?"

"That's right, miss."

"I don't understand."

He looked back to his family for an answer to her bewilderment. Apparently the reason should have been obvious. "Why, you're *revered*, miss Avonwood."

Those were the words that took her back a thousand years, and not in the form of an inconvenient flashback. It was before the curse. It was before the dragon. It was during the time when she was a respected Soul-Summoner living in Keswing and helping out at the tavern-turned-infirmary with her mother.

That word had been used before to describe her. *Revered*. She loved the sound of it as it passed through the lips. It was the absolute opposite of what she felt she was now—*despised*. Clive had been a special circumstance—a man who tried to understand her and love her. But these people were strangers. They had never met her. They had never laughed with her, cried with her, or shared a meal or an argument with her. All they had was her reputation and for some farfetched, outlandish reason, they respected her for it. They *revered* her for it.

"Why?" she asked, not liking the way her voice was faltering. Too many memories were trying to push their way through her mind at once. "Why would you revere *me*?"

Again, he looked to his family for answers but quickly turned around when he realized he would find none. "Because you're the one who's going to save the world." He said a lot in just a short sentence.

She glanced toward Clive for reassurance but he was as confounded as she was. "And just what makes you think I can do that?" she asked Pendar.

"You are going to raise up all these dead bodies. They are going to live again and march against Mydian. You're bringing hope to the Ruinites and the Lylussians. Somehow, Kersey Avonwood, you've united gods in a way that no man or divinity has ever done. You should be proud."

That made her smile. She couldn't believe her ears. Someone thought she should be proud. Those small words were enough to make her want to finish this—to build this army and let it wash over the land in a torrent that would leave Mydian helpless, beaten, and dying. She was ready to get to work—to raise the dead—and even if she had to pull them each up by hand, she was going to do it.

She snatched Aneesa's book from her sack and held it up. There was a gentle chorus of *oohs* and *ahhs* as they admired its simple beauty. This was an historic day and every mortal here would remember it for the rest of his or her life.

"Go up to the tower," Pendar said, directing her attention to the steps that led to the balcony. "You'll be able to see the land better from there."

She took his advice and grabbed Clive's hand, then hurried up the crumbling staircase. The tower was incredibly elevated, but once at the top, the view was breathtaking. Their attention however, wasn't on the panoramic landscape or the aesthetically pleasing ocean view.

It was on the hundreds of people cheering below them.

There were Ruinites in tents and on blankets along the jagged cliffs, watching her, waiting for her to cast her powerful spell like an audience awaiting a play. A *revered* play. Their congregation—their eagerness and acceptance of what she was gave her incredible strength. Although the spell was difficult and the circumstances were important, she knew she wouldn't fail.

Beyond the camping Ruinites, Kersey could see the battered landscape for miles and miles. It was mostly downhill and offered nothing more exciting than an occasional burnt tree or skeletal bush. The land looked soft and uneven and she knew that only a few feet beneath it, there were thousands upon thousands of dead soldiers—good and bad men and women—waiting to be freed from their muddy tomb.

The Ruinites cheered when they saw the blazing halo over her head and she had to fight to keep their distracting yells and shouts out of her mind. She immediately let the voices of the dead flood around her. This was the largest surge of spiritual whispering she'd ever encountered.

It would have been impossible to answer any of them. They were all so jumbled—so mismatched and odd-shaped that the voices were nothing more than gibberish. However, their desire to walk again—to serve her and be rid of the wretched ground that the world threw over top of them—came to her mind with an unwavering clarity.

Kersey flipped the pages until she came to rest at the *Symbian Range*. This was what the gods had been fighting over. It was what Daegin had died for. Sadly, it was what Avery had also died for. Although it didn't ignite the war, it surely propelled Ruin into starting it.

The sun was just starting to settle for the evening when Kersey began to speak aloud the words to the *Range* spell. Every little sound died down to a quiet whisper. The Ruinites were watching with great interest. Clive was holding his breath and she could sense his heart speed up. There was so much ancient magic surging through her—it entered from her mind and flowed out of her fingertips. It took hold of her like no spell had ever taken hold in the past. Her healing spells—the cures and the resurrects—were simple incantations compared to the complexity of the *Range*.

Kersey was lost to the words of the spell. Her feet lifted off of the bell tower's balcony and the magic carried her into the air. She didn't stop speaking—couldn't stop—and the magic kept her dangling, like a star to guide the dead from their resting places.

As the last word left her mouth, a white flame shot from her fingertips, her mouth, and her eyes. It carried across the barren landscape and lit the twilight sky with a brilliant glow that lasted for only a moment and then was no more. There was a massive tremble across the ground that shook the foundation of the Drakish temple and even rang the bell. A murmur of cries, cheers, and chants rang out from below as the watching Ruinites got to their feet and looked around. Kersey settled back down on the balcony, very much out of breath and very much drenched with sweat. Her fingers had literally burned themselves into the cover of the book.

All eyes were turned to the countryside now. Pendar and his family ran up to the balcony and the group watched the open horizon for a sign of the spell's success.

At first, nothing happened. The Ruinites probably thought the violent shudder and the bright flash of light were nothing more than an elaborate fizzle, but then Clive was the first to see it.

"Over there!" he screamed, pointing far off to the north.

There were vines snaking out of the ground. Kersey could feel them—could feel their slivering movement in her mind. It was *growing*. Those little slithers were seeping into her thoughts and under her control. Beneath the ground, for miles and miles around, they were bringing everything back to life.

Moans broke the overall silence of the fleeing afternoon. With the vines came the long dead corpses of Mydian and Lyluss' armies.

They were easy to tell apart—mainly because the Lylussians' armor hurt to look at.

It started in the front. The dead that were buried the closest—no more than five or ten feet from the nearest Ruinites—started pulling themselves from the ground. Several men and women rushed to their aid and helped them free. There weren't enough Ruinites to help them all—probably weren't enough in all of Mystyria. Rows upon rows of dead soldiers broke through the surface and stood on legs that hadn't been used in a thousand years. Nearly every corpse was little more than a skeleton—a thin, bony figure that was wrapped in corroded armor and sporting a broken or bent sword.

In only a few minutes time, the landscape for as far as the eye could see was moving. There were dead men and women everywhere and it was starting to grow disconcerting for the Ruinites. They had never seen such a thing—no one had. Even Clive, who had been with her every moment of the journey, marveled by the sheer number of undead soldiers breaking through the ground.

The causalities of the war weren't limited to men and women, either. There were horses, dolgathas, and swoopdrakes. There were even a couple of adult red and green dragons that ripped through the ground and hammered onto the surface. They shook the dirt from their bony heads and looked around—probably wondering how they went from fighting for Mydian to being here at the command of a representative for Ruin.

It would take time to raise them all, Kersey noted to herself. She could still feel them waking from their slumber a mile away. By her estimations, the Kragspire stretched nearly fifty miles in every direction. The full Gothmirk army wouldn't be ready until several hours—most likely around sundown. If Mydian's Crossback vampires were near—they would attack at the perfect time—when

Kersey's army was at full strength. However, she didn't think the god of the Underworld would attack in such an open, highly visible battleground.

"So now what?" Clive asked, watching the legions form rank and turn to face Kersey. She was just as clueless as he was.

"We wait for Ruin to tell us where to go."

"I'll bet he'll want to take Crynsia back," Pendar said, and then pointed north, past the waves of undead. "After all, it's only an hour's gallop that way and the fighting has already begun."

"It has?" Clive asked.

"Oh indeed," Pendar said. "Mydianites are attacking Ruinites wherever they are found. We were driven from our homes." He pointed to the happy congregation below him. "Mydian has overthrown Crynsia. I'm guessing he'll reinforce it and wait for you."

"It almost sounds like a trap," Clive said, obviously not seeing the bigger picture of what was happening.

"Ruin will want to take it back," Kersey stated flatly. "But it is a diversion."

"How can you be so sure?" Pendar wondered.

"Mydian has garrisoned troops at Crynsia in hopes that I'll send my army northward, or at least part of it. Either way, it is his intention to thin the force that will head to Bloodgate." She pointed to the south, in the direction of the city of the Black.

Kersey knew very little of battle tactics but this much was clear. Mydian was going to protect Bloodgate—and the Martax at all costs. The Crossbacks and the hundreds of thousands of soldiers at his disposal would all be thrown unsympathetically into the line of fire in order to keep her from taking one step closer to his unholy city.

"When was such a wedge driven between the Ruinites and Mydianites?" Clive asked. "I can understand why gods war. They war because they are jealous of one another's power. But their servants ..." His voice trailed off. "I would have assumed Mydian's servants would be more forthcoming with Ruin's."

"Is that right?" Pendar said, a hint of sarcasm in his voice. He turned and called out a name and before Kersey knew who it was, she heard the click-clack of tiny feet across the marble floor. It was the little girl she'd seen earlier.

Pendar knelt down next to her and wrapped his arms tightly around her tiny body. She smiled but couldn't stop looking up at Kersey—who only offered an awkward, sheepish grin.

He turned to Clive and then took his daughter by the hand and held it out. "This is how *forthcoming* Mydian's servants are." The little girl's fingers had been cleanly sliced off—all the way down to the first joint. What remained was a stub of a hand that had healed with various scars and bruises. Kersey and Clive both grimaced at the sight but she suddenly understood every ounce of his hatred toward the dark god and his minions.

"Are you soldiers?" Clive asked him. Kersey had noticed the pair of daggers tucked into his boot.

"Indeed we are," he said, leading his daughter back down the stairs. His family was standing out front, watching the hypnotic slither of the vines as they toiled the ground—uprooting the dead like meat hooks.

"Will you be marching with us?" Kersey asked.

"Until we fall off the edge of the map, milady." His smile was so caring, so comforting. Ruinites were normally evil, sadistic people by nature who were no better than Mydianites. For once, Kersey didn't believe that. She was once a priestess of Lyluss and after the curse, she turned into something so dark—so twisted and abominable that the vileness inside of the Mydianites paled in comparison to her.

If she could find forgiveness and acceptance, then so could these people—no matter what god they chose to serve. Everyone deserved that one little word:

Redemption.

.23.

Unlikely Reinforcement

By the time the sun disappeared beneath the Elandiran horizon, it was too late for Dyne to realize she had left the lanterns below deck. It was dreadfully dark—the moon's silvery light barely bled through the spotted clouds. Only the rippling glow of the waves crashing around their vanishing ship kept them from being in total blackness.

The stillness of the night was as equally eerie. After days of being over water, Dyne had learned to block the sound of the waves out of her mind. Now all she heard was the cracking of wood under them and the heavy breathing of Lorne. She wanted to see lights in the distant—just something that she could shout at to come and pluck them from being taken under by a sinking vessel and into the waiting maws of sharks.

They were still nearby, as best she could tell. Their brittle jaws had a very distinctive clap whenever they opened and shut and that sound resonated from time to time. She kept her ankles tucked close to her body, feeling that the tip of the bow was all that was left now. In only a few minutes time, the *Murder* would be completely submerged, and they would be in the water, blind, and fighting an enemy that wouldn't give up.

"I suppose this is it," Lorne said. She could hear him unsheathe a blade. "Alive not even a week and already I'm headed back to the Underworld."

"If it makes you feel better, this'll make *twice* I've died this week. Well, in my head, anyway." She couldn't help but find the humor in it.

"No, it doesn't at all," he said, but she could tell he was smiling. Somehow, in the dark, she knew.

"I'm sorry I wasn't better than this," Dyne offered. She felt responsible for what was about to happen to them and she didn't know why. She had led Lorne out of a happy life in the Underworld and right into harm's way. There was a time when that would have been funny to her, but not today. Centuries later and her strong, yet feeble heart was making her feel guilt. She should have been cursing its defects but she couldn't. On yet another front, she had failed.

"You've nothing to be sorry about," he said from the darkness.

Dyne lowered her head and laid it against her knees. "Yes I do," she weakly managed.

There was a long silence that followed—a dead air that lingered over her and made the dismal circumstances all the more unbearable. Lorne was staring at her, waiting for her to elaborate on what she meant. Those words were harder to say than thank you.

"I'm sorry I didn't believe you earlier. I know now that you never took Hannah's things. I just . . ." Her voice trailed off, her mind no longer able to comprehend what her mortal heart felt.

"You just did what any loving mother would have done. You sought retaliation for something you saw unjust."

She was smiling so broadly by his answer and she felt the heat rush to her face. It was embarrassing for her to express that type of joy. Those words made her so happy—so content that she forgot for a moment the trouble they were in.

There was a loud snap below Dyne's feet and she crawled backwards to the top of the bow. The water swished around in front of them, splashing up to their ankles. For just a moment the moon slipped out from behind the shadow of the clouds and she could see the horrible visage of the shark as it came right for her.

A small gasp escaped her as she instinctively grabbed onto Lorne's arm and hoisted herself higher on the bow. Her back was flush with the railing. The creature came several feet out of the water and landed on the deck in front of them and Lorne started hacking wildly with his dagger. There was no blood, nor any movement. It was already dead when it landed near their laps.

Just then, the moon's light caught a glint of something—it was long and made of metal and was jutting from the top of the shark's skull. Something moved the creature around and without warning, the metal spear jerked from its head. Dyne and Lorne followed the glimmering weapon up and noticed the stars and clouds had faded on the horizon to the east. There was nothing but a vast emptiness in front of them, as if the entire sea, sky, and all that the two contained simply vanished.

It took a moment to realize there was a ship by their side.

Dyne was the first to notice. She made out the intricate crossing of the rigging and could tell there were black sails, just like on the *Murder*. At first she was hopeful that the rest of the *Phantom Seven* had caught up, but noticed this was a completely unheard of ship once she made out the raised letters. This vessel called itself *'Lyluss' Bane'*. Perhaps not a Mydianite ship, but clearly a friend, nonetheless.

It wasn't as large as the *Murder*, but it was still quite long. Some of the crew was standing by the railing—mortals who were dressed in blackened leather sporting the Mydianite seal across the breast. The bridge was completely enclosed and there were cannons lining the second deck.

There was a robed figure hanging from the side of the railing, the spear in his hand. He reminded Dyne of the *Shadow* back in Gloomrift. Arctis had used a robe that leaked smoke from the hood to conceal his identity. The feeling she got from him was the same she got from this seemingly helpful person.

"Is this all that remains of the *Black Murder's* crew?" he asked in a powerful voice.

"We are the only mortals left. The rest are below us, sleeping," Dyne answered.

For a moment the robed figure simply looked at them, or so she thought. His hidden eyes and hidden intentions were quite puzzling, but after a long pause, he reached his hand out and said, "Well come aboard, then."

Dyne hesitated for just a moment but Lorne put a comforting hand on her back and urged her on. It felt so alien, but after today's rendering of unknown feelings, she was ready to accept it.

As soon as her hand joined with the robed man's, he pulled her onto the deck with more strength than was needed. A tiny cry escaped her as his angry hands dragged her down the deck, away from the floating remains of the *Murder*.

"Hey!" she heard Lorne yell as she was hauled across. Her legs flailed and she tried to break the robed man's grip but he wouldn't budge. From the corner of her eyes, she spotted a few men step in front and usher Lorne to the far end of the ship.

"Where are you taking me?" Dyne screamed, feeling the coarse woodwork of the deck slide beneath her. Her body was faced up, eyes on the sky and then suddenly, it was gone. She was looking up at a wooden ceiling and the dim glow of a crystal chandelier.

The robed man lifted her up by the arms and sat her down in a hard, wobbly chair and then circled around a table to seat himself. Dyne bolted up, ready to lunge across and show him what a bad idea it had been to treat her so roughly, but he simply put a hand to her face and shoved her back into the seat.

There was a great commotion outside. Dyne looked through the stained glass windows and saw several figures walking past the cabin. Suddenly, one was thrown against the wall, rattling the chandelier above her. It was Laraek.

"We're all Mydianites here! What is your business?" he asked. "Please don't hurt my wife!"

Dyne spotted the towering, slender form of Eva right next to him. The remaining four vampires and Lorne were out of sight, but their wails of anger could be heard around the corner.

"Who is Laraek serving?" came the commanding voice of the man across the table. He pulled out a pipe that magically lit itself and then inserted the bit into his unseen mouth.

"Who are you?"

"That isn't important," he said. "I just pulled you from certain death so you could serve the Master a little while longer on Mystyria. Now who is Laraek serving?"

"Why is this so important to Mydian? Is Laraek the only one who's ever betrayed him?" She pounded her fist against the rickety table.

"Not at all," he said, a puff of smoke curling from the dark recesses of his hood. "There is another. But she'll be dealt with shortly. I'm going to ask you once more before I toss you and your friend out there back into the Elandiran. Who does Laraek serve?"

"Are you going to kill him? Is that all you're waiting for? You want me to tell you which god is going to be another threat to the Master and then you're going to go right outside and jab a blade into his heart. Am I right?"

"That you are, sweet girl, that you are. Laraek deserves to die a traitor's death and so he shall. But let us first learn whose servants need butchered and what temples need destroyed other than Lyluss and Ruin's."

Dyne looked down into her lap and thought hard about what she was going to say. She didn't know who this man was. All she did know was that she didn't owe him a thing. She still loved Laraek and even though he had hurt her so many times, it was her own heart that caused the pain.

"I haven't found out yet," she said.

"You're lying, girl." He sat the pipe down and leaned in.

"I most certainly am not," she said, folding her arms across. She pursed her lips and raised an eyebrow, coaxing him for another question.

"Why? Why must you weak-minded women go out of your way to save something that is no longer there? I can see it in your eyes." He looked out through the stained glass window and found Laraek, leaning against the railing, a little calmer now that the crewmen had no doubt explained their business. "And I can see it in his. Whatever the spark is that you think still lingers after three centuries has vanished."

Dyne felt the heat rush from her face. She buried her shaking hands in her lap and brushed her pouch as she did. For a moment, she had forgotten all about the keys and the Boudian family crest that she found in Laraek's cabin. This strange robed man knew many things, but she wasn't about to betray herself.

"Your heart has been shattered by this man. Deliver it back to him." The robed man's relentless pursuit of the truth continued on.

"I don't know who he is serving. You can choose to believe me or not," she said.

For a moment, he sat there, still as a statue and said nothing. He drummed his fingers on the table and occasionally peered out the window, clearly unsatisfied with that answer.

"Not it is," he said. "You're lucky that Mydian still thinks you are of value or else you'd be hugging an anchor right now on the bottom of the Elandiran."

"And Laraek?" she asked, assuming the worst.

"Well *somebody* has to find out who he is working for and until Mydian has someone new to watch him, you're to continue your job."

Dyne smiled and offered a mock salute. The way the robed man's shoulders slumped told her that he was the least bit amused. "Get out," he said, pointing to the door.

She couldn't help but let a small grin surface. It felt like she was in control again, if only temporarily. Mydian had put her back on Mystyria for a reason and he wasn't going to just let one of his own kill her so easily.

Everyone was sitting on deck, listening to the last remaining shark snap helplessly at the hull of the ship. Lorne gave her a brief smile that let her know he was alright. Laraek and Eva were huddled against one another, leaning over the railing. He was running his fingers through her hair and together they shared a somber expression as they watched the last of the *Murder* disappear. It was now only a blank spot of undisturbed water.

There was so much lost—so much beneath the Elandiran that they would never see again. Eva's baby crib was entombed in a watery grave. The vampires no doubt left their menial possessions—shirts, socks, lockets from loved ones, and Laraek thought his precious keys were thousands of feet beneath them.

Dyne tried not to look into his eyes as she passed by him. She only wanted to go over and sit next to Lorne but his warm hand wrapped around her arm.

"I found this," Laraek said, handing her a soaked Nighteye. It was dripping water but she gave it a try and was happy to see that it still worked just fine. "It was down there," he said, pointing over the railing.

"Thank you," she meekly said. He ran his fingers through his drenched hair and gave a gentle nod. There was something there—something that made her feel at ease, as if he was trying to rekindle a happy thought. She wanted to talk to him now, away from the madness, away from the robed man, away from Lorne, and away from Eva. That wasn't likely to happen.

"You can thank Lord Mydian that you're all still alive. He sent me to rescue you." The robed man stepped out on deck and addressed the soaked vampires.

"And we thank you for that," Laraek said. He turned and looked over the railing. "There's something . . . *precious* I need from my ship before we head off."

Dyne exchanged an uneasy glance with Lorne.

"Your ship is sitting on the bottom of the Elandiran and I'm sure you don't want to venture down that far. Besides, we are needed elsewhere." The robed man turned to the bridge and yelled, "Off we go!"

There was a sudden jolt as the ship began to move. Crewmen were toiling all over the deck but with their dark clothing and the starless, black night, it was nearly impossible to see them.

Lorne raised an eyebrow to the robed savior. Dyne settled down next to him and eyed him with the same scrutiny. Why had Mydian sent a ship to rescue *them*?

"If I may ask, what is the rush?" Laraek asked. "Kersey has probably made it to the Kragspire by now."

The robed figure chuckled and settled against the wall. "Oh, and she has. I would imagine her army is quite grand, as well." He looked to the horizon, to the direction they were headed and seemed to sigh. "But you have failed and Mydian no longer needs you chasing her. I have been pulled from Crynsia to kill her."

The man produced a small, purple marble from thin air and tossed it over the side of the ship. Dyne and Lorne followed the glowing gem but thought nothing else of it. That had been just another strange occurrence on a mountain of oddities.

"Then where are we going?" Lorne asked.

"Back to Crynsia. Mydian has taken over and we need your help to keep it that way," the man said.

"What?" Dyne said, the outrage thick in her voice as she got to her feet. "I've spent every waking hour since my arrival trying to kill Kersey and take this damn book and now I'm being forced to do guard duty in a city I could care less about?"

"That's exactly right, my dear." The robed man was probably smiling beneath his hood.

Dyne was so angry from being forced to do such a menial task that she didn't see the water swirling off the starboard side of their ship. It was glowing with a slight purple haze and was growing faster, stronger, and deeper with each pass.

"Everyone hold on to something," he said, ushering Dyne away. She emitted a low growl and latched onto the railing when she saw the purple light coming from the water.

The *Bane* was pulled into the cyclone and the bow suddenly plummeted. For a moment, they were completely vertical and just when she thought their ship was going to be descending into a torrent of water that would close in around them, they completely leveled out. The sea calmed, the purple haze faded, and there were lights hanging impossibly in the air.

She pulled out her Nighteye and was shocked to find that they were no longer on the open sea. They were in some sort of tunnel, with bricks high above and to their sides. Lanterns hung from hooks along the rounded ceiling and the entire crew of the *Bane* stepped up on the first deck. There were people in the distance, standing on a platform that the ship was quickly approaching. The robed man had just transported the entire vessel.

Men in Mydianite armor stepped up to the *Bane* and threw a wooden plank across. Dyne was the first one off and was never so happy to be on solid ground. *It didn't even feel this good in Tharg*, she thought. Now that she had the keys she felt a small victory.

There was a narrow walkway that ran the entire length of the tunnel. Dyne looked to the far end through the Nighteye and saw the open sea past a stone entrance. Apparently this was some sort of secret harbor meant to hide Mydianite ships.

"This way," the man in the robe said, pulling the magical lens from her eye. She was really starting to dislike their rescuer. "There's nothing out there but miles of sea and I'm sure you've had your fill."

Lorne nodded in agreement and let him lead them to the opening at the other end. There were muddy steps that ran alongside a massive pipe that absorbed the water from the harbor. It was dark and once a heavy breeze slapped Dyne across the face, she knew they were outside. This place smelled of *blood*.

There was a city far off in the distance that she recognized as Crynsia. Its towering grey walls were in ruins and she spotted several flaming boulders lighting up the night sky. The distant sounds of war could be heard—swords scraping, innocents crying, and structures that had endured for ages being demolished. The robed man's portal had taken them just beyond the bloodshed.

"What do you see?" the robed man asked her.

"What?" she wondered, not taking her eyes off the battle to the north.

"You're fond of your little seeing glass. Tell me, what do you see next to you?" His voice was low and ominous with a bit of an antagonistic tone.

She pulled her Nighteye up and looked around. There were mountains to the south—high, jagged cliffs that created virtually an impenetrable wall around Crynsia. Those types of mountains were a nightmare for soldiers. To the east, there was more water—the Elandiran where their ship had just come from. But to the west was something that startled her so badly that she dropped the lens. Luckily, the robed man caught it before it could shatter against the ground.

There were vampires standing all around, quiet, unmoving, and facing the group by the tunnel exit. It wasn't just a few either. Even with the visible power of the Nighteye, Dyne couldn't see where the rows ended. They started all the way back at the mountains in the distance. This reminded her of the armies she commanded in the second War—hundreds of thousands of men and women who made up a sea of faces.

These were Crossbacks. Their gnarled fangs and void-filled eyes were unmistakable. Few were wearing full suits of armor and even fewer had weapons. They didn't seem to care about Dyne and her crew but they did keep their attention on the robed man. He was the one they served.

"Quite impressive, yes?" he said, patting one of them on the head as if it were a puppy.

"Where did you find so many soldiers to convert to vampirism?" Laraek asked.

"It wasn't very difficult, I assure you. We scoured the prisons, asylums, orphanages, and shelters of North Corscus. No one will miss these degenerate rejects," the robed man waved toward the legion of sightless abominations. Several were only a little older than children. "They are more valuable this way and they have finally been given a purpose other than being a constant, parasitic leech on society."

"So this is Mydian's big plan?" Dyne asked. "Take an army of a hundred thousand and try to subdue an army of a half-million?"

"You lack so much faith in Lord Mydian," he said.

"No, I only have faith in common sense," she said. "You're not going to stop her with this. You're only going to slow her and make her angrier."

"Exactly. Mydian is only trying to save Bloodgate. These creatures will thin her army enough so that our forces there can easily repel her." He stepped closer to Dyne and added, "And you know *nothing* of her anger. It will destroy her."

A small brigade of horses came barreling out of the gates of Crynsia. Dyne readied her sword and turned to face them.

"Sir!" one of them called to the robed man. "I have news from the Kragspire."

There were about ten men, each atop a beautiful black mare. Some held the reins to another horse and Dyne knew this was their escort back into Crynsia. Her mind had been made up. She wasn't going to just let this man and his army have their way.

"Has Kersey started to move?" the robed man asked.

"It isn't about her, milord. It's the Felornites. They've sent the Dragon Clan from Addystiir to hunt her."

Felorn's chief city was Addystiir, a large, dilapidated settlement in the mountains that was on the other side of the continent, west of Boudia.

Dyne nervously shifted her eyes to Laraek. He must have known this attack was coming.

"She wants the book back," the robed man said. "Ruin plucked it right out from under her in Tharg as it was being transferred to Fyrl Jonath. She thinks she can step into the middle of the battle and come out with the spoils."

"We can help you," Dyne said. "We want a chance to kill her."

"We'll make sure Mydian ends up with the book," Lorne added.

"I'm sure you would," the robed man said with a hint of sarcasm. "But you are going back to Crynsia and make sure the Ruinites don't get their city back."

"This is ridiculous!" Dyne blurted out. "I've been chasing her from the beginning and now you, whoever you are, come along and try to take her right out from under m—"

Her voice trailed off when he flipped his hood back. Everyone seemed content to see his face but Dyne knew a lot more than they did. They hadn't carried around a bust of his head for a hundred years. They didn't steal a painting of him in Bloodgate. They certainly didn't realize that the spear he held was actually a lance. Dyne had drawn a mental picture of this man in her head long ago and now, centuries later, she saw just how accurate it was. He was one of the *Ten*. One of the Greater Overlords.

He was Brin Todrich.

He put his hand on Dyne's shoulder and looked at her with his deep, penetrating eyes. "Trust me, dear girl. I've been looking for her *much* longer than you."

The horsemen handed off their reins to Laraek and his vampires and then headed back to the turmoil of Crynsia. Brin took one and climbed atop it and then faced his Crossbacks.

"Who wants to kill for the Master tonight?" he screamed. "Leave their blood alone, lest you want to end up a pile of ash. Overcome them with strength. Break their back and necks!" There was a low cheer that normal people would have made when the offer didn't seem very enticing. The Crossbacks however were ecstatic by the prospect but only lacked the awareness to show great emotion.

Dyne threw herself up on a horse and waited for her companions to do the same. Laraek appeared angered by the whole situation, as did Eva. Lorne had the look in his eyes—the look that said he wanted the title of, 'Killer of Kersey,' to take back to the Underworld.

"Head back to Crynsia," Brin told them.

Dyne reached out and grabbed his wrist. He turned around, a look of pure evil in his eyes. It was so much deeper than hers.

"Why are you doing this? Why do you even care to go after her?"

He smiled and Dyne felt her skin crawl by his sudden display of fangs. It was the eeriest, creepiest, gesture she'd ever known. She suddenly wanted to be out of his presence.

"Call it 'unfinished business'," he said, and then left.

The footfalls of a hundred thousand men and women were like tiny quakes with each step. They sounded in perfect repetition and Dyne thought she could feel her heart beat in the same succession.

"Let's go," Laraek said, turning his mount toward Crynsia.

"So that's it then?" Dyne asked.

"We have orders," Eva said.

"And? We're simply walking away from this? Brin Todrich is going to get credit for the kill that we laid claim to. And what of the Felornites? Are we just going to let them swoop down and take the book from us, as well?"

"What do you suggest?" Eva asked. "That we tag along with his army and hope he doesn't notice?"

"No," she said, and then turned to her companion. "Lorne, do you remember the Clearfork trail?"

"Yeah, it's that way, about two miles," he said, pointing off to the west where the Crossbacks were still obscuring.

"What is the Clearfork trail?" Laraek asked.

"It's a path that cuts through the mountains and ends up at the Dolga River. It goes right through the Kragspire. The four of us can catch up to Kersey before Brin can get his army up there."

"And just what are we going to do once we reach her?" Laraek asked, waving his vampires off. The remaining souls of the *Murder* turned their mounts and headed out toward Crynsia. "I suppose the four of us are going to walk through her half-million-strong army and kill her?"

"Kersey is waiting at the summit, I'm sure. There is a Drakish temple up there and it was probably the first thing she came to after the Gap. We can reach it from the path and probably avoid most of her Gothmirks." Dyne was amazed by how her memory of North Corscus held up after all the years.

"Mydian won't be too happy about all of this," Eva said.

"Nonsense. If we stop her from reaching his beloved city and keep the Felornites from getting the book, I'm sure he'll be *overjoyed.*"

After a moment's hesitation, Laraek looked to his wife for approval. Her relaxed stance and folded arms told him that she wasn't pleased with the idea but she nodded nonetheless.

"Let's go then," he said to the group.

Just before he could head off, Dyne noisily cleared her throat. Laraek spun his mare back around and saw the scorn in her eyes. She wasn't going anywhere under his lead.

"We're not on the *Black Murder* anymore, dear," she said, whipping the reins of the horse, and as she passed by him added, "You follow *me.*"

.24.

Declaration

The Ruinites were some of the most hospitable people Clive had ever known. Living in Southern Corscus, he had been taught that all peoples from the north were evil, corrupt, and not to be trusted. For the most part, that was true. But these common folk—divided and torn, were *good*. They only wanted what everyone else wanted and that was to survive.

Pendar was a good man, an honorable husband and a wonderful father to three children. His only crime had been owning a pub in a district that the Mydianites wanted to control. His home in Crynsia, his tavern, and one of his sisters had been taken simply because he didn't want to leave. Clive completely related.

It wasn't because of Kersey. All of the bad things that had happened over the past few days weren't her fault. Every single drop of blame rested on Mydian's shoulders. It was because of his relentless pursuit of her that made Clive lose everything he held dear.

"I have a gift for the two of you," Pendar said, holding out two leather cuirasses. Clive eyed the symbol on the chest and saw a spiked skull with a dove by its temple. It was some sort of collaboration of Ruin and Lyluss' insignias.

"What's this?" Kersey asked.

"This symbolizes our unity," Pendar said, handing her one of the chestplates. "Lyluss and Ruin. The most unlikely union in the history of Mystyria."

"Does it hurt?" Clive asked her, pointing to the dove across the front. It wasn't completely Lyluss' insignia, but it was symbolic to her nonetheless.

Kersey winced just a little but flashed him a warm smile. "Not much. I can live with it."

"You two can change in the tent over there," Pendar said, pointing to the large wolf-skin dwelling that was situated by the ruined Drakish temple.

Both headed off in that direction but once they reached the door, Kersey held the flap back and said, "After you."

He smiled and shifted the armor to the other hand and said, "You go first. I'll wait."

She grinned from ear to ear and stepped in. Clive pushed the flap over the tent and listened to her as she slipped the wet and bloodied dress off. "Your heart is beating so fast," she said from within.

He put a steady hand to his chest and cleared his throat, slightly embarrassed. The heat flustered his face and he turned to watch the dead birds gathering on the steeple of the Drakish temple.

Kersey pulled the flap from his fingers and stepped out, the shiny black armor now adorning her tiny frame. Her hair was pulled back off of her neck and she wore a pleated skirt that showed her thin, pale legs. There were daggers lining her boots and a small pouch hung at her side, the spell book safely wrapped inside. Clive couldn't help but look at her exposed neckline. This was the first time he had seen so much of her *flesh*.

"Your turn," she smiled, breaking him from his entranced awe. Her dainty fingers held the flap up for him and she waved to the interior of the tent. Clive's face was turning red and he could only nod as he ducked and went in.

It only took him a few minutes to change. He had very little possessions other than the slacks he'd had on for days. Pendar gave him a nice long sword that was adorned with Ruinite symbolism and he thought of how mad Nalia would be that he was using something that didn't have Quillian's likeness on it. But then again, he was truly fighting for Kersey. All of the other gods came second to her.

When he stepped back out, the first thing he noticed was the smell of charred flesh. It was wafting up the mountain, through the trees and into their camp in heavy bursts. The crowding Ruinites gathered around and watched as the Gothmirks in the distance continued to rise.

It was night now, so the flames on the horizon were easy to see.

There were large beasts circling overhead. They weren't as big as the Pack Dragons, but they were still enormous. Clive could see the glinting sparkle of their scales. They were white dragons—pearlscale to be exact. On their backs were men and women who threw spears toward the cluster of Ruinites. From the maws of the beasts spewed angry fire into the troves of undead. Clive had no idea who these riders were.

"Everyone into the temple!" Pendar shouted. He took his daughter by the hand and pulled her away.

The undead in the distance were in ruins—their charred, smoking bodies ambled around like mindless denizens. Kersey was growing frustrated by her Gothmirks' inability to fight back. Several vines broke through the bloody ground and latched onto a few of the low-flying dragons but the massive beasts easily ripped free and continued their assault.

A volley of spears suddenly struck the ground in front of where Clive was standing. Two pearlscale dragons swept by, their tails whipping through the tops of the trees.

Kersey picked up her lance from a pile of weapons and headed down the hill toward her blazing minions. "These are Felorn's dragons," she told Clive as he followed behind.

"Felornites? What do they want?"

"The book, of course. But I'm not going to let them take down half my army in an attempt to get it. Stand back."

"Kers, don't do this!" he said, looking toward the sky. There had to be at least ten of them, belching fire from their mouths and laying waste to her defenseless minions. One of them spotted her and cried out in rallying support. It circled around and deftly headed up the hill toward her.

Its rider brought it close to the ground, shaving the treetops as if they weren't even there. The massive beast's talons were outstretched as it descended right for her, ready to rip her apart.

"Kers, move!" Clive screamed, holding his sword out toward the oncoming dragon.

She looked at him with a simple calm that made him feel at ease. She was so beautiful, yet so powerful. "Have you forgot just what I was a slayer of?"

Just as the creature reached their position, Clive hurtled out of the way. Kersey leaped into the air and landed on the saddle, just behind the rider. As the dragon sailed away, he watched as she drove her lance into his back and tossed him aside. She grabbed onto the reins and fought to keep the creature stable as it tried its best to expel the unwanted guest from its back.

Clive watched them fly far off, beyond the treeline and once they were out of view, he heard an ear-piercing wail that seemed to draw attention from all the others. Kersey's dragon was headed into the ground, fire spewing from its maw in random bursts. There was flaming forestry all around them, creating a vibrant, orange glow that made the battle below look like stage theatrics.

The pearlscale crashed into the cliff, about a hundred yards away, blood painting its shiny white scales. A loud crack followed by a low, guttural growl marked its death.

Then, just as quickly as it had crashed, it picked itself up and took to flight, although it looked erratic due to a broken wing.

Clive could only see Kersey's lance in the darkness. The surrounding forest fires cast an ominous glint across it, but that was all he needed. He could see that ominous glint leaping from dragon to dragon, killing the rider, then the creature. They were dropping from the sky like quail. In only a matter of seconds, Kersey had managed to create her own aerial army. All of the dragons were bloodied and disembodied and only three of them were able to fly after her wrath. The rest hobbled around, tearing trees down to make a path for their massive wingspan. It didn't matter. What did matter was that they were all on *her* side now.

She hopped onto the back of the beast with the best wings and allowed it to carry her back to Clive's position. The Ruinites cowering in the temple cheered in victory and rushed out to greet her.

Clive sheathed his sword and smiled over her triumphant defeat of twelve dragons in only a few seconds. He looked down and patted the hilt of his blade and said to himself, "Maybe I'll one day actually get to *help* her."

Kersey jumped off her mount and stroked the side of the undead dragon. The pearlscales may have been one of the most evil of all breeds, but they were certainly beautiful. It was a tragedy that Dargas would allow them to be so easily corrupted to the destructive will of Felorn.

Clive was standing there, awestruck at the sight of seeing one of them so up-close. Or perhaps he was astonished by the way she felled so many so quickly. She had been given a long time to perfect her dragon slaying techniques.

Most of the woods around them were ablaze, the smell of charred embers and flesh thick in the air. The Ruinites were suited up, ready to march in whatever direction their god decided to send them. Even the Gothmirks, still smoking and dropping soil from their shoulders seemed to turn an interested ear to the heavens.

"What are you thinking?" she asked her friend who sat next to her.

Clive had been running his dagger through the dirt, making stick figures. He looked up, clearly taken aback by her question. "What?"

"What are you thinking about, right now?" she repeated.

He twirled the blade between his fingers as he stopped to think about it. "I'm thinking about how much things have changed in the last few days. I'm thinking about how a week ago, I was sitting behind a desk stamping my seal on criminal reports. Now look at me."

"I'm sorry," she said, looking away.

"No, no, Kers, don't be sorry," he said, getting to his feet. He pulled her chin up so she had to look into his eyes. "This is the best thing that has ever happened to me. *You* are the best thing that has ever happened to me." He let her go and turned around to look across the rows of undead. "I had been searching for something for so long and could never find it. I passed it every morning as I made my rounds through the prison. It was you, sitting there in a cell, never talking, and never watching. You were right under my nose the entire time and I was too self-absorbed and too embedded in my work and empty life to notice."

"Clive," she breathed. "If I'd have known this was how you felt, I would have probably been a different person for the last fifteen years. I—"

"—but I didn't feel this way," he interrupted. "Not then. It took my sister's death, my house burning to the ground, and the constant deadly shadow that has been hanging on our every mile for me to be this way."

She wanted to tell him again what she had said in the boat. She did in fact love him. Now, thousands of miles from where she first met him, she knew she couldn't live without him. Her only goal in life had been to survive. She *had* to survive. That goal had changed. She no longer cared about her well-being. If she died tonight and Mydian claimed her soul, she would have been fine with it. Now, all she wanted was for Clive to be happy and find the peace he deserved. So badly, she wanted that for him.

Just before she could say anything, the Gothmirk dragon stood up and said, "just look at you!" in a happy, cheerful voice.

Well, happy and cheerful for Ruin.

The surrounding Ruinites applauded and clamored by the sudden presentation of their god and crowded around to listen.

"Just as you wanted, eh?" Clive said.

"Oh very," the dragon spoke. Its breath was still warm and smelled of fetid meat. A dim light burned inside its throat. "I am quite proud of you, Kersey Avonwood."

"Then I assume I am finished?" she asked.

The dragon chuckled, its long, slender neck rippling like a snake. "Almost, my child, almost."

Kersey unfolded her arms and cocked her head to the side. "What do you mean by *almost*?"

"This army was risen for one reason and that reason is war." He pointed his talon toward the hill where hundreds of thousands of creatures swarmed. "I thought I'd give you the honor of declaring it."

She smiled. This was something that the gods normally did. It made her ecstatic with joy to be the first stepping-stone in the siege against Mydian.

There was a thunderous boom that shook the land, nearly bringing everyone to their knees. A bright light shone through the clouds and hit the ground in a shimmering pillar. When the blaze was gone, there was a lone figure standing by their side, within a pulsing ring of white light.

It was obviously a woman, although the visor of her helmet was down. She wore the most beautifully crafted armor Kersey had ever seen. It was bright silver with white etchings and the insignia across the chest was a glowing scale. This was Dormi, the goddess of justice. She stepped out of the ring and approached the awestruck vampiress.

"Kersey Avonwood," she said in a stern voice.

Kersey bowed.

"I believe there is something you wish to say to me?"

She looked once to Clive and then to Ruin who nodded his large, reptilian head. There would certainly be no turning back now. This would mark the end of many people but she had to remember that it had to be done. Mydian had to be stopped.

With a strong voice, she bellowed out across the masses of waiting undead soldiers. "In the name of Ruin, god of the dead and Lyluss, goddess of good, I declare war on Mydian, god of the Underworld, as well as his servants, his interests, and his allies."

"There is no Lylussian representative here," Dormi said, then turned to Ruin. "Do you accept Kersey's declaration on your own behalf?"

"Oh, I most certainly do," the dragon said.

"Then by the order of Telsis, I deem Mystyria in a state of *War*. The days ahead shall be known as the third War of Balance." Dormi threw her hands into the air and as the cheers of the Ruinites picked up, she disappeared into a shimmering mirage.

"That's it then," Clive said. "Mystyria is now forever changed."

"For the better, my boy, for the better," Ruin said. He pulled Kersey close with his enormous wing. "I'm grateful of you, child. You've done well for yourself and everything you love. Your family would be *proud* of you."

"I hardly doubt my mother and father would be proud that I just made a declaration of war, but thank you. Now, our agreement?"

"Of course. Mydian will hold no chains around your soul. Lyluss and I are ready to fight to our own deaths to keep you out of his domain. You needn't worry about anything."

"Thank you," she breathed and knelt in the dirt.

"I want you to meet someone," Ruin said, pointing to the sudden part between the waves of undead. A skeletal figure riding an equally skeletal wilderbear rushed up the path to the Drakish temple.

He had been dead a long time. The vines did very little to heal his charred bones and it was incredible that the footfalls of his mount didn't shatter him completely. This creature couldn't possibly be much help.

"Kersey, meet Kier Deathhook."

Kier was a legend. He was Ruin's first necromancer, long ago when the gods were feuding on Mystyria in the shackles of mortality. He was credited with raising the first undead.

"What exactly is he going to do?" Kersey asked.

"He will be leading the army from here. You've done your job. I want you to go off and be happy."

Those words reached into her soul and awakened something that was supposed to be dead. She looked at Clive and could see the happiness well inside him. His heart was beating so fast and his eyes shone such an eagerness to accept what Ruin said.

"Thank you again, Ruin," she said, bowing deeply.

"The pleasure is all mine. It has been an honor to know you, Kersey Avonwood. I'll see you again one day, if only for a moment." With his last words to her, the dragon's head slammed against the rock, only to be lifted back up an instant later with the curse of the Gothmirk.

Pendar hugged his wife and kissed his children and then joined ranks with the undead. He smiled and saluted Kersey as his kinsmen followed him down the hill and toward the north—toward Crynsia.

The waves of undead parted to let the mortals in the middle and joined them in their slow march. They were quiet and moved with a repetition that looked very unnatural. The larger beasts—the dragons and dolgathas—marked the scale of grandeur with their heavy footfalls.

Don't be so hasty to run off, came the voice of Kier in Kersey's mind. *I've come from Crynsia and have seen the woman you are interested in.*

"The blond woman with the vampires? She's alive?"

Oh yes, quite alive. Dyne, they call her. She is with three others and they are headed this way. If you wish to talk to her, you need to take the northern trail to intercept her. They will be nearing your minions shortly and the fighting shall begin.

"We have to go," Kersey said to Clive, climbing atop the dragon and settling into the saddle. She reached out her hand and helped him up. There was a plain, uneasy look on his face and she knew he'd never ridden on the back of anything in his life.

Be mindful once you reach them, Kersey Avonwood, Kiel said. *There is a Felornite spy in their midst.*

.25.

Three-Century Secret

The Clearfork trail was remarkably clear, as its name implied. It was wide enough for wagons and smooth enough for galloping at high speed. Thick trees lined the edges of the path, their foliage blotting out the moon like a shield. Dyne couldn't see a thing, but the horses knew where to go. There were things beyond the wood that kept them on the trail.

Most of the time, merchants used the Clearfork as a quick route between Crynsia and Xenthia to the south. Wagons could easily travel the kempt path and not have to worry about sinking up to the carriage in muddy, blood-infested soil. Any other time, Clearfork would have been bustling with jaunting carriages and soldiers-in-training, but not tonight. News of the vast apocalyptic army of Gothmirks had spread—and coaxed people to stay at home.

Dyne was a fast rider. She always had been. In Boudia, she had a small mare named Delph that she would use to race the Stretch. It was a mile long loop that started around her home, passed the graveyard, and then up by the academy. Eventually it came back around and she would have her father time her from the porch.

Delph had never needed to go so fast for so long as the mount beneath her now.

It was unnervingly quiet. That was the reason she hated the undead. The rotting creatures had some sort of natural ability to stay silent as they intently pursued their prey. There could be half a million standing in the weeds just beyond the treeline and she would have never known.

"Look!" Lorne whispered as loud as possible.

The oblivious three whipped their heads to the right and caught a glimpse of a lantern bouncing heavy on the rough terrain. There were footfalls but they didn't sound like a horse. The rider didn't use the path; they were far out within the trees where death was surely lingering.

When the lantern got closer, Dyne saw it was tethered to the saddle of a skeletal wilderbear. The creature's ivory bones glinted in the warm glow of the light. It was wearing bronze armor and it threw its head up and snorted.

Atop its back was a man—a skeleton. He wore a dark robe and held the reins in his clenched, bony hands. For just a moment, he looked over in the direction of the huddled group but for some reason he didn't seem interested. Instead, he whipped the reins and hurried on ahead.

"He has to be a messenger," said Dyne.

"Because of the lantern?" Laraek asked.

"No, because he didn't stop and fight us," Lorne finished, watching the last of the light fade into the dark.

"If we follow, maybe he'll lead us to Kersey," Dyne said, kicking her horse with her heel.

The path ran alongside where the galloping Gothmirk had traveled but he had been much faster than the four pursuing him.

His lantern was but a memory now. That didn't deter Dyne one bit. She kept hammering down on the reins, coaxing all the speed she could out of her panting mount.

After around half an hour of riding, the Clearfork came to the junction for which it was named. There was a high road and a low road, both which led to the summit in the Kragspire. Along the low road, however, there were chasm spiders—as large as a man's head, that lived in tiny webs along the ground. That way was rarely traveled and rightly so. It was much safer to take the high road, the one that ran up the cliff and overlooked the chasm.

There was a sudden rustling in the leaves and Dyne pulled her sword. She turned her mount around full-circle and saw nothing but her three, clueless companions. They were up on the cliff, next to the dark ravine that held nothing but death. The wind was blowing slightly and the few trees that chose to grow from the rocky, barren ground were being tossed aside.

A thought occurred to her the moment she started on the path of Clearfork. If Kersey's power had been stretched to great lengths, could she have been able to raise the dead this far south of her? Perhaps the magic weakened as it went out and the corpses took longer to reanimate the further away. The answer came quite fast in the form of a scuttling, undead arachnid.

A swarm of bony chasm spiders crawled up from the ravine and scurried across the rocks toward the four mares. The first wave latched onto Lorne's horse, startling the black steed and sending it up on its rear haunches in an aggravated neigh. He fought to control it but the pain in its legs and the fear in its eyes caused it to bolt.

There were more Gothmirks than Dyne had thought. She saw a few humans, a bear, even a pair of enormous scorpions. She watched Lorne's horse carry him away into the darkness but she couldn't let the same thing happen to her. Leaning over in the saddle, she swung wildly, tearing away at the chasm spiders that got near her.

Laraek and Eva pulled their blades out and hopped from their mounts. It was dreadfully dark but being so high up on the cliff made the treeline sparse. The moon's silvery light cast a dull glow on the fight.

Dyne could hear Lorne far off in the distance. He was attacking someone—some*thing*, and she felt a small bit of relief that the horse didn't carry him to his death over the edge of the cliff.

Eva pushed Dyne out of the way of an oncoming bear and slashed across its meaty side. She nodded her thanks to the vampiress and let her continue the fight further up the cliff. Laraek stayed nearby, skewering the spiders with simple flourishes. The smell of their insides reminded her of rotten cabbage.

A Gothmirk woman—a young girl with horrible burns across her face and neck stepped up to her with a scythe leveled at her head. Dyne ducked the narrow blade and thrust her own into the creature's gut. She ripped through bone, muscle and flesh until there was nothing left but two halves of a twitching torso. The death of the monster wasn't important or noticed. Dyne was too busy wondering about the brilliant blue light against her side.

Laraek yelled out in pain and she turned to see that the keys were hanging halfway out of her pouch. There were vibrant sparks erupting around them as they gently touched the flesh on his elbow. Dyne cursed herself for letting this happen. She remembered back when the same kind of key hung around Hannah's neck. The little girl had to hold it because Dyne couldn't. Lylussian wards were placed upon it to harm vampires. Such a ward had been placed on these three, as well.

"What was that?" Laraek asked, inspecting the bleeding wound.

Dyne gave him a cold look. He knew exactly what 'that' was. He had been searching all around Mystyria for them. She was lucky that his initial response wasn't to take them by force. A small part of her was suddenly afraid—afraid that he might try and hurt her but she kept the blade out in front as she produced the small, adorned keys.

"Don't play me for a fool any longer," she yelled. The tip of her sword was resting against his neck. For the moment, the advancing Gothmirks had slowed. They took interest in the horses and left the squabbling mortal and vampire alone.

"What are you talking about, Dyne? What are those?" He gingerly pointed to the clenched keys that were making her knuckles turn white.

"*These* are why you've been carting your ship all around Mystyria," she informed. "You found one in Hope's Covenant, one in Skyhaven, and one in Davinshire. You need the book to tell you where to look for the last one, am I right? You've been doing Felorn's work!"

Laraek's increasingly puzzled face starting to work on her nerves. She hated liars, especially one that she had a history with that had been built on honesty. There was a small, fleeting pain that she felt deep in her heart. How could the man she loved so much have turned out this way?

"I don't know where you're drawing these conclusions, Dyne," Laraek said. "But please just put the blade down."

"Stop lying to me! I should kill you right now," she breathed. "For betraying *my* trust." There was a slight weakness in her eyes when she added, "I loved you, Laraek."

His eyes flickered from hers to the side and Dyne realized too late that someone was approaching from behind. She felt the cold, bloodied steel of a blade being drawn across her throat, a small tug of pressure pulling her into the strong embrace of the woman behind her.

"Put your sword down," Eva purred into her ear.

Dyne shot Laraek a look that would have made a normal man turn and run. With great hesitation, she drove her blade into the ground. It wobbled for just a second before Eva threw her aside.

Laraek sighed and kissed his wife on the cheek as he kept his sword trained on Dyne. She spit dust from her mouth and looked up to see the two cohorts looking at her with disdain. Her former lover's eyes weren't as foul and haughty as she would have thought they'd be.

"I think she's been through a lot these last few days, Eva," Laraek said, turning to his wife. "She's gone mad."

He looked to the kneeling woman and then to the three keys sprawled across the rocky ground. His brow furrowed in what Dyne thought was confusion. Taking both hands, he pulled himself away from his wife and said, "Hope's Covenant, Davinshire, and Skyhaven. Love, aren't those the cities you've been to this past year in hopes of finding us a child?"

Dyne couldn't see her face but she realized faster than Laraek that Eva had just been caught. The vampiress would lead them on no more. A sudden weight lifted when she realized he was innocent—that he had been in the dark and just as blind as everyone else. The commander of the *Black Murder* had been a front—a scapegoat—for her devious acts. She had been using the ship's resources and protection under false pretenses of stealing a baby. In each city she had only had one thing in mind—to find the keys to Gloomrift.

"Eva?" Laraek asked her when she failed to say anything. His face turned to a scowl—the realization that the wool had been pulled over his eyes—had been for the entire length of their sham marriage but it was quickly replaced by one of pain and anguish.

Eva backed up and Dyne could see her dagger wedged firmly into her husband's chest. He tried to scream through bloody lips but she wrenched the blade to the side and shoved him over the edge of the ravine. His cry ended abruptly when he hit the chasm floor far below.

Dyne was overcome by grief but it was but a mere shadow to her anger. She had been lied to, led to believe her former lover was a bad man. This woman had been using him from the beginning. She had invented a longing for children and that angered Dyne even more. She had used that against Laraek to fund her excursions into Mystyria, in order to find the keys. The Lylussians, as well as Mydian, truly believed he was the one responsible for stealing Lady Good's property and had hunted him because of this wench.

"I suppose thanks are in order," she said, turning around and drawing her sword. "I thought I'd have to make a deal with the god of the sea to get those keys back. Thank you for rescuing them from the doomed ship."

"Why are you doing this?" Dyne asked from across the cliff. She cast an anxious eye into the darkness behind her and could still hear the clamor of swords. *Hurry up, Lorne,* she thought.

"Why? Because my goddess wants it so," Eva said, as if the answer should have been obvious. "Felorn wants inside of Gloomrift."

"How long have you eyed Laraek and the *Phantom Seven*? I'm sure you've planned this for awhile now."

"Well I've eyed Laraek for three centuries. I can remember the first time I saw him. It was back in Boudia, at the fair I do believe."

She brought the pommel of her sword to rest on her chin, mocking a deep thought. Her eyes lit up in exaggerated excitement. "That's the same day I first saw *you*!"

"You're lying," Dyne said coldly. "I assure you we've never met. I would have certainly remembered you."

"Of course you would have," Eva pointed out. "That's why we didn't actually talk. Felorn told me where to find my useless, pitiful father and in exchange, I would serve her." She twirled her sword a bit and approached Dyne, but the fight wasn't in her just yet. "I found him and his family and butchered them a week later."

"What?" Dyne asked, her heart fluttering.

"We are half-sisters, Dyne. Your father was *my* father. Thank the gods that Arctis Moonbridge never learned of me or else I'd have been drawn up inside of Mydian's plans to raise that damned dragon."

"This isn't possible."

"It isn't? But I *feel* you, just like you felt your little girl years ago. You are my blood," Eva said, a fabricated grimace across her face. "Your father was a missionary who frequented Bloodgate and no, it was not for Mydian. It was for my mother. She loved him! She gave him a child and what did he do to repay her? He abandoned her, threatened to kill her if she told anyone of their affair, and went back to his family in Boudia. Your family!"

Dyne couldn't believe what she was hearing. It was true that her father took many excursions to Bloodgate but she would have never thought this was the reason. Eva was probably born around the same time that she was.

"You killed my family?" she asked.

"That I did," Eva triumphantly said. "Your father ruined my life. Later, he decided he wanted my mother silenced, so he came back to Bloodgate and burnt our house down. Only she wasn't there. It was just my two boys and I. Your father took away my children! He let them burn because he didn't want his affair to be made public!" She gazed up to the heavens with glassy, weakened eyes and smiled. "I see now from whom you get it. Wrecking families, I mean. Your father was an expert at such things."

"And Laraek?" Dyne asked, eyeing the cliff. "Why did his family have to die, as well?"

Her head dropped in what appeared to be sadness but at this point, Dyne wasn't ready to believe any of her actions or moods. "I never knew jealousy until I saw you. When I saw the two of you at the fair . . . I wanted what you had. The love of a man." Her tone suddenly grew fierce and angry and she screamed, "You had all of the things that I should have had! Love and a normal family! If I couldn't have them, no one could. Not even my half-sister."

"You murdered both of our families because you wanted revenge against my father?" Dyne asked, her voice a little weaker.

"And I would have killed the two of you as well but Mydian stepped in and turned you both to vampires. That's when I stumbled upon the power and protection of the *Phantom Seven*. I knew Laraek would be of better use alive." She smiled in gentle satisfaction and added, "And I also found the love I needed."

"Yes, well, you just stabbed that love in the chest, sweetie," Dyne pointed over the cliff.

"No matter," Eva said emotionlessly. "Without his precious ship to keep me hidden, funded and safe, he's useless. Besides, my life has been devoted to Felorn, not man. I've finally done my job. Now I can go home and reap the rewards."

"So your longing for a child . . . it was all just a guise?" The thought of something so vile made Dyne's skin crawl.

"Not at all," Eva said. "I *will* find another child. But I have to make sure my goddess gets her way first. I'm sure you know how such contracts work."

Dyne smirked. She was upset over her family but those memories were distant and the hurt was a cold numb. Eva already had a long list of reasons to die and she just kept adding to them by the minute.

She unfastened her pouch and threw it into Dyne's arms. She pointed to the keys and said, "Pick them up. Put them in there."

Dyne gave her a sneer but knelt down to do as she asked. After all, she was pointing the bad end of a blade right into her chest. Eva thought she was in control. She thought that things were going to be this simple and that Dyne was going to simply put her hands up and admit defeat. The vampiress should have been wise enough to see what was coming.

With a quick flick of her wrist, Dyne shoved the keys into her face. The vampiress howled in pain and lost the grip on her sword. Bright blue sparks ripped through the dark night as her face and neck were singed by holy magic. Both women toppled backwards and Dyne landed on top, still thrusting two of the shiny trinkets into her cheeks.

Eva brought her leg up and used the leverage to force her attacker off. Dyne rolled to the side and plucked her sword from the rocks. The vampiress followed form and grabbed her own. She ran fingers through her matted hair and regained her composure, despite the horrid burns on her face and neck.

"I was going to kill you quick like your useless lover down there," she pointed over the ravine, "but you've convinced me that such a death is too good for you."

"Oh? Well you haven't convinced *me*," Dyne pointed across her chest.

The vampiress charged, thrusting straight down toward Dyne's head. She quickly dodged, jumping aside just as the blade bit into the ground. She whirled around and kicked Eva's arm, forcing her back long enough so she could regain her footing.

Eva dodged two of Dyne's slices, both passing her ear by inches. She pulled a dagger out and tossed it, but it simply sailed past and disappeared into the darkness.

Their fight grew more intense—both had traded finesse for brute force. Dyne gripped Adella's sword with both hands and heaved with all her might. She met Eva's blade in the air and struggled to gain the upper hand. After a second of losing ground against the strength of a vampire, Dyne kicked her in the mid-section, sending her flying a few feet toward the cliff.

Eva circled around, clearly uneasy about being so close to the steep edge. She slashed toward the ground, her blade grazing the side of Dyne's armor. The hardened leather was so magically strong that it spit a few sparks as if made of metal. For a brief moment, the seemingly ordinary cuirass enthralled the vampiress but that was all the advantage Dyne needed. She had used such distractions many times and it worked just as well three-hundred years later.

With the strength of a giant, she hacked the vampiress' right arm off. The blade and appendage fell heavily to the ground. Eva screamed as her stump rained blood but she pulled a second sword from its sheath along her hip and kept ready.

There was desperation in her eyes now. Dyne had seen this before. When her enemies had abandoned all hope—be it a turn in the battle, the death of a comrade, or a severe wound—it was inevitable that the fight was over. Eva lost interest in Dyne—and in the keys—and turned around with every intention of running off—

—but there was a squatting, undead dragon blocking her way.

Kersey and her mortal friend sat on its saddled back, simply watching the fight. The Overlord hopped from her perch and approached Eva, who was horrified. Her bloody fingers did little to slow the current pouring from her stump.

Kersey spun her around and said into her ear, "I think Dyne would like to finish this." She gave her a mighty shove back into the fight.

Dyne was dumbfounded for just a moment but it didn't last when Eva realized this would truly be to the death. She lunged with failing strength and missed by several feet. It was but a quick effort to jab the blade into the vampiress' chest and fish out her heart.

"Felorn will find you," Eva spat through bloody lips.

"I surely hope she does," Dyne said, severing the beating heart with a forceful tug. Eva, the three-hundred year old thief and murderess died in a brilliant, dizzying display of light.

Quickly, Dyne gathered up the keys, keeping a watchful eye on Kersey. She was holding her lance out but she wasn't making any type of advancement. That worried her more. Everyone had some sort of fighting style, a battle plan, but this woman did not.

"So I hope you have closure now," Kersey said, taking no further steps.

"What would it matter to you?" Dyne angrily yelled, stuffing the last of the keys into her sack. "I know your kind. I've killed evil like you before."

Kersey's face was emotionless, as she seemed to ponder something. Her hair was tied back and the spotted moonlight cast her skin in a somber, white glow. "I'm different. I wish to *help* you."

Dyne chuckled. It was the most ridiculous thing she'd ever heard. "Help me? And just how would you help *me*?"

"I know what it's like to lose everything. You were taken from your home, your friends, and your family and thrust into the life of a vampire and still, to this day, you are being forced to work against your will. At the very least, I'd like to offer my hand of friendship in knowing that we both share the same hatred for Mydian."

"You know nothing about me," Dyne growled.

"I know that you feel as betrayed by the Master as I do, and because of that, you and I are alike."

Dyne couldn't believe that she'd had the opportunity to meet two Greater Overlords in her life and they had both said 'alike'. Just because they were old enough to rack up more problems than the rest of the world, it didn't make them like those around them. Dyne and everyone else could never be like these creatures—the fountain of evil they bathed in was too deep and too rich.

"What do you say?" Kersey asked, slowly stepping forward with her hand outstretched. The mortal on the dragon's back looked on with unbroken interest.

For a second, Dyne accepted what she said. She had not one friend—one ally in the world other than Lorne. The sounds of the battle were growing distant and she wondered if she'd even see him again. At that moment, Dyne felt more alone and more vulnerable than she had ever felt in her life. It was like she was standing naked in the streets and being pelted with rocks. For the first time, she wanted a friend—someone who shared her thoughts, her feelings, and who would never turn their back no matter what circumstance arose.

But there was another part of Dyne's complicated personality.

She wanted the thrill of killing a second Overlord. It was in her blood. Through tiresome travel, countless battles, and betraying circumstances she had made it this far. Dyne deserved to feel every minute of her blade being wedged right into Kersey's breast. It was such a torn decision and she wondered just how much of her vampiric nature her soul retained. She was, after all, a creature of habit.

Her heart and mind picked the latter.

With a violent swing, Dyne lashed out and ripped a deep tear on Kersey's armor. A small bit of blood poured from the dark metal and she simply closed her eyes, as if fighting a minor irritation. The mortal on the dragon gasped and started off but she held her hands up to keep him back.

"Is this really what you want to do?" Kersey asked.

"Of course it is," Dyne answered.

"Why do you feel you must kill me?"

"Because I have to succeed at *something*!" Dyne blurted out. She suddenly felt so exposed.

"There are other ways to be successful," Kersey said.

"Not for me."

Kersey sighed and held her lance out. "Well let's be done with this."

Dyne ripped across the lance with the blunt of her blade, sparks flying wildly in the gentle breeze. The two women circled around as the Overlord kept retreating. She constantly rained down blows but Kersey didn't try to fight back, as if toying with her—and that made her even angrier.

"Don't do this, Dyne. Mydian doesn't deserve your soul." Kersey pushed her off without so much as a strain. "You could be doing good work for some other god who appreciates you."

"Like Lyluss or Ruin?" she mocked.

"Perhaps. They aren't as bad as you were probably brought up to believe." Kersey said.

"I have family in the Underworld," Dyne said. "So either way, that's where I'm headed."

Kersey lowered her head in a tired defeat. "I'm sorry you couldn't see reason. Just don't let Mydian pull your strings when you make it back there."

Dyne brought her blade down hard against her lance and for a moment, she thought she had the strength to push her to the ground. It had looked like the Overlord's resolve had weakened—that her force had been dwindled by the outcome of Dyne's decision.

That was completely wrong.

Kersey pushed back with more strength than ten men could muster. Dyne flew through the air and landed solidly on the edge of the cliff and then rolled to the side. She let go of her sword and fought to grab on to something—anything, and keep from tumbling over into the darkness, right on top of Laraek. Her sword—the priceless blade of Adella slid right over and disappeared into the ravine in a fleeting glint of light.

Dyne struggled to hold on as she dangled over the chasm. She couldn't see anything below other than a blackened void. Somewhere down there was Laraek's remains.

There were Gothmirks closing in. She looked past Kersey, past the dragon, and up the hill to the waves of movement. They were marching north, probably toward Crynsia. This battle was lost before it even began.

"Give me your hand!" Kersey yelled, dropping her lance and stepping up to the edge of the cliff. Dyne looked up and saw something that gave her hope, even if she was a moment from death's doorway. If she died here today, she wouldn't be a complete failure, after all.

With a shaky hand, she let go of the rock and hoisted herself up toward Kersey's outstretched arm. She gritted her teeth as her nails dug into the ground to keep her steady. Kersey kept her foot firmly planted on the edge of the cliff and reached as far as she could. Their fingers danced inches from grabbing distance and then, without warning, Dyne did something totally unexpected.

She abandoned the reaching woman's hand and grabbed the dagger from Kersey's boot. She pulled it out and in one quick slash, cut the pouch along her waist. The Overlord looked perplexed but she knew what was happening when she saw the little red book slip out and drop into the waiting arms of the woman falling from the cliff.

Dyne released the knife and the cliff, and wrapped her arms tightly around the book as she fell, letting the darkness of the ravine close in around her.

.26.

The Rage of the Vampire

Kersey muttered a silent curse beneath her breath as her quick hands fetched the pouch before it went over. She checked the coins inside and stuffed it beneath her armor. Dyne had been so foolish. The book wasn't even important now and she traded her life for it. Clearly, some people couldn't be reasoned with, she thought. But alas, at least Kersey finally realized what it was like to feel 'compassion' for one's enemies.

There were undead all around now, their lazy feet kicking up dust from the rocks as they passed by. They moved in waves—a large, pounding collection of footsteps that echoed along the cliff's edge. There were a few freshly dead bodies in the throng now, apparent opposition they met along the way.

"I'm sorry, Kersey," Clive said, jumping from the squatting dragon.

"For what?" she wondered, running fingers through her dirty hair.

"I've only been your heavy baggage this entire trip. Sure, I killed a few vampires in Tharg, but you'd have probably been here days sooner and with much less emotional turmoil." He couldn't bring himself to look up at her.

"Hey," she said in a warm, gentle voice. She touched his chin with her cold fingers and raised his face. "You saved my life back in Tharg. Daegin could have had me if not for you." She turned her back and gazed out beyond the chasm. "And besides, just because you don't get to stick your blade in everything that comes at me doesn't mean you're not *useful*."

"I don't know if I believe that," he said, crossing his arms over.

"Well you should. You mean the world to me. I wouldn't have had the courage to take one step out of Tharg if not for you. In every triumph I've known, you've been responsible."

Clive looked like he wanted to say something—to perhaps offer another rebuttal to her words but a loud screeching from the north broke the stillness of the night. The pearlscale dragon lifted itself off the ground and headed for the noise. All of the Gothmirks turned to face it and the vines trailing along the ground rattled like coins in a jar.

There were vampires running up the hill toward her. Their fangs were gnarled and their faces were white and bloated with dead blood that did not move. Their running was stiff and labored and they held their hands outstretched, their only weapon being stringy fingers. Kersey wasn't afraid of them, but she knew that this many would slow the army down—and *that* was something she wasn't going to let happen.

They didn't even seem interested in her. These creatures had been bred for one thing: to destroy her Gothmirks. Most of the Crossbacks passed by, paying no mind as they dug into the bony undead and ripped them apart like twigs. There were a few flashes of light as the Gothmirks took advantage and Kersey kept a weathered eye over her shoulder to Clive.

He was taking care of himself. The abominable Crossbacks didn't even have a chance. His sword passed through them with such finesse—such grace that it looked like he had hunted them his whole life. They weren't very interested in him either, but they did fight back when he attacked.

Kersey cut them down as they ran past. It was like she was invisible—a silent, hidden killing force that ripped the life from them as they went to find prey. Something in their subconscious made them part away from her—to draw toward the edges of the cliff and let her pass through with a wider margin. She thought they had changed tactics or had grown tired of being cut down so easily. In truth, they were moving aside so a rider on horseback could pass through.

Her eyes met his.

For the first time in a thousand years the old feelings of fear, of anger, and of a life-long bitterness snaked its way to the surface. The world around her melted as if undergoing another trance but she was more lucid than she'd ever been in her life. All of the sounds, both small and large flooded away and was replaced by the beating of her heart. She could feel and follow each drop of her own blood. It was rushing to her face in a heavy torrent.

"Brin," she breathed, no louder than a growl. He had the smug, self-loving smile splayed across his face that she'd learned to loathe. It had only been from memories but it was enough to make her dream of stabbing it away from thought.

He jumped off his horse and stood there, next to an array of mangled, twisted trees that overlooked the ravine. They were probably just as old as the two that lingered beneath their withered shelter.

Her chest started hurting and for a moment, she thought she was going to lose the hold on her lance. If she dropped it, she feared the feelings of vulnerability—of helplessness would creep back up and kill her. She wasn't going to allow that to happen. Not again. That pain in her chest was the anger. It was that small bit that she never let go of. It was the reason she could still be in the spot she was standing and not run away, cowering to a prison like she should have been. That small trickle of anger—of rage had just been awakened, and until the one before her was dead, it wouldn't go back to sleep.

There was a pounding at her temples and suddenly her hair caught fire. It didn't burn her flesh nor did it feel hot. It was only there as a manifestation of her fury. Under different circumstances it would have probably been a beautiful, golden glow that clung to her head like auburn locks. Now, it was a twisted, blazing crown that signified her undying hatred.

Tiny flames also danced along her fingertips. They created golden contours in the air as she moved. Even small spots of fire burned on the ground with each step she took like little orange stepping-stones marking a trail to her most hated man. Her skin darkened, as well as her eyes. Small, black dots reflected shimmering flames as she stared at him with an unbroken vigilance.

Vines broke from the ground and started ripping the vampires up around them. There were sporadic wisps of white light as a mosaic of flashing death erupted all around. The tendrils themselves even felt her anger and sprouted thick, slime-covered thorns that pierced flesh like the steel of a dagger.

Brin looked around at the devastating power of her vinery and then back to her sudden transformation. He smiled and then heartily laughed. Never in this world would he allow her to ever think she had the upper hand. Men like him only wanted women weak, on their knees, and begging for their lives. Men like Brin Todrich usually got their way and men like him weren't used to being fought back.

Today he would be taught a lesson.

"When I was told that it was you that forged this grand army in Ruin's name, I just had to come and see it for myself," Brin said, twirling his lance with careful grace.

Kersey didn't even think she could talk right now. The words in her throat wanted to all come out at once. She wanted to tear him apart with her voice but he had to know her pain first.

"Everything I became was because of you!" she screamed, aiming her lance at his head. "I lived a life of torment for a thousand years because of the things you did to me!" A tear tried to escape her eye but it only made it to her cheek, where it sizzled away.

"You're not talking about the cavern, are you?" he asked with dismissal. "Don't lie, girl. You *loved* what happened in there."

She began to tremble so badly that her hair looked like a blazing beacon that had been picked up by the wind. His words had gotten the best of her before, but not today. For too long she had thought of this day and for too long she had dreamed of what tonight's events would be like. He was already dead. He just didn't know it yet.

"Look at me!" she screamed. "This is your mess!" Her voice turned cold, almost seductive. "Now come fix it."

She looked at her lance and then back at him. He was standing at defense, ready to be assaulted by a rage-driven woman who would blindly die out of sheer revenge. With a gentle nod, she tossed her weapon aside. It was too good for him.

Kersey balled her hands into fists and charged.

Brin jabbed with his lance but she hopped over and slid along it to deliver a violent blow across his cheek. Blood rained from the wound her dry knuckles caused and for just a moment he was stunned by her quickly changed tactics and guile. His wicked grin didn't take long to resurface.

She stepped back and let him come to her. With the strength of a god, he slashed across the ground in an attempt to sever her legs. The lance grinded along the rocks and she jumped and landed at just the right moment. As he pulled to free his weapon, she kicked him across the nose, causing him to fall back against the ground and lose the hold on his lance.

"I'm going to do what I should have done all those years ago," Brin cursed from the ground. He spit blood into his hand and flipped back to his feet.

Kersey raced over and kicked his lance over the edge of the ravine. His eyes lit up in brief fear but that quickly faded. Men like Brin didn't fear anything, despite how the odds looked.

"No matter," he said, watching the last of his priceless lance fall over the edge. "As you recall, I do my best work with my hands." He cracked his knuckles and approached with a most malicious stare.

His thick, brawny hands wrapped around her arms and for just a moment she was startled. The memories of the cavern were creeping back up on her and she felt that a flashback was about to make its presence known. She didn't need to be thinking about the last time his hands were around her. If she lost her conscious mind, he would kill her. Or worse than that, he would do *it* again.

She found her clear mind came with a rattled brain. With enough force to split a pumpkin, Kersey slammed her face right into his. Blood gushed from the open wound on his nose as he faltered back a step. Taking advantage of his momentary disarray, she kicked him to the ground.

Rubbing her own nose, she said, "That's a little trick I picked up from you."

His eyes were so angered now. Brin was finally starting to feel a piece of the rage that had been stored inside her soul. His fangs grew to his bottom lip and a bright, cold flame danced in his eyes. There was nothing scarier on Mystyria than two Greater Overlords fighting at the height of their fury.

He feigned a kick and when she dodged, he wrapped tight fingers around her throat. She reached up and dug at his hand, tearing the flesh away from his forearm like it was wrapping paper. There was a small flicker in his eye as he registered pain but the determination to kill her was too great.

A tight hand found its way to her left breast, beneath her armor and stayed there. The color and feeling in her face suddenly left. He was smiling in gentle satisfaction that she was about to die. For just a moment, she believed she would.

"Mydian once told me that when you die, he's going to do what I did every single day. Be proud, Kersey," Brin's fingers were pressing hard against her chest. "You're going to be the Master's whore!"

With that, his sharp fingernails dug into her flesh, ignoring the restraint of skin, muscle and bone and found their way into her chest cavity. Kersey let out a rippling scream that made the fire around her head burn with an unbridled ferocity. Brin's fingers were wrapped around her heart. Blood—her blood, was spurting down her chest in thick streams.

Her head fell back and the world around her started to move. For just a moment she could see the fires of the Underworld. She could see the pillars of Mydian's necropolis and the walls of Castle

Hiriam. Mystyria was but a fading vision of a world she spent a millennium on and then was gone. Clive, however, was not going to let that be her fate.

From the corner of her eye, she saw him approach. Brin was too fixated on her—too eager to send her straight to his dark lord that he didn't see him step up and slash hard across his wrist.

"Clive, no!" she screamed as Brin's severed arm dropped her to the ground. The entire limb disappeared in a brilliant flash and then blew away. She panted heavily as the gaping hole in her chest slowly began to mend.

Brin had recovered her lance and was battling her friend. Golden sparks rained down with each heavy blow and it was obvious Clive didn't have the strength in his arms to keep up. He had the strength in his heart and that was all that mattered. Any other mortal would have turned their back and walked off. Why get involved in something so vile—something that had been brewing for centuries? His remarkable heart was what killed him.

It was but a simple flourish that allowed Brin to disarm his combatant. Clive's sword disappeared over the ravine like so many other things tonight. The Overlord twirled the lance once and then plunged it into his gut.

"No!" Kersey screamed from the ground. She was holding large handfuls of her own blood. Brin held her friend up, feet dangling inches from the ground. He simply tossed him aside and turned to her, a wide, evil grin across his face.

"Oh, was that someone significant?" Brin asked in mock sorrow. "And here I thought *we* had something special." He touched his chest with his bloody stump.

That had been the last straw. Maybe she wasn't strong enough to kill him. Perhaps her rage and rampant hatred for him wasn't a match for his strength and training. But now, her undying anger was coupled with the fear of losing the one she loved most. Together, those two things would be the end of Brin Todrich. Her chalice of power had just been filled to overflowing and the wine of vengeance was about to wash over him.

The large hole in her chest was gone. There was a small puddle of blood beneath her and she stood on wobbly legs. Fire burned all around her in each spot she had stepped. Brin kept his arm up to slow the flow of blood but he was still holding her lance out.

Kersey approached and delivered a solid kick into his midsection. He tried to swat her off with the lance, but she tucked it beneath her arm and kicked again. She couldn't pull her eyes off of her dying friend on the ground but at the same time, she wasn't going to let Brin catch her off-guard and distracted.

She brought her heavy boot down again, this time across his elbow. The sound of the break was so satisfying. A thin scream escaped his throat but it didn't last. After a moment, he snapped it back into place and the break healed. What was important however, was that he was now disarmed.

Kersey reached up and dug her fingers into his face. The tiny flames at her nails singed his flesh. He grabbed her around the throat and tried to force her into kneeling but she wasn't about to go down. Her nails scraped the flesh from his face, down to his neck, and across his chest. They tore the simple cloth shirt like strips of paper. Again, he screamed out as tiny, red trails were left across his body like someone had just yanked a rake across him.

She grabbed at his face and pulled him back by the hair. Her balled fist smashed into him repeatedly until his lips sputtered scarlet. Kersey had even managed to break off his fangs, which could only grow back when he slept. Brin would never get such a pleasure again.

Her fingers tugged at the flesh around his eyes. Piece by piece, she was pealing him like an apple. There were small wisps of smoke as her blazing nails made contact with his skin.

Brin tumbled back and with her fingernails so firmly planted beneath his flesh, she went with him. There was a loud, mangled ripping sound from behind him and the flash of red across his eyes revealed some great pain. Blood spewed from his lips in new waves and she retracted her hands and stood on the cliff's edge.

They were right against the ravine. The wind had picked up and was blowing the withering tree that Brin was pressed against. A low creak sounded from the ground and the rocks at her feet shifted. The tree leaned a little closer into the abyss. Kersey could see something poking from Brin's chest, slightly pushing his mangled shirt up.

She smiled in eager satisfaction as she pulled his garment away and saw the dark, crimson wood of the tree lodged in his chest. There was a gentle pulse that pushed his ravaged flesh out in a steady beat. The limb of the faltering tree had pierced right through his heart.

He sat there and looked up at her, death in his eyes and a fleeting strength in his body. His blood—his life-force continued to flow out of the bleeding stump of his arm. There was a violent twitch as he desperately tried to keep his weight off of the tree. Too much moving and he might go over the ravine or even make the puncture wound in his heart worse.

Kersey's anger died down and with it, the manifestation of her rage and anguish. The blazing hair, the flame-lit fingertips and the dark skin and eyes melted away as she became herself again. Brin was still smiling, despicable and loathsome to the end.

"There's still hope to save your soul," he said through cracked lips. "Just turn this army around and send it after Ruin or Lyluss. Mydian says he'll let you live in peace." His various wounds began to heal themselves again, save for the one in his chest. With the tree lodged inside, the gash could not mend.

Kersey laughed, but it came out tired and uninterested. "Oh really? And the Master doesn't want me for a whore, then?" she said. "My soul is *already* safe. And I'm happy with my life now. It's going to get better without the looming thought of you hanging around."

"Don't be stupid, Kersey. I've told you this before. You can't have a normal life. No one is ever going to have you after all you've done!" The tree groaned again, its trunk shifting even closer to the blackened void.

"That's where you're wrong," she breathed. "I *was* loved again." She looked over to her unmoving friend and then back to the one she hated. "Life threw me a good turn. Lyluss is a good god and my faith in her is restored. Tell that to Mydian when you see him."

With a renewed strength and resolve, Kersey reached out and pushed on his shoulders. He screamed out and grabbed onto her wrists as she slid him back against the branch. The heart—the beating treasure that was myth and legend on Mystyria—was pushed out through his flesh and with a sickly, wet snap, it ripped from his chest.

The cleansing light washed over as his body melted away into white ash. His weight suddenly went from heavy to non-existent. Kersey found herself slipping and landing against the branch. Without even a moment's hesitation, she bounced back onto the safety of the rock but the tree, as well as the pronged heart, went over.

"No!" she screamed, reaching out to grab it. Her vines tried to form a net to save it, but it was too late. Her eyes welled with tears as her best chance to save Clive's life escaped her grasp.

She crawled over to where he laid, a low moan thick in his throat. He was still alive. There was dark, crimson blood at the corners of his mouth and his tongue was painted just the same. A huge gaping hole went through his chest and followed all the way to his back. His left arm and leg twitched like a nervous stick and she knew the lance had pierced something important.

"Kers," he muttered with a gurgle.

"Don't move," she coaxed, running her fingers through his sweat-matted hair.

"Thank you," he breathed.

"For what?" she cried. "All I did was take you miles from home and let this happen."

"No," he said and placed a cold hand over hers. "You showed me what love was capable of. Wherever I'm bound, I'll always remember you for it."

"Clive, don't talk like that!" she screamed. There were tiny drops of blood running down with her tears. Suddenly, she smiled, as if remembering a long lost forgotten antidote that would take this affliction away from him. In a way, that's what it was.

"I can *save* you," she said, letting her fangs grow down to her bottom lip. She turned his head gently to the side and ran her fingers across his clammy neck. He swallowed a large lump in his throat.

"No!" he said with a firm voice. "Not that way. I'm finished Kersey. Just let me go."

"I can't do that!" she yelled, her fangs shrinking back to the corners of her mouth.

"Just promise me one thing, okay?" He squeezed her arm and she nodded. "Promise you won't try to raise me. I don't want to be one of those ... *things*."

He motioned toward the Gothmirks. Kersey had tried the same thing with Avery with no success. Lyluss wouldn't let her resurrect a soul from another realm. She wanted her burly friend restored, but she only managed to make him just like all the others—walking death that was a mere shadow of his former self.

Clive's eyes rolled back into his head as the last of his blood drained over the rocks.

"Clive!" Kersey managed through thick sobs. She pulled him up and locked her arms around him. His body was cold and she felt the stillness of him—the absence of a beating heart. Her only friends had been Avery and Clive, now, only days apart, they were both gone.

She laid him back down and gently cradled his head. Her shaky fingers ran over his face and closed his eyes. There was still so much going on around her—the thousands of Crossbacks and the hundreds of thousands of Gothmirks. She didn't pay attention to either of them. They were insignificant. *Everything* was insignificant now.

"Please forgive me, Clive," she said, more to herself than to her departed friend. She straightened his corpse and placed her hands at his temples. "But I have to *try*."

.27.

Somber Remembrance

Dyne rolled over and coughed, blood spewing from her cracked lips as she did. The armor had saved her. She bounced twice on her way to the bottom and finally ended up on her back at the very end. A chasm spider crawled over her leg and inspected her for a moment before scurrying away. Apparently it realized its prey was so close to death that it didn't matter.

She sat up and looked around but there was nothing in the blurry darkness. Her sword was lying in a puddle of mud on the other side of the chasm floor and she held the book between her clenched fingers. It was a miracle that she kept it all the way down. Quickly she stuffed it into the pouch next to the keys and attempted to get up.

That was a mistake.

Sharp pain erupted from her shin, sending needles of torment up her thigh. She sat back down and realized there would be no walking with a broken leg. Dyne muttered a curse and surveyed her surroundings. All she could do was try and crawl to safety.

First, she retrieved her sword. Although she didn't have the strength, nor the spirit to fight, she felt safer with it by her side.

Once it was slid into its sheath, she started off on her knees, toward the north. It would be an impossible crawl to Crynsia, but perhaps someone allied with Mydian would see her and offer to help.

Would Mydianites even help me now? she asked herself. News would travel quickly of what she was carrying. The Ruinites, the Lylussians, the Felornites, *and* the Mydianites were probably all chasing her by now. She wasn't safe anywhere, from anyone.

And where was Lorne? Had her friend been killed by the onslaught of Gothmirks? She surely hoped not, but in the back of her mind she feared for the worst. Dyne was on her own now, in a world that would turn its back on her and destined to a merciless realm that would do the same.

Someone grabbed her from behind and she started at the touch. Quickly, she whirled around, ignoring the massive pain in her leg and faced her once lover.

Laraek was still alive.

He was hanging on by a thread. She knelt in front and held him up to face her. There was blood everywhere and the blade was still sticking from his chest. She was too scared to touch it—too afraid that one wrong twist would sever his heart and he would be ash in her hands.

"I thought you were dead," she said.

"Did you get her? Did you kill that betraying harlot?" he asked with a weakened tone.

"I did," Dyne said. "Laraek, she *killed* our parents! It was her!"

"Why? Why would she do that?" he asked.

"Because my father abandoned her mother. Eva and I were half-sisters."

"I suppose you feel differently about Lord Mydian now? He didn't do a thing to our families, after all."

"No, but I don't think he sent me back from the dead just to spy on you. Kersey was onto something. Mydian has a greater purpose for me being here."

"What about the keys?" Laraek asked, obviously not even caring as to why she had been picked to climb aboard his vessel back in Pelopha.

"I have them."

"Dyne, you have to turn them over to the Mydianites. Everyone will be after you now. Felorn isn't going to want to be known as the true instigator of the war. She is going to want you silenced."

She bit her lip at that suggestion but said nothing. Instead, she pulled the book out and waved it before him. "Better late than never," she said with a forced smile. "Laraek, I'm so sorry that I didn't trust you. I thought . . . I thought you had betrayed me."

A cold hand stroked her face. She closed her eyes and fought to suppress her tears. "It's ok. You were right on the *Murder*. I do still love you. I think I only chose Eva because she was a constant reminder of *you*."

"Well you didn't choose Eva, love, she chose *you*. That foul creature was scheming against you long before the two of you met."

"I suppose you're right." His head dropped and he said, "Dyne, there was something aboard the ship . . . something precious that I wanted you to have, but now it's gone."

"Do you mean this?" she asked, pulling out the crumpled family crest. The way his eyes lit up told her that it was exactly what he wanted. This was why he wanted Brin to let them inspect the wreckage of the *Murder*.

"I'm glad you found it," he weakly said. He balled it up and clenched it with strength that was quickly fleeing. "I had it made the day of the fair."

"So what do I do now?" she asked, forcing memories away like the pain in her leg.

"We. What do we do now," he corrected. "I'm not going to let the gods bully you around. I'm coming with you. I will make sure—"

His words abruptly ended when Dyne heard a loud *'whoosh'* from behind and above. There was a tremendous pain near the break in her leg. She looked down and saw a thick, metal stake wedged just above her kneecap. Her eyes followed it up and saw that it had entered through Laraek's back and exploded through his chest. The pointed end lodged itself in Dyne's already painful leg.

"Laraek!" she cried, just as four spiked prongs ejected from the sides of the shaft. They embedded themselves within the flesh of his chest and in one quick motion, he jerked back by a chain, over the rocks and up to a ledge where he was assaulted by an unseen attacker.

She'd seen that weapon before.

There were the sounds of a struggle—of metal scraping and grunts and then suddenly a helmet flew up and bounced down the rocks and ended up right by Dyne's feet. It was the adorned headpiece of the Lylussian priest that had hunted Laraek for weeks.

Rocks slid down the cliff as the fight grew more chaotic. Dyne desperately watched the mountain and the inability to see what was going on was driving her mad. She put her hands to her face and screamed when the bright flash signifying Laraek's death cast a shadow across the rocks. A figure stepped through his dispersing ash, quickly alerted by Dyne's sudden outburst.

Small, dainty hands grabbed hold of the rocks up above and a face peeked over the edge. Her beating heart seemed to stop for a moment. She had seen that face before—over and over since her rebirth on Mystyria, only now it was weathered with age and shaped by time. It gave her comfort and was the only reference of innocence she had ever known. It was a young woman, probably eighteen years, with a fair complexion and red hair with blond streaks. The look on her face was a wearisome anger that soon sprouted with surprise. There was also a ruggedness to her. A large gash ran the length of her chin and ended at her bottom lip. Dyne was equally as shocked and astonished. She didn't know how to react—didn't know how to think clearly with this kind of muddled confusion pulling her mind in separate ways.

She felt herself go faint and just before she lost consciousness, she looked up at the girl and uttered her name.

"Hannah."

.28.

Hope for the Future

The sound of the ocean wasn't normally this soothing, especially under these kinds of circumstances, he thought. The padded sand surrounding his body and fingertips were so gentle and so fine. As he opened his eyes and took it all in, he realized that he was in a much different place—a very distant, very unique place.

It was a sunny and warm day. There were thick, voluminous clouds ambling by in the blue sky above but there was no sun. The light's source was mysterious, but comforting, nonetheless. A green bird with bright purple and yellow spots was flying low over the beach and he questioned if such a thing even existed.

Clive sat up and looked out to the ocean in front of him. The water was so green—so pure and untainted and he knew that something like that didn't exist on Mystyria. Even the sands of the beach were tinted a light blue—giving this realm a unique otherworldly flair.

He was wearing a white, unblemished robe. There was no pain in his chest now. Up until today, the worst physical agony he had ever endured came in the form of a broken leg due to a faulty step of a wagon. A thick blade through the torso certainly held precedence now. But the hurt, the blood, and the heartache were just tiny memories that were whispering in the back of his mind. He didn't feel an ounce of the pain, didn't see a drop of the blood, and didn't feel uneasy due to the fact that he was dead.

This was the Davertere Utopia. It was Quillian's home realm and the place where her people were rewarded after death.

"Clive," a voice breathed behind him. The scenic beauty and majesty of the realm weren't even enough to keep his attention when *that* voice called his name. He whirled around, casting blue sand all over and stood to face her.

"Nalia!" he cried. Tears weren't a part of this world. No matter how much he wanted to, they just wouldn't run down his face. It was for good reason. There was no cause in this wonderful afterlife to be sad.

She was so beautiful. Her long, auburn hair was tied up and draped across her shoulder. She was wearing an elegant, white dress that was frilled with blue diamonds and golden braids. Clive had never seen her so happy and so physically healthy. Her eyes were piercing and gentle, not red and baggy from the stress of work. Her dainty fingernails were painted blue, not dirty and grimy from being Fyrl's unappreciated aid.

Most of all, she looked genuinely excited to see him. She lifted her dress and ran to him. He wrapped his arms around her and lifted her into the air, kissing her along the neck and cheek as he did. Nalia giggled and returned it.

For a moment, Clive stood there, hands on her cheeks, looking into her eyes as if making sure this wasn't a dream. Or was it? He certainly lost a lot of blood after he decided to intervene and help Kersey.

"This is no dream," Nalia answered for him. "I'm just as real as you are." Her voice was so sweet and innocent.

"Nalia, where is mother and father? Nana and grandpa?" He looked past her to the towering white castle that had to be Davertere Keep, the home of Quillian herself. From the beach, it was impossible to see the dotted houses and dwellings of her loyal followers.

"They're all up in town, Clive," she smiled, but it faded just a little.

He took notice of her sudden dismay and asked, "Nalia, what's the matter?"

If she could have cried, she probably would have been. Clive could see in her eyes that something was eating at her—that she just couldn't bear to say what it was she had to say. Somehow, she managed to gather the strength.

"You're not dead yet, Clive."

He pulled himself away from her. "I'm not?"

"No, you're not," came a gentle voice from behind him.

He jerked around and saw there was another woman on the beach. He knew who it was—knew *exactly* because of all the drawings and depictions of her scattered throughout Mystyria.

It was Lyluss, Quillian's companion.

She was just as beautiful as Nalia. Her hair was long and blond with streaks of silver running through it. Her porcelain skin and sharp blue eyes looked like those of an oil painting. She was wearing a light blue dress that was full of white, intricate motifs. There was a faint, bluish-white aura surrounding her that made Clive want to drop to his knees.

"I'm glad to finally meet you, Clive," she said, taking a step toward him. She didn't even leave footprints in the sand. "Nalia is such a humble servant of the Heavenly Nurse. I knew you'd be just as forthcoming."

"Where is Quillian?" he asked.

"I'm everywhere," a voice answered high above. The three on the beach turned to look at the sky and Clive spotted a cloud that seemed to pulse and vibrate with each word. "I'm also glad to finally meet you, Clive. We've been interested in talking to you for quite some time now."

"Talk? With me?" He was completely dumbfounded.

"First, I would like to commend you on being such a loyal and humble servant, dear Clive." Quillian's voice boomed from the sky and turned the cloud a bright green with each syllable. "But my words have no meaning here. Lyluss has instructions for you."

He turned to Lady Good and smiled. It was unique how a turn of events could happen so quickly.

"I want to thank you, Clive," she said, and crept closer.

"Thank me? I've done nothing for you," he admitted.

"Oh, but you have, child." She giggled and looked to the heavens where another laugh bellowed. "You've helped me realize that one of my servants deserves a second chance. Without you, Kersey would have surely perished by now. Mydian would have sank his claws into her and Mystyria would have lost a legendary hero."

"I've done nothing but get in the way the entire time. I couldn't even kill Brin when I had the chance." Nalia shook her head and Clive thought he was about to get a severe reprimand.

"No, no," Lyluss countered. "You have helped to sort her demons. Kersey's redemption is because of the selfless effort of you."

"I don't know," he said.

"I do," she said flatly. "It broke my heart to have to curse her all those years ago, but now, thanks to you, she is the woman she once was. She is the esteemed, revered Soul-Summoner."

"We want you to thank her for us, Clive," came Quillian's booming voice in the clouds. "With her help, and the help of Ruin, we will topple Mydian and restore Mystyria to its former glory."

Clive nodded. He looked to Nalia with a defeated gaze that he didn't think was possible in this world. "I suppose I'm going back now, aren't I?"

She bowed her head and said nothing. Lyluss put a warm, comforting hand on his shoulder and pulled him around. Her eyes were so sympathetic—so moving and still *so* strong. "You'll see her again, Clive. I promise you this."

"And I promise it, as well," Quillian boomed. "You can't lose with the power of *two* gods on your side, dear boy."

"Kiss your sister," Lyluss told him.

He faced Nalia again—the last time until the fateful day when he actually would die. He put one hand on her shoulder and one on her chin and raised her head. She was just as sad, just as somber as he was but the two both knew the truth. They would see each other when the time came. "I love you, Nalia," he said and planted his lips against hers.

"I love you too, big brother," she managed through the kiss. Lyluss was looking up to the clouds, smiling in adoration of such a holy, pure thing that was quickly fading from Mystyria.

Clive pulled himself away from her and faced Lady Good. "Again, thank you, Clive." Her tone turned serious and she grabbed his shoulders and drew him in. "I have something for you to give Kersey when you see her." With that said, Lyluss kissed him—a strong, deep kiss that lasted several seconds and held Clive's body inert. There was a bright light that snaked its way up through her throat, over her lips and passed into him. It was *power*. He didn't know what purpose it served but he did know it felt *strong*. Her kiss made his knees weak.

As the two separated from one another, the entire world—the blue sand, the green water, Lady Good, Nalia, and the Heavenly Nurse in the sky all faded away into a shower of a brilliant, blinding white light.

With a frenzy of wheezing coughs, Clive sat up. Kersey's eyes mounted with tears as she wrapped her hands around her friend in the tightest embrace that wouldn't crush him. Blue sparks fizzled across his slacks and shirt.

He pulled himself away and inspected the wound. It was gone. His fingers danced over the blood that clung to his chest hair and he was marveled by how his body had been healed.

"You did it!" he told her.

She was squatting on her knees and couldn't help but clap her hands together in sheer excitement. "Lyluss has forgiven me!" she said. "I have her power back!"

"That you do," Clive reassured. "I got to speak with her."

"You did?" she asked, but figured as much. Clive worshipped Quillian, Lyluss' companion. The two shared each other's world and mingled with each other's servants.

Clive went on to tell her about how he was able to talk to Nalia one last time and the things that Lyluss and Quillian spoke of. She couldn't believe her ears. The gods were actually proud of her. The entire time she thought she was only doing things to save her own skin—her own soul, but she had actually sculpted Mystyria into a better place. The good gods were set to take control of the world and Kersey was to thank.

"And I have something else for you, from Lyluss." Clive reached out and put his hands to her cheeks. She closed her eyes and felt the warmth emanating from him. It was so lovely. All of the pain she had inflicted upon herself would gladly be traded for something this precious. This *pure*.

He leaned up and kissed her. His hand found its way to the nape of her neck and pulled her close. She moaned silently as his mouth glided over hers, a vibrant warmth suddenly rising.

From squinted eyes, she caught the glimpse of a small white light travel from his mouth to hers and in an instant, it grew so bright that she had to look away for a moment. She separated herself from the wonderful kiss and licked her lips. He was smiling and didn't have the slightest idea of what had just happened.

"Gods, I can't believe it!" she yelled, rising to her feet. She pulled Clive up. His clueless expression was quite cute. "Lyluss' curse has been lifted!"

"You mean?"

"I can go in her churches, see her symbols, and benefit from her blessings. I can *serve* her again."

"That's wonderful news, Kers. I'm so happy for you." His smile was warm and genuine and completely out of place considering the battle was still raging all around them. "So what do we do now?" he asked.

She grinned from ear to ear with silent satisfaction and jingled the sack of coins. He followed her bouncing pack and remembered just how much money she had stowed away. A vampire of a thousand years was able to save a lot of coin.

"We've done our part in this war," she said, looking out to the horizon. There was no way he'd be able to see it the way she could. "Others will follow in our footsteps and shape it further." She took his hands and pulled him close. "I say we find the quietest place in the realms, the furthest from war and the closest to peace and live there."

She pondered that thought with great interest. That did sound wonderful—too wonderful for her to even imagine. In time, she would learn. After his entire struggle, Clive was going to have a good life for the rest of his days. She would see to that. In turn, she would be happier than she'd been since her childhood days back in Keswing. They completed each other and today, on the shaping of Mystyria, their story would end.

"I love you, Kers," Clive said.

She stood on his toes to reach him and returned, "I love you, too." They shared a kiss, a warm embrace, and a knowledge that despite the growing darkness the war would bring, theirs would be a life full of happiness and deserved seclusion.

.29.

Mommy

The battle had grown so chaotic. There were white flashes of light all over the cliffs making it look like a violent thunderstorm, despite the moderately clear night. Gothmirks ran in swarms, their guttural cries from moaning lips echoing down in the ravine like a somber war-cry. There weren't even any Lylussians here, but it didn't matter. Mydian and Felorn were both retreating from the unending wall of undead. Kersey's forces pushed north and like a rake, everything in its path.

For a long time, she simply sat there, watching the unconscious woman below with questioning, sad, and angered eyes. A few spiders scurried over her but paid her no mind. The sounds of the war above were fading out—drawing closer to Crynsia and away from the now unimportant Kragspire.

Hannah fidgeted with *Spira-Sian*, the upgraded weapon she had taken from her father. It had proved useful time and again, just as it had for him. She wanted to hunt again—to go on to her next mark, but she couldn't. All of her insecurities, her inadequacies were because of the person lying on the bottom of the ravine. It paralyzed her with uncertainty.

She flipped around and sat against the cool rock of the cliff. Her eyes fixed on the opening ahead—the same path she had silently descended to get to this spot where she took her shot. The commander of the *Phantom Seven* had been her target for months, an innocent who had taken the fall for his mischievous wife. Never would she have guessed who one of his crewmen had been.

How long had mommy been with him? Hannah cursed herself for even calling her that. She wasn't a mommy to anyone, certainly not *her*. Her name was Dyne—a liar, an emotionally abusive vampire, and an abomination who had twisted, sickly intentions of living. How could anyone want to choose a vampire's life for a little girl?

After the attack on the *Black Murder* in the air, Hannah thought for sure that death was coming once her mount was hit. No matter, though. Lady Good would have looked after her. She had been watching, there in the sky, and had whispered into a rogue swoopdrake's ear. That beast saved her life and allowed her to continue the pursuit.

Everyone else had been killed. Laraek, Dyne and their misfit crew had murdered all that Hannah had called a friend. Some were students at the Lylussian Academy in Keswing with her. Others were children she knew growing up, after her father had taken her away and placed her in—what he thought—was a normal life.

With that thought in mind, she pulled out a small bag of glowing rocks and opened it. These were the last things he gave her before she set out after the *Seven*, weeks ago when Lady Good deemed its commander a thief.

She sprinkled the rocks across the ground and before so much as a bounce, they started swirling like a cyclone. The stones started sparkling and dimming, creating an intensifying pattern that shimmered and vibrated until they were spinning in a large oval.

The dark, dank cliff behind it melted away and several people appeared inside, sitting around a fire. There were Lylussian banners up and a large, ornate table adorned the center of the room. Large tallow candles cast everyone in a tired, orange glow. One man in the middle saw his daughter and came rushing to the edge of the portal.

"Hannah!" he screamed, seeing her for the first time in over two months.

"Hello, father," she returned, smiling with a bit of warmth.

"What happened to your leg?" Tranas asked, looking at the large gash that cut through her armor near the ankle. She had completely forgotten about the spear that nearly ripped her foot off.

"I'm fine. How is everyone there?" Hannah looked past him and could see her friends, Daniel and Elana, as well as their mother Sky. Near the rear of the room, in a large, overstuffed chair sat Sigmon, one of her father's friends. He was the only vampire she had ever known to love—mostly because of his vast differences from his wretched brethren. There were several Lylussian priests darting to and fro, carrying maps, books, and whatever else they needed in the pursuit of readying Lady Good for the war. Everyone looked so happy to see her.

"We are good. Other than having to deal with constant house checks. We've managed to stay hidden with no problem, though. Are you finished?"

"The commander is dead," she answered. "He wasn't even the one responsible and the keys weren't on him."

"Then check his ship," Tranas said. "They have to be there."

"I believe that Kersey may have taken care of the *Murder*. There was very little crew left."

"Hannah, we can't let Mydian have those, we have to be su—"

"You never trust in what I say!" she yelled, wishing she hadn't. Independence was too much a part of her and it made bad things come out of her mouth like clockwork.

"I'm sorry, dear," Tranas said, the large bags beneath his eyes growing darker. He sat himself down in front of the portal.

"It doesn't matter anyway, you still have the one they need." She pointed to the chain that hung around his neck where the key dangled across his chest.

"Look, we can deal with this later. You've done your job. Now come home." He stood up and waited for her to pass through.

Just then, a horse's neigh broke through the silence of the night. Several spiders scurried by the cliff and disappeared into the holes that littered the wall. Hannah rose up and looked down to the ravine floor and saw Dyne being lifted onto a horse.

The man who gave her nightmares still to this day was alive, as well. They had been returned to Mystyria, as mortals. Lorne looked around, but didn't see her. He noticed the Lylussian helmet sitting a few inches from his mare's leg but thought nothing of it. Instead, he kicked the beast in the side and sent it galloping down the ravine, toward the north.

Hannah turned back around and swallowed hard. This was a difficult decision to make. She lived a poor example of a life. Through so much trauma as a youth and then an underdeveloped adolescence, she sometimes felt like a walking Glowbomb. The pieces of her mind and life weren't securely glued together. One of those reasons was standing in the portal, waiting for her to walk through and be a few thousand miles from this place. The other was unconscious, on a horse and galloping off.

She could deal with her father later. Right now, she needed closure.

"I'm sorry, father," she said, waving the portal away. "But I have a new job."

.30.

The Fate of Mystyria

The epitome of evil resided in a realm known as Nubetas. It had always been that way and after the days when Mystyria and the heavens crumbled to dust, it would *still* be that way. Both mortals and gods feared its ruler; his reputation preceded him with incredible truth. He was Drak, the Bane of Holiness.

Mydian passed beyond the Underworld and into Nubetas, the dank and foreboding fortress of spikes. It was calm, just as it always was around the castle. There were far off screams, mirroring the agony and turmoil of his own world. Drak's domain was far more threatening and Mydian envied it. Not many powers in the universe could conjure such fear and wickedness as the Dark Child of evil.

A pair of Drakish Golems stepped up to block Mydian as he tried to enter the fortress of spikes, their jagged metal skin reflecting the blood red lanterns along the wall. They looked upon the Lord of the Underworld with the eyes of an enemy—of denizens who thought their god wouldn't want a meeting with such a lowly deity.

"Out of my way," Mydian growled, waving his hand to the side. The Golems twisted and compacted, dropping their glowing spears. Their metallic cries and violent shuttering stopped as he crushed their bodies with the will of his mind and the anger of his voice. He stepped over the flattened metal and headed toward Drak's foyer.

There was blood dripping from the ceiling of the massive antechamber. Mydian paid it no mind and continued across, spotting a man in the next room over. A large grin found its way to the Dark Lord's mouth but it was forced. Everything hung in the balance now. Hopefully Drak would be forthcoming.

"Too long you've let Mystyria go to the dogs," the bitter voice of evil said. He turned around and gazed upon Mydian with cold, reptilian eyes. His red hair was tied in a war knot to the side and his dark skin was almost eerily black. There was a tactful, questioning look in his eyes but Mydian knew it was all part of his disarming demeanor.

"Mystyria is in grave danger, Drak." Mydian didn't like the way the admittance of defeat tasted in his mouth. It was the simple truth and the unholy god of evil was going to have to be motivated to care about the mortal realm once more. If it continued toward the path of righteousness, both of the gods standing in the room would be dead within weeks.

"This I can see," he said, waving his hands toward the ceiling. The droplets of blood continued to fall, already creating a thin sheen of scarlet across the floor, the desks, and the voluminous bookcases. "The blood of the innocents has already started to fill my domain. Isn't it wonderful?"

"I just learned from a . . . wrongly accused servant of mine that even Felorn has betrayed me. As a matter of fact, nearly all of the gods have turned on me. I've come here for your help," Mydian said.

"Is that so?" Drak said, leaning against a sturdy table. His nimble fingers drew lines across the film of blood. "And just what did you do to upset them so?"

"Nothing that I haven't done before," he admitted. "But this time is different. This time . . . they are joining forces."

Drak paced the dark room for just a moment, leaving bloody footprints across the green tile. His brow was furrowed in thought and he stroked his chin, leaving red splotches in his stubble. "I've been away from Mystyria for a long time, Mydian. And this isn't my problem. Besides, I'm no longer needed there."

"That's where you are wrong," Mydian said. "You have just as many servants today as you had years ago when you decided to let the world forget you existed. Now is the time to show them your strength, your resolve. Evil is about to be stomped out like a fire."

"I've been away from Mystyria but I still feel its presence. The wicked are still running the world." Drak put his hands up and closed his eyes, as if drawing in the very air around him. "Just what makes you think *this* is fading?"

"Ruin and Lyluss have united against me. They have put aside their differences long enough to pound my cities, kill my servants, and destroy my interests."

"Ruin has . . . *joined* Lyluss?" Drak's voice was almost a whisper, as if the very words choked him.

"That he has," Mydian said. "Together they have enough soldiers, weapons, and influence to rip all of our temples apart. If we don't do something, there will be no Underworld. Nor will there be a *Nubetas*."

"But Ruin is supposed to be one of us!" Drak spat. A chorus of screeches and cries erupted from an unseen force around them. "He is betraying his nature by joining with the likes of Lyluss."

"And we can't let him get away with that, right?" Drak was a blunt instrument when it came to good and evil. He felt that the two were as opposite as night and day and should have never mixed, nor coexisted. Evil prevailed and good was for the weak.

Mydian crept close to Drak, the god of evil's eyes were piercing, red and distant. He was thinking on things from the beginning of time—the era where he walked Mystyria as a mortal and showed the world what true evil was about.

"Gather your troops and whatever weapons you have at your disposal. We can use them and send Lyluss and Ruin back to the depths from which they crawled." He put a strong hand to Drak's shoulder and pulled him around to face him. "What do you say?"

A thin, creepy smile ran across the evil god's face. He returned the strong grasp and nodded with great resolution. "Let's go take back Mystyria, brother."

About the Author

Hubert is the son of artist, Hubert H. Mullins. Rage of the Vampire is his second novel, the follow-up to The Vampires of Hope's Covenant. He is an avid animal lover and spends most of his time working with them. Hubert resides in Welch, WV and is hard at work on concluding the adventures of Dyne, her enemies, and her friends.